Dear Reader:

In HarperPaperbacks's continuing effort to publish the best romantic fiction at the best value, we have taken the unusual step of pricing nine of our summer Monogram titles at the affordable cost of $3.99. Written by some of the most popular and bestselling romance writers today, these are magical and exciting stories that we hope you will take to your hearts and treasure for a long time.

Open the pages of these wonderful books and give yourself the gift of a reading experience like no other. HarperPaperbacks is delighted to present nine extraordinary novels—at a very attractive price—by favorite authors who can bring the world of love alive for you.

Sincerely,

Carolyn Marino

Carolyn Marino
Editorial Director
HarperPaperbacks

Harper
Monogram

Misbegotten

 TAMARA LEIGH

HarperPaperbacks
A Division of HarperCollinsPublishers

This is a work of fiction. The characters, incidents, and
dialogues are products of the author's imagination and are
not to be construed as real. Any resemblance to actual events
or persons, living or dead, is entirely coincidental.

HarperPaperbacks *A Division of* HarperCollins*Publishers*
           10 East 53rd Street, New York, N.Y. 10022

Copyright © 1996 by Tammy Schmanski
All rights reserved. No part of this book may be used or
reproduced in any manner whatsoever without written
permission of the publisher, except in the case of brief
quotations embodied in critical articles and reviews. For
information address HarperCollins*Publishers*,
10 East 53rd Street, New York, N.Y. 10022.

Cover illustration by Jean Monti

First printing: July 1996

Printed in the United States of America

HarperPaperbacks, HarperMonogram, and colophon are
trademarks of HarperCollins*Publishers*

❖ 10 9 8 7 6 5 4 3 2 1

This one is for the belle of North Carolina—
my mother, Zola.
You taught me life, inspired me with your strength,
showed me the power of persistence, and shared the
wisdom of your years. But of all these, your love is
the greatest gift of all.

1

England, Spring of 1348

He hated the waiting. It made him feel like a vulture circling above an animal that has yet to drag its last breath. But that was what he did— waited for his brother to die so the promises made him would finally be fulfilled.

Heaving a sigh of disgust, Liam swiveled on his heel and strode back toward the opposite end of the great hall. In the past quarter hour, he had paced this same stretch more than a dozen times, scattering the rushes until he had worn a path down to the flooring. Now he did so twice more: past the hearth and stairwell, past the trestle tables and benches stacked against the wall, past the raised dais upon which the lord's high seat awaited him. . .

He halted. Patience, he reminded himself. What were a few hours compared to the past six years? By the morrow, Maynard would take the death pall and all would be as it should have been from the beginning. Liam, bastard-born of Montgomery Fawke, would attain his rightful place as lord of Ashlingford. A baron.

He closed his eyes on the thought. Though he'd shouldered the responsibility of the barony all these years, the title had belonged to his young half brother. But it was Liam who oversaw the immense demesne, supervised the accounts, met the needs of his brother's people, and managed to keep Maynard himself in funds enough to satisfy his excessive way of life. All would be different now, Liam vowed. Never again would anyone control his destiny. . .

"William."

Deep in thought, Liam had not heard his uncle approach. He turned and looked across at the man who refused to call him by the name given him by his Irish mother. A man who was of the holy church and yet had doubtless known more women than had Liam.

Ivo stood at the base of the stairs, his priest's vestments creased from hours spent praying for his nephew, his gaze as accusing as when he had this noon arrived at Ashlingford. "It gnaws at you, doesn't it?" he said.

Liam stared hard at him.

"I speak of all the waiting, of course," Ivo added, though no explanation was necessary.

Although there was truth in what he said, Liam's anger flared at this man's baiting of him. But it was no different from usual. There had never been and would never be any liking between him and his uncle,

Ivo having long ago made known his hatred of his bastard nephew. For the priest there was only Maynard.

"What is it you want?" Liam asked.

"I come from Maynard."

Liam waited for him to continue, but when he did not, asked, "He is dead?"

As if his were a secret that might change the course of the world, an uncommon light entered Ivo's eyes. "You must be patient, my son. 'Twill happen soon enough."

Suspicion merged with anger. "Then what have you come for?" Liam snapped.

Ivo crossed his arms over his chest. "The baron has refused confession and the taking of the Last Sacrament until he has spoken with you. He asks that you attend him at once."

As Maynard had earlier denied him entrance to his death chamber, Liam's suspicions grew. What more was there to talk about that had not already been discussed? What provisions that had not already been made? What knowledge that had yet to be imparted? Something pleasing to Ivo, he concluded, which could only mean all was not as it should be. "I will follow," he said.

With a nod, his uncle lifted his robes and mounted the steps.

Liam watched him go, and only when the stairway stood in its own shadow did he stir. Praying that it would all be over soon, he took the stairs two at a time to the first landing and strode down the corridor and into the chamber.

Instantly, Maynard's gaze fell upon him. "Liam." He spoke barely above a whisper. "Come."

As Liam stepped forward, he glanced at the woman who sat beside Maynard's bed. With her gnarled hands pressing a bunched kerchief to her eyes, she wept. Emma had been with Maynard since his birth. As his wet nurse and later his nursemaid, she had known him better than Anya, his own mother—and had certainly loved him more. However, in spite of her loyalty to the legitimate son, she was always kind to Liam, which was more than most had been.

Standing alongside Ivo, Liam looked down at his brother's pitifully battered body stretched out on the bedclothes. Though it was he who had carried Maynard up to the donjon and laid him upon his bed, the physician had immediately ordered everyone from the chamber. Liam had not had time to see what injuries lay beneath his brother's tunic, but he knew they would be the death of him.

Maynard's collarbone jutted out at a peculiar angle, and where the left side of his lower rib cage ought to have been, there was only a depression, the bones having broken inward. However, it was neither of these injuries that drained the life from him, but deep bruises covering nearly his entire abdomen. Maynard was drowning in the blood of his torn internal organs.

"I am dying," he rasped, the hint of a drunken slur still on his tongue. "But you know that, don't you?"

Liam looked at Maynard's beautiful face. The golden hair was tarnished by dirt, the skin drained of color by the stalking of death. Though he knew better than to feel compassion or pity for this man with whom he'd shared only a father, emotions lurched within him. "I know," he said.

It seemed an effort, but Maynard smiled. "I thought it would be me burying you," he murmured. "Thought I would . . . outlive you."

Liam reflected on his brother's reckless life. Maynard had lived as if he would never die. "And then not have had to keep your vow to me," he said.

"Ah, you know me well."

"I do."

"Will you—" Maynard broke off as pain engulfed him. However, by the time the physician reached his side, it had abated. Waving the man away, he asked, "Will you take a wife now, Liam?"

"I will." Though Liam had intended to wed before this time, the affairs of the barony had always been too pressing. Also, in the back of his mind had been the possibility that Maynard might go back on his word—that he might marry and produce an heir after vowing he would not. But now, intentional or otherwise, it appeared he had kept his side of the bargain. In exchange for Liam's years of managing the barony, which had abundantly financed Maynard's ventures and exploits, Ashlingford would become Liam's. Of course, there was still the matter of Ivo's secret. . . .

"Will she be Irish?" Maynard asked.

With a snort of disgust, Ivo shook his head.

So now it was Maynard's turn to bait him, Liam thought. Although it would have served him better all these years to have turned his back on his mother's people—to have used William, the English form of the name his mother gave him, and refused association with the Irish—he had not. Nevertheless, it was true that the woman he married would be of the English side of him, for Ashlingford needed a lady of that noble blood. "Nay," he said. "I will marry English."

"At least in that hope Maynard may rest in peace," Ivo muttered.

It took every bit of Liam's will to keep his fists at his sides and not set upon the holy man.

"That is good," Maynard said. "Thin the Irish out of your line." Though long ago he had learned to keep his mouth closed on his loathing for Liam, now that he was dying he dared where normally he never would.

Liam clenched his fists tighter, the muscles in his hands straining as he fought to control the temper he was well known for, a temper foretold by the red of his hair. "I am pleased that you approve," he said.

Maynard let his lids close a moment and then dragged them back open. "How is your head?" he asked, a gleam of satisfaction in his eyes.

Liam needed no reminder of the blow Maynard had dealt him across the back of his skull when the younger man had come to steal from the barony's coffers last eventide, no reminder at all. Upon regaining consciousness he had felt such an explosion of pain he had nearly been blinded by it—and still the swelling throbbed fiercely. "I will live," he said.

Maynard smiled and beckoned. "Bend near me, brother. I have something to tell you."

Ivo shifted restlessly and turned his face away.

Still, Liam could see the upward tug of his mouth—triumphant—and he rubbed the chain of his crucifix between his fingers as he always did to curb his impatience. Aye, here was what the priest had been waiting for, Liam realized: the secret revealed.

Feeling a tightness in his chest, Liam leaned near his brother.

"Closer," Maynard whispered, the stench of drink upon his breath.

Liam ground his teeth together and turned his ear to his brother's mouth.

"I have won, you bastard," Maynard said in a rasping voice. "'Tis not you who will gain Ashlingford, but my son."

The words knelling through him, Liam slowly straightened. "The barony is more rightfully mine than any of the misbegotten sons you have sown on village women," he said. "Should you try to name one of them heir, I vow to petition the king for the baronage. And he will not deny me, Maynard."

"You think I speak of those dirty little whelps?" his brother said scornfully. "I assure you I do not."

Liam felt something drop out of him. Was it his soul? "Who?" he demanded.

With a long-drawn sigh, Maynard closed his eyes. "Ah, I am enjoying this immensely," he murmured. "One of the few pleasures left me."

"Speak," Liam ordered.

"Liam!" Emma reproved, past her sobbing. "Your brother lies dying, and you—"

"He will die the sooner, by my hands, if he does not tell me. Who, Maynard?"

Opening his eyes, he met Liam's gaze. "My legitimate son," he said.

Though he knew it to be the truth the moment it was spoken, Liam repeated, "Legitimate?"

Maynard laughed, but only for a moment before he was overcome with a hacking cough. Finally, the spasm subsided, leaving his pallid face flecked with drops of blood. "So you see," he said, "you have given yourself for naught. Six years of your life. And I thank you for every one of them, *brother*."

Liam felt as if turned to stone. *For naught.* Without his knowledge Maynard had wed some woman and produced an heir, a legitimate son who would claim all that should be Liam's. A fury so deep it threatened to consume every last particle of his being spread through him. It poured into his angry fists, gripped his heart, filled his belly, and tightened every muscle in his body. In that instant he might have killed both Maynard and Ivo, had there not been the English in him to cool his blood.

How could this have happened without his knowledge? How had he not been alerted to what his brother intended? There had been no reading of the banns to announce Maynard's marriage—at least not anywhere near Ashlingford.

Liam grabbed the thread of hope dangling before him. As church law decreed that a marriage between a man and a woman from different parishes must be publicly announced in both, Maynard's marriage might yet be declared void and his son illegitimate. However, the fragile thread snapped with his next thought. No doubt Maynard had purchased a special license to allow him to be wed without announcing it beforehand. And the substantial amount required to buy such dispensation would have been doled out, unwittingly, by Liam.

Thinking Ivo must have been involved, Liam turned to him. "You knew of this?"

The flush of embarrassment creeping up the priest's neck and stealing into his cheeks said otherwise. Though he had long prided himself on being indispensable to Maynard, his nephew must not have confided in him about his marriage—worse, had not enlisted him to help work the deception.

"It surprises you I did it on my own, does it not?" Maynard asked.

Liam looked down at him.

His brother chuckled past a gurgling in his throat. "I am not the fool you think I am, Liam. Of course, you may continue on at Ashlingford to serve my son as you have served me."

Liam's deadly emotions rose again. "Where is the gold you stole from me last eve?" he demanded.

Maynard shifted his gaze to Ivo, then back to Liam. "Stole?" he repeated. "From you? As baron of Ashlingford, I took naught that was not already mine."

Fighting to hold back his Irish temper, Liam asked again, "Where is it?"

Maynard affected a frown of uncertainty, then with effort patted a searching hand across his waist. "Fancy that . . . gone," he said.

Ivo knew where it was, Liam knew. Recognizing that if he stayed any longer he would make good his threat upon Maynard's life—useless as it would be—he pivoted and strode toward the doorway.

"His name is Oliver," Maynard called to his back.

Liam halted but did not turn around.

"Oliver Fawke," Maynard said with smug satisfaction. "He will be three years old at summer's end."

Dragging in air, Liam asked, "And your wife?"

"She is Lady Joslyn of—" Maynard broke off as another bout of coughing assailed him.

Liam waited.

"Of Rosemoor," Maynard finished.

This explained why Maynard's marriage had gone unnoticed. Rosemoor lay far to the south, so any reading of the banns—had they been read—would not have reached Ashlingford, nor would word have reached the barony. Especially as Maynard had not wished it.

Needing to hear no more, Liam continued from the chamber.

"Do you not want to watch me die?" Maynard asked, but in the next instant choked on his own mockery.

Glancing back, Liam settled his gaze on his brother's writhing body. "You are already dead," he said, and strode down the corridor toward the stairs.

"You bas—" The groan that broke Maynard's words ascended to a high-pitched wail.

Liam tried not to hear it, not to care that his brother was in the throes of death, but still it made him falter. Standing before the stairs, he bent his head and clenched his fists at his sides. He would not think of the brother whom he had once felt great affection for, he told himself. He would not dwell on the one who, as a child, had revered him. Only the Maynard of this last day would he ever again allow in his mind: Maynard the man. And never would he mourn him. Never.

With the sounds of his brother's final groans resounding off the stone walls, Liam forced himself to descend the steps and start across the great hall. However, on reaching the doorway, a silent beckoning caused him to halt his stride. Knowing what it was, he resisted but in the end looked over his shoulder and settled his gaze on the elaborately carved high seat that only the lord of Ashlingford could fill. It awaited him—as it had for more than six long years. And the wait was not yet over.

Feeling betrayed and betrayed again, Liam stepped outside into a sunless spring afternoon that bit him with its chill wind. As he looked across the bailey to the land beyond that should have been his, he did not at first see the gathering at the base of the donjon steps. However, their murmurs dragged him from the mire of what should have been and what was.

"The baron is dead," he announced, knowing that if Maynard's life was not over in this moment, it would be in the next.

The murmur swelled to a din, though not because the castle folk suffered great loss at the death of their lord. They were merely surprised. Although during the first twenty years of his life Liam had numerous times had to prove himself past his Irish blood, it was to him these people had grown loyal, him they regarded as their lord, not the philandering baron of Ashlingford.

Liam drew a deep breath. Nay, his bid for the barony was not finished. This was his destiny. It belonged to him, and he would not so easily hand it over to the child Maynard had made in order to steal it from him.

Descending the steps, he called for his men and then strode along the path that opened before him. On all sides he was besieged by questioning eyes, but he met none of them. Soon enough they would learn of Maynard's deathbed disclosure.

In the outermost bailey, a half dozen men on his heels, Liam shouted for horses and provisions. Then, still saying nothing of his intentions, he headed for the smithy.

"Sir Liam!" a familiar voice exclaimed. "What commotion is this?"

Liam's thoughts jerked to a halt. Swinging around, he looked at the man who was guiding his mount into the bailey.

Sir John offered him a grin, swung himself down from his destrier, and tossed the reins to his squire.

Liam had forgotten that the knight, being vassal and keeper of the lesser castle of Duns, had been expected this day to discuss his accounts. But no longer did it matter. After sending his men on to the smithy with orders that their weapons be sharpened for travel, he strode to where John stood picking at the fingers of his gloves.

"Surely you are not leaving," the knight said. "We've business to discuss and . . . " He trailed off as his gaze settled on Liam. "Something is amiss?"

"Maynard is dead."

Leaving the glove dangling from the end of his hand, Sir John said, "Dead? Good God, Liam, how?"

"Rode his horse into a ravine last eve."

"But how can that be? He was as capable a rider as any."

Liam raised an eyebrow.

Understanding, the knight answered his own question with as much disgust as he'd always had for the baron of Ashlingford. "Drunk."

Liam nodded.

"You found him?"

"Nay, he climbed out of the ravine and walked the distance himself."

As if he referred to a horse, John asked, "Did he linger long?"

Liam refused himself the image of his brother lying prostrate and broken on the bed. "Long enough."

With a knowing nod, John said, "Gave you a time of it, did he?" He returned his attention to the removal of his gloves. "Well at least 'tis over with. Ashlingford is now truly yours, Liam—I suppose I shall henceforth have to call you 'lord.'"

There was only one whom Liam trusted more than this knight—his steward, Sir Hugh—but still he collared the expression of his rage. Eventually, it would have to be released, but not now. "Ashlingford is not mine," he said. "Yet."

"I do not understand."

"Maynard has left behind a son, a legitimate son."

The knight's eyes widened. "Impossible. He cannot have wed without your knowing. The banns—"

"May have been read at Rosemoor, where he wed, or not at all."

"A special license, then," John murmured. "But even so, we all know of his arrangement with you. He—"

Liam cut him off. "I ride south within the hour. Do you ride with me?"

"Of course, but what do you intend?"

What *did* he intend? "To take back what is mine," he said, and then pivoted on his heel and left the knight staring after him.

*   *   *

"William!"

Dragging on the reins, Liam stayed his mount before the drawbridge. The dozen men chosen to accompany him did the same and turned with him to face the interloper.

Just as the horse Ivo rode was far too fine for a priest, the sword girded about his hip was also misplaced. But it was all that Ivo was and had ever been. Now aged forty and nine, the once-handsome man lived life with God on his lips, warring on his mind, and greed in his heart. He was a man of the church in name only.

Straining to suppress his anger, Liam asked, "Have you not someone to bury?"

Ivo halted his destrier before Liam. "I do," he snarled, the whites of his eyes veined red with the strain of tears he had wept over Maynard. "But as your journey will not wait, neither will mine."

"Go, then."

"Ah, but I go with you." A bitter smile etched Ivo's hard mouth.

Liam was surprised that his uncle did not first go to seek the coins Maynard had left somewhere behind. As it was a considerable sum—the greatest portion of Ashlingford's coffers—it could only mean it was hidden well enough that it could wait. "I do not require your priest's services," he said.

With the jewels of his crucifix catching sunlight, Ivo said, "I do not offer them."

Lord, but he was near to losing control! Liam thought. So near to releasing all that was pent up inside him. However, feeling the shifting unease of his men—who feared the letting of holy blood—Liam reminded himself that, in name or not, he was still their lord. "You are not needed," he said again.

"'Tis to Rosemoor you go, is it not?"

"It is."

Ivo inclined his head. "Then I am needed."

"And I ask you, for what?"

"To ensure the safety of Maynard's heir—that he reaches Ashlingford alive."

Alive. As if Liam might resort to murder to attain what was already his! Resenting the accusation, which was as obvious as if it had been spoken, Liam said, "And you think he will not?"

"Many are the unfortunate accidents that befall children in travel." Ivo lifted his palms heavenward. "I would simply ensure that none of them befall Oliver."

"As I will not be traveling with him, I assure you your worries are unfounded, uncle," Liam said, his voice level despite his emotions. "I go to Rosemoor only to verify the child's existence—and the validity of Maynard's marriage."

"And then?"

"You are far too learned to ask such a foolish question."

"You will go to London to petition the king for the barony?"

Liam left Ivo's question unanswered. "Stay and bury your beloved nephew," he said. "No harm will come to the child."

Ivo smirked. "Let us be certain, hmm?" He impelled his horse forward and over the drawbridge.

Though it was a great temptation to overpower his uncle and lock him in one of the gatehouse rooms until he returned, Liam knew he would have the church to answer to. Nay, let the old devil come along, he grudgingly decided. Soon enough Ivo would regret his interference.

Liam thrust his destrier ahead of the others. "We ride!" he shouted.

2

"Do not touch."

"Why?"

"It has thorns." She touched the base of the plant's spine. "See?"

"Uh-huh."

"And if you catch your finger on it, 'twill hurt quite badly."

"Why?"

"Because . . . " Joslyn sighed. "Ah, Oliver, I have told you before."

"Tell me 'gain."

She tapped a gloved finger to his mud-smudged nose. "Nay, I will not, young man. Now along with you."

Heaving an exaggerated sigh, Oliver turned and headed back across the garden.

"And take your bucket," Joslyn called after him.

He scooped it up and toted it back to the corner of the walled garden he had minutes earlier abandoned, a patch of earth ravaged by numerous holes and heaps of dirt. Then, issuing another sigh clearly intended for his mother's ears, he plopped down and set about dirtying those rare inches of himself that were still clean.

Joslyn smiled. From the top of his golden head to the small toes he curled into the dirt he was hers, every dear and dirty bit of him. Her heart lightened, she turned back to the rosebush she had been in the midst of transplanting when he had come to her with his many questions. However, she had only just begun to pack the roots when a distant sound caught her regard. Sitting back on her heels, she tried to identify what it was that traveled not only on the air but which could also be felt through the earth.

Horses, she named the vibration beneath her knees. But why at such speed when it was not permitted within the walls of the village? Though none would speak against their lord making such a ride, never had her father done so—even when he was in his cups. Of course, something might have happened to warrant it, something that brought her father from London when it was yet three days before he was expected home again.

Joslyn stood.

"Mama?"

Glancing behind, she saw that Oliver had also risen. "'Tis naught," she told him. "Stay here."

"I come too."

"Nay, I will be back in a moment."

"But I want—"

"Stay here," she said more firmly.

His lower lip jutted out, but a shake of his mother's head set him back on his rear end.

Hoping he would not disobey her, which he'd been doing ever since he turned two, Joslyn walked to the gate and around to the front of the manor house. Shading her eyes with her hand, she scanned the village before her, but all she saw were people coming out of their homes to see for themselves what was happening—as were the manor servants behind Joslyn.

Concluding that it must be her father and his men come with bad tidings, for surely any others in such great number would have been turned away at the village gates, Joslyn lifted her skirts and started across the green, which was still sodden from yesterday's rainfall. However, she was only a quarter of the way across it when the riders rode into sight. Out of the village they came, to turn onto the road leading to the manor.

Joslyn faltered. Though they were still distant, she could see it was not her father at the fore. Instead, the sun shone on one who sat taller in the saddle than was possible for Humphrey Reynard—and whose head was crowned with hair of red.

God, he had come!

For what seemed an eternity, Joslyn stood rooted to the spot, her mind awash with what it meant. In the end, though, it came down to one thing: her son.

Fear racing through her, she turned and began running toward the garden. *Faster!* she commanded her legs. She had to reach Oliver first—get him inside before it was too late. Lord, how she wished this once he had disobeyed her and followed! As there was no entrance into the manor from the garden, she would have to retrieve him and then retrace her steps.

Alarmed, the servants called to Joslyn, but she could make no sense of their words. She hadn't time. "Oliver!" she screamed.

In her frantic flight, she slipped twice on the wet green but quickly regained her footing and continued to the garden. Within, she paused only long enough to locate Oliver. He stood looking across at her with wide, curious eyes—exactly where she had left him.

"Mama?" he asked.

Praying for wings, Joslyn rushed forward, gathered him into her arms, and ran back to the gate. However, she had only taken a step out of the garden when her gaze lit on one rider who had broken away from the others and was this moment heading across the green toward her. He must have seen her, she realized. Must have guessed who she was.

Measuring the distance from the manor door to the man whose red hair proclaimed him to be Liam Fawke, Joslyn realized it was futile. Never would she make it, especially carrying Oliver. But what then? She could not simply stand here and allow this man to do what he intended, and neither could she scale the back wall, for it was too high.

"Who's that?" Oliver asked, looking toward the thundering horse with its red-haired knight.

A thought struck Joslyn. Leaving Oliver's question unanswered, she turned back into the garden and ran to where she had earlier noticed a portion of crumbling wall in need of repair. If she and Oliver could squeeze through it, the thick wood beyond the village wall would provide a refuge.

Setting Oliver down, she dropped to all fours and pushed aside the stones. Unfortunately, the hole was only big enough for Oliver to pass through. But it would do.

She turned to where her son stood watching her and said, "Listen to me, Oliver. There is a bad man coming and you must hide."

"A bad man?"

She nodded. "Do you remember—"

"The red knight?"

Needing to impress the urgency of the matter on him, she pulled him toward her and tilted his chin up. "Aye, the red knight. Now, do you remember the old oak, the one by the stream with the large hollow in its trunk?"

"Uh-huh."

"I want you to crawl through here—" she nodded to the breach in the wall— "and run as fast as you can to the postern gate." Unless someone had closed it during the past hour, it ought still to be open. "Go into the wood and hide yourself inside the oak. I will—"

"But there's bugs in it. You said I could not—"

"This is different, Oliver. You must hide there so the bad man cannot find you. Do you understand?"

Clearly not all of it, but he nodded.

Pulling him into her arms, Joslyn squeezed him tight and pressed a kiss to his brow. "Go now," she said, pushing him toward the hole. "I will come for you shortly."

Oliver lowered himself to his knees. "Will he hurt you, Mama?" he asked.

Managing a smile she hoped was reassuring, she shook her head. "Nay, he will not. Now hurry."

Once his small bottom disappeared and she heard the beat of his feet over the ground, Joslyn straight-

ened and retrieved the rake she had earlier discarded.
Then she ran back across the garden, pressed herself
against the wall alongside the gate, and raised her
weapon.

Though Joslyn expected Liam Fawke to propel his
mount into the garden as recklessly as he had over the
green, he did not. Instead, he reined in before the open
gateway, the destrier's heavy breathing and the
shadow it and its rider threw over the ground the only
proof of their presence.

Liam Fawke was no unseasoned knight, Joslyn
acknowledged, for he obviously suspected what
he could not see through the gateway. Just as
good, though, for the longer he stayed without,
the more time Oliver had to reach the wood. However, in the next instant, the horse bolted into the
garden.

Too late, Joslyn swung at the man's back and
landed a blow to the air that nearly lost her the rake.
Splintering her hands on the wooden handle, she
raised her crude weapon again as the knight wheeled
his horse around to face her.

And what an unexpected sight he was! Joslyn had
known him only by the red hair Maynard had told
her of: the Irish in him. From that, and from her husband's tales of this cruel and treacherous man, she
had envisioned a far different person from the one
before her now. The bastard brother Maynard had
described had been neither so tall nor so broad-
shouldered. He'd been older, and certainly had not
possessed a handsome face beneath his red hair.
Joslyn had pictured that hair as being long and
unkempt, rather than groomed as it was—cut short
above his ears but longer in back where it curled

over his collar. Lord, he looked more the gentleman than the knave of Maynard's tales. But he was dangerous. . . .

From the woman's flight across the manor green, Liam had guessed she was the Lady Joslyn and that she ran from him to hide her son. But now that he saw her up close, he knew this could not be the woman whom Maynard had wed and bedded, for the creature who stood before him wielding a rake would have held no appeal for his brother.

From the crooked veil atop her head, which had loosed strands of blackest hair, to the hem of her drab skirts, she was streaked with dirt—including her face and throat. A village woman, perhaps, but certainly not of the manor. She must have run simply out of fear.

"He is dead," she stated, the first to break the silence.

Frowning, Liam searched her eyes. They were a brilliant amber.

She tilted her smudged chin higher. "He said you would come," she continued, in a voice and manner at odds with her appearance. "He said you would try to murder me and my child. Is that what you intend, Liam Fawke?"

It *was* she. The shock was difficult for Liam to contain. Perhaps cleaned up, Maynard's wife might be somewhat presentable, but there seemed nothing about her to attract a man. Lord, who even knew what figure she possessed beneath those dirty, ungirded garments?

"Is it?" she asked again.

Liam had to think back to what she had said— Maynard had warned her that if he came it would be with murderous intent. "Where is the boy?" he demanded.

"First you will answer my question," she said. "What are your intentions?"

She was stalling for time, Liam realized. "To claim what is mine," he said, allowing her what he could well afford.

"Ashlingford."

He inclined his head.

"Then I am correct in believing Maynard is dead?"

"He is."

She lowered her lids over those incredible eyes—the only remarkable thing about her—but when she lifted them again, there was no sign of grieving there.

She was cold, Liam concluded. Unfeeling. Just as Maynard had been. It was this, then, that had drawn them together. Like attracted like. "You seem hardly saddened by the news, my lady," he remarked, though he nearly laughed aloud at having bestowed the title on one who could not possibly look less the noble-woman.

Her amber eyes flashed at him. "As you do not know me, Sir Liam," she said, "do not attempt to judge me."

But he did know her. What more needed to be told about the woman than that she had wed Maynard? Of course, she may have had no choice. Though some women had a say in whom they wed, most did not.

"What are your intentions toward my son?" she repeated.

Liam prodded his destrier nearer her, provoking her into raising the rake higher.

"Come no closer," she warned.

Turning his mount sideways, he looked down the length of her weapon and into her eyes. Aye, as a mother protecting her babe, she would use it if need be—even if in vain. "On the morrow I ride to London to put my case before the king," he said. "Oliver will accompany me."

"Why?"

It was true Liam had not planned to do this when Ivo had questioned him about it, but the more he pondered, the more it appealed to him. Let the king see for himself the heir Maynard had named. Let him decide if a barony of the magnitude and importance of Ashlingford belonged in the hands of a child. "Where is he?" he asked.

A satisfied gleam entered her eyes. "Where you cannot touch him."

"In spite of what you think of me," Liam said, "no harm will come to your son."

Her eyes said she did not believe him.

Liam gestured to the rake. "Do you plan to use that?"

"If I must."

There was something almost humorous about the situation, Liam thought. What would his father have said of an armed and mounted knight facing off a bedraggled waif whose only defense was a rusty old rake? "Put it down, Lady Joslyn," he said. "You need not fear me."

"Needn't I? You are not a stranger to me, Liam Fawke. I know the man you are."

Maynard had made certain of that. "Then what makes you think that silly thing will prevent me from taking what I have come for? Am I not armed?"

Her gaze fell first to the thrusting sword that hung on the front of his saddle, then to the shorter sword suspended from his hip belt, and last to his dagger.

"Were I the murderer Maynard led you to believe," he continued, "I assure you that you would not still be standing where you are now."

She must have known it was the truth, but still she refused to give up her weapon. "I will not allow you to take my son."

Liam was about to assure her again of the boy's safety when he heard beyond the garden walls a child's voice raised in protest. "But I have him already," he said.

Fear flooding her eyes, Joslyn dropped the rake and ran from the garden.

Liam prodded his destrier forward and followed her around to the rear of the manor, where Sir John and three other knights rode toward them.

"Nay!" Joslyn cried as she lunged toward the squirming, screeching child beneath John's arm.

Liam turned his destrier into her path. "You will be trampled underfoot," he warned.

Snapping her head back, she leveled all her loathing at him. "That would fit well with your plans, would it not?"

Liam gripped the reins tighter but, rather than argue his character, turned his eyes forward again. She would believe what Maynard had told her before she would ever believe the words of a stranger, and as it was unlikely Liam would have occasion to disprove his brother's lies, it would be a waste of time even to try.

As Sir John drew near, Liam got his first glimpse of

this child who was Maynard's. Though it hardly seemed possible, the boy was even filthier than his mother.

"Mama!" he howled, catching sight of her. Then he stretched out his arms as if he thought she might fly into them.

A moment later, Sir John brought his horse alongside Liam's. "He bites," the knight grumbled.

Joslyn reached to take her son from him. "Give him to me," she demanded.

At John's questioning look, Liam shook his head.

Catching the exchange, Joslyn turned her angry gaze on Liam. However, she did not argue the matter—quite likely fearing it would upset the child even more. "'Tis all right," she said, patting Oliver's knee.

Although her touch and nearness comforted him enough to still his fitful movements, he continued to reach for her.

"If you promise to keep your teeth to yourself, boy," Sir John said, "you may share my saddle with me."

Oliver stilled, and after a long silence of weighing the merits of remaining beneath the man's arm against those of being allowed to sit on the exquisitely worked saddle, he nodded agreement.

As the child was settled between Sir John's thighs, Liam said, "So this filthy little urchin is Oliver."

The boy jerked his head up, giving Liam his first real look at him. "I am not little!" he declared, his fear replaced by bright-eyed outrage.

Liam needed no more confirmation that the child was Maynard's. Cleaned, his hair would be as golden as Maynard's had been, and visible beneath the layers of dirt he bore the same distinctive forehead and jaw as had the generations of Fawkes before him. True, the coloring of his eyes was given him by his mother, but their shape was unmistakably Maynard's—and Liam's.

Suddenly, Oliver's outrage slipped away. His jaw dropping wide, he pointed a finger at Liam and declared, "The bad man, Mama!"

The bad man . . . ? Liam glanced down at Joslyn. However, she averted her gaze.

"He will not hurt you, Oliver," she assured him.

The boy mulled it over a moment, then asked Liam, "Will you hurt my mama?"

Something about his childish concern dragged a smile from Liam. "Nay, Oliver, I am not the bad man your mother thinks me to be. I am your Uncle Liam, the brother of your father."

Oliver cocked his head to the side. "My father?"

"This really isn't necessary, is it?" Joslyn interjected.

Liam ignored her. "How old are you, boy?" he asked.

Thoughtfully, Oliver raised a hand before his face, uncurled one finger, a second one, chewed his bottom lip a moment, then thrust his hand toward Liam. "One . . . two," he said. "See?"

Liam sought Joslyn's gaze. "Let us go inside."

Her eyebrows arched. "Surely you do not expect me to welcome you into my father's home?"

His tolerance nearly spent, Liam leaned down from his mount so she could better feel his words. However, the scent wafting off her surprised him into speechlessness. Instead of the rank odors of an unclean body, she smelled of earth and wood and, beneath that, a hint of roses. Rosewater, he thought, which meant she had recently bathed.

Remembering himself, he looked into her indignant eyes. "If you would prefer, I will simply take Oliver up before me and continue on my way," he said, though he had no intention of doing such a thing. Not only would it be unwise to have tales of abduction following him to London, but he must first verify the boy's claim on Ashlingford—that Oliver was, indeed, legitimate born.

"Of course not," Joslyn said quietly, his threat taming the defiance out of her.

"Then to the manor?"

Grudgingly, she nodded.

Liam urged his destrier around, but in the next instant checked the animal's progress and leveled his gaze on the men riding toward him. Sir Gregory and, ahead of him, Ivo.

Insufferable priest! The past two days of hard riding should have tired the man who was twenty years older than Liam, but Ivo had kept pace the entire way. Thus, in order to take Rosemoor without his uncle's interference, Liam had been forced to trickery.

After Ivo had gained them entrance into the village in the name of the church, Liam had set Sir Gregory on him, and in the ensuing fray he and the rest of his men had ridden on the manor.

Clearly angered at having been left behind, Ivo dragged his horse to a cruel halt and turned to his bastard nephew. However, he did not utter the words pressing at the back of his colorless lips as he must have wanted. Instead, he cursorily searched the small gathering before him and a moment later eyed the unlikely woman who stood alongside Sir John's mount. "Where is your mistress, girl?" he demanded.

Liam smiled.

Raising her chin again, Joslyn said, "You are mistaken, Father. I am—"

"Lady Joslyn Fawke," Liam finished for her. "Maynard's widow."

The disbelief rising on Ivo's face offered a rare glimpse of the usually arrogant, self-assured man.

"And here is Maynard's son," Liam continued. "Oliver Fawke."

Recovering from his momentary surprise, Ivo looked to the unkempt boy. However, in spite of the boy's appearance, some of the harshness drained from the priest's eyes. "Maynard's son," he murmured.

"And who are you?" Joslyn asked.

He was a long time in pulling his gaze from Oliver. "I am Father Ivo," he finally said. "Maynard's uncle."

"Ivo?" Joslyn echoed.

Liam heard the hope in her voice. Clearly, Maynard had told her of his beloved uncle, and in him she now saw a possible ally. More than possible, Liam knew. If need be, Ivo would defend Oliver's right to Ashlingford all the way to the papacy.

The anger in Liam surfacing again, he barked, "We will continue this inside," and spurred his destrier forward.

At the manor steps, he was met by uncertain, hand-wringing servants and the handful of men he had ordered to position themselves there in the event of trouble. But trouble would not come from the manor, he saw, as he looked behind him. It would come from the villagers, who were now massed on the road Liam and his men had taken. Their weapons implements such as Joslyn had tried to use against him, they came to ensure that all was well at their lord's manor.

"Lady Joslyn," Liam called to her as she neared, "go to your people and tell them naught is amiss. Instruct them to return to their homes."

The rebellion that flared in her eyes smoldered in the next instant. As Sir John still had possession of her son, she had no choice but to do as she was told. To Oliver she said, "The knight has a fine horse, does he not?"

He nodded with enthusiasm. "Bigger'n A-papa's."

"Aye, much bigger than your grandfather's horse. Do you think you can watch him while I go down the road to talk to the villagers? I shan't be long."

A tiny frown gathering between his eyes, Oliver looked back at Sir John. "You not a bad man?" he asked.

With a smile twitching at the corner of his mouth, the knight shook his head.

Oliver looked back at his mother. "A'right," he agreed. "I watch the horse."

Sending Liam a warning look, Joslyn started toward the road.

Liam glanced at Sir Gregory, who'd so recently served him well, and only then noticed the bleeding cut tracing the man's cheekbone. No doubt Ivo's nasty dagger had done that, though surely his uncle would have preferred to pierce the young knight's breast than the trivial flesh of his face. "Sir Gregory," he said, "accompany Lady Joslyn."

Joslyn halted, but though she must have wanted to say something quite badly, she drew herself stiffly erect and continued on as if she went alone.

3

Liam Fawke's eyes.

They were the first Joslyn saw when she stepped into the hall. They bored through her and then shifted to the knight who had accompanied her down the road to speak with the villagers.

Disquiet shuddered up her spine. She had heard it said a fine horse could make a man, but such was not the case with Maynard's brother, for even without his great destrier beneath him, he was an imposing presence. Not that he was unusually tall. It was just that his broad shoulders coming out from beneath the mantle, and the muscled legs defined beneath the material of his chausses, set him so far apart from the others.

Hating every inch of him, Joslyn began searching for her son. However, she did not have to look far—only down. The little boy stood in Sir Liam's shadow, his eyes fixed on the man towering over him.

Though the desire to call him to her was strong, Joslyn quelled it and walked forward with as much dignity as was possible in her soiled gardening attire. On her heels, Sir Gregory followed—no doubt to report on her conversation with the villagers. How Joslyn wished there had been some way to alert her father's people as to what had truly transpired, but fear for Oliver's well-being curbed her tongue.

Liam Fawke had not won, though, she told herself as she spotted Father Ivo where he stood warming himself before the hearth. From Maynard she knew of the priest's staunch loyalty to her husband, and though he had been surprised by her appearance, in his eyes had been the promise of an ally.

"Mama!" Oliver exclaimed.

Ignoring Liam, Joslyn stepped to her son and gratefully accepted the small hand he slid into hers. Lord, but it felt wonderful. There had been a moment when she feared she might never touch him again. Bending down, she asked, "Did you tend the knight's horse well?"

He bobbed his head up and down, "Unca Liam let me touch his sword!"

Joslyn flinched at the affectionate title of "uncle" he so innocently bestowed on one who sought to steal his birthright—one who might even have murdered Oliver's father in order to do so, she reminded herself. "Is that so?" she asked.

"Aye, an' his dagger too."

Although she felt Liam's eyes on her again, she continued to ignore him.

"He's a great knight," Oliver continued.

Joslyn raised an eyebrow. "Is that what he told you?"

"Nay, Sir John told me." He pointed to a man who stood nearby—the same who'd snatched Oliver from his flight toward the woods and taken him onto his horse.

"I see," Joslyn murmured. As she straightened, out of the corner of her eye she saw Liam turn to Sir Gregory.

"Thirsty, Mama," Oliver said, his voice loud enough to make it impossible for Joslyn to hear Sir Liam's exchange with his man.

It mattered not, though, for there was naught the knight could report that might anger Liam Fawke, Joslyn assured herself. Turning, she motioned one of the servants forward. "Clare."

"Aye, my lady?" Clare asked.

"Bring some honey milk for my son," Joslyn said. Then, remembering she was the lady of her father's house, she added grudgingly, "and ale for the men."

"It has already been sent for—the ale, I mean," Clare said, "but I will fetch the honey milk."

"Sent for?"

"Aye, Sir Liam called for it."

Of course. Resentment rolling through her, Joslyn leveled all of it on the cur's back. "Fine."

"Hungry, too," Oliver piped up.

It was early for supper, but Joslyn could see no reason not to have it over and done with. "Tell Cook to prepare some cold meats and cheeses," she ordered the serving girl, "and to warm some bread. Then find someone to help you move the tables and benches out from the walls."

"Aye, my lady. Anything more?"

"Nay, that is enough."

With a bob of her head, Clare turned and started back across the hall.

Although the thought of a bath beckoned mightily to Joslyn, she decided that a washbasin would suffice until this eve, when she could linger in the tub. "Let us go wash ourselves and change our clothes," she said to Oliver, "and when we are finished, you will have your drink—"

"Clare," Liam called to the girl.

Grinding her teeth, Joslyn looked over her shoulder at where he stood.

The girl offered him a pretty smile. "Aye, my lord?"

"You may tell Cook not to hurry. The ale will suffice until the lady has had her bath." Liam's gaze flicked to Joslyn, dismissed her, and returned to Clare.

"Very well, my lord."

Joslyn's control snapped. "Nay, Clare, tell Cook to prepare the meal with all speed," she said. "My son and I are hungry."

The girl was startled, but seeing something in her mistress's face that she had not seen before, she nodded and scurried toward the kitchens.

Joslyn hardly noticed the quiet that fell over the hall as she stared at Liam and silently dared him to countermand her. In fact, for the longest time it seemed they were the only two in the room: the Irish bastard and the defiant widow.

Staring across the three strides that separated him from Joslyn, Liam's annoyance ebbed as something uninvited stirred in him. As unbecoming and filthy as

Joslyn was, he felt a peculiar oneness with this lady, who was not placid and proper as she should have been, and who was certainly not as cold as he'd first believed. She was unlike any English lady he had ever known. Indeed, she seemed to have a bit of the Irish in her.

That last thought made Liam smile . . . and smile wider. Throwing back his head, he laughed the first laugh he had enjoyed in as long as he could remember and was soon joined by his men.

A moment later, the arrival of servants bearing pitchers of ale caused the din to subside.

"And what is it you find so amusing, Sir Liam?" Joslyn demanded.

Liam quaffed his tankard of ale before answering her. "'Tis amusing that Maynard would choose you for a wife when he professed to so hate spirit in a woman," he said, "and yet you could not be more like my mother, whom he hated."

Though he had not meant it as an insult, she took it as such. "The difference is, Sir Liam" —she spoke between set teeth— "Maynard married me. Unlike your father, who refused to wed your mother. *My* son is legitimate. Unlike you. And Oliver is the heir of Ashlingford. Again, unlike you."

Silence descended, expressions froze, and tankards hung on the air like drops of steel dew.

Had Liam not earlier had the laughter to temper his sudden surge of anger, he knew he would surely have erupted, but he once again repressed what was inside him. "Are you finished, Lady Joslyn?" he asked.

If she feared him—which she should have—she did not show it. "Quite," she said. Then, something catching her eye, she shifted her gaze to the hearth.

Liam looked around in time to catch the slight shake of Ivo's head, a warning that she had gone too far. The man knew him well. Joslyn would be wise to heed his counsel.

The tables and benches having been positioned during the pouring of the ale, Liam strode toward them. "Meal," he said.

With Oliver seated on her right and Father Ivo on her left, Joslyn stared at the food before her. The supper was without flavor, though only because she could not put her mind to it. She was far too preoccupied with this day's events to know what passed her lips, and too fearful of Liam's plans to pay any heed as to whether or not Oliver put anything past his.

Shaking off her troubled thoughts, she looked to where her son had come up on his knees to search out choice morsels from her trencher.

Filthy little urchin, Liam had called him—and it could not have been more true. Oliver had been pleased to sit at table wearing his garden dirt, never before having been allowed to do such a thing.

What would her father say of his grandson if he walked in at this moment? Joslyn wondered. But more, what would he say of his daughter, who had not only allowed it but looked the urchin herself? He would be horrified, though with a tankard or two of ale in him, he would perhaps find humor in it.

"Lady, I fear you tread too heavily."

The unexpectedness of the whisper near her ear

startled Joslyn. She looked into the mature but still handsome face of Father Ivo.

"Pardon?" she asked.

"Do not push the bastard," he said from behind the hand towel he pressed to his mouth. "All will come right if you allow me to prepare Oliver's way."

She glanced to where Liam sat, across the table and three persons down from her. Though his eyes were on the goblet he held, he appeared to be listening to the knight beside him. "How?" she asked. "I—"

"Speak no more. I will come to you this eve and explain."

Her thoughts running ahead, a spring of hope beginning to flow, Joslyn nodded.

"My uncle is an interesting man, do you not think, Lady Joslyn?" Liam asked.

She was caught. Hiding her surprise behind a falsely composed face, she looked into his lucid green eyes. "As we are hardly well acquainted," she said, "I cannot say, can I?"

His smile was cutting. For certain he could not know what had been said between his uncle and her, but he knew it was of him. "Ah, but I'm sure you will become close friends," he said. "Don't you agree, Ivo?"

Ignoring his question, the priest stuffed a piece of cheese in his mouth and began chewing it with great thought.

Seeking another path down which to lead Sir Liam, Joslyn asked what she had yet to know. "How came you into the village?"

"At least in this my uncle was useful," he said.

"In the name of the church, he gained us admittance when we would otherwise have been turned away."

"And had you been turned away?"

He considered her query a moment, then shrugged. "I suppose I would have waited for night and then scaled the walls."

But still he would have come for Oliver. "I see," she murmured, and looked back at her trencher.

Sometime later, Joslyn was again dragged from her thoughts, this time by the arrival in the hall of a man she knew well: Father Paul, the priest who had ministered to the people of Rosemoor for the past twenty or more years and had presided over the vows she and Maynard had spoken. Led forward by one of Liam's men, the rumpled priest looked questioningly about him and seemed relieved to lay eyes upon Joslyn—but only for a moment, before he noticed her dreadful appearance.

Standing, Joslyn took a step toward him.

"Regain your seat, Lady Joslyn," Liam ordered.

She looked across and saw in his eyes a warning—one she badly wanted to defy. However, knowing there was naught to be gained in doing so, she turned back to the bench and slowly lowered herself.

While the priest waited to be told the reason he had been brought to the manor, Liam ordered his men from the hall. Lingering only long enough to gather their tankards of ale and picked-over platters of viands, they complied.

With only Father Ivo, Father Paul, Joslyn, and Oliver remaining, Liam walked around the table.

"Where'd they go?" Oliver asked.

"Outside." Joslyn spoke low.

"Why?"

"Because . . . " Realizing she was about to be drawn into another of his endless queries, she shook her head. "I will tell you later."

With a sigh, he returned to scavenging her plate.

"I apologize for rousing you from your church so late in the day, Father," Sir Liam said, "but I have good reason."

The priest eyed him. "I expect you do. And you are?"

"Sir Liam Fawke. Half brother to Lady Joslyn's husband, who is now departed."

Crossing himself, Father Paul looked past Liam and cast his sympathetic gaze upon Joslyn.

She bowed her head in acceptance of his condolences for a man neither of them had known well.

"What is it you want of me, my son?" Father Paul asked.

"There is the question of who stands to inherit my brother's estates."

Folding his hands before him, the priest nodded toward the tables. "I believe it would be Oliver."

Joslyn saw a muscle jerk in Liam's jaw. He was not pleased. "Then the child is legitimate born?" he asked.

Joslyn leaped up. How dare Liam Fawke suggest her son had been born out of wedlock, that she had lain with Maynard without having first spoken vows! However, before she could voice her resentment, Father Ivo gripped her arm and urged her back down.

"It matters not," he whispered.

She drew a shaky breath. He was right, of course. There was naught to be gained in going against Sir Liam again. At least not yet.

"Of course Oliver is legitimate," the priest said. "'Tis Lady Joslyn we speak of, sir, not a common trollop."

"When was she wed to my brother?"

"The year of our Lord 1344," he said. "The end of autumn, was it not, Lady Joslyn?"

Clenching her jaw so tight it made her teeth ache, she nodded.

"Aye," the priest continued. "There were leaves upon the ground and a storm in the making. I remember it well."

"Was the marriage recorded?"

"Certainly. No marriage or birth in Rosemoor goes unwritten. By my own hand it was inscribed in the church docket."

"And the banns were read prior to the ceremony?"

The priest shook his head. "Nay, a special license was obtained to forego the reading."

Whatever coursed through Liam's mind, it boded no good for Joslyn and Oliver. Eyes narrowing and nostrils flaring, he said, "I would see the license and the church docket."

"I do not lie, Sir Liam," Father Paul objected, "and neither am I so old I cannot remember."

"I will see them."

Though the man of God looked near to arguing the matter, he drew a calming breath and nodded. "They are at the church. If you like, I will show you."

Liam looked around at his uncle. "Do you come?"

Father Ivo rose. "It surprises me that you would even ask, William."

For a moment, Joslyn foundered over the calling of his nephew by another name, but then remembered Maynard mentioning his brother's refusal to take the English form of Liam. "William." She mouthed the name and tried again to fit her tongue around it. Nay, not at all fitting for the man she had these past hours come to loathe and fear. Liam Fawke would never be William. Looking up, she was startled to discover him watching her—no doubt having seen her play over the name he refused.

"Lady Joslyn," he said, "I would ask that you remain inside the manor until my return."

It was more than a request. It was an order that would undoubtedly be enforced by his men. "And if I do not?" she asked, daring where Father Ivo would have warned her not to.

His gaze narrowing, he said, "You are free to move about the manor."

She simply could not help herself. Standing, Joslyn grasped either side of her skirt and bowed low. "I am most grateful, sir knight," she said. "Your thoughtfulness is beyond measure."

A deep silence met this mocking reply, followed shortly by the sound of boots over the floor. Glancing up from her obeisance, Joslyn watched Liam stride from the hall. Then he was gone, leaving the two priests and her to stare at the empty space he left behind.

Straightening, Joslyn shifted her attention to Father Ivo, expecting him to admonish her again for goading Liam. However, all he did was frown hard at her before following his nephew.

Meeting Father Paul's reproving gaze, Joslyn said, "I tried, Father, but still it came."

"As it always does," he said, his eyes reflecting memories of past mischiefs. Then he turned and left her and Oliver to be the only occupants of the hall.

4

They were prisoners in their own home, Joslyn realized as she stepped from the wooden tub and into the towel her maid held for her. But what would Sir Liam's return from the church make them? With verification of her marriage to Maynard and Oliver's legitimacy established, what would he do?

Though when he had ridden on the manor she had believed murder to be his intent, having thought on it this past hour, she realized it had been an irrational fear. If misfortune befell them— especially so soon following Maynard's death—it would be too obvious who had done the deed. Sir Liam would gain naught and might well lose his life. She sensed Father Ivo would make certain of that.

"You may go," Joslyn told the maid as she slipped her arms into the sleeves of her robe. "I will put Oliver to bed myself."

"Very good, my lady." Gathering Joslyn's and Oliver's soiled garments, the woman left.

Joslyn walked to the table where she had earlier set out her sewing kit. From it she removed the finest of her needles and began to pick at the splinters she'd taken in both palms while wielding the rake this afternoon. Every one of them Liam Fawke's fault.

"I've done it, Mama!" Oliver cried a few minutes later.

A wooden top careened across the floor where he had cleared the rushes.

"My, but you have," she said, "and all by yourself."

"Aye," he agreed, pride brimming over.

Realizing she'd given Oliver too little of her attention these past hours, Joslyn set the needle atop the table and went to his side.

As they watched, the top whirled toward the rushes, grazed the bordering pieces, corrected its course, and moved back onto the bare floor. However, it had lost its momentum. "Quick, spin it again ere it falls," Joslyn prompted.

Cornering the wobbly toy as if it were a beast to be tamed, Oliver whipped it with his stick and set it to spinning again. Unfortunately, it spun away and beneath the bed.

Oliver groaned.

Joslyn ruffled his damp hair. "Fetch it and you may try once more ere I tuck you in."

His scrubbed cheeks plumping like shiny apples, he smiled and went down on his hands and knees beside the bed.

She would have to tell him, Joslyn thought. Though Oliver knew about his father, he had not *known* him. Only once following Oliver's birth had

Maynard come to see his son, and as the child had been barely a year old, Oliver could not possibly remember the handful of hours his father had spent with him. He knew only of his existence, which was hardly less than Joslyn had known of the man.

She sighed. If only she could grieve for her husband, squeeze a tear from behind her eye for the man who had fathered her son. But there had been nothing more to their relationship than Oliver. Nothing.

Lost in her thoughts, it was a moment before she heard the light tapping. "Who goes?" she asked as she crossed to the door.

"'Tis I, Father Ivo," a voice whispered through the doorjamb.

He had returned from the church, meaning Liam Fawke was likely to have returned as well.

"May I enter?"

Joslyn glanced down at her robe, then behind her, to where Oliver's searching made him oblivious to their caller.

Thoughtfully, she nipped her bottom lip. Though Father Ivo had told her he would come to her this eve, surely they might talk as well tomorrow. "I am readying for bed," she said. "Can it not wait till the morrow?"

"Nay, it cannot."

"But—"

"Make haste, someone comes," he hissed.

Knowing it would not do for the priest to be caught lingering outside her door, Joslyn pulled it open.

With a rustle of robes, Father Ivo slipped in.

Joslyn closed the door and leaned back against it,

then met Father Ivo's eyes, which gleamed with an appreciation she had never seen in Father Paul's.

"Why, you are not without comeliness, lady," he said.

Self-consciously, Joslyn pulled her robe tighter and nodded to the tub of water. "'Tis quite a miracle a soak and a scrub can work," she said.

"A miracle indeed."

Uncomfortable beneath his continued scrutiny, she walked to where Oliver stood, top in hand and a frown on his face. "Are you going to try it again?" she asked, nodding to the top.

He pointed to the priest. "What's he doin' here?"

"Father Ivo has come to speak with me. It shan't take long." Though Joslyn expected him to ask why, he surprised her by bending down to work his top again.

Joslyn turned to face Father Ivo. "The docket was in order?"

He nodded. "As expected."

"And Sir Liam? What had he to say?"

"Naught." He lowered himself into a nearby chair.

Ignoring that propriety should have seen her seated first, Joslyn remained standing. "Then?" she prompted.

He steepled his hands before his face. "You know you can trust me, do you not?"

All Joslyn knew was that Maynard had trusted him—but only to a point, for he had not told his uncle of his marriage. "You were loyal to my husband," she answered.

"As I will be to you, lady."

"How?"

"I offer you the protection of the church. With me, you and Maynard's son will be safe."

As if Oliver were not *her* son as well, Joslyn reflected. "Safe?" she repeated. "From your nephew?"

"Nephew," Ivo scoffed. "William is no more nephew to me than I am uncle to him."

"You are his father's brother."

"*Maynard* was my nephew," he said, his mouth trembling with sudden emotion. "William is a bastard, and that is all."

Although from what Maynard had told her, and what she'd seen this day, Joslyn shouldn't have been surprised, she was nevertheless taken aback by the priest's vehemence. What had his misbegotten nephew done to deserve such loathing? "Is he responsible for Maynard's death?" she asked.

His eyes darkened ominously. "He is."

Joslyn's blood ran cold. Had she been foolishly secure in believing Maynard's brother would not move against Oliver and her? "But if he killed his brother, why—"

"I did not say he killed Maynard," Father Ivo snapped, coming up out of the chair, "but he is as responsible as if he had."

"I do not understand."

"Mama?" Oliver asked, his concerned face materializing next to Joslyn.

"All is well," she told him, forcing a smile. "Are you ready for me to tuck you in?"

He shook his head. "One more time, please."

"One more time," she echoed, and looked back at Father Ivo. "Tell me," she said.

He opened his mouth as if to do so, but closed it in the next instant. "As William will soon discover me gone and come searching, it will have to wait."

The thought of Liam Fawke coming into her chamber and seeing her attired in her robe, her hair wet about her shoulders and her feet bare, was disconcerting.

"I will come for you and Oliver at midnight, after the changing of the guard," Father Ivo said.

"Why?"

"We will seek an audience with King Edward, you and I. Oliver's right to Ashlingford must be secured ere William reaches London and attempts to convince the king otherwise."

"I do not know that I wish to claim the barony for Oliver," Joslyn said, having spent the past hour dragging the idea back and forth.

"But of course you will claim it!" Ivo exclaimed. "It belongs to him as Maynard's son."

"And *my* son," she reminded him, annoyed that he again disregarded her part in bringing Oliver into the world.

The priest was silent a long moment, his only movement that of his fingers as he repeatedly drew the chain of his crucifix through them. "Aye, yours and Maynard's," he acceded with a nod. "Of course."

Appeased yet wary, Joslyn reached out and lightly skimmed a hand over Oliver's bent head. "I fear for him," she murmured.

Father Ivo stepped near her. "Once the king acknowledges the rightful heir of Ashlingford, we will send William away. He will not be able to touch Oliver, nor will he, knowing that suspicion would fall first on him."

"Still, I—"

"What has Oliver if you deny him his birthright?" Ivo demanded, his voice rising. "A meager manor when 'tis an immense barony he should one day rule?"

Not even Rosemoor, Joslyn thought. It was to her

wayfaring brother the manor would pass when her father died. There would be nothing for her son.

"'Tis not your decision to make," Father Ivo continued more gently, "but Oliver's."

And he was too young to even care. "But how can Ashlingford be managed without a lord?" she asked. "It will be many years ere Oliver is ready to assume his place there."

As if this had not occurred to him, Father Ivo contemplated the floor for a long moment. Then he turned, clasped his hands behind his back, and walked across the chamber. At the opposite wall he paused and pivoted. "I will do it," he said finally.

"You?"

"If it pleases you, lady, I will manage the barony for Oliver until he is of an age to bear the responsibility himself."

Joslyn closed her eyes. It was true. She had no right to take from Oliver what belonged to him. Ashlingford was his future. "Very well," she said. "We will accompany you."

Father Ivo's mouth curved almost into a smile. "Midnight," he said, and walked to the door. "Have you a court gown?" he asked over his shoulder.

"A court gown?"

He raised his eyebrows, reminding her of her earlier attire. "You must charm the king, Lady Joslyn, not shock him."

She nodded. "I have one." At least she hoped it would suffice.

"Midnight," he said again, opening the door a crack.

"Father Ivo?"

He glanced back at her.

"What of Sir Liam's men? How do you intend to get past them?"

He closed his hand around the hilt of the sword that looked so out of place against his priestly vestments. "Of the church I may be," he said, "but I am not without resources."

Then he would shed blood? A holy man? Nay, she could not allow blood on either her or Oliver's hands. Would not.

As if he read her thoughts, Father Ivo shook his head. "By the flat, not the edge," he said. "No blood will I draw." He opened the door wider and slipped out.

By the flat? Joslyn pondered, but a moment later threw the worrisome question off. So long as he did not kill. With no time to waste, she hurried to her chest and threw back the lid.

The flat of the blade striking the soldier's brow produced no more than a choked protest, and then the man crumpled to the ground.

Ivo held his sword horizontally, one gloved hand gripping the hilt, the other the end of the blade as he stared down at his victim. Then he dropped to his haunches. Having more of a care for his weapon than the hapless man it had downed, he gently laid the sword aside and proceeded to remove a rope and rag from inside his mantle.

From the shadows, Joslyn watched as he deftly trussed the man hand and foot, gagged him, and dragged him into the bushes—as if he'd done it many times before.

"Come," Ivo urged, his voice a harsh whisper in

the night. Leading the way, he set off across the expanse of moonlit green before the manor.

Passing by the unfortunate soldier with Oliver fast asleep against her shoulder, Joslyn grimaced. Though no blood had been shed of the two the priest had thus far overwhelmed, each would bear an unsightly swelling in the middle of his forehead and a dreadful throbbing there when he regained consciousness.

Joslyn felt guilty for the punishment they would surely reap in having allowed her and Oliver to escape. She could not even begin to imagine Liam Fawke's anger.

Quickening her steps to keep up with Father Ivo, she held Oliver tight for fear she might lose her footing and drop him. But her feet knew well where she trod, even in spots the moonlight failed to reach. Born at Rosemoor Manor, she'd taken her first steps over this same ground, played the games of youth upon it, and, as she'd grown older, daydreamed as she strolled it.

But the daydreaming was done now, she reflected, as she stepped off the green and onto the road. Maynard Fawke, and now his bastard brother, had stolen that innocence from her. Now she was a widow with a child, about to make an arduous journey to secure a future she did not want. But for Oliver she would do it.

"Hurry," Father Ivo called over his shoulder.

Though they both wore black mantles to clothe them in the shadows of night, the light of the half moon would reveal them to any sharp eye that might be watching. Great as Joslyn's burden was, bearing both Oliver and a bundle of their belongings, she stretched her stride to match the priest's. Finally, upon reaching the streets of the village that hid them from sight of the manor, Father Ivo slowed.

"Where are the horses?" Joslyn asked.

"At the gates. Father Paul will have them in readiness for us."

She faltered. "Father Paul?" It surprised her that he would become involved in this. Though no one could question his loyalty to her father, he had always been cautious in the extreme. She could not imagine him stealing into Rosemoor's stables to bring forth their horses—and doing so without being caught by Liam's men!

Ivo read her thoughts. "He does not do it alone," The priest assured her.

This certainly made a bit more sense, but not wholly, for Father Paul was not one to risk the lives of others either. "I still cannot imagine he would have agreed," she said.

"He understands the gravity of the situation. Oliver's future hangs on William's whim."

"Aye, but—"

"As you will find when we go before the king," Ivo interrupted, "I am a very persuasive man, Lady Joslyn."

And, as she was quickly learning, nothing like Father Paul. In fact, Maynard's uncle hardly seemed of the church at all. But then, she had been sheltered most of her life and knew little beyond Rosemoor. Mayhap it was Father Paul who was different.

Through the sleeping village they wound, and at the gates found the priest waiting for them in the glow of a single torch. Beside him stood two villagers, Bartholomew holding the reins to Ivo's warhorse,

Carle the reins of the dappled palfrey that belonged to Joslyn.

Father Paul stepped toward Ivo. "All has been made ready," he said, his concerned gaze glancing off Joslyn. "Though I do still wonder if 'twould not be better to await the return of Lady Joslyn's father, that he might deal with this himself. Word has been sent to him of the baron's death, and—"

"Nay, 'twill be too late when he arrives." Ivo spoke sharply. "Do we not go this night, William will take the child with him on the morrow."

Though his face continued to reflect uncertainty, Father Paul nodded. "I suppose you are right." He turned to Joslyn. "Should you not meet up with your sire on the road to London, I will send him to you there."

She nodded. "A prayer, Father?"

He stepped forward to grant her request, but Ivo's next words denied it. "We must leave at once," he insisted. "Let us mount up and be gone from here." Taking the reins from Bartholomew, he gained the saddle as easily as any well-trained knight.

Though annoyance flickered across Father Paul's face, he acceded to the other priest's wishes. "When you are gone, I will speak prayers for you and Oliver before the altar," he assured Joslyn.

"I thank you," she said, She walked past him and put Oliver into Carle's arms. Turning aside Bartholomew's offer to assist her in mounting, she gave the bundle to him, put a slippered foot into the stirrup, and settled herself atop her palfrey. Once her belongings were secured to the back of her saddle, Carle passed Oliver up. Unfortunately, it jostled the child out of his sleep.

"Mama?"

"Hush, little one," she soothed, "you are dreaming."

"I am?"

"Um-hmm."

With a sigh, Oliver nestled against her side and slid back into sleep.

Pulling the blanket and her mantle more closely around him to protect him against the chill of the night ride, Joslyn looked up at Ivo. "We are ready," she said.

"Open the gate," he ordered.

With a grunt, Bartholomew pushed one of two large doors outward.

Immediately, Ivo's horse surged forward and passed through the portal.

Joslyn would have followed, but Father Paul stepped to her side and covered her hand with his. "God be with you," he said, "but beware a man who makes his life in the shadow of the church."

She frowned. "Father Ivo?"

"'Tis not only Sir Liam who covets what belongs to another."

Though Joslyn would have liked to hear more, the priest turned and walked away.

There was nothing left to do but to follow Ivo and mull over the priest's warning. She urged her horse forward.

"Godspeed, my lady!" Carle called after her.

"Godspeed," echoed Bartholomew.

Liam stood on two thresholds—that of the chamber Joslyn shared with her son and that of an anger which rivaled what he had felt when Maynard revealed his deceit.

The Lady Joslyn and her son were gone, and they were not alone. Gone with them was Ivo.

Among the first to awaken, Liam had immediately noticed his uncle's absence. As Ivo was not partial to rising before late morning, Liam had known something was amiss and had wasted no time in raising the alarm. His knights scattering, he had come abovestairs to confirm the reality of his suspicions: During the night, Ivo and Joslyn had stolen Oliver from the manor. Undoubtedly their destination was London, where they would seek an audience with the king to plead the child's right to Ashlingford.

Thwarted yet again. "God almighty!" Liam shouted. What stupidity to think Ivo could be kept in his place by soldiers with half the priest's experience. What foolishness to believe Joslyn would not endanger her child for a barony. What—

Something among the rushes caught Liam's eye. Interrupting the richly deserved self-condemnation, he crossed the small chamber and bent beside the bed to pick up the object: a top. He'd had one himself, at Oliver's age, and then passed it on to Maynard after growing too old for it. He still remembered . . .

Shaking his head, Liam broke the memory into a thousand pieces and turned toward the door. However, something made him pause—something in this place that wafted to his senses and teetered on the fringes of his knowing.

Frowning, he turned back to the bed. Though the covers were in slight disarray, he knew Joslyn had not slept there last night. More likely she had sat propped against the pillows, waiting for Ivo to come for them.

Breathing the air, Liam caught the faint scent again. Curiosity momentarily replacing anger, he lifted the sheet to his nose: roses, just as when he'd leaned down from his destrier and smelled them upon her. However, this time it was not earth and wood mingled with the flowers, but the sweet smell of a woman. A woman who had defied and deceived him.

Dropping the sheet, Liam strode to the door. It was time to ride.

5

"You wish to know how Maynard died?" a soft voice asked.

Having thought herself alone in the chapel, Joslyn started with surprise. "Father Ivo?" she said.

"Aye, 'tis I, child."

Unclasping her folded hands, Joslyn looked toward the lit candles whence his voice issued. "I thought myself alone," she said, meeting his gaze among the flames.

"One is never alone in the house of the Lord, Lady Joslyn."

A shiver of disquiet stole up her spine. Wishing Father Ivo would come out from behind the candles that made him appear so sinister, she rose from where she had spent the past hour of evening kneeling in prayer. "Of course not," she said.

"You are fearful. I felt it the moment I entered His sanctuary."

"Have I not cause to be?"

He inclined his head. "More cause than you know, lady." Which he obviously intended to make known to her here.

Their day-long ride to London having been made nearly without pause, Joslyn had not had the chance to inquire further into Maynard's death. However, now that they were settled in the manor of an acquaintance of Father Ivo's, she hoped finally to learn of the role Liam Fawke had played in his brother's death. "Tell me of Maynard," she invited.

Stepping from behind the candles, the priest's face turned familiar again. "Do sit, Lady Joslyn."

Though she would rather have stood, she lowered herself back to the bench.

Without hurry, Father Ivo walked forward and sat down beside her. "It is true that my nephew—your husband—was not without sin," he began. "As you know, he drank far too much and was loose with his coin."

As she had known too well, Joslyn reflected.

"But I tell you now, Maynard was driven to it."

"Driven to it?"

"Aye, William shamelessly encouraged his brother's drinking and gambling, for the drink kept Maynard vulnerable, while the need for betting money humbled him into begging it from his own coffers. This gave William power over the barony of Ashlingford, you see, power he still hungers for."

Joslyn had heard the same story from Maynard during the few times he had come to Rosemoor before the marriage. Beaten down by his brother, he had been forced to turn over the management of the estates to him. And each day that passed had seen more and more taken until all that remained to

Maynard was a worthless title. "I have never understood why Maynard did not appeal to the king to have his brother removed," she said.

"You ask that after meeting the bastard?"

Aye, Liam Fawke riding across the green toward her had certainly struck fear in her, Joslyn admitted to herself, but could not even the king subdue him?

"He is a dangerous man, Lady Joslyn," Ivo said. "Why else would Maynard have kept Oliver a secret from him?"

He had said he feared for his son's life, but all the more reason to have dealt with his illegitimate brother. "What of Maynard's death?" Joslyn asked.

"As I told you, though William did not kill Maynard by his own hand, he is as responsible as if he had." Ivo paused a moment before continuing. "Ere Maynard died, he told me that he and William had had an argument the night before, which started Maynard drinking. It was about money. William withheld it from Maynard when every last coin of it was his." He shook his head. "Too much drink in him to think right, Maynard called for his destrier, and, rather than challenge him, William allowed him to ride out into the night with his blood full of drink. Always William could drive him to act rashly."

"What happened?"

"Shortly after leaving the castle, Maynard was thrown from his horse into a ravine, and though he climbed out of it and returned to Ashlingford on foot, his injuries were mortal."

Now Joslyn understood. Not by Liam Fawke's hand but through his devices. Still, though her fear of the man was certainly well founded, she could not help but conclude that Maynard was also to blame for his death. After all, he had been a man of twenty-and-six years, fully grown and responsible for his own actions.

With a glimmer of tears in his eyes, the priest looked down at his hands. "Some hours later he died of inner bleeding. In my arms." The unmistakable pain in the last words he spoke strained his voice so it was hardly recognizable.

Father Ivo had truly cared for his nephew, Joslyn knew. He had been the one person Maynard had been able to depend on. Moved to feel for her husband as she had not while he was alive—but more, for this man who had loved him—she said, "I am so sorry."

Father Ivo looked at her. "The one who should be sorry is William," he said, his anger flickering back to life. "He stole your husband, and more: the father of your son."

Husband . . . father. . . . Inwardly, Joslyn sighed. Neither of those things had Maynard been. However, there was little to gain in revealing to the priest the truth of her marriage. Not knowing what else to say, she rose to leave.

"The bastard will pay one hundredfold for what he has done!" Father Ivo shouted, his words drenched in vengeance.

Joslyn was stunned that he, a priest, would speak such words—especially in a place of worship. "Father Ivo, I know you are grieving," she said, attempting to calm him, "but—"

"You know naught." Pushing to his feet, he thrust so near her she took a reflexive step backward. "You did not love him, did you?"

Quelling the desire to flee, Joslyn met his gaze. She could not lie. "Nay, as with many a marriage, ours was not consummated out of love. It was for the getting of an heir."

He stared long and hard at her. Then, without further word, he turned away.

Eager to take her leave, Joslyn walked quickly to the chapel door, but before exiting, she stole a look behind.

Facing the altar, his hand upon the hilt of his sword where it hung at his side, Maynard's uncle looked anything but a man of God. He looked a man of war—not by the flat, but by the edge.

Joslyn crossed the room once more before pausing in front of a large mirror hung on the wall. As her reflection had earlier startled her, it did so again, casting back a likeness that was not at all that of Joslyn of Rosemoor.

The maid Ivo sent to her had plaited her black hair on either side of her head, pinned it over her ears, and circled her brow with a metal fillet to hold all in place. If that were not extravagant enough, the woman had then attached mesh cylinders to either side of the fillet and therein encased the plaits. And that had only been the beginning of the transformation.

Lowering her gaze, Joslyn fingered the belt of jeweled, articulated metal plaques draped about her hips. Fastened over the fitted undergown—the coat hardy—it was revealed through the large armholes of a velvet outer garment that extended from below her shoulders to just beneath the line of her hips. Court dress, Ivo had called the garments; he'd had them delivered to her after rejecting the gown she had produced to wear before the king. But to Joslyn they were more simply described as excessive. Never had she felt so proper and pretentious, or so constrained.

She sighed. If not for Maynard's death, all this would be unnecessary. It would have been he who installed Oliver as his heir, not she. Never would she have had to ride on London with Liam Fawke in pursuit, never would she have had to don such uncomfortable wear, and never would she have had to wait two days to go before a king she would have preferred to know from a distance.

"Ah, Maynard," she whispered. "Why?"

The door across the room swung inward. "Lady Joslyn Fawke, Father Ivo." The king's man addressed them. "His Majesty will grant you an audience now."

The moment had arrived.

Her heart lurching in her chest, Joslyn turned to where Father Ivo rose from the padded settle he had occupied this past half hour. Though she had hoped her father would return to the city in time to stand with her before the king, it was not to be. Thus, she would have to content herself with the priest.

His robes crisp but for the creases of his sitting, Ivo stepped forward and put a hand beneath her elbow. "Come, my lady."

Clutching the woolen mantle folded over her arm, she allowed him to lead her from the room and into a great hall the likes of which she had only before heard described.

Why, a half dozen of Rosemoor's halls would fit into this one, she marveled as she looked upon the spacious splendor. Mayhap more. And the ornamentation!

Hardly noticing the king's men positioned around the edges, Joslyn absorbed it all with the wide-eyed disbelief of a child. Everywhere, rich stuffs covered walls and floor, their brilliant fabrics pleasing to the eye and tempting to the touch. Even the benches and settles were draped with lengths of costly material she simply could not imagine seating herself upon.

Joslyn might have lost herself deeper in the grandeur had her gaze not fallen next upon the man seated in the high-backed chair of state.

The King of England, Edward III.

He looked positively bored. That was the first thing she noticed about him. His handsome head propped on one hand, a leg swinging to and fro, he looked as if he would rather be any other place than here, listening to the petty arguments of his nobles.

As Joslyn and Ivo crossed toward the raised dais, Edward shifted restlessly on the throne, cupped his chin in his palm, stayed the swinging of the one leg, and began tapping the foot of the other. Though he must surely have known of their presence, all the while he stared at a place far to the left of him. And then he yawned.

Having heretofore envisioned the king as one whose nearness to God transcended such human character, Joslyn nearly laughed, but in the next instant she reminded herself of the seriousness of the situation. Suppressing her amusement, she halted alongside Father Ivo where he'd come to stand before the king.

"Your Majesty, the Lady Joslyn Fawke and Father Ivo," the herald announced.

Together, Joslyn and Ivo bowed before the king, a

much-practiced exercise Ivo had insisted that Joslyn master to perfection.

"Arise," Edward said in a bored voice.

Irritation shot through Joslyn as she straightened, for the king still had not looked at them. All that bowing for naught.

After a long moment, Edward shifted again, plucked at the thick pile of his velvet tunic, and finally turned his gaze on Ivo. There it rested briefly before moving to Joslyn. And suddenly light came into his eyes. A slight smile unfolded on his lips as he perused her twice over; then he straightened on his throne and stilled his restless movements.

"Lady Joslyn Fawke," he said, almost questioningly.

She dipped her head in acknowledgment.

His smile was wider when she looked up, but then, as if remembering himself, he cleared his throat. "Ashlingford, is it?" he asked.

"Aye, Your Majesty," Ivo answered, a queer tightness in his voice.

Obviously, he was as displeased by the king's appreciation of her as she was uncomfortable with it, Joslyn thought. For all her misgivings about the priest, his concern for her well-being was reassuring.

King Edward leaned forward, his gaze steady upon Joslyn. "I have reviewed your petition for the acknowledgment of your son as heir to his father's holdings," he said, "as I have also reviewed Sir Liam Fawke's."

He expected a response from her, but before Joslyn could formulate one, Ivo prompted, "And your determination, Your Majesty?"

Irritation flashed across the king's brow. "I have not yet made one."

"But Your Majesty, 'tis clearly Oliver Fawke who has the rightful claim to Ashlingford," Ivo protested. "He is of his father's loins, legitimate born, whereas William Fawke is a bastard—"

"That he is," King Edward interjected, almost as if the circumstances of Liam's birth were of little consequence to him.

"He seeks to steal the child's birthright," Ivo continued.

It becoming increasingly clear that Ivo was not being well received by the king, Joslyn hastily interceded. "Your Majesty, it was my departed husband's greatest desire that our son, Oliver, succeed him as baron of Ashlingford. Liam Fawke has no legitimate claim to the barony."

"Ah, but 'tis said it was promised to him, lady."

Promised to him? Joslyn faltered over that. Whatever did the king mean?

"By whom?" Ivo demanded.

The king arched an eyebrow at him. "By your nephew, Maynard, of course."

Ivo threw his hands into the air. "What lies does William tell now? Never have I heard such before, and neither would I believe it had I."

"No less than a dozen men of good standing have signed this petition," Edward said, lifting the parchment from his lap, "each attesting to knowledge of the pledge made by Maynard Fawke to Liam Fawke six years past. Each stating that Maynard agreed he would leave no legitimate heir when he died and that his brother would succeed him."

"Your Majesty, 'tis utter nonsense," Ivo said.

Seeing the clouds gathering in the king's eyes, Joslyn stepped forward. "I do not understand, Your Majesty. What pledge do you speak of?"

"Seven years past, a similar petition was brought before me," he began, settling back upon his throne as if the telling might take some time, "though it was to determine whether Liam Fawke or his younger brother, Maynard, should succeed as baron."

This had not been part of the story Joslyn's husband had poured out to her. Never had he told her his succession had been questioned. The news could not have been more disturbing.

"You see," King Edward continued, "their father had named Liam as his heir, but Father Ivo and Lady Anya, Maynard's mother, challenged the elder son's claim based on his illegitimacy."

Understanding opened up within Joslyn. It was no wonder Liam believed his right to Ashlingford stronger than Oliver's. Perhaps it was. "But you awarded the barony to Maynard."

"I did. As he had been born in wedlock and was of noble birth both sides of him, it seemed the right decision."

Hearing the regret in his voice, Joslyn prompted, "And it was not?"

The king frowned. "Maynard failed me. In less than a year, Ashlingford's revenues dropped to less than half, there was much quarreling among the vassals and villagers, and word was that its baron was fast emptying the demesne coffers with his excessive gambling and cavorting."

Gambling. The very thing that had caused Joslyn to wed Maynard. "And what of Sir Liam, Your Majesty?" she asked.

"Knowing of my great displeasure, your husband convinced his brother to return to Ashlingford and manage the estates for him."

So Liam Fawke had not forced his brother to turn management of the estates over to him as Father Ivo and Maynard had led her to believe. It had been given to him willingly. All that Joslyn had believed about her husband and his relationship with his illegitimate brother was beginning to crumble. "And he claims that in exchange for this, Maynard promised him the barony?" she asked. Would her husband have agreed to such terms? It hardly seemed possible.

"'Tis what the Ashlingford knights attest to, though not until two days past had I heard tell of it myself."

What to believe? Joslyn wondered. That Liam Fawke had gathered false witnesses to him to gain Ashlingford? Or that her husband had made a promise he'd had no intention of keeping?

"Even were this true, which 'tis not, Your Majesty"—Ivo returned to the conversation— "William is still illegitimate. He can have no legal claim upon Ashlingford, especially when there is Oliver."

Edward shifted his gaze to the priest. "Perhaps," he murmured.

"But surely you are not seriously considering awarding the barony to William," Ivo said.

"I am."

Though the priest must have wanted badly to send up a cry of even greater protest, he compressed his lips, closed his hand over the dangling crucifix, and averted his gaze.

How Joslyn would have liked to walk away from

this, to surrender all to Liam Fawke and return with Oliver to the security and comfort of Rosemoor! But Father Ivo's words came back to her: It was not her decision to make. "And what of my son, Your Majesty?" she asked. "He is the legitimate issue of Baron Maynard Fawke."

"You were married by special license, were you not?"

She nodded.

"Have you never questioned the reason, lady, that your husband did not wish it to be publicly known he had wed you?"

"I had no reason to question it, for he told me he feared for the life of any heir that might be born of our union. He said his brother might seek the child's death to gain the barony for himself."

Edward frowned. "Though I cannot say I know Sir Liam well, I find that difficult to believe of him."

Ought she to tell him how Liam Fawke had ridden on Rosemoor? Joslyn wondered. How he had threatened to steal Oliver away from her? Nay, for though Liam Fawke had frightened her, that was all he had done.

"Convince me that I should confer the barony upon your child, Lady Joslyn," King Edward said, "and I will."

Joslyn blinked with surprise. How was she to do that? "I know not what else to say that has not already been said, Your Majesty, except that on his deathbed, my husband named Oliver his heir and Father Ivo bore witness to it."

"I did," the priest concurred.

"The child is but two years old," Edward reminded them.

"Three come summer," Ivo said.

"Two, three," the king muttered, "he is still a child. Incapable of running a barony as vast and vital as Ashlingford." He looked upon Joslyn again. "Surely you do not propose to oversee Ashlingford yourself, Lady Joslyn?"

She? Lord, the thought had never even occurred to her. It was true she could read, write, and compute numbers and for years had kept her father's books for him, but Rosemoor was tiny compared to Ashlingford. Still, perhaps—

"Until Oliver comes of age and responsibility," Father Ivo said, stepping forward, "I have offered to manage the estates for him, Your Majesty."

"You?" King Edward exclaimed. "A man of God?"

"A man of God, but also of Ashlingford. Lest you forget, Your Majesty, I am also a Fawke. Though much of my life has been spent doing the work of the Lord, I know the barony better than any."

"And you think yourself capable of managing it?"

"I do."

"Better than Sir Liam?"

Ivo's answer came after a slight hesitation. "Aye."

The king looked anything but convinced. "Did you not assist Maynard in managing the demesne ere Sir Liam was returned to it?" he asked.

Ivo's skin crept with color. "Only in keeping the books, Your Majesty. My nephew did not consult me on any matters of great importance. He was stubborn that way."

"Yet he later allowed Sir Liam to make those same decisions for him," the king reflected aloud. "The half brother for whom he had no liking."

"I—" Ivo began.

King Edward held up a silencing hand. "I have made my decision."

Joslyn was jolted by his abruptness. Considering his exchange with Father Ivo, it could only mean he had determined that Liam Fawke was more suited to the barony of Ashlingford than a child figurehead and a priest. Thus all had been for naught; Oliver's birthright would be taken from him. However, she felt little regret over the king's decision, for it was he, and not she, who would deny her son the estates. Now she and Oliver could return to Rosemoor and a life that placed neither of them in danger.

The king turned to the man who had earlier brought Joslyn and Ivo into the great hall. "Summon Sir Liam."

Joslyn gasped. Though she had known Liam was in the city, she had not thought she would have to face him here, and certainly not before the king. To be exposed again to his mockery as he was given the title of baron would not be pleasant. She watched the king's man cross the hall to a door opposite the one she and Ivo had entered through.

King Edward beckoned her to the dais. "Come, Lady Joslyn, stand by my side."

For what reason? she wondered. That she might more fully face Liam's arrogance? "But I—"

"Come," he ordered, brooking no argument.

Lifting her skirts, Joslyn stepped up to the platform and tightly clasped her hands before her. She would show Liam Fawke no fear, she vowed. Neither would she show defeat. Let him gloat over his victory, deserved or not, for she would give him no further satisfaction.

"You have judged me wrong," King Edward murmured.

"Your Majesty?"

"Patience," he said, and looked at the man emerging from the side room. Liam Fawke.

6

He was in trouble. Liam knew it the moment he laid eyes on the woman who stood to the right of the king. Though surely only God could have arranged this, it was none other than Joslyn Fawke who stared across at him. With her chin lifted proudly and her hands clasped before her, she looked every bit the noblewoman she had not seemed at Rosemoor. By divine intervention she had been transformed from plain, dirty, and ill-mannered to lovely and genteel. And though the spirited woman of three days past might still be in her eyes, Liam was certain of one thing: No contentious words or baiting would pass those lips. Not in the presence of the king.

Lord, but he was in trouble!

As he traversed the hall, Sir John following, he continued to hold Joslyn's stare. She seemed so confident, so assured that the wiles she had worked on the king would see her son named Ashlingford's heir.

Would King Edward steal Liam's right to the barony a second time? Would he risk the revenues of Ashlingford again, this time knowingly?

Positioning himself to the right of Ivo, Liam moved through the formalities of introduction and veneration as if outside himself, his gaze returning time and again to Joslyn. But it was more than her transformation that drew his attention. It was a searching for something just out of reach—a feeling in the oldest part of him that she held the answer to some unanswered question.

"Are you with us, Sir Liam?"

He shifted his gaze to the king. "I am, Your Majesty."

"There is something you find particularly interesting about Lady Joslyn?" Edward asked.

It was not idle talk Liam was here for, but he knew he must indulge the king—and himself—a bit. "Interesting?" he repeated. "Nay, only surprising."

"And how is that?"

"'Tis just that her appearance is wholly different from what I previously saw of her." In the next instant, he felt her gaze stab him.

The king leaned forward. "Tell," he prompted, his eyes shining with keen interest.

Joslyn had spun Edward well around her little finger, Liam concluded, with no small amount of contempt. Obviously, the king's concern for her went well beyond the duties of his office. Would she lie with him this eve if he awarded Ashlingford to Oliver?

Looking again at Joslyn, Liam found himself liking the way her eyes stood, large with outrage. Aye, 'twas far better than the self-possession she had exuded only minutes earlier. Returning his attention to Edward, he said, "It would not be gentlemanly of me to carry tales, my king. Suffice it to say that this lady is much improved over the one I met at Rosemoor."

Edward frowned a moment, then smiled. "So she is at her best for me, hmm?"

In Joslyn's eyes Liam saw all the things she would have liked to say to him but could not. He slid his gaze over her flushed countenance, the rapid rise and fall of her chest, her hips embraced by a jeweled belt, her slippers peeking from beneath her skirts. "Aye, her best," he agreed.

With a satisfied chuckle, the king reclined upon his throne. "Then to business," he announced.

Knowing this day would decide the rest of his life for him, Liam reminded himself of the control he must keep regardless of what was said.

"Sir Liam, I have considered your petition for hereditary right over Ashlingford," Edward said, "and admit that yours is a defensible claim. There is much to consider with a barony the size of Ashlingford. Mine is not a decision easily arrived at."

Then the decision was made, meaning Edward would listen to no further argument on the subject.

"As you have ever been a loyal vassal," the king continued, "willful at times, but otherwise obedient, and are known to be honorable and just, I am inclined to believe the men who have corroborated the vow made to you by your brother. However, there is more to consider than a promise made by a desperate man."

Ivo stood straighter, Joslyn jerked with surprise, and Sir John muttered beneath his breath, "Good God!"

Liam held the king's gaze. The question of who would succeed Maynard was no more. In his foolishness, Edward had decided to award the barony to a child incapable of wiping his own nose, a child born of Maynard's deception, sustained and strengthened by the treacherous Ivo and the illusive Joslyn. Damn them both! Damn them to perdition!

So strong were the feelings coursing through Liam that he nearly missed the king's nod to the senior guard—no doubt signaling the man to prepare himself and his men for Liam's reaction. Obviously, Edward had not forgotten what Liam was capable of.

"Nobility descends from nobility, Sir Liam," King Edward said, "and though one half of you is of your father, the other . . . " He hesitated, almost apologetically. "The other is of the common."

What he did not say, but surely considered, was that it was not just any "common" blood in Liam, it was that of the Irish.

Fury causing his heart to pound hot blood through every vein, Liam forced himself to wait on the king when what he wanted was to rage over this mark that was ever upon his brow. But by all that was holy, he would not be ashamed of the circumstances of his birth!

"Thus, though the child of Maynard Fawke is yet too young to take up the barony, I have decided that 'tis to him Ashlingford should pass." Edward settled his forearms to the arms of his throne and waited for Liam's response.

Though Liam continued to stare at the king, he sensed the triumph shining out of the eyes his uncle turned on him.

How was he to respond to the king's pronouncement? Liam wondered. Should he rage as he had seven years past when the king had first taken his birthright from him? Turn on Ivo as he'd done that day?

He clenched his fists. Then it had taken four guards and their weapons to bring him down and drag him from the hall. How many would it take this day, should he unleash his ripening rage? And why not? He had nothing left to lose.

As much as Liam needed to release the fury of these wasted years, he held it in with the hard-won reminder that he was no longer the rash twenty-two-year-old he'd been then. True, he would leave London as landless as he'd left it seven years before, but this time with dignity. This time not as the volatile Irish bastard he'd been called, but as the dispassionate Englishman.

"I am pleased to see you have gained control of your emotions, Sir Liam," King Edward commented.

Liam dipped his head. "And now I would ask your leave, Your Majesty."

"In due course. There are yet matters to be resolved."

Liam cursed silently. Damnation, but he wanted to be away from here! To put the breadth of England between himself and all those present—most especially the woman who had given Maynard the means to triumph over him this day. He stared hard at Joslyn. Although her face reflected wide-eyed uncertainty, Liam knew she must be alive with the victory she had gained over him. God, but she was truly worthy of Maynard.

"Do not think I am unaware of your value, Sir Liam," Edward said, "for most certainly I am. Thus, I have a proposal for you."

"A proposal, sire?" Liam repeated, surprising himself that he could speak past the constriction in his throat.

"Aye. As I am loath to jeopardize the revenues of the barony, I would naturally like to see you continue in the same capacity as you served your brother."

Joslyn could hardly breathe, her throat nearly closing as the king's words dug themselves deeper into her consciousness. Lord, let him not mean it. Let this be but a cruel game. Looking across at Liam, she glimpsed his own surprise before he hid it behind a hard jaw and eyes like flint.

Finally, Ivo recovered from his shock. "B—but Your Majesty," he sputtered. "I am willing to manage the estates for the child until he comes of age."

"'Tis Sir Liam I want," Edward said.

Liam had never seen his uncle look more flustered. Ah, the poor man's plans gone awry. And what of Joslyn Fawke? Steering his gaze to her, he saw the fear upon her face. Almost amusing. Though he had no intention of accepting the king's proposal—providing it was that and not an order—he found himself asking, "And in return how am I to be compensated, Your Majesty?"

Looking as if he enjoyed these three whose destinies were his to control, the king smiled. "This eve there will come into my hall many who vie for the barony of Thornemede. You know it, do you not, Sir Liam?"

Of course he knew it, though it was hardly a barony any longer. Half a day's ride from Ashlingford, Thornemede had fallen into disuse. Its aged baron, who had outlived both his sons, was now dead as well. Was this, then, what the king offered, a squandered barony for a thriving one twice its size? "I know Thornemede," Liam said.

"Though the men who wish it for themselves will eat my meat, swill my wine, and flatter me in all manner of ways," Edward said, "'tis you I will give it to, do you agree to manage Ashlingford for your brother's son until he is of age."

A barony. But not the one that was his. Not the one his father intended for him, the one Liam had broke sweat upon and bettered ten times over for the day he would be named its lord.

"Thornemede is not so great as Ashlingford," King Edward added, "but it is respectable and will support the many generations that spring from your loins, Sir Liam. A baron you will finally be, and your son and his son thereafter."

Nay, Liam decided, let the king live with his decision and all its consequences. He wanted naught more to do with Ashlingford. Instead he would return to the tournaments, where he had gone following Edward's decree seven years earlier. Having spent a year besting other knights and filling his chests with winnings with which he'd intended to purchase his own estates, he had later poured the monies into Ashlingford to set aright Maynard's misuse of its revenues. This time would be different.

"With your permission, Your Majesty," Liam said, "I beg to decline your most generous offer."

"And if I make it an order?"

"I would ask that you do not."

The king considered him a long moment before nodding. "I will allow you that."

Ivo's sigh was heard by all.

"But tell me," Edward continued. "What would change your mind?"

It was on Liam's tongue to tell him that naught

would change his mind when a voice crept in. Here was his chance for revenge. Lord, how sweet and tempting. How perfect the opportunity to put Ivo in his place. And as for Joslyn . . . ?

Pride be damned, revenge be had; he would accept the king and, in doing so, rob his uncle of the power he so lusted after and Joslyn his convenient absence. Food for a vengeful soul hungering to be fed.

"Concessions?" the king asked.

The negotiation could not have progressed better had Liam declined Edward in order to gain such. "Though it has the name," he said, "Thornemede is hardly a barony, Your Majesty."

"Its castle is of stone and sturdy; it can be rebuilt," Edward said, though he certainly knew that was not what Liam referred to.

"And the monies to do so? 'Tis my understanding that Thornemede's coffers are weighted only by dust."

Edward scratched his temple. "The lands are rich. They will produce again. And, of course, there is the wool."

Providing the sheep had not all been slaughtered to feed mouths left hungry by poor crops, Liam added silently. "And until then?" he asked.

Clearing his throat, Ivo shifted foot to foot, obviously uncomfortable with Liam's questions.

"I see," Edward said. "All right, if you accept my proposal, I will give you three years to turn Thornemede profitable again and, till then, issue a writ exempting you from taxes."

Good, but not enough. Knowing he would prick the king's ire, Liam pressed on. "Surely Your Majesty knows it will take more than that to restore Thornemede."

Edward's nostrils flared. "What are you asking, Sir Liam? That I finance the barony for you when there are others who would pay me for the privilege of gaining it for themselves?"

"Not you, Your Majesty, but Ashlingford. One tenth of its receipts for my service to that barony should suffice."

"One tenth!" Ivo exclaimed. Crimson flooding his face, he hurried to the dais. "'Tis robbery, Your Majesty!"

"Stand away, priest," the king ordered.

"Surely, sire, you can see what harm would be done the barony do you allow this vengeful man to return to Ashlingford," Ivo said. "And to take such a large portion of the receipts! You cannot do this."

With that last bit, Ivo had crossed a line that few with any sense would have dared step over. "Can I not?" Edward spoke between clenched teeth. "Though you appear to have forgotten it, *Father Ivo*, I am the king. I do as I please."

"Of course, sire," Ivo said, his eyes darting left and right as a guard each side of him began to advance. "it is just that—"

"It matters not to me whether you take your leave of my hall on your own or are carried from it," the king snarled.

The priest had only a moment to decide before the guards reached him. Spinning around, he evaded them and hastened to the side room where he and Joslyn had awaited their summons. A moment later, the door slammed closed behind him.

"One tenth," the king repeated thoughtfully.

Steepling his hands, he looked up, no doubt calculating the impact it would have on his own revenues from the barony. "Very well," he concluded, "one tenth it is, but only after my taxes have first been paid."

This was still more than Liam had expected him to accede to. "Then, if it pleases Your Majesty, I would be honored to accept your proposal," he said with a bow.

Edward smiled, then leaned forward conspiratorially. "I would have given more, Sir Liam," he said.

"More, sire?"

He grinned. "As I said, I know your worth. So you see, 'tis I who have won, not you."

So this had been little more than a game for the king. In less than a half hour he had assured both his revenues and his amusement.

With the terrible realization that his decision had been driven by his thirst for revenge, Liam said tightly, "With your permission, I will take your leave now, Your Majesty."

"Regrets?" the king asked.

Too many to number. "I have accepted your proposal, Your Majesty, and so it will be."

"So it will," Edward echoed, and waved Liam away. "Your leave granted."

Liam looked one last time at Joslyn.

She met his gaze straight on.

Aye, she would be difficult, ever interfering with his management of Ashlingford, but he would soon show the scheming woman her place. Like it or not, he was now lord to her lady, even if only in name.

Snapping a bow to his king, Liam started across the hall. Following him, Sir John's footsteps patterned his own.

"Sir Liam," Edward called to him as he passed through the doors held wide by two men.

Reluctantly, Liam halted.

"We will expect you in our hall for dinner," the king said. "Do not disappoint us."

It was an order, not a request. Holding in his resentment, Liam said, "I would be honored," and withdrew.

Joslyn felt as if her strength had run out through the soles of her feet. For what seemed like hours she had fought to maintain her composure during the veiled revelations and unanswered questions. To have Liam Fawke gone at last from her sight was such a relief it nearly dropped her to her knees.

"Ashlingford is Oliver's," the king said. "What have you to say, Lady Joslyn?"

She met his inquiring eyes. Though she knew she should be grateful to him for having accepted her son as Maynard's successor, she could only feel discomfort. "I am most grateful, Your Majesty."

He studied her for a long thoughtful moment. "I am not so sure you are."

She cursed herself for being so easily read. "'Tis just that I worry over the safety of my child to be in the company of a man who hates him so, sire."

"Sir Liam does not hate your son. Surely you know that?"

Impulsively, Joslyn lowered herself to her knees beside his throne. "But I do not," she said. "He has every reason to wish ill upon Oliver, every reason to do him harm. Pray, Your Majesty, give Sir Liam the barony of Thornemede, but do not send him to Ashlingford."

His mouth softening, Edward reached forward and

cupped her chin in his palm. "Lady," he said, "'tis your departed husband and his uncle who bear the burden of Sir Liam's anger, and for good reason, not an innocent child."

His touch frightened her, made her want to wrench back. However, for fear of offending him, she forced herself to be still. "I would like to believe that, sire, but I cannot."

He rubbed his thumb across her jaw before abruptly dropping his hand from her. "You can," he said, shifting his gaze to the great seal ring set upon his finger. "I would not jeopardize your son if I believed Sir Liam would attempt to injure him. Look elsewhere for your enemies, lady."

Defeated, Joslyn stood.

Pushing back a lock of golden hair that had crept over his brow, Edward moved his gaze down her figure. "You will, of course, stay to dinner," he said.

"But I could not possibly," Joslyn said, without thinking. "There is Oliver, and he is—"

"Father Ivo will care for him."

"I . . . I would prefer to care for him myself, Your Majesty," she said, the desire to return to her son only just greater than the desire to avoid coming anywhere near Sir Liam again.

"Do you argue with me, Lady Joslyn?" King Edward asked, his voice ominously level.

Her insides churning, she shifted her gaze to her hands. "I suppose I do. I humbly beg your pardon."

He grunted, then captured the regard of one of his knights. "Sir Miles, see that a chamber is prepared for the Lady Joslyn."

She started. A chamber? But she already had accommodation. More, she had promised Oliver she would be away only a short time, and now to return to him past dark? It was unthinkable.

"Your Majesty, I do not need a—"

He frowned.

Inwardly, Joslyn cursed the power of men. As if by divine right, they bent others to their will. What price, then, would she pay for the king's generosity?

"And now I have further business to attend to, Lady Joslyn," Edward said, as he reached for one of several parchments that lay on the table beside him. Without looking at her again, he unrolled the document and began scanning its contents.

Her leave given her, Joslyn bowed, stepped from the dais, and followed Sir Miles from the hall.

7

A short time later, Joslyn found herself alone in a magnificent chamber.

Past the ornately draped bed she paced, between two beckoning chairs, over a rug plush beneath her feet, and back again. Then, her plan formed, she halted. Though she knew she risked the wrath of the king if found out, she felt she must see Oliver to assure herself and him that all was well.

Taking up the mantle she hoped would allow her to leave this place unnoticed, she walked to the door, pulled it open a space, and looked out into the corridor. It was blessedly empty.

To leave the tower palace concealed in the mantle proved far easier than Joslyn would have guessed. Joining with several women servants, none of whom received more than a cursory glance from any of the guards, she followed them outside. What did not bear thinking on was how she was to later return unnoticed and make her way back into the palace.

Passing over the second of three drawbridges behind a procession of carts, hay wains, piemakers, and fishmongers, Joslyn peered up from beneath the hood of her mantle. Ahead loomed the first bastion of the stronghold's defense, the last she must pass in order to reach the outside. Appropriately named the Lion Tower, it was a massive structure liberally studded with armed officers and men-at-arms.

As Joslyn swept her gaze right, her eyes clashed with those of a young soldier, and in his she saw suspicion. Fortunately, in the next instant he was distracted by a commoner whose cart toppled over, loosing an excited swarm of chickens from their woven cages.

Pushing past the others, Joslyn reached the final drawbridge at last, and a moment later her feet were upon it. But not until her slippers were dusted with the dirt of the road leading toward the city did she expel the last of her breath.

Heavenly Father, she had done it! Her mind reeled. She had slipped free of the king and would soon be with her son. Pausing only once to hitch her skirts up out of sight, she soon found herself in a city she did not know. But she was certain she could find again the monastery where she and Ivo had left Oliver that morning.

Winding west, Joslyn hurried past crowded shops capped with cramped housing, people who called to her to touch and taste their wares, and children who played in the streets as if there were fields of green beneath their feet.

Suddenly, the street Joslyn traversed ended, leaving her with the choice of turning either left or right.

Right, she decided. However, it wasn't long before the decision proved a poor one, for the street grew narrower and darker for want of sunlight, and its smell worsened the deeper she went.

Though she would have preferred to find the monastery without compromising the commoner she pretended to be, she finally accepted that she would have to ask someone to set her aright. But who? Pausing before a shop offering fish that smelled well past consumption, Joslyn looked about for a woman whom she might approach.

With men all around her, many of whom had stopped to cast eyes upon her as if she were something edible, Joslyn experienced a panic not unlike that when Liam Fawke had ridden his great destrier across the green of Rosemoor. Huddling deeper into the folds of her mantle, she looked back the way she had come. She could—

A sudden screech brought her head around. There in a window of the third floor up from the street stood a woman with breasts half bared and a bearded man in her embrace. Their laughter merging, the two lovers dropped out of sight.

Fear gripped Joslyn. This was a place of drink and ill repute she had come into, a place where no lady would even dare toss her slipper.

"Whatcha hidin' yerself fer, girl?" a gruff voice asked.

Startled, Joslyn jumped back and came hard up against a reeking barrel of fish.

"Ye an ugly one?" he pressed. "I don't mind, ye know."

And well he shouldn't, Joslyn thought, as she stole a glimpse of his thick jowls and pockmarked face.

"Same to me," he continued, "specially if it costs me less." He reached for her hood. "Now let me see ye."

Desperate to elude him, Joslyn sidestepped.

"Unfriendly, eh?" The man clamped a hand around her arm. "I may not be handsome and strappin', but my coin's good, and so's what I got 'tween my legs."

Joslyn had never before been spoken to in such a manner, but somehow she managed to get past her shock to formulate the only reply that might save her from this beast. "I've the pox."

With disease a thing more to be feared than a dagger to one's breast—especially with word arriving daily of the great plague that had spread out of the Mediterranean and was now ravaging France—the man abruptly released her.

Offering up fervent thanks to God, Joslyn started back down the street. However, her retreat was soon thwarted.

"The whore's with the pox!" the man shouted.

Immediately, those who feared to be crossed by her shadow shrank away, and those whose anger was greater than their fear began pelting her with anything at hand.

Joslyn began running, but a moment later was arrested by a stone that struck her square in the back. Dropped to her knees, she bent under the terrible pain. However, her instinct for survival stood her back up to face the half dozen men advancing on her. Thinking the only way out would be to go deeper down this forbidding street, she swung around to flee opposite. But it was not to be, for there with two others came the man who had sought to have her. Which was worse, she wondered, to be murdered or defiled?

Murdered, Oliver would have no one, but defiled she might yet return to him. God be with her.

Tossing back her hood, Joslyn lifted her chin to reveal the nobility imparted to her today by the maid Father Ivo had sent her.

The gesture had the desired effect. Stupefied, her assailants halted. And in that, Joslyn saw one other possibility. Though it would most likely prove futile, she lifted her mantle and ran on legs that had always known how to move quickly. Slipping past the three men, she raced up the street.

The shouts behind told Joslyn of the men's recovery; the pounding of their feet warned her of their pursuit. Though she managed to maintain her distance—and even gain a little—she knew it would not be enough to escape unless she veered onto one of the side streets. Turning sharply left, she increased her stride and, when another street opened up to the right, turned onto it. However, she soon realized her mistake. It was not a street at all but an alley, dark and without exit.

Whirling around to flee, in the next instant she pressed herself back against the wall. Too late. Her precious lead was lost. As she watched, a hand pressed to her mouth to suppress her labored breathing, a half dozen men ran past her hiding place.

She had eluded them, but for how long? Knowing they might return when no further sign was found of her ahead, Joslyn stepped toward the opening. However, a moment later a figure turned into the alley.

Dear God, she was found out!

With nowhere to go, she retreated deeper into the alley as the man stepped forward, and shortly found herself backed against the far wall, with the distance between her and her pursuer closing steadily.

Where were the others? she wondered. Was it possible this man was the only one to have seen her turn this way? Was she to be spared the greater horror of the many for the one? Focusing on him, she tried to see beyond the shadows he wore as near him as his clothes, but he remained faceless.

She would not scream, Joslyn promised herself, for to do so might bring the other men running. Squeezing her eyes closed, she began praying for a deliverance that would be nothing short of a miracle if it was granted her. However, the moment hard fingers curled around her upper arm, a sound came from her mouth unlike any to issue from it since she had crossed out of childhood into womanhood.

Immediately, a large hand clamped over her mouth, catching her scream in a calloused palm.

Heavenly Father, protect me, she beseeched silently. Protect Oliver if I meet my death this day. Protect—

"Fool woman! What were you thinking?" a voice snapped in her ear.

It was a voice Joslyn knew. Opening her eyes, she stared up at the man whose features she could barely see in the darkness. Was it possible?

"I ought to have left you to them," he said, anger deepening his voice.

It *was* he: Liam Fawke! But the relief flooding through Joslyn was short-lived with the reminder that this man was as much an enemy as the strangers who had chased her into this place, and as likely to do her harm as any one of them. Heart pounding, she began struggling against his hands.

"Holy rood! 'Tis Liam Fawke, Lady Joslyn," he said.

Joslyn continued to kick and strain away from him.

Muttering thick curses, Liam drove her back against the wall and pressed the weight of his body into hers. "Enough," he commanded.

She jerked her head to the side, but he thwarted her attempt to dislodge his hand from her mouth by pulling her chin back around.

"Hear me, Joslyn." He spoke with urgency. "You are safe."

Realizing she could do nothing at present to escape, she stilled. Perhaps, she thought, her submission might lull Liam into a false sense of security and allow her to catch him unawares.

"I am going to remove my hand now," he said. "You will not scream. Understood?"

She nodded.

Slowly, he withdrew it from her mouth. "Better," he said. Then he pulled slightly away.

Though Joslyn had hoped for more, she knew it was likely the best chance she would ever have of escaping him. Moving her leg into position, she lifted her foot from the ground. She had never done it before, but she had seen it once—and it had been very effective. She brought her knee hard up into Liam's groin.

His shout pained her ears, but rather than release her, he fell heavily against her.

God, she had failed! If he had not been going to kill her before, he certainly would now. Fear pumping through her veins and lending her greater strength than before, she took up her struggle again—twisting, pushing, and straining to free herself, jabbing with her elbows and clawing with her nails. But it was as useless as before. Liam was too large a man and too determined to hold on to her. She slackened.

His breathing heavy, Liam lifted his head from where he'd pressed his brow to the wall. "Damnation, woman! You really think I mean to do you harm, don't you?"

"I will not die easily for you, Liam Fawke," she said.

Still recovering from the blow, he did not immediately respond. "Nay, I do not imagine you would," he finally said. "I will count it my good fortune that I do not seek your death."

"Do you not?"

"If murder were my intent, *Lady* Joslyn, I would slit your throat this moment. However, in spite of what you think of me, I am not a murderer—nor one to take what does not belong to me."

As she and Oliver were taking from him what he believed was his. Lord, what *might* be his, she admitted. "Then what do you intend?" she asked.

"'Tis my unfortunate lot that should any ill befall you or your son I am the one whom suspicion will come upon," he said. "Thus it falls to me to ensure your safety—and by my word, that I will do."

But he could hardly be blamed did she meet her end out of his hands, she thought. Indeed, why hadn't he left her to her fate as he'd done with Maynard when he'd ridden from the castle with too much drink in him?

Maintaining his hold on her, Liam stepped back. "We must leave this place lest those men return," he said, and began pulling her down the alley.

Had she misjudged him? Joslyn wondered. Had all

Maynard's stories been the same as his husbandly devotion, shallow and false? Stepping into the street after Liam, she was surprised when, in the next instant, he dragged her back into the alley.

"God's wounds!" Liam swore beneath his breath, his hand going to the hilt of his sword.

Their din preceding them, the unsavory men had turned back down the street bordering the alley. "Check 'em all," one shouted. "Gotta be hidin' here somewhere."

They would soon discover her and Liam, Joslyn realized. However, Liam did not allow her to contemplate the consequences for long. Pulling her deeper into the alley, he turned her against the wall and wrenched the metal fillet with its mesh cylinders from her head.

"What are you doing?" she gasped.

"Playing a part," he muttered, "as will you." Raking his fingers through her pinned hair, he quickly loosed the plaits and sent her hair falling past her shoulders. Then he pressed his body to hers, lifted her chin, and bent his head. "Pretend you like it," he whispered. A moment later, his mouth covered hers.

Joslyn was shocked. Nothing in her twenty-one years of life had prepared her for this, not the innocent kisses of her early years, and certainly not the dispassionate ones of the man who had been her husband. Nothing . . .

No gentleness about him, Liam urged her mouth open beneath his, drew a hand down her back, and grasped her buttocks.

A ripple of sensation leaping across her spine, Joslyn loosed a small sound. Liam took it from her and gave back a husky groan. Next, he slid his mouth off hers and trailed its moist warmth down her neck. "Put your arms around me," he said.

Joslyn's hesitation was a moment later met by a shout from the mouth of the alley. They were discovered, and with that realization she began to understand the charade she must also play if they were to convince her pursuers they had stumbled on something not of their concern. Still, it hardly made sense that Liam would go as far as he did with the shadows obscuring them. Especially the kiss.

"Now!" he ordered.

Obediently, she slid one arm around his waist, the other across his shoulder, then dropped her head back and sighed.

When the man at the end of the alley stepped forward, Liam jerked his head around. "Who goes?" he asked in a guttural accent that could not possibly be mistaken for noble, his voice shaded with drink he had not had. The dim light of the alley also hid his attire, which otherwise would have made a lie of him.

The man halted. "Lookin' fer a lady," he said. "A noblewoman who came this way."

"Noblewoman." Liam spat. "Yer dreamin', man, ain't no lady ever come near Whore's Way."

Whore's Way. Lord, no wonder she'd been approached to sell herself, Joslyn realized.

As the other men gathered behind him, the man demanded, "Who's that with ye?"

"Ain't no lady, eh, my love?" With that, Liam jerked a handful of Joslyn's hair, urging her to respond.

"Go on with ye," she tossed at the men, affecting an unrefined accent she prayed would be believed. "I got good money to make, and I canna do it with ye standin' there gapin' like fools." Jesu! Where had that come from? The words had slid off her tongue as if common to it.

Trying to see deeper into the shadows, the man at the end of the alley leaned forward.

"Ye heard the wench," Liam said. "Be gone."

The man hesitated and took a step forward.

Unsheathing his dagger, Liam lifted it to catch the light above his head. "I won't be tellin' ye again," he warned. "Ye can have her when I'm finished but not before."

Trying not to think of the blood that might be shed at any moment, Joslyn swallowed hard. "Aye, do ye got enough coin," she said. "I don't do nothin' fer free." And she held her breath.

A long uncomfortable silence followed. Then, mumbling something, the man swung about and started out of the alley. "Not here," he announced to the others. "Jus' a whore turnin' her trade."

Grumbling their disappointment, the men withdrew.

As the silence returned, one part of Joslyn eased while the other—that still in contact with Liam— tensed further. She tried to ignore his solid chest against her feminine one, his stony thighs trapping hers between them, but something in the recesses of her knowing roused.

Thinking herself depraved to feel anything but fear for this man, she lowered her arms to her sides. However, Liam continued to hold her. Surely it was safe for him to release her now. After all, the danger was past. Wasn't it? She looked up at his unmoving face.

Though Liam's gaze was more felt than seen, the

thumb he brushed across her lower lip was unmistakable. Nay, the danger was not past.

"I see Maynard neglected your mouth," he said softly, reminding her of the intimacy they had just shared and which she'd hardly known how to respond to—an intimacy that, as a woman who'd borne her husband a child, she ought to have had more experience with. "What else did he neglect?"

A thousand untried emotions winging through her, Joslyn curled her hands into fists so tight they hurt. "I do not know what you mean."

Liam lowered his face near hers, the hair upon his brow grazing her forehead. "He wanted you only for what you could give him that could take from me," he said. "Isn't that true, Joslyn?"

Briefly, she closed her eyes. Aye, it was true. There was no other reason Maynard had wed and bedded her.

"There was no pleasure in it, was there?" Liam pressed.

No love, no pleasure, only the conception of an heir. But never would she admit it, her marriage having been too much a mockery as it was. She set her chin high. "We should leave here," she said. Unfortunately, the defiant gesture brought her mouth nearer Liam's and his breath upon hers.

"Should we?"

A peculiar ache growing in her breasts, she said, "They might return."

"Nay, they will not. Are you going to answer me, Joslyn?"

Feeling cornered and ready to burst with the straining of her senses, she snapped, "I most certainly am not. And do not be so free with the use of my given name, Sir Liam. If you so soon forget, I am *Lady* Joslyn Fawke, your brother's widow."

Such power did mere words have that in the next instant Liam released her. "As if I could forget," he said. Sheathing his dagger, he turned from her and strode the reach of the alley. "Do not dawdle, *Lady* Joslyn," he called over his shoulder. "The tower awaits."

The tower. She hurried after him. "It is not to the tower I wish to go," she said, stepping into the street.

"That much is obvious, but it is where I am taking you."

She grasped his arm through the short mantle he wore. "I promised Oliver I would return to him after the noon hour," she said. "He will be frightened if I do not."

Liam halted in the middle of the street, looking down at where she held him and then into her eyes. "You worry for his safety, do you not?"

She released him. "Of course I do."

"Though I do not think it will console you much, Lady Joslyn, I have sent a man to watch over the monastery to assure no ill befalls your son."

How did Liam, the one from whom she had thought to hide Oliver, know where her son was? Her worry doubled. "Nay, I cannot say it consoles me," she said, "which is why I would see for myself that he is well—and assure him I am well also."

Liam shook his head. "I regret it will have to wait."

"For you, perhaps," she said, turning and starting up the street. However, Liam caught her and pulled her back around.

"In this place, Lady Joslyn," he said, his gaze

intense, "it would not be taken amiss for a man to carry a woman over his shoulder. Which would you prefer, to be carried or to go forward on your own feet?"

He would do it, she knew. The threat was there in his eyes. Still, what of Oliver? "Sir Liam, if there were any good in you—"

"Which you do not believe."

"—you would take me to my son first." To Joslyn's surprise, something akin to wavering crossed his face. But that was all.

"You will have to trust me in this," he said. "Oliver is safe—as are you. I give you my word."

In that moment, something turned in Joslyn. Something whispered to her that Liam did not lie. King Edward had not been mistaken about this man when he assured her Liam was no threat to Oliver.

"Which is it to be?" he asked.

She would have to trust him. "I shall walk," she said.

Releasing her, Liam reached forward, dragged her hood over her head, and turned away. "Come."

8

Liam led Joslyn through a series of small side streets she did not recognize until they reached the market street she had first traversed. There, mounted and holding the reins to Liam's destrier, was Sir John.

"I was beginning to think I might have to come in after you," he said.

Liam made no comment, nor did he give Joslyn any warning before lifting her into the saddle of his destrier. She was still struggling for words when he swung up and settled himself behind her. However, her protest fell away as the warmth of his thighs pressed against her, nudging the sleeping thing inside her that he'd first awakened in the alley. "I can walk," she finally managed to say, trying very hard to put from her mind the feel of this dangerous man.

"You can," he agreed. Then he wrapped an arm around her waist and left Sir John to follow behind them.

Halfway to the palace, Liam felt Joslyn move to

look around at him. "How did you know I had gone from the tower?" she asked. "I thought you long departed when I left."

He did not answer immediately. Then he said, "As I had other business to attend to, my departure from the palace was delayed."

"You followed me?"

"Aye."

"How did you know it was me?"

Remembering the bent figure that had at first seemed an old woman, Liam said, "You passed by me—near enough to brush my sleeve."

"But I was cloaked."

Cloaked but unmistakable. Tempted to say what he should not, Liam leaned forward and put his mouth near her ear. "When you do not smell of dirt, my lady," he said softly, breathing her in again, "the scent of roses lingers about you. 'Twas how I knew you had gone down the alley."

She stiffened further, but still the shudder she must have tried hard to suppress quaked through her.

He affected her, Liam knew—had known it ere he had even put his mouth to hers. But, be damned, she also affected him, and in that direction lay naught but trouble.

"I am not the only one to bathe in rosewater," she said, her voice tight. "Many ladies use it."

"Ladies, but few if any commoners," he said, reminding her of the disguise she had adopted.

"It could have been another lady."

He ought to let it go, Liam knew, but could not. "Nay, Joslyn, it smells different on you. Your skin." Sliding his hand more deeply around her, he pressed his fingers into her waist.

She jerked against his hand.

Lord, but she was so different from the woman who had seemed without form or figure when she'd swung a rake at him, Liam mused. Never would he have guessed so feminine a shape was hidden beneath those filthy garments.

"Will you tell the king I left the palace?" she asked, obvious in her ploy to change the subject.

Liam smiled wryly. It was just as well, for his body was beginning to answer his thoughts. Shifting in the saddle, he loosened his hold on her. "Nay, for I am sure he is already very much aware of your absence."

"I do not see how. Dinner is yet a time away."

Was she truly so naive as to believe the barony came to her son without recompense? Liam wondered. So blind that she had not seen the desire Queen Philippa's faithless husband had shown for her? Nay, she was neither of those things, for he himself had witnessed the confidence she exuded when she stood beside the king. And when word reached him that Edward had given her an apartment at the palace, it had only confirmed what should not have needed confirming. For certain, Joslyn knew what was expected of her—though Liam did not understand why she had risked the king's wrath to go to her son. "You know I do not refer to dinner," he said.

Joslyn grew so still Liam could not even feel her breathing against him. Then she twisted around. "I know what you are thinking," she said, outraged, "but you are wrong."

Such fire in her amber eyes, Liam thought. As if it were he who had done what the king intended. "Nay," he said, "you are the one who is wrong. Wrong to believe you can promise a man as powerful as the king something and then leave him with empty hands."

She turned three shades of heat, one after the other. "I promised him naught."

"Not even with your eyes?"

In the next instant, those same eyes grew even larger. "You are a despicable cur, Liam Fawke. Never would I sell myself for that bit of land you lust after."

Now it was Liam's turn to feel fury. Dragging on the reins, he brought the destrier to a halt. "That 'bit of land' is a barony, Lady Joslyn. It is called Ashlingford, and it is among the most profitable in all of England."

She stared at him a long moment before looking away. "I know," she said. "The truth is, I had hoped the king would decide on you, rather than Oliver. That my son and I might return to Rosemoor as we were before you came."

Her lies only angered Liam more. "Which is why you stole from the manor in the middle of night to put your claim before the king?" he said.

"Father Ivo told me it was not my decision to make. That Ashlingford was Oliver's birthright and I had no right to take it from him."

It sounded like his uncle, Liam reflected—indeed, most assuredly Ivo had been behind the plan—but he simply could not believe Joslyn preferred a paltry manor to a princely barony. "In that my uncle is right," he said. "No one has the right to decide another's fate." As twice now the king had decided Liam's.

Joslyn must have understood his meaning, for she said no more.

Ignoring Sir John's raised eyebrows, Liam commanded his destrier forward, and not until they reached the tower did either speak again.

"Prepare yourself, lady," Liam said softly, "for the king does not take kindly to spurning."

She looked over her shoulder. "No doubt you hope he will take Ashlingford from Oliver for what I have done."

A grim smile twisted the corners of his mouth. "Hope," he repeated, rolling the word on his tongue. "'Twill take far more than that to return the barony to its rightful heir."

Joslyn wanted to ask what he meant but did not. There was no need to taunt him any further. Whatever his reason, he had saved her from those men when he could more easily have left her to them.

So deep in thought was she that she did not notice they were before the palace, nor that Liam had dismounted, until he reached up and lifted her down from his destrier.

On her feet, Joslyn tilted her head back and met Liam's gaze. "I have not thanked you for delivering me free of that place," she said.

"I do not expect you to."

"But I do thank you."

"Methinks there will be many an occasion for you to thank me, Joslyn Fawke," Liam said, and nudged her forward. "The king awaits you."

The guards before the palace gates eyed Joslyn as she advanced, and then one of them separated himself from the others. "What be your business at the palace?" he asked.

"I am Lady Joslyn Fawke." She pulled the hood back to reveal her tangle of black hair. "I am a guest of the king."

The guard blinked with surprise. "We have been searching for you," he said. "It was made known to us not a half hour past that—"

"But now she is returned," Liam said from behind Joslyn. "May we proceed?"

The guard stepped back. "Of course."

Inside the palace, an ornately robed man with disapproving eyes led Joslyn and Liam to the great hall. "Wait here," he said, then nodded for the guards to open the doors. A moment later, they were pulled closed behind him.

Very much aware of Liam where he stood silent at her side, Joslyn stared straight ahead. What would be her punishment for having left the palace without permission? she wondered. She did not have long to ponder it before the doors opened again.

Bowing, the robed man backed out of the hall, gesturing for Joslyn and Liam to go forth.

Drawing a deep breath, Joslyn stepped inside.

King Edward was not alone.

"Father!" Joslyn exclaimed. Forgetting propriety and her sorry disarray, she hurried across the hall and went into the arms her parent had no choice but to open to her. "I feared you might not come," she spoke into his shoulder. "The message was sent you three days past. I—"

"Joslyn, the king," Humphrey Reynard reminded her, his tone gently admonishing. Pulling back, he turned Joslyn with him to face Edward upon his throne. "'Twould appear my daughter is found, Your Majesty," he said.

Fearing what she would find in the king's gaze, Joslyn bowed low and then lifted her face and stared into his angry eyes. Was he angry because, as Liam had suggested, she had not been available to "thank" him for Ashlingford? Or only because she had defied him?

"Aye, found," King Edward said, "and by Sir Liam, no doubt." He looked to where Liam stood, to the right of Joslyn and her father. "What is the meaning of this?" he demanded.

"I think the lady can better tell it than I," Liam answered.

Once again besieged by the king's regard, Joslyn swallowed hard. "Your Majesty, 'tis not that I wished to disobey you, only that, under the circumstances, I was worried for my son's well-being. I had to see him. Unfortunately, in leaving the palace I became lost in the city, until Sir Liam happened upon me and brought me here."

Her explanation was not well received. "So you thought me a liar when I assured you your son would be safe," the king said.

"Nay, I . . . " How to explain it to a man such as he? "I am a mother, Your Majesty. What else would you have me say?"

Menacingly, the king leaned forward. "I—"

"Only a mother can understand another mother, my dear," a sweet voice said from behind. "You waste your breath upon these men."

Startled by one who dared to interrupt the king's admonishing, Joslyn looked around at the woman crossing the hall toward them.

Queen Philippa. It had to be. And what a sight she was! Though Joslyn had heard it said that the queen was of fairest face and kindliest disposition, such words hardly did her justice. She was a strikingly pretty woman. Her eyes twinkled like stars in a clear night sky, her cheeks glowed with a smile that looked never to turn downward, and her face was the face of an angel. Though she was on the plump side, it did not detract from her beauty.

Pausing before Joslyn and her father, Queen Philippa reached forward and took Joslyn's hands in hers. "I am most relieved you are returned to us safe, Lady Joslyn," she said. "Your disappearance caused quite a tumult. All manner of imaginings had I for what fate might have befallen you."

Belatedly, Joslyn lowered herself before her queen.

Philippa urged her back up. Then, with a smile and a pat to Joslyn's shoulder, she turned and crossed to the dais, where her husband sat with furrowed brow and down-turned mouth. "The poor thing is in dire need of a bath and a maid, would you not say, my lord?"

King Edward dragged his gaze from Joslyn to the woman he had made his wife, and though he must have tried to maintain his displeasure, a softening came into his eyes. "I would say she is far more in need of correction," he grumbled. "The witless woman left the palace without escort, and then lost herself in the streets of the city."

"As you have more important affairs to attend to, my lord, you may be assured I will deal with this myself," Queen Philippa said. Then, as if the matter was settled, she turned and stepped down from the dais. "Come, Lady Joslyn. We must talk most seriously, you and I."

How had she so easily slipped out from beneath the king's wrath? Joslyn wondered, in awe of the power this woman appeared to wield over the king of England. Stealing a glance at Edward, she saw his smooth brow had creased again—as if he questioned what had just occurred—but he did not call his wife back. Instead, he said, "I am placing you in the care of my queen, Lady Joslyn, but be warned that no more of your behavior of this day will I tolerate. Am I understood?"

"You are, Your Majesty."

He waved her away. "I've more important affairs to attend to," he said, announcing what the queen had reminded him of.

In silence, Joslyn, her father, and Liam followed the queen from the hall and into the antechamber.

Joslyn turned to the man whose cheeks bloomed with the color of too much drinking. "Father, you must go to Oliver," she said in a low voice. "He is at—"

"I know where he is. I was readying to leave for the monastery when you returned." Sweeping his gaze over her, he shook his head. "Good God, Jossie, what did you think you were doing going into the city alone? You could have been . . . " He sighed. "I should have taken the strap to you more often when you were young."

As if he had *ever* taken the strap to her, Joslyn reflected. "The king has named Oliver heir of Ashlingford over Liam Fawke," she whispered.

"Aye, 'twas what I was told."

"Then you know I fear for Oliver."

Humphrey Reynard looked past her to where Liam stood. "I do," he said, "though I wonder why this man would rescue you when he could very well have left you to your fate."

"I also wonder at it," Joslyn said.

Her father shook his head. "Had I only not been delayed in returning to Lon—"

"Why *were* you delayed?"

He hesitated. "Ah, daughter, though it grieves me to admit it, the delay was not in returning to London but in leaving it in the first place."

"And how is that?"

"The message came belated to me."

"But it was sent directly to you at Lord Tyberville's manor."

He shifted foot to foot. "Aye, it was, but I was not there when it arrived, and when finally it reached me . . ." He shrugged. "I returned to Rosemoor only to discover you long gone from there."

She ought to have known. "A game, Father?"

He shrugged. "'Tis in my blood. You know that. I—"

"Come, Lady Joslyn," Queen Philippa beckoned from the stairway. "We have much to do ere meal time."

Humphrey Reynard could not have asked for a better excuse to slip away.

With an obedient nod to the queen, Joslyn looked one last time into her father's lined face. "You will go to Oliver directly, won't you?" she asked.

"Of course." He pressed her hands between his. "Worry no more on it, Jossie."

Still, she would, though not as before when there had been only Liam Fawke and Father Ivo to watch him. The child was more precious to her than anything else in her world. Stepping back from her father, Joslyn resisted looking toward Liam. However, she had barely started forward when he called to her.

"Lady Joslyn."

She looked over her shoulder. "Sir Liam?"

He pushed off the sideboard he had been leaning against but came no nearer. "I always keep my word," he said, a peculiar light in his eyes that might have been anger had Joslyn not already witnessed that emotion in them.

And why wasn't it anger? Surely he must be unhappy that King Edward had not punished her for her disobedience. "Your word?" she asked.

"My word," he repeated. Then, addressing her father, he said, "I will accompany you to the monastery."

To Joslyn's chagrin, Humphrey Reynard accepted Liam's offer—if it could be called an offer. Crossing to the stairs, she followed the queen's ascent, but faltered when she realized Liam's "word" referred to the assurance he had given in the dark streets of London that she and Oliver were safe with him. She sighed. How comforting if only she could believe it.

So enmeshed in her thoughts was Joslyn that she did not realize where she was until the queen pushed open a door and ushered her into a chamber of such grandeur it dazzled the eyes.

"My apartments," Queen Philippa announced. Turning, she faced Joslyn while a maid lifted her ermine-edged mantle from her shoulders. "And your quarters for the duration of your stay with us."

Joslyn gaped. She was to share this place with the queen as if she were one of her attendant ladies? As her own mantle was removed, she noticed at the far end of the chamber a group of five colorfully garbed women gathered before a softly flickering fire. Although they all held lengths of worked cloth in one hand and a needle in the other, they appeared more

intent on conversation than on adding even a stitch to
their embroidery.

"I would be honored, Your Majesty," Joslyn said,
"but I have been given an apartment of my own."

"You were, but this is where you will sleep and
occupy yourself henceforth."

Did the queen suspect what Liam believed? Joslyn
fretted. Had King Edward intended to visit Joslyn in
that apartment? Worse, did the queen think Joslyn
had invited him to come to her? Wishing fervently to
defend herself but knowing it would be improper to
do so, she simply said, "I thank you, my lady."

The queen smiled and looked over her shoulder to
the woman who had taken her mantle. "Send for
water," she bade her. "The Lady Joslyn is in desperate
need of a bath."

Until that moment, Joslyn had forgotten her
appearance, but now it came back to her. Lord, she
was before a queen, and soon to be among the most
noble of her ladies.

"And now I will present you," the queen said as
she stepped past Joslyn.

Joslyn looked down at the gown she wore. True, it
had taken little of the abuse which her mantle, slippers, and hair had been subject to, but still it showed
traces of her flight through those filthy streets. "I am
hardly presentable," she said.

"Ah, child," the queen murmured, as if speaking to
an awkward daughter, "simply smile and none will
find anything amiss."

Hoping Philippa was right, Joslyn followed the
regal woman into the first of what appeared to be
four chambers.

"Ladies," the queen called to them.

Immediately, all five looked around in surprise. Then they rose from their stools, bowed, and murmured greetings to their queen.

"We've a guest, ladies," Philippa said. "Lady Joslyn Fawke, soon to be of the barony of Ashlingford now that her son has been named its heir."

"Ashlingford," one lady said. "Then 'tis not the Irish bastard who will inherit?"

Queen Philippa swiftly interceded. "Unbeknown to any, the Lady Joslyn was wed to Baron Maynard Fawke some years ago. As their son is quite young, Sir Liam will continue to manage the barony as he did for his brother."

It amazed Joslyn that the queen was so well apprised of the situation. What else did she know?

A sweet-faced young woman who could be no more than sixteen summers of age leaned toward a lady older by several. "'Tis a pity the Irishman did not inherit," she whispered. "He is quite handsome, and a fine husband he would have made with such a barony."

Another of the ladies asked, "You have seen him?"

The young woman's cheeks warmed with embarrassment at having been overheard. "From a . . . a distance."

"And how is that, Lady Cedra?" Queen Philippa asked, disapproval in her tone.

Looking thrice more shamed by the queen's question, Cedra bit her bottom lip and shifted her gaze to her clasped hands. "Ah, my queen, truly I did not mean to listen in upon your conversation with Sir Liam, but when I came upon you in the garden late this morn, my ears could not throw back what they had already heard."

So this was the business that had delayed Liam's departure from the palace.

"You should always make your presence known." The queen's reprimand was a motherly one. "'Tis unseemly in a lady to skulk among other people's conversations."

Contrite, Lady Cedra bent her head. "I beg your forgiveness."

Queen Philippa regarded her a moment longer, then stepped forward and tipped her chin up. "All I ask is that you remember this lesson," she said. "'Tis of no good if you forget it."

"I will remember, Your Majesty."

The queen smiled again. Then, as if the incident had never occurred, she began introducing Joslyn to each of the ladies. "Lady Cedra, as you know." She nodded to the woman. "And this is Lady Amilie, beside her Lady Justina, and these two are the elder Lady Ellen and the younger Lady Ellen."

Two Ellens. Mother and daughter? Joslyn wondered. But nay, though one was definitely older than the other, there could be no more than a half dozen years' difference between them.

"Sisters." Queen Philippa answered the unspoken question. "Their mother so loved the name."

"And why is Lady Joslyn in such disarray?" the tall thin-faced Lady Amilie asked.

Slipping a wink to Joslyn, Queen Philippa said, "I fear the lady sees herself as something of an adventuress. She thinks naught of exploring the city on her own."

"Oh . . . my!" Lady Cedra breathed louder than the others. "Alone?"

The queen chuckled. "As you can see, there is

much to do ere she takes her place at the barony—
and less than a day in which to do it, for on the morrow she and her son journey to Ashlingford."

Joslyn's heart lurched. So they would go directly to
their new home without first returning to Rosemoor.

"I daresay there is much to do." Lady Amilie
voiced clear disdain. "A lady would never even think
of leaving the palace without a considerable escort. I
know I would not."

Reaching forward, Queen Philippa gently tweaked
the woman's cheek. "Just as a lady would never
accept a scoundrel's invitation to tryst beneath the
stairs, hmm?" she said, laughter on the edge of her
voice.

Lady Amilie colored.

"But enough of this," the queen said. She looked
back at Joslyn. "Remove your garments and give them
to Lady Justina. Then we will have you into a bath."

Joslyn had never been overly modest, but neither
had she ever gone unclothed before any other than
her maid.

"I've a robe you may don until the bathwater
arrives," the queen said, as if reading her thoughts.

"Thank you, Your Majesty."

"I will do her hair," Lady Cedra offered.

"I will read to her while she bathes," the younger
Lady Ellen said.

"And I?" The elder Ellen shrugged. "Ah, well, I
suppose there is naught left for me but to stroll the
garden."

"Naught but for you and Amilie to tend me," the
queen reminded her.

The woman bowed her head. "But of course."

"Enjoy your bath, my dear," Queen Philippa told

Joslyn. "We will talk afterward." She turned away and left the chamber, Amilie and the elder Ellen following.

Wondering what else the queen wished to talk to her about, Joslyn began to undress.

9

"*Do not think I am unaware* of my husband's appetites," Queen Philippa said.

Joslyn started with surprise. Bathed, perfumed, garbed, and groomed, she had been savoring these few moments of solitude when the queen had stole behind her without warning.

"Your Majesty?" she asked, turning to face her.

Resplendent in red velvet, the queen smiled. Still, there was a bitter tug to her lips that had not been there before. "I speak of the apartment, of course," she said.

With dread understanding, Joslyn forced herself to hold the queen's gaze when what she wanted most was to look away. Liam had said, and now Philippa confirmed, that King Edward had intended to come to her for recompense.

But did that mean Liam had lost Ashlingford for no other reason than that Joslyn had appealed to the king? Lord, she prayed not—unless, of course, it meant King Edward might reconsider his ruling. Surely she could not be blamed for the loss of Oliver's birthright if the king changed his mind, for even had she not recklessly strayed from the palace, she would have refused Edward had he come to her.

"I had to leave the apartment," Joslyn said, "to assure my son and myself that all was well."

The queen stared at her. "Then you did not know what my husband planned?"

What a quandary Joslyn found herself in. "I suppose I should have known," she admitted, remembering the way the king had looked at her and, later, touched her, "but all I could think of was Oliver."

As if searching for the truth in her words, Queen Philippa considered her a moment longer. "When word was brought me that my husband had installed you in that apartment, I must admit I was angry, but no more than usual. You see, Lady Joslyn, I love my lord very much, and I am certain he loves me, but it is difficult for him to pass by a lovely face when it is so easily in his power to enjoy it." With a sigh, she caught up the loose ends of her girdle and began rubbing the gold beads threaded upon it between her fingers. "'Tis a shameful thing to admit, but I was relieved to hear you had disappeared from the palace."

"It was the king who discovered me missing?"

"Nay, but he would have, had your father's arrival not brought it to light first."

"So you brought me to your apartments," Joslyn concluded.

Queen Philippa turned and walked to the flickering fire. "Self-serving, hmm?" she mused, putting her hands out to warm them. "Aye, Lady Joslyn. 'Tis rare that I am able to manage my husband's infidelities, but in your case I saw the opportunity and took it. Quite unashamedly, I might add."

"Even if— " how to say it? — "I would not have . . . "

Queen Philippa turned back. "Now that I have met you, my dear," she said, a smile returning to her face, "I can see I need not have worried." She stepped forward and patted Joslyn's shoulder. "Think no more on it. All is as it should be. On the morrow you will be on your way to your new home, and this need never be mentioned again."

Joslyn was tempted to appeal to the queen for assistance in the matter of Ashlingford, but she did not. Providing King Edward was not so angered with her that he bestowed the barony upon Liam Fawke, the matter was settled. Naught to be gained from complaining. "I thank you, Your Majesty," she murmured.

"And I you," Philippa answered. Then, almost to herself, she said, "Methinks Sir Liam is very wrong about you."

Joslyn should have let it pass but could not help herself. "How do you know Sir Liam?" she asked. "What I mean is, Lady Cedra said you were with him in the garden this morn."

Philippa chuckled. "Wondering if I am as unfaithful to my husband as he is to me?" Before Joslyn could protest, she shook her head. "I jest. Do not fear to have offended me." With a long sigh, she lowered herself into a plump armchair that looked never to have been sat upon. "As we've yet a few minutes," she said, "I will explain. I was at my husband's side seven years ago when Sir Liam and his brother came before the crown to argue whose right over Ashlingford was the greater. Myself, I thought it was

Sir Liam whose claim ought to have been honored—even though he was not legitimate born."

"Because his father had named him heir?"

"That is part of it. After all, an astute man knows his sons better than they know themselves, and the old baron was indeed wise."

"And the other part?"

The queen shrugged. "Though it was more a feeling than anything else, it seemed to me Sir Liam was the more honorable. That he was honest and responsible, whereas his brother . . . " She frowned. "I am sorry, Lady Joslyn. I forget you were wed to Maynard Fawke."

"I do not require an apology. Truly, I am grateful for the insight you have given me into a man I know so little."

Philippa nodded. "I thought it was that way, but still it is not proper for me to tell you who your husband was when I knew him not. As I was saying, I was present when my lord decreed that Ashlingford should pass to the legitimate son. Throughout the proceedings, Liam Fawke had been so calm and confident that when he lost control of himself following the pronouncement, no one was prepared. Like a lion, he raged, and though that might have been the worst of it, his foolish uncle taunted him. 'Tis astonishing that one man could capture such strength in anger, but it took three—nay, four—of the guard to pull him off Father Ivo and drag him from the hall."

The images rushing through Joslyn's mind caused fear to run up her spine. She could well imagine Liam's anger. "What happened?" she asked softly.

"The king was so infuriated by Sir Liam's behavior

that he ordered him imprisoned in the Beauchamp Tower, a prison few men leave alive. It is a most serious matter to be sent there."

Hardly realizing she did so, Joslyn rubbed her hands up and down her arms to smooth the fine hairs that had risen there. "And was he taken to the tower?"

The queen smiled. "Nay, but only because I humbled myself and pleaded for him."

"You did? But why?"

She sighed. "He is a handsome man, would you not say?"

The question caught Joslyn unaware. "I . . . well, I suppose . . . "

"He is. Mayhap you do not see it now, but when you fear him less, you will hardly be able to overlook it."

The truth was, Joslyn already knew it—and more. Though she tried to suppress the memory, she saw him again in her mind, his face so near hers she could feel the touch of his mouth again. Suddenly short of breath, she said, "I cannot believe you went to his aid simply because he was pleasing to the eye, Your Majesty."

"I did not. As I have said, I felt for Sir Liam. I believed him wronged. Thus, in my mind he was justified in voicing his feelings, dangerous as they were."

"And the king pardoned him?"

"Aye, after I begged him to. And since then I have affirmed that it was the right thing to do, for I have come to know Sir Liam as a man with years of hurt behind and before him. A man aching to be understood." Thoughtfully, she traced a finger down a pleat of her lustrous skirts. "'Tis true he has a temper, Lady

Joslyn, but I beseech you, do not let that shadow the good of him."

Then the queen also believed she need not fear him, Joslyn thought. But how could she not? Even with all she had learned this day, Liam till unsettled her. Lord, never would she forget his ride on Rosemoor Manor. Like the devil he had come to shatter her snug little life, and like the devil the king had this day set him upon her shoulder to darken the rest of her days.

"Of this I am certain," the queen continued, "Sir Liam is as honorable today as he was seven years ago."

"Though angrier," Joslyn pointed out.

Regret settled in the fine grooves of the queen's face. "Aye, angrier. The future promised him has been taken a second time." She shook her head. "'Tis a cruel life he has been dealt."

Made all the more cruel by an innocent little boy who had yet to know of the tumult he had caused simply by being born. "Yet you think he will remain honorable?" Joslyn asked.

Without a moment's pondering, the queen answered, "I know it." Then she stood, smoothed her skirts into place, and started from the chamber. "Ladies," she called, "pull your noses from the door and let us be to dinner."

There was a shuffling behind the closed door of the apartment into which the women had earlier gone to prepare themselves, a calculated moment of silence, and then the door was pulled open. Each looking as innocent as a cat with a feather stuck between its claws, the five women filed out.

What a strange life. An empty life, Joslyn thought.

Would it be the same at Ashlingford? A sudden yearning for Rosemoor filling her belly, she forced her thoughts of Liam aside and followed the queen and her entourage from the apartments.

"Let us have music!" King Edward shouted.

The tedious meal over with, and now the ceremony whereby Liam had sworn fealty to the king as the new baron of Thornemede, the minstrels in the galleries positioned their instruments and struck up a merry tune.

The commotion that followed was an opportunity Joslyn could not allow to pass her by. Overwhelmed and in need of fresh air, she rose from the bench she had occupied these past three hours and walked stiffly to the doors standing open to the left of the dais.

The soldier who stood guard there swept his gaze over her but allowed her to pass unhindered.

Stepping out onto the balcony, Joslyn looked across an expanse of lawn bordered by flowers. Even lit by a clouded sky it was lovely, so open and serene in contrast to the hall behind.

A breeze coursed gently over her brow, bringing with it the scent of rain. She sighed. Just a few minutes, she told herself, and then she would return to the hall with its throng of people and suffocating noise. Longing for Rosemoor, she crossed to the railing and leaned her elbows upon it.

"You are thinking of slipping away again, Lady Joslyn?" A voice too soon intruded upon her sanctuary.

Liam. As he had not said a word to her throughout the meal they had shared at the same trencher, it surprised her that he would now seek her out. Keeping her back to him, she said, "Would I dare?"

"I think you would."

If there were a chance of succeeding, but there was not. Joslyn looked over her shoulder at where Liam stood in the doorway, his red hair darkened by the gray day. "I love my son very much, Sir Liam," she said, and then hastily substituted his new title. "Lord Fawke."

He considered her a moment. "I know."

Against the backdrop of merriment within the hall, an uncomfortable silence descended between them. Liam strode to the railing.

Though a space separated them, Joslyn found his nearness unsettling—even more so than when they had eaten side by side, ignoring each other. He was ignoring her no longer, though, his green gaze steadfast upon her.

"You are a baron now," Joslyn said, groping for something—anything—to turn back the silence.

Liam inclined his head. "I am," he said, his voice tight.

But not of the barony he wanted.

Although she knew she ought not to care, Joslyn felt for him—ever a bastard to men of noble birth. When she had sat beside Liam during the king's pronouncement that Thornemede would be awarded to him, she had heard murmurs of discontent among those of the nobility who had wanted the barony for themselves. Though Liam had shown no reaction to their resentment, he could not have been oblivious to it.

As if remembering it himself, the emotions he held so near to him came into his eyes—fleeting, but seen by Joslyn in that moment of unguardedness.

She knew it was a mistake the moment she lifted her hand, but she could not help herself. Reaching up, she laid her fingers against Liam's jaw.

Roses. The delicate scent flooded Liam's senses and went straight to the heart of him. He fought it, tried to explain it away as mere fleshly need, but it was a losing battle. There was something about Joslyn. Something . . .

Leaving the tenderness of her eyes, he looked lower, and beneath his gaze her lips parted softly. Only vaguely aware of what he did, he bent his head.

"Liam?" she breathed, uncertain.

Why uncertain? As if arising from a dream, he blinked. Then, focusing on her mouth that was only a moment away, jerked back. God's rood! What possessed him? He did not want his brother's wife. Certainly not. The witch was pulling him in, like a spider to a fly. Damned roses!

Though, in fact, more angry with himself than Joslyn, Liam growled, "There is an answer to your need, Lady, but I am not it."

Her brilliant eyes widened with surprise a moment before outrage flared from their depths. "I assure you 'tis not need that made me do so foolish a thing," she snapped, fisting the hand that had touched him. "And were it, I most certainly would not turn to one such as you."

"A bastard."

"You know that is not what I mean!" she exclaimed.

"Do I not?"

"Nay, you do not. 'Twas not want that I felt for you, Lord Fawke, but . . . but something you do not understand."

"Pity?"

As if groping for a reply, she opened her mouth, closed it, opened it again. "As I said, you do not understand. 'Tis not in you to understand."

"Nay, it is not," he agreed, "but neither is it in you to understand *me*, Lady Joslyn. So do not attempt it."

And what was she to say to that? Joslyn wondered. That she had no intention of trying to fathom the man beneath the fury? Nay, it would only be a lie, for already she battled a strong desire to learn more about Liam Fawke—to understand his hurt and pain, and perhaps help him. . . .

Lord, she was only getting herself deeper into this mess. The best possible thing for her to do would be simply to ignore this man. But how was that possible when he would be so often at Ashlingford?

"We will be missed," Liam said. He turned on his heel and strode from the balcony as the first drops of rain began to fall.

Telling herself that what had nearly happened did not matter—that she was eternally grateful Liam had not put his mouth upon hers—Joslyn followed.

10

With anxious eyes, Josyln searched the crowd approaching the tower for the pixie-faced child she had lost so much sleep over. It being the first time she and Oliver had been parted overnight, she had tossed and turned on her wonderfully plump pallet, catching only snatches of rest between the hours of worry. Soon, though, they would be reunited—if only to begin a journey that boded no good for either of them.

With that thought, Joslyn glanced at the man mounted on the horse beside hers. Neither she nor Liam had spoken a word to each other since being brought together again a half hour past. As each understood what was between them, enough having been made clear on the balcony yesterday, conversation was unnecessary. They would avoid each other as much as possible, speak as few words as was feasible, and live their lives as separately as was practical. Still, Joslyn wished there were some way to make peace with him.

However, there was no more time to ponder her situation, for suddenly Father Ivo and the knight Liam had set to watch over Oliver appeared behind a procession of hay wains. But where was . . . ?

There. Humphrey Reynard rode behind the two men, and in his arms was a wonder-struck Oliver. Riding on the front of his grandfather's saddle, the little boy did not at first notice his mother ahead of him, so in awe was he of the magnificently walled tower.

Joslyn urged her mount forward. To her immense relief, Liam and his men did not follow, and Father Ivo and the knight continued past her. It would be difficult enough to bid her father farewell without having any of them watching over her shoulder.

"Mama, does a giant live there?" was the first thing out of Oliver's mouth when finally he noticed her. Not "Why didn't you come back yesterday?" or "I was frightened," as she expected. He seemed to have taken her absence in stride, as if it were an everyday occurrence. Of course, it must have been a comfort for him to have had his grandfather arrive at the monastery, but she realized he was also growing up. Perhaps she needed him more than he needed her.

Still, Joslyn could not have been more grateful that Oliver appeared untouched and unworried by the promise she had been unable to keep. "A giant?" she mused, guiding her palfrey alongside her father's. "'Tis true a mighty man lives there, Oliver, but he is not quite a giant."

"But nearly, huh?" He pleaded for her to feed his childish imagination.

Her arms aching to hold him, she smiled. "Very nearly."

As she reached to accept him from his grandfather, Oliver asked, "An' a dragon? He lives there too?"

Folding him in her arms, Joslyn nodded against his golden head. "Oh, most certainly, Oliver." She savored the feel of her little boy in her arms for as long as he would allow it; it was not long enough. Growing restless, he pulled back, grasped the ties of her mantle, and pensively drew them through his hands.

"We goin' to Ashaford now?" he asked. "A-papa said we were."

A-papa. His child's familiar for "grandfather." She smiled. Aye, he was growing up, but he could be called her little boy for many years yet. Smoothing a hand over his round head, she said, "Aye, we go to Ashlingford. 'Twill be a great journey—an adventure. Are you excited?"

He shrugged a shoulder. "A-papa say he not goin' with us," he mumbled, his lower lip beginning to jut.

She looked across at her father. "But he will come visit us soon, won't you, Father?"

"Of course I will," he said, his voice more jovial than the mood reflected in his eyes.

He would be a lonely man at Rosemoor with both of them gone, Joslyn knew. Lonelier than he had been these past years since his son had left the manor.

Oliver eyed him. "You will?"

Reaching across, Humphrey tapped his grandson's nose. "Aye, my boy."

Oliver grinned.

"We must be on our way," Joslyn said. Turning Oliver around, she settled him on the fore of her saddle. "'Tis a long ride to Ashlingford." She looked up and met her father's gaze.

"I will . . . miss you," he said, blinking against a moisture that had come into his eyes.

Her heart swelling for the words so clearly drawn from deep inside him, Joslyn reached across and put her hand over his. "As we will miss you," she said.

He tried to smile, then gave it up and laid his other hand over their two. "I am going to find your brother, Jossie," he said. Then, seeing the surprised look on her face, he added, "It is time."

Then some good *would* come of her and Oliver leaving Rosemoor. Faced with the prospect of being utterly alone, her father would relinquish his pride and bring Richard home—providing her brother agreed. Though Humphrey Reynard could not be said to be a cruel man, when his beloved wife died he had begun drinking heavily to ease his loneliness. The first two years following her death he had often drunk himself into fits of rage, but not once had he turned his grieving upon his daughter.

It was his son who had gotten in his way and been given punishment that was not his due. Thus, Richard Reynard had taken to the road, which had finally jolted Humphrey out of his reckless behavior. Though he still drank more than was good for him, not since the night his son left had he lost control of himself.

"I am pleased," Joslyn said, her throat constricting.

He gave a crooked smile. "I only hope I shall be. Richard is more stubborn than even I."

That was true, but they had to begin somewhere if ever they were to mend what had been broken. "You will send news when he is home again?" she asked.

He nodded, then looked beyond her.

Joslyn followed his gaze.

Liam Fawke and his men were advancing. Knowing it was time to part, Joslyn started to withdraw her hand from her father's. However, he clasped it tighter.

"I do not think I like that priest," he said.

"I will be cautious," she assured him.

He nodded. "As for the bastard, methinks he may not be the man Maynard led us to believe."

What had transpired between her father and Liam when they rode to the monastery yesterday? she wondered, then abruptly set aside her pondering. There was no time to discuss it. "Perhaps," she said, pulling her hand free. "In time we will know."

With a sigh, her father shifted around and removed the bundle tied to the back of his saddle. "Your belongings," he said. Leaning sideways, he secured it to Joslyn's saddle. "I collected them first thing this morn."

"I had nearly forgotten," she said, grateful that she could later change into the comfort of her own garments.

Humphrey Reynard straightened. "God be with you, daughter," he said, his voice gruff with emotion. Then he turned his horse back toward the city.

"Love you, A-papa," Oliver called after him.

He hesitated, but a moment later looked over his shoulder.

Joslyn saw the struggle on his face—the yearning

to profess his own feelings for Oliver—but in the end he only winked and lifted a hand in farewell.

Oliver did the same.

Out of the wood they came, thundering like an angry storm across a clear sky.

There was no time to think—and hardly time to react. Tightening her arm around Oliver, who instantly jolted awake, Joslyn dragged on the reins to jerk her palfrey's head right. It lurched forward but carried her less than two strides before faltering and pulling left.

There was nowhere to go, Joslyn realized. They were all around and among them now. Their voices loud, their weapons catching sun on silvered blades, twenty or more brigands set themselves upon the Ashlingford knights. And soon they would be upon her and Oliver.

Her heart slamming so loudly she could put no sense to what Oliver was saying, Joslyn looked to the one who might prove himself their savior. But Liam was nowhere to be seen.

Then a terrible thought struck her: Liam was behind this attack. Here was the means by which he would rid himself of her and Oliver and gain Ashlingford for himself.

"Mama?" Oliver squeaked, his fear echoing hers.

With an unexplainable pain in her center, she eyed the bordering woods they could not possibly hope to reach, then met her son's wide-eyed gaze with a lie of confidence. "Hold to me," she said, knowing that if she did not at least try to save them, their fate was spoken for.

Obediently, he turned and wrapped both arms around her waist. It went no further than that, though, for in the next instant they were dragged from their horse and onto another. For a moment Joslyn believed an attacker had swept down upon them, and then those feelings learned in the alley told her different. It was Liam Fawke who held them. Liam Fawke keeping his word.

"Do not fight me," he growled, tightening his arm around her.

Joslyn opened her mouth to tell him she had no intention of doing so, but a cry somewhere between a wail and a scream stopped the words. Jerking her eyes left, she saw one of the brigands racing toward them on a horse lathered with exertion, his raised sword piercing the air before him.

Liam tensed, and then answered the other's charge by guiding his destrier around, dragging his thrusting sword from its scabbard, and raising it to meet the enemy.

Instinctively, Joslyn hunched over Oliver and a moment later felt the impact straight through her bones. Then the next blow, and one after it. Like the beat of a smithy's hammer, the song of steel rang in her ears. But this was no weapon being forged. It was the reason for the forging: death.

A sudden moisture flecked Joslyn's brow. Knowing that rain could not fall from a cloudless sky, she began to pray as she could not remember ever having prayed.

"To the devil with you!" Liam shouted, his body following the thrust of his sword forward.

The air split with an enraged cry of pain. But whose? Joslyn wondered, her heart swelling so large she thought it might burst. Though she could not believe it was Liam whose life had just been laid waste, her motherly instinct prepared her to take the brunt of their fall from Oliver.

The fall never came.

Suddenly they were moving again, the gust of Liam's breath in Joslyn's hair, the bunched muscles of his chest pressing against her back. He lived.

"Thank you, Lord," she murmured, and opened her eyes to see they had crossed into a shaded wood.

Liam did not go far. Instead, with an urgency that spoke to Joslyn of further bloodshed, he halted his destrier beside an outcropping of boulders and, without any gentleness, lifted her down.

"Get behind the boulders and stay there," he ordered as she stumbled back under the burden of Oliver. "I will return for you when 'tis done."

Her footing still uncertain, Joslyn lifted her chin and met his stare—but only for a moment before a shout on the edge of the wood announced the arrival of two more brigands.

"Now!" Liam bellowed, his gaze turning fierce.

He was another man, she saw in that instant, a man to be feared even if he had just saved their lives. Was this now the knight who had raged at King Edward seven years past when his birthright had been given to another?

Realizing his rage might be loosed on her did she not do as he commanded, Joslyn ran forward and dropped behind the first boulder. Then, peering over the top, she watched as Liam remounted and rode back toward the fray.

"Scared, Mama," Oliver said into her shoulder.

For fear he might look up and witness the bloody

clash soon to be upon Liam, she pressed a hand to the back of his head to hold his face against her body. "All is well," she soothed. "All is well."

Liam glanced toward the road where the Ashlingford knights appeared to be holding their own against the attackers, then shifted his gaze to the first brigand, a man much his own size, though older, who looked to be a worthy opponent.

Drawing back his sword, Liam slammed its edge across the other's. "For six years of naught!" he shouted, Maynard's deathbed taunt returning to him.

The brigand jerked sideways from the impact but managed to hold the saddle.

Driving his destrier past him, Liam set himself upon the second attacker, but at the moment their swords should have met, he listed far left of his opponent and swept his weapon downward. "For the lies!" he bellowed.

A squawk not unlike that of an incensed bird was evidence that he had found the soft belly of the brigand, who wore no chain mail to deflect the blow. The crimson upon Liam's blade confirmed it.

Leaving the mortally wounded man to his death, Liam wheeled his mount around to engage the first brigand a second time, and a moment later they crossed swords again. This time, though, neither blade gave, causing both horses to rear beneath the strain of the locked weapons.

One dangerous emotion after another clamoring to be set free, Liam met his opponent's gaze, saw a like anger there, and answered it by forcing the other man's sword away.

As the horses settled back to the ground, the brigand countered with a stroke that grated loudly across

Liam's mail shirt, then he heaved forward in an attempt to push his blade through the links. However, it was Liam who broke flesh first, his blade slicing through the man's exposed thigh.

With a fierce snarl, the brigand leaned sideways in his saddle, lifted his injured leg, and thrust his booted foot toward Liam's chest in an attempt to unseat him.

Grabbing his leg, Liam shoved him backward.

The brigand wavered on the edge of his saddle, his free hand grasping at his destrier's mane to right himself, but a moment later he plummeted to the mossy earth.

Although the time it took for him to recover would have been sufficient for Liam to run him through, the deceit of these past six years demanded more than an easy end. True, it was neither Maynard nor Ivo fallen before Liam—both far more deserving of his vengeance—but here was the means of release he needed so badly.

Fitting his hand more precisely around the hilt of his weapon, the familiarity of the worn leather against his palm and fingers focusing him, Liam dismounted.

On his feet again in spite of the gaping wound in his leg, the man beckoned Liam forward. "Come on, bastard," he challenged, the smirk of knowing on his lips.

Bastard? Aye, Liam acknowledged the truth of what he had suspected. This attack was by design. But whose? One of the disgruntled noblemen who had sought to make Thornemede his own? Or a man who wished Liam as far from Ashlingford as possible, and what better place than the grave? Though it could be either, Liam was drawn nearer to the possibility that it was his uncle. No matter how many of the attackers Ivo slaughtered, they would die having done a service for him. Unfortunately for Ivo, Liam had no intention of obliging him. Death would not take him this day.

Liam lunged toward the jeering man and, with one stroke, severed a dozen links of his shabby chain-mail tunic.

The man staggered back a step.

But Liam wanted more from him than spilled blood. He wanted satisfaction, and satisfaction he would have. "I still stand," he taunted his opponent.

The words spurted new strength through the man, and a moment later Liam was trading blows with him again.

Time and again Liam colored his blade with a life that would soon be forfeit, filled his ears with sounds of suffering that echoed the years inside him, and shouted his victories with a voice that rose to the heavens only to fall back. When the brigand foolishly swung wide, opening himself to death, Liam even then did not finish him off. Instead he allowed the man breath to recover before stroking his blade downward on his opponent's sword arm.

His face contorting with pain, the brigand retaliated with a sloppy slice, but one that earned him a small victory.

Oddly, Liam did not feel the pain in his forearm. Instead, he sensed only warmth as the blood flowed from the wound and trickled down his wrist. Turning his attention to the sword swinging toward him, he fended it off with a stroke carried high, forced the man's blade above his head, and leaned into him.

"You or me?" he asked between clenched teeth.

Uncertainty passed over the man's face. However, in the next instant something dashed it away—a glance behind. "You," he rasped, baring his teeth with renewed confidence.

Liam knew without looking around what had restored the man's spirit; others were coming to his aid. Knowing a greater challenge awaited him, he nodded. "Then we are done," he said, and, as if dreaming it, watched as he closed his left hand over his right upon his sword's hilt. Like a mother whispering "hush" in the night, his blade glided down and off the other's sword and so easily slid into place.

Pain widened the other man's mouth, and then he dropped to the ground.

It had been years since he'd taken someone's life, Liam realized, as he looked down upon the breathless man, and this day he had already taken three. But even as loathing for what he had done filled him, he swung around and deflected the blow of the brigand who charged him on horseback. However, there was no time to turn away the weapon of the one who followed the first—a weapon not unlike a club but differing in that its head was covered with iron spikes: a mace. Liam jerked back to avoid it, but though he spared himself a crushed skull, it caught him across the jaw.

Whooping loudly, the brigand rode past.

This time there was pain, the easing of Liam's anger in the face of death causing him to feel the blow as he had not with his first injury. Feeling both now, he looked to the two attackers, who had turned their horses about and were starting back toward him. They would kill him, he knew—either by sword or beneath the hooves of their horses.

Knowing that if he did not draw again on his anger he was as dead as the man at his feet, Liam looked into that raw place inside him where strength lay. *Maynard*, he reminded himself. *Ivo. Anya. Ashlingford.* Like a storm, the rage of years blew over him again, and when the brigands swept down upon him he was ready for them.

Wielding his sword with one hand, Liam reached with the other for the dagger upon his belt. It slid free and a moment later sailed through the air. Years of practice had perfected his left-handed throw—so perfect, in fact, that it struck the brigand swinging the mace exactly where he intended.

Grabbing his chest, the man fell backward and met death as he hit the ground.

Too soon the other brigand was upon Liam. In the path of the rushing horse, a sword leveled at his chest, Liam spread his legs, raised his weapon, and at the last possible moment leapt to the side and swung his sword. The man was unprepared for the blow, which caught him mid-back, and though his chain mail spared his blood, the impact lurched him forward.

The human side of Liam lost in the violence, the animal in him calculating his prey, he bolted after the brigand and fought as he had never fought before. He forced the man down from his horse, across the floor of the wood, and onto the road, and when the Ashlingford knights came forward to offer their assistance, he acknowledged them only long enough to shout them back. Their own battles won, they retreated to watch from a distance the man who should have been their lord prove himself more than worthy of the title. And finally, with the last of his great anger, Liam laid the brigand down.

The man fell without so much as a groan, turned his gaze to the heavens, and eased where he lay.

Looking about at the strewn bodies, Liam saw that not all the attackers were accounted for. Either they had fled with the realization they were the weaker force, or they had regrouped to attempt another ambush farther up the road.

The Ashlingford knights had not escaped unscathed, the rent shirts of mail and slashed chausses revealing injuries not unlike those Liam had sustained. None was dead, however—as near a miracle as Liam had ever seen. Only Sir Gregory had fallen, and he appeared still very much alive where he sat propped against a rock, a hand to the wound in his side.

Liam fastened his gaze upon Ivo, where he stood to the right of a cut and scraped Sir John. Though his face mirrored repentance for the lives he had taken with his unholy sword, Liam knew his remorse was not truly for them but for what they had not accomplished. The bastard nephew still lived and would yet return to Ashlingford.

Liam had thought his anger spent, but it rose again to flex his hand upon his sword. One more life, just one more, he thought, stepping forward. What better place for a mock priest to die than upon the battlefield he had most likely created himself? There would not be any among the Ashlingford knights who would object did he perish among his equals.

But there was Joslyn. . . .

Liam looked toward the wood. She was still there, but did she cower behind the boulder? Or were her eyes this moment fixed upon him, ready to witness what would seem to her a heinous crime? Damnation!

Suppressing the desire to finish Ivo now, Liam captured his uncle's gaze and sent him a message that could not have been more clear were it spoken. Then he returned his sullied sword to its scabbard and turned back toward the wood.

Several of the Ashlingford knights followed him, all keeping silent as if commanded. Hardly had Liam set foot into the wood when, across the distance, he saw Joslyn where she stood before the boulders—no cowering lady, she—her bearing solid and upright but for the little boy huddled in her arms.

Liam again reflected on his brother's choice of wife. What an odd match Maynard had made, he who had preferred his women simpering and needy—even if only acting the part. Joslyn seemed as far from that type of woman as could be. She was strong, though not as strong as she might have liked him to believe, Liam realized, as he drew near and saw in her haunted eyes the things she had just seen and heard.

Though it should not have touched him, in that instant a thousand regrets flooded him for what she had witnessed. From the moment he had turned from her, he had plunged so deeply into the heinous battle to survive that he had forgotten her very existence. He had—

Nay. It was just as well that he had put her from his mind, for had he tried to shield her from the warrior in him he would surely have given up his life for it. And it mattered not what she thought of him. After all, he owed her no explanation for who he was and what he had done.

"You are well?" he asked.

She stared at him a long moment before nodding, then shifted her gaze to his bloody jaw. Her lids flickered, but she did not swoon as many a lady might. Instead, she lowered her gaze to the marks of battle adorning his chain mail. "You are injured," she said softly.

"Are you ready to ride, Lady Joslyn?" he asked.

"I am ready," she answered, wanting to be as far from this place as possible.

"Can I look now, Mama?" Oliver asked, starting to pull back from her.

"Not yet," she replied, seeing beyond Liam the scattered bodies his men were examining. Throughout the fighting she had pressed her palms to Oliver's ears to prevent him from hearing the battle and death cries. She would not now allow him to see the result of this day's clash.

"I will carry the boy if you like." Liam surprised her with his offer.

Instinctively, Joslyn tightened her hold on Oliver. "Nay, I will carry him," she said, knowing she insulted Liam in not trusting her with her son, but also needing to hold on to this little life that had never before been so near danger. So near death.

He turned away before she could see his reaction. "Then let us be gone," he said, heading out of the wood.

They had hardly covered any ground before one of the knights called to him, "This one's alive!"

Halting, Liam looked behind him at Joslyn. "One of the knights will assist you in mounting," he said, and motioned for her to continue on to the road.

It being enough to look upon one injured man, Joslyn had no desire to see another, and that one most likely near death. Lifting her skirts higher, she swept past him toward her horse.

Liam wondered what was in her mind as he stared after her, but he pushed his ponderings aside and strode to where the knights looked down upon one of the attackers—the first man Liam had put his sword through.

There was no hope for the brigand, Liam saw; it was only a matter of time before he lay as dead as the others. But something might be learned from him ere he passed on.

Going down onto his haunches, he demanded, "Who hired you, man?"

Cradling his belly, the brigand turned his ashen face to Liam and slowly curled a grim smile at him. "Why, the devil himself," he whispered. "You . . . you know him, don't you?"

Aye, he knew Ivo, but was he the devil referred to? "I am sure I do," Liam replied, "but why don't you tell me anyway."

"You'd like that, eh?" The brigand choked.

"More than you can know."

"And what be my reward?" The man's eyes sparkled with the irony of pocketing something he would have no use of in hell.

"A grave," Liam offered. "Else you are left as pickings for the beasts of the wood."

The man's lids fluttered closed over his eyes. "I will have to think on it a moment."

"You will be dead by then."

With effort, the brigand opened his eyes far enough to peer at Liam. Then he nodded. However, whatever he intended to say was in the next instant severed from him by the sweep of a dagger that laid open the great vein in his neck.

11

"*God would not have* made him to suffer so," Ivo said, wiping his blade as he straightened. "'Tis merciful to speedily deliver a dying man from his tortured end. Did I not teach you that, William?"

Liam had not seen it coming, his uncle having appeared behind him unnoticed. With a roar, he drew his sword and lunged to his feet, but when he would finally have put an end to Ivo, another thwarted him.

Sir John caught Liam's sword arm. "Think, Liam," he entreated. "Think!"

God, how could he think after all that had happened this day? When what he wanted most in this world was to rid himself of this one last demon?

"The church will be upon you if you shed his blood," John reminded him.

Grudgingly, Liam nodded and, when John released him, lowered his sword. "'Tis not over with, *uncle*," he said. "By all that I am, this day you will account for."

Shock and outrage swelled on Ivo's face. "You think I did this?" he demanded.

"I *know* it," Liam said, and pivoted away before he lost control of himself again.

"You dare accuse a holy man of making death upon God's people?" Ivo shouted after him.

Liam knew he ought to walk away, but he turned back. "You are hardly holy with the blood of those you have this day slain all upon you," he said.

Ivo's nostrils flared. "Look to the noblemen who lost Thornemede to a bastard," he said viciously. "There you will find the one responsible for this."

Instead, Liam looked to each of the four knights who stood around the dead man, and saw in their eyes that they also believed Ivo responsible. Contenting himself with that, he turned and tramped back across the wood pausing only to retrieve his dagger from the man he had felled with it.

Resuming his stride, he glanced at his bloodied forearm. Though the gash was wide, it was not deep. In fact, the bleeding had all but stopped. As for his jaw . . . ? He fingered it. Aye, it would need attention, and certainly stitches.

Liam swung into his saddle and instructed the others to mount up. "Sir Robert," he called.

The man guided his horse alongside Liam's. "My lord?"

"We will pass the night at Settling Castle to tend to the worst of these injuries. As you appear to have fared better than the rest of us, I wish you to ride on to Ashlingford and tell them of our arrival, that they might prepare for it; then I would have you continue to Thornemede and inform the castle folk that their new baron will arrive a fortnight hence."

The knight inclined his head. "I will do it. Anything else, Lord Fawke?"

How strange to hear himself called such, Liam thought. "Nay, that is all."

With a press of his heels and a slap of the reins, the knight set off down the road.

Though Liam had every intention of riding straight past Joslyn where she was mounted ahead—of leaving her to follow behind—the sight of Oliver still hugged tight to her made him draw in the reins.

"Frightened?" he asked, indicating the little boy.

Through her stupor came a flicker of surprise that Liam would express concern for her son. "He does not understand," she said in a low voice. "I would not allow him to see, or hear, yet 'tis as if he did."

"He feels your fear. Thus it has become his own."

A frown puckered her brow. "Mayhap," she said.

Why he should care, Liam didn't know, but suddenly he did. Still, there was naught he could do about it, he reminded himself. He started to urge his mount forward, but then remembered what he carried in his pouch: the top, which he had taken from the rushes of Joslyn's chamber.

He pulled it out, and in the next instant silently cursed himself. Damn, he made himself look a fool. But it could not be undone. "Boy," he called to Oliver, "I've something here for you. Would you like it?"

The child stirred in his mother's arms, then peeked up from her shoulder. "Mama!" he exclaimed. "'Tis the top A-papa made for me."

"So it is," she murmured.

"Would you like it, Oliver?" Liam asked.

The boy nodded. "Aye." He reached to take it. "Have you my stick too?"

"I fear not, but another can be made."

Clasping his toy to him as if it were the dearest thing in the world, Oliver looked up at Liam for the first time. In the next instant, his joy dissolved. "Ooh," he breathed.

Liam had forgotten about his jaw. Uncertain whether it was awe or fear the little boy was feeling, he berated himself for having allowed the child to witness that which his mother had tried to shield him from, and said the first thing that came to mind. "I'll not wrestle that bear again." As a child he had loved to have tales of beasts told to him. Now if only Oliver was as intrigued . . .

"'Twas a bear?" Oliver asked, his eyes growing round.

"It was," Liam said, "and a bigger one I've yet to meet." He glanced at Joslyn, but rather than seeing reproach in her gaze as he expected, there shone relief.

"Tell me," Oliver urged.

Behind, Liam heard the knights drawing near. "Mayhap this eve," he said. "'Tis time for us to ride again."

"I wanna hear it," Oliver pleaded.

"This eve." Joslyn spoke firmly.

"Nay, now," he pressed, his jaw thrusting stubbornly outward with his lip.

"Only a few hours more, Oliver," Liam said. "Then I shall tell you all about it. Everything."

Oliver thought a moment, battled with his childish desires, and said, "Promise?"

From somewhere deep within him, Liam dragged out a smile. "'Tis my knightly vow to you," he said. Wondering what he was doing making promises to this child of Maynard's who had taken Ashlingford from him, he gathered the reins again.

"Lord Fawke," Joslyn said.

He looked over his shoulder at her.

"I thank you," she said, and urged her palfrey forward.

Joslyn knew she would never forget the way Oliver sat cross-legged on his pallet listening raptly to Liam's tale of the bear who had come out of the wood to challenge the knights, or how Oliver slowly inched closer to Liam until he finally made it onto his uncle's lap.

At first, Liam had seemed uncomfortable with the child, exchanging a look of disquiet with Joslyn, but before long his arm had gone around the little boy and he had resumed his lively rendering of the tale. In that moment, Joslyn had sensed something very different about Liam. Though it could not be called calm, there was a certain quieting about him—as if the anger that had seemed to emanate from every pore of him had dimmed. Was it possible?

When Oliver was fast asleep, Liam gently laid him down upon the mattress and drew the blanket up over him.

Was this the same man she had once feared? Joslyn wondered. The one she had been told would murder her son to gain Ashlingford? Or did that man exist only in the minds of Maynard and his uncle?

Straightening, Liam turned to where she stood beside the four-postered bed she would this night share with the three daughters of their host.

"It was a wonderful story," Joslyn said, somewhat embarrassed to pay him the compliment. "You are good with him."

"There was a time when I was good with Maynard too," he remarked. "But then he grew up."

Joslyn detected regret in his voice. Had there been a time when animosity had not existed between the two brothers?

"I must return downstairs," Liam said.

As Joslyn must also do. She nodded. "I will be down shortly."

And then Liam was gone, leaving the door ajar behind him.

Bending down beside Oliver, Joslyn tucked the bedclothes around him as she did each night. Content, he sighed, snuggled more deeply into the mattress, then surprised Joslyn by opening his eyes.

"Mama," he said, his voice thick with sleep, "I like him."

"Lord Fawke?"

"Unca Liam," he corrected her. "Do you?"

"Like him? Of course," she said, realizing as soon as she spoke that it was not as much a lie as she had thought.

An angelic smile touching his lips, Oliver closed his eyes and a moment later returned to the arms of sleep.

Although Joslyn would have preferred to stay with him, she knew she was expected to return to the hall. Regretful, she leaned forward, pressed a kiss to Oliver's smooth cheek, and turned away.

The hall was abuzz with conversation, but hardly had Joslyn stepped off the stairs when she was accosted by Father Ivo.

"We must speak," he said.

She met his urgent gaze. "On the morrow, perhaps? It is late and—"

"'Tis about Oliver."

Concern stirring in her, she asked, "What of him?"

Ivo opened his mouth as if to explain, but a glance over his shoulder had him shaking his head. "Elsewhere," he said. "We cannot speak here."

Joslyn knew who had silenced him. Looking past the priest, she briefly settled her gaze on Liam where he sat before the hearth, conversing with Settling's lord. "Very well," she acquiesced.

Pivoting around, Ivo led her across the hall.

As Joslyn had thought he meant to speak with her in one of the alcoves, she faltered when he started down the passageway that connected the hall with the kitchens.

"Come," he urged, looking around.

"Can we not speak here?"

"Nay, outside. There we will have privacy."

"But there is privacy here," she pointed out, the passageway empty but for them.

"It only appears so. Come, Lady Joslyn."

Grudgingly, she followed him through the kitchens, then outside into a moonless night lit only by torches set about the bailey.

Because father Ivo's clerical robes identified him, they were allowed to pass unhindered by the guards. Reaching the wall walk overlooking the wooded side of the castle, the priest drew to a halt before an embrasure.

As Joslyn had no mantle to warm her against the chill night, she folded her arms across her chest. "What about Oliver?" she prompted.

Ivo stared at her a long moment. "Methinks he was meant to die this day."

"Die?"

"And you as well."

"What makes you believe that?" she asked, having gladly accepted what had been advanced during the evening meal by Settling's lord—that the brigands had been sent by one or more of the noblemen who wished Thornemede for themselves, and it was Liam's death they sought. Considering the number of men who had set themselves upon him, it made sense to Joslyn.

"I know William well," Ivo answered. "'Tis Ashlingford he seeks, and Ashlingford he will take if he is not sent from it. Forever."

"But it was he who delivered Oliver and me to safety," Joslyn said. "He who was attacked."

"He is not foolish, Lady Joslyn. If ever he is to hold Ashlingford, your deaths cannot touch him. 'Twas only a guise he affected."

"Nay," Joslyn said, certain the priest was wrong. "'Tis true that I feared he was behind the raid when first we were attacked and I could find no sight of him, but then he appeared. Had he intended to murder us, he could easily have done so then."

Joslyn sensed Ivo's anger even before he spoke it. "You do not wish to know the truth, do you?" he demanded.

Recalling the untruths both he and Maynard had told her—the things they had led her to believe—Joslyn could not help herself. "I *do* wish to know the truth," she said, "but I do not think I will get it from you, Father Ivo."

"You say I lie, then?" he exclaimed, astonishment

thinning his anger. "I do not wear these vestments for comfort, Lady Joslyn." Seizing the crucifix from where it hung low on his chest, he thrust it near her face. "I am a holy man," he said. "A man of God. A man of prayer and comfort."

Joslyn looked past the crucifix, with its jewels that could feed a thousand hungry mouths, and into Ivo's eyes. "A man who should have told me the truth about Ashlingford," she reminded him. "Neither you nor Maynard ever told me the old baron intended for his estates to go to his elder son—or that once Maynard was awarded them it was he who gave control of the barony to his brother. You had me believe it was stolen from Maynard."

"But it was!" Ivo cried. "'Tis true Maynard agreed to install William at Ashlingford that he might administer the barony in his stead, but that was all. Never did he intend for William to take control, and most certainly he did not agree that in exchange for the bastard's services he would leave Ashlingford to Liam upon his death. I tell you, lady, William is the devil himself. Had his plans not gone awry, I would this day have buried you and your son."

Joslyn shook her head. "That Liam—Lord Fawke—" she hastily corrected herself, "is responsible for the raid cannot be the truth."

"Liam, is it now?" Ivo snapped.

Berating herself for the slip, Joslyn returned to the safer subject of the raid. "It must have been one of those who lost Thornemede to Lord Fawke who ordered the raid," she said.

Stepping from the embrasure, Father Ivo turned a harsh hand around Joslyn's arm. "Methinks forbidden longings speak from your mouth and twist your good judgment, lady," he snarled. "Do you so soon forget? In the eyes of the church Maynard's brother has become yours—bastard though he is."

Joslyn gasped. "How dare you suggest . . . " Clenching her hands into fists, she said, "You are wrong."

"I pray that I am."

His touch was foul. Joslyn tried to pull her arm free, but Ivo only gripped her tighter. "Unhand me," she demanded.

As if suddenly remembering himself, he complied. "I am only trying to protect you and my . . . great-nephew," he said. "Unfortunately, devotion for Maynard has made me act rashly where I otherwise would not have." He paused, seemed to grope for his next words, and said, "I pray you will forgive me, lady."

He waited for her to do so, but the words he had spoken were still too fresh. "Good eve, Father," she said, stepping around him and leaning into the embrasure.

The silence dragged out until finally Ivo said, "'Tis your son who is at stake here, Lady Joslyn. Do not forget that." Then he walked away.

Joslyn listened for his footsteps to recede and, with the last, propped her elbows on the shelf of the embrasure and buried her head in her hands. Never had she believed she would arrive at such a terrible place in her life. If only—

A sound to her left entered her consciousness. Thinking Ivo returned, though for what purpose she did not even care to ponder, she drew back and looked down the wall walk. Peering closely, she saw a shadow moving among shadows along the wall. "Father Ivo?" she queried.

No answer. Shortly, the shadow took the shape of a man, but one of greater proportions than the priest. Mayhap a guard, she ventured, suddenly wary.

"I am Lady Joslyn," she announced, hoping for the same courtesy, "a guest of your lord." But hardly had she said it when that new sense of hers suggested she had guessed wrong—and was a moment later confirmed when Liam Fawke stepped into the light.

"What are you doing here?" she asked.

Unlike when he had bent over the little boy who had begged a tale from him, he looked sinister in the bare light, his jaw swollen and crossed by numerous stitches, his eyes glittering darkly.

He continued toward her, finally halting so near she could feel the warmth of his broad body. "I am but seeing to your safety, Lady Joslyn," he answered, his voice deep as the night, "and keeping an eye on my dear uncle."

She took a step back from him. "You were listening to our conversation," she accused him.

"I was," he said, no shame in his admission.

"All of it?"

"Nearly."

Though at the moment Joslyn could not recall every word that had passed between her and Father Ivo, she knew far too much had been said of Liam. Too, there was the priest's accusation that she desired his nephew—the reason he believed she defended Liam against any involvement in the raid. "'Tis past time I retired for the night," she said, starting past him.

He stepped into her path, causing her to brush against him.

Joslyn's breath caught on the sensations that sung through her. They had hardly touched, and yet it was as if they had embraced. Shaken, she stepped back.

"My uncle has had his say, Lady Joslyn," Liam said, "and now I will have mine."

Seeing no way past him without an argument that would likely take as long as what he wished to say to her, Joslyn acquiesced. "Please be quick with it."

A long uncomfortable moment passed before he spoke. "It is not greed that drives me to Ashlingford," he began. "'Tis birthright—a promise made long ago by a father to his son. A son he loved nearly as much as he loved the woman who birthed the misbegotten child. But though Ashlingford is a part of me as surely as my own arms, and now stolen twice from me, I would not murder for it."

"I know you would not," Joslyn said.

The light in Liam's gaze flickered over her. "Yet you believed me responsible for the raid."

"Only in the beginning," she admitted. "I searched for you, but you were nowhere to be seen."

In Liam's silence she felt his resentment, but when he spoke again it was not reflected in his voice. "Though Ivo would have you think it is I you should fear, Joslyn, I tell you it is he you ought to keep your distance from. A priest's garments he may wear, but never has a man been farther from God than Ivo."

"Now 'tis you who seeks to make me fear *him*," Joslyn observed.

"With good reason, I assure you."

"Tell me the reason."

"Suffice it to say that he who accuses me of having

hired the brigands to murder you and your son is the very one who put coin in their pockets—coin to murder the bastard nephew he wishes to be rid of."

Joslyn was stunned. "You are saying your uncle planned it? Good God, but you and your uncle are more alike than you can know. Neither of you will even consider the most obvious place for the blame. Surely it was one of the nobles who wished Thornemede for himself."

If he was offended at being likened to the man he hated, he controlled it. "I had entertained that idea myself," he said, "but then, in the middle of a confession I was extracting from the one brigand we found alive, Ivo slit the man's throat. I knew then."

Joslyn felt as if the ground had been pulled out from beneath her. What greater evidence of the involvement of Ivo in the raid than that he had slain the brigand ere the man could confess his last? Feeling suddenly ill, she pressed her back to the wall for support.

"I do not know what to believe," she murmured, wanting no more to rest her head upon a pillow but to burrow beneath one. "He is your uncle—of your blood."

"As you should know by now, blood has naught to do with anything," Liam said. "It has all to do with greed. A powerful emotion."

Had Ivo ordered the raid? Joslyn wondered. Was his hate for Liam truly that great? Not wanting to believe it, she shook her head. "I am sorry, Lord Fawke. Mayhap I am a fool, but I cannot believe the raid was Father Ivo's doing—just as I do not believe it was yours." She prepared herself for his anger, but it did not come.

"You do not have to believe it," Liam said. "All I ask is that you not close your eyes to the possibility. As Thornemede is likely to take me away often, I will not always be at Ashlingford to protect you from my uncle's scheming."

His words struck a chord within her. "Could it be you care, Lord Fawke?" she asked, but in the next instant knew she should never have said it.

Liam's anger resurfaced. "As I have told you," he growled, "if any harm should befall you or your son, 'tis likely the blame will be put on me. Do not mistake my concern for anything more than that, *Lady Joslyn*."

Embarrassment caused Joslyn to respond with like anger. "How foolish of me to believe you might actually have a heart, Liam Fawke," she snapped. "Why, you are more empty than even Maynard was." She skirted him and headed for the steps that would return her to the bailey, but had barely made it halfway down when Liam seized her arm, turned her around, and pushed her back against the wall.

"More empty than Maynard?" he whispered, his breath tinged with the sweet wine he had drunk at table. "Let me show you how *empty* I am." And he lowered his head.

Knowing what he intended, Joslyn jerked her chin to the side. However, rather than being deterred, Liam put his mouth against her ear—not forcefully, but with a sudden gentleness that contrasted sharply with his anger.

Joslyn was unprepared for the sensation, so much so, in fact, that with her mind urging her to flight, her body countered with a treachery she had not known it was capable of. As Liam's breath fanned her sensitive skin, tendrils of pleasure wound through her and warmed her insides. "Nay." She mouthed the only protest she could manage, but even to her ears it sounded more like a sigh.

And then Liam pressed his body into hers, letting her feel all that he was. "Empty?" he repeated, his voice grown so husky it was hardly recognizable. Without waiting for an answer, he began tracing her ear with his tongue. But that was not all. While Joslyn's emotions clambered one atop the other, he curved a hand around her hip and pulled her forward the last breath that stood between them.

With his male member hard against her belly, and growing harder with each breath she took, a queer sound not unlike the mewling of a kitten parted Joslyn's lips. Never had she been touched like this, never had fires leapt within her, and never had she known so great an ache in that place she had thought untouchable.

She thrilled to the fitting of her body with Liam's. It was if they had been made to become one. His hardness to her softness. His man to her woman. She turned her face to him, inviting him to kiss her.

Liam accepted. Pressing his lips to hers, he urged her mouth open.

With a resonant groan shuddering out of her, Joslyn touched her tongue to his and thus began a dance so sensual it was as if they were already joined. Knowing want so strong it nearly made her cry out, she dug her nails into Liam's arms.

He murmured something into her mouth, slid his hand up her side and closed his fingers around her breast. Her response guiding him, he found her taut nipple through her gown and squeezed it between thumb and forefinger.

Joslyn whimpered.

Liam slid his mouth off hers and trailed it downward until he reached that wonderfully sensitive place between neck and shoulder. Gently, he sank his teeth into her flesh.

"Liam," she gasped, her body quaking.

"The same as Maynard?" he asked.

What had he to do with this? she wondered through a haze of longing. "Nay." She sighed, wishing Liam would only continue what he'd begun. "Ah, nay."

But he had no intention of going any further. He was done with her. That realization came too late to save Joslyn from humiliation when the bewilderment finally cleared and she found herself now pressed against the wall rather than against the man who had filled her every sense with desire.

Grateful for the dark, she gathered her shredded pride about her and lifted her gaze to where Liam stood silhouetted against the sky. "You are despicable," she said, her voice hardly more than a whisper.

"But not empty," he reminded her.

His words pained her as surely as if he had struck her. "Though you can . . . do that to me," she said, "it does not prove you have a heart, Liam Fawke. It only proves you know women."

"As did Maynard," he said softly. "Yet he never made you feel what you have this night."

To deny it would only make her seem a shrew, Joslyn knew. Best she not even address it. "I assure you, I'll not feel it again with the likes of you," she said.

He took a step toward her. "Is that a challenge, Joslyn? One you wish me to take up?"

"No challenge, *Lord* Fawke," she said. "I'll simply not be bothered by you anymore."

The low rumble of his laughter raised the fine hairs on the back of her neck. "Ah, Joslyn," he said, "were it any man other than Maynard who'd had you, I might be tempted to teach you what your body has been waiting for."

His words made her feel dirty—as if in lying with her husband she had whored herself.

"But as you are now made my sister," Liam continued, "'twould be unseemly."

Though his dangerous anger appeared to have vented itself, it was apparent he had yet to deal with bitterness.

"Teach someone who cares not whether 'tis a heart you possess or a stone," Joslyn snapped. She descended the remainder of the steps and crossed the bailey with the longest stride her legs could take.

Liam watched her go, then dragged a hand down his face. "Damn," he muttered. He had not meant to kiss her, but the witch had pushed him to it, as had this ever-growing desire to touch her and better know the mystery of her. When she had drawn the likeness between himself and Ivo, he had wanted to shake her but had kept his arms at his sides, knowing that if he touched her he might be tempted out of his anger. Then she had compared him to Maynard, accusing him of being empty when each moment spent with her since their encounter in the alley filled him with longing—longing for one forbidden to him not only by the church but by the knowledge she had first been Maynard's.

Liam was grateful for the reminder of whose wife she had been, for that had been the only thing holding him from her when she'd been drowning in his arms, the eager press of her body calling to the very depths of his desire. Aye, otherwise he might now be inside her, teaching her about him and learning about her. And that could never be.

12

"'Tis bigger'n Rosemoor, Mama."

Trying not to feel Liam where he stood beside her, Joslyn angled her head back to follow Oliver's gaze. Aye, Ashlingford's castle was grand, she silently agreed—magnificent, even, with its white- and blue-washed exterior and its soaring interior—but it was not home. Would it ever be?

Her thoughts drifted to Maynard. He had grown up here, walked the floor she now stood upon, and lived among the discreet wealth adorning the great hall, but hardly had he spoken of it. Previous to this day, all Joslyn had known of the castle was that Rosemoor was pitiful in comparison, for the handful of times Maynard had visited the manor he had complained incessantly about its modest size and lack of grandeur. Now she knew why.

"Can I have my own room?" Oliver asked.

"I am sure the donjon is large enough," Joslyn said,

smiling to soften her answer, "but *you* are not, dear boy."

He stamped his foot. "Want my own room!"

"Oliver," she warned, leveling one of her practiced looks at him.

Poised on the edge of rebellion, he wrinkled his nose, pursed his mouth, and clenched his hands into fists.

Inwardly, Joslyn groaned. It was rare that he behaved this way, good-natured as he was, but since leaving Settling Castle two days past, Liam's push to reach Ashlingford had left her son little time to be a child. Tired of sitting a horse with naught to do but ask why and roll his top between his hands, he had grown increasingly fractious, building toward the tantrum that looked about ready to break.

Thinking to distract him, Joslyn bent down and caught his hands in hers. "Would you like to meet everyone now?" she asked. "They are most anxious to meet you."

She knew it was a lie she told him, for the moment they had passed over the drawbridge and into the bailey she had sensed disapproval among the people, the knight Liam had sent ahead having brought them news of the king's decree. Even had it been spoken aloud, it could not have been more obvious that it was Liam these people were loyal to—he whom they wished to be their lord. But as Joslyn had no choice in the matter, neither had they.

Tugging free of her, Oliver stepped back and crossed his arms over his chest. "Nay," he said. "Don't wanna."

Other than yield to him, there seemed little

Joslyn could do. He would simply have to vent himself before they could continue with the formalities.

With a glance at those who watched, Joslyn felt regret for what was about to happen. It would certainly win none of them over to their side. Indeed, it would reinforce what they already thought of Maynard's successor.

"I am sorry, Oliver," she said, "but your own room will have to wait until you are older."

His chin quivered and his eyes filled with tears, but just as he opened his mouth to cry out his disappointment, Liam plucked him from the floor and into his arms.

"Your mother is right," he said, "but that does not mean you cannot see the room that will be yours when you are old enough for it. Would you like to do that?"

Oliver's mouth turned up. "Can I?"

Liam nodded. "But first I am going to ask a favor of you."

Joslyn did not know what to think of this turn of events, but at least she was not alone. Shifting restlessly and murmuring among themselves, the castle folk stared at the unlikely twosome. Here was the man who had just lost his last bid for Ashlingford, and in his arms the child who had taken it from him.

"What?" Oliver asked.

Leaning forward, Liam whispered something in his ear. "Think you can do that?" he asked.

Oliver sighed. "A'right, but then I wanna see my room."

Liam nodded. "Ready?"

"Uh-huh."

Sparing Joslyn no more than a glance, Liam strode toward the gathering and began introducing Oliver.

From the sideboard where drink had been set out for the returning knights, Ivo stood with tankard in hand and looked from Joslyn to William and back to Joslyn. Unmoving, her profile reflected an emotion Ivo would have loved to slap from her face as she stared after the bastard and her son. Then she stepped forward to be included in the introductions.

Damn her! Ivo silently cursed. She had no right to look at any man that way, most especially William. The greedy bastard was luring her ever nearer an unholy union—luring his brother's naive widow into his bed by pretending he cared for her son. But Ivo wasn't fooled.

Oliver's happy, chattering voice dragged Ivo from his thoughts. Down from Liam's arms, the child stood before Emma, who had creaked down onto her haunches to welcome Maynard's son. With her rumpled face aglow as it had not been for years, the old woman nodded at Oliver's excited string of mispronounced words, smiled, arched her eyebrows at him, and touched him as often as possible.

She was likely to be the only one other than himself to welcome Oliver's arrival at Ashlingford, Ivo thought. The others would just as soon see the evidence of Maynard's existence disappear. Thus it fell to him to serve as the child's protector. Who better to watch over Oliver than one who regarded him as much his own son as one sprung from his seed? Ivo was hard pressed not to laugh at that last thought. Aye, it was time for him to make Ashlingford his permanent residence.

Joslyn sighed. Except for the woman who had been Maynard's nurse, no one had seemed genuinely pleased to meet the future baron. In fact, had Liam not appeared so accepting of her son, Joslyn thought it likely Oliver would have been greeted by naught but cold stares and speechless mouths. But Liam's unspoken message having been received by all, the servants and retainers did their best to welcome the unwanted child into their midst, even that great bald-headed man who was Ashlingford's steward: Sir Hugh, wasn't it? Still, there had been some who had appeared to waver on the edge of succumbing to the little one's innocent charm. Joslyn hoped time would bring them around.

"I trust it meets with your approval?" Liam asked, startling her out of her worrisome thoughts.

She saw that Oliver was once again perched on his arm. "My approval?" she echoed.

He raised an eyebrow. "Ashlingford."

Of course. This being the first time they had spoken to one another since that bitter night when Liam had shown her just how "empty" he was, Joslyn floundered to find the right words. "It is beautiful," she said. "I would not have guessed it to be."

"Maynard did not tell you?"

Cursing herself for saying more than necessary, Joslyn braved Liam's gaze again. "He did not speak often of his home," she said. His few visits to Rosemoor had chiefly been spent at the table with her father, gambling the day and night away, and throughout he had spoken of little but the bastard brother who had stolen the barony from him. Now, though, Joslyn knew much of what he had said to have been lies. Would time prove the rest lies as well?

Liam surprised Joslyn by letting the matter rest.
Turning his gaze upon Oliver, who had listened to the
exchange with curiosity puckering his brow, he
asked, "Are you ready now to see the solar that will
one day be yours?"

Instantly, Oliver's forehead smoothed. "Aye,
now!"

Stepping past Joslyn, Liam strode to the stairway
and disappeared from sight.

Joslyn felt a yearning for home as she stared at barren stairs that were twice the width of Rosemoor's.
Lord, but this place was large! she reflected. How
was she ever to make a home of it for Oliver?

"Fool woman!" Ivo snapped.

She looked around at him. "What have I done to
displease you, Father Ivo?" she asked, her dislike of
him swelling.

"Think you naught of allowing Maynard's son to
be alone with the one who seeks his death?" he
demanded.

Though quiet followed, Joslyn knew they were not
alone. Lingering servants listened and watched to see
what her reaction would be to his accusing words.
She set her chin up a notch. "Liam Fawke will do him
no harm," she said with conviction.

Ivo stepped toward her as if he intended to lay a
hand to her, but he clenched his fist instead. "Then as
your mind is otherwise occupied, it falls to me to protect Maynard's son." He started for the stairs.

Joslyn knew what he implied—that her love for
Oliver was not so great as her desire for Liam. "I have
not asked for your help," she said, "nor will I, Father
Ivo."

He paused. "You have not, but Maynard asked it

of me, and now I will honor the vow I made him to safeguard his heir."

"Is that all he is to you? An heir?"

Ivo's fervent gaze turned flat. "Nay, he is more than that," he said. "Far more than that." Then he mounted the stairs.

Was there to be no peace at Ashlingford for her? Joslyn wondered. Was she to raise up her son with this priest's hatred hovering over one shoulder, the temptation of Liam Fawke over the other? With a sigh and a shake of her head, she slid her gaze to where Emma hovered nearby.

The old woman stepped forward. "Something is amiss, child?" she asked in a voice graveled by age.

Though Joslyn felt comfortable with this woman who had taken so readily to Oliver, especially as she exuded such genuine warmth and acceptance, she wondered if she could speak to her of her misgivings regarding the priest. She thought on it a moment longer, then replied, "I do not trust Father Ivo. I believe his hate for his nephew consumes him. And I do not understand why."

"You are right," Emma said. "He holds it as dearly to him as his own arms and legs."

"But why? All because Liam is of less than noble birth? 'Tis not as if it were his own doing."

With a sigh, Emma gently laid a hand to Joslyn's shoulder. "We will talk of it, you and I," she said, "but now is not the time. Come, and I will show you to your chamber."

Suddenly weary from three days spent in the saddle, with its incessant creak and groan, Joslyn allowed herself to be guided from the hall and up the stairs. However, at the first landing the sound of Oliver's gleeful voice echoing from the right pulled Joslyn that way.

"Do not worry about him," Emma said, urging her opposite. "Liam will not allow this loathing he and his uncle have for each other to touch the boy."

Though Joslyn felt this was true of Liam, she was not so certain of Ivo. "Oliver should nap," she said. "It has been a long journey and—"

"And he is quite tired of being still," Emma reminded her. "Let him enjoy himself and he will sleep well tonight. Surely there can be no harm in that."

Joslyn wavered.

"I will go to him as soon as you are settled down for a rest," Emma assured her.

Joslyn sighed. "Very well."

Turning left down the corridor, Emma led her to the modestly appointed, yet elegant chamber that had been made ready for her. "'Twas the Lady Anya's," she murmured.

Maynard's mother. As with nearly everything that had to do with her departed husband, Joslyn knew very little of the woman. Only two things had ever been made clear about Anya Fawke: She had been revered by her son for her strong will, and her death so soon after his father's had been a bitter blow.

Wanting to know more that she might come to understand these people better, Joslyn asked, "You and Lady Anya were friends?"

Emma's eyebrows jumped. "Friends?" she repeated on a bubble of forced laughter. Then, her disbelief fading into sadness, she shook her head. "Nay, but we knew each other's secrets well."

Joslyn wished the woman would continue, but she did not. "Maynard told me of her death. The tragedy of its coming so soon after his father's."

Emma stood silent a moment and then walked to the bed. "It *was* tragic," she said, as she turned back the coverlet.

"Her heart, was it not?"

"It was."

The woman could not have made it more clear that she did not wish to speak of Lady Anya. With a sigh, Joslyn stepped to where Emma bent over the bed, her aged hands plumping the pillows. "Emma," she said, "there is so much I need to know, not only about Father Ivo but also about Oliver's father and his family. Will you tell me of them?"

Emma stilled. "You wish to hear from an old woman like me?"

"I do. Otherwise 'twill be Father Ivo who tells me, and I do not know what to believe of him."

Turning from her task, Emma met Joslyn's imploring gaze. "Aye, it would be better did I tell you," she conceded, "but now you must rest."

Joslyn could not argue with that. "Of course," she said, fatigue dragging at her limbs. "Later, then."

With a small smile, Emma reached forward and pulled the tie of Joslyn's mantle loose.

"Will I sleep here when I'm bigger?" Oliver asked, one small hand patting the mattress, the other holding tight to his top.

Liam pulled his gaze from where Ivo watched at the solar doorway. "Aye, you will," he answered, his enmity for Ivo lessening as he looked into the innocence of Oliver's face. "When you become a man and lord of all Ashlingford, it will be your bed."

As soon as he spoke it, Liam heard the echo of his father's voice saying the same to him nearly twenty-five years past, making a promise he'd not known would never be kept.

"That's a long way away, huh?" Oliver asked.

Having lost the thread of conversation, Liam frowned. "What is a long time away, Oliver?"

"When I'm a man and lord of Asha'ford."

"Not as long as you think," Liam said, remembering how brief his own childhood had been. Always there had been someone forcing him to grow up faster than the other children: the enmity of Ivo, the jealousy of Anya, even the expectations his father had for him.

Fingering the coverlet, Oliver said, "Wish I could sleep here now."

"Would you like me to lift you up so that you may know how it will feel when you come to it a man?"

Oliver's eyes popped wide open. "Aye!"

Liam lifted him beneath the arms and sat him upon the mattress—just as his own father had done with him all those years ago.

"'Tis big," Oliver said, looking around him. "You sleep here now?"

Though it should have roused Liam to anger, for he had never slept here as he should have, he felt only regret. "Nay, it was your father's bed," he said.

"Oh." Oliver tilted his head to the side and frowned. "My papa sleep here till it's my turn?"

At first Liam did not understand his question, but then he realized the boy was unaware of his father's death. Lord, why hadn't Joslyn told him? he wondered. True, it should be gently said regardless of Oliver's relationship with Maynard, but the boy was old enough to understand some of it. However, it was not his place to do it, so Liam searched for words to get around Oliver's question.

But Ivo was not of the same mind. "Nay, he does not sleep here anymore, Oliver," he said, stepping into the chamber. "Did your mother not tell you that he died?"

Were it not for the boy, Liam would have loudly cursed his uncle's lack of delicacy. Always, Ivo had dealt with children in this manner, as if they had the minds of adults—the same as he'd treated both Liam and Maynard during their childhood.

"He dead?" Oliver repeated, uncertainty rolling into his bright eyes like clouds across a clear sky.

Throwing Ivo a look of warning, Liam said to Oliver, "Your father has—"

"I will tell the boy, William," Ivo interrupted. "He should hear it from one who loved his father, not one who—"

Liam swung around to face him.

Abruptly, Ivo halted. "Keep your temper about you, Irish," he said low-voiced.

"You will leave now," Liam said between clenched teeth.

"Else?"

Lord, but he was tempted, Liam thought, as he eyed his uncle's vulnerable jaw. But not in front of Oliver.

"Father Ivo," someone behind called to him.

It was sweet old Emma, come to put out the spark ere it turned to flame.

"What is it?" Ivo demanded.

As always, she was unruffled by his displeasure. "My soul is in need of prayer," she said, her gaze steady on him. "Lord Fawke can talk to the child while you and I address the Lord."

Ivo was slow to respond, his tension overflowing into the chamber. In the end, though, he left the solar with a backward warning glance to Liam.

Liam stared at the empty doorway, pondering what his father had on more than one occasion pondered himself: the bending of Ivo to Emma's will. Though Montgomery Fawke had once suggested that Ivo was taken with Emma, it had been his real belief—as it was Liam's—that the woman was privy to a secret Ivo did not wish told. If so, knowing Emma, Liam predicted she would take it with her to the grave.

Liam sat down on the mattress beside Oliver. "You wish to know about your father?" he asked.

His confusion evident, Oliver said, "Papa's gone?"

"Aye, Oliver, he is gone."

"Why?"

Damn Ivo for putting him in this situation! Had his uncle left it to the boy's mother to tell him, he could now be out upon the land ensuring that all was in order on the barony. "He had an accident," he said, rising above his unease to choose his words carefully. "Your father was riding his horse and fell from it."

"An' died?" Oliver said, though Liam knew he could not possibly grasp the full meaning.

"He did."

"Why?"

Liam wondered at his question. Why had Maynard fallen from his horse? Or why—

"Was it God, Unca Liam?" Oliver asked, his hand creeping onto Liam's thigh.

"God?"

Oliver nodded. "I had a kit-cat an' he died too. Mama said it was 'cause God needed him to guard His gates. Was it God, Unca Liam?"

Liam found himself answering as he would never have believed himself capable of doing. "Aye, God needed a mighty warrior in heaven," he said, "so he called your father to Him."

It seemed exactly the reassurance Oliver needed. "Then that's a'right he died, huh? He's happy there."

Providing it was in heaven and not in hell that Maynard had landed. Liam's thoughts turned dark again. Truly, he could not believe God would be merciful with one such as his brother. However, as if to prove him wrong, Oliver began rolling the top between his hands. He was so like Maynard had been as a boy. So innocent and sweet.

Liam closed his eyes. Maynard had been accepting of his bastard brother when he was too young to know otherwise. In fact, at first he had adored the brother whom he too soon learned to hate.

"You sad?" Oliver guilelessly brought Liam back to him.

Liam opened his eyes. "A little."

"Why?"

That one word was nearly enough to push back all of Liam's pain with laughter. Throughout the journey to Ashlingford, he had listened to Oliver ask it over and over again of his mother. Her answers, and her son's persistence, had made him smile when he had not thought a single smile left in him. "I am just remembering your father—my brother," he said.

"You loved my papa?"

Liam was about to lie and tell Oliver he had when

he realized it was not a lie. He *had* loved his little
brother, and Maynard loved him. There was no lie in
that—only in the years that had followed. "I did," he
said.

Oliver nodded, then surprised Liam by asking,
"Who gonna be my papa now? You, Unca Liam?"

Liam nearly choked. He a father to Maynard's
son? A husband to Maynard's wife? Not only forbidden but impossible. "Nay, Oliver," he said, "but I will
be your friend." For as long as the boy was not cor-
rupted by Ivo, he added to himself, but mayhap that
would not happen with Joslyn present.

Oliver pondered a moment. "Why?"

Feeling as if the burden of ages was lifted from
him—even if only for these few moments—Liam
laughed. And Oliver began to giggle.

Ivo wanted to scream. As his gaze followed the old
bitch across the hall, he wished her dead with every
last particle of his being. She was a curse unto him,
having darkened his days from the first, and she
would continue to darken them until he found some
way to rid himself of her. But once again she had
made it impossible for him to seek her end.
Dissatisfied with what she already used to control
him, she had gone further. Too far.

Opening his palm, Ivo looked at the coins Emma
had triumphantly dropped into it and slowly curled
his fingers back over them. "Burn in hell, you old
bitch!" he rasped.

Instead, it was he who felt the heat. A fire growing
in his head, he dropped it back against the wall and

rolled his eyes up to the ceiling. The wily old hag. Had he known she'd been listening to Maynard's deathbed confession, he would not have been so eager to accompany Liam to Rosemoor. Instead, he would have followed later—after he'd first claimed what was his.

God, but he needed a woman! Any woman would do. Intending to find one, he pushed off the wall, but in the next instant stayed himself with the remembrance of the coins grown warm in his palm. For a moment he was tempted to fling them against the far wall, but he restrained himself with the reminder that though they were few compared to the whole, they were enough to keep him for at least a month—and quite well. His hands trembling with a fury that needed to be spent soon, he dropped the money into his purse and then crossed the hall.

13

They hardly knew him, but still the two children were drawn to where he stood before the fire pit.

"Sir Liam." The older boy greeted him.

Liam smiled. "How are you, Michael?"

"Very good, sire."

"And you, Emrys?"

The four-year-old paused to tug on his chausses, which were torn at the knee. "My leg hurts, sire," he said. "Fell down."

"And how did you do that?"

Emrys grinned. "Chasin' Gertie."

"Why were you chasing her? She's much smaller than you—only two years old."

"She had my ball and wouldn't give it back."

"Ah," Liam said. "You didn't hurt her, did you?"

He shook his head. "Nay, sire."

Liam saw that the little girl who trailed behind the boys looked to have suffered no ill. "And Gertrude," he said. "How are you?"

She gave him a quick smile, then sank her teeth into her bottom lip and averted her gaze to the dirt floor.

Glancing across the single-room dwelling, Liam looked to where the man and woman stood watching quietly. The woman was pregnant again, and from the rise of her skirts around her middle he figured she was likely to deliver within the next month. Inwardly, Liam groaned. These three not included, she already had four children of her own. How was she going to manage with eight?

He looked at each of the three children and saw what he saw whenever he looked at Oliver: Maynard's face in theirs. Here was a portion of the seed Maynard had so carelessly scattered. The misbegotten. Over the past five years, Liam had brought each of them to this family. Michael had been the first, coming here after his mother had died birthing her second child. Then Emrys had come, who lost his mother when she fell beneath the plow. Last, there was little Gertrude. A year ago, her mother had run off with a merchant, leaving her daughter behind.

With a sigh, Liam opened the pouch he held, took out three coins, and pressed one into each of the children's palms. Amid gleeful shouts, he strode across the room and handed the pouch to the man. "Send word if you need more," he said, and left.

Lifting her head from the pillow, Joslyn looked at the morning sunlight streaming in through the window. She had slept the remainder of the day and then the night through, she realized.

"Mama."

Twisting her head around, she looked into her son's face where he rested his chin on the mattress. "Would you like to come up?" she asked.

With a shake of his head, he lowered his gaze to the coverlet and began running his fingers over its rumpled surface. "'Tis not so big a bed as Papa's," he said.

Though disappointed by his lack of interest in joining her, Joslyn asked, "Isn't it?"

"Nay!" he exclaimed. "Papa's is" —Stepping back, he threw his arms wide— "big as this room."

Joslyn smiled. "Really?"

"Uh-huh."

She lowered her feet to the floor and stood. "You will have to show it to me later."

"I will."

Kneeling, Joslyn held her arms out to him. "First a morning hug, and then we will dress and go belowstairs to break our fast."

As expected, Oliver played with her. Lowering his head so she could not see the smile tugging at his mouth, he crossed his arms over his chest and peeked at her from beneath his lashes.

"Not even a little hug?" Joslyn pleaded.

He shook his head.

Knowing well the response he sought, she sighed heavily and feigned a pout.

With a giggle of glee, Oliver lunged forward and fell against her. Joslyn hugged him tight, thus ending the morning ritual begun six months past.

"Hungry," Oliver said, emerging from her embrace.

As she stood, Joslyn swept searching eyes over the chamber for sight of their clothing.

Oliver pointed to the iron-banded chest at the foot of the bed. "Emma put 'em there," he said.

She walked to the chest and lifted the lid. To the right lay a small, neatly folded pile of boy's clothing, and to the left an assortment of women's garments. She frowned. "These are not ours, Oliver. Do you know what Emma has done with our clothes?"

"Washin' 'em, but we can wear these."

"Did she tell you that?"

"Uh-huh."

Though Joslyn would have preferred their own garments to those of strangers, she really had no choice. They could not go belowstairs scantily dressed as they were.

After dressing Oliver, she chose the plainest of the gowns—which was still far more lavish than anything she owned. However, as she lifted it above her head to draw it on, something fell to her brow and from there to the floor.

Frowning, Joslyn searched out the object from where it glinted among the rushes, bent down, and retrieved it.

"What is it, Mama?" Oliver asked.

She turned it front to back. "'Tis a coin," she said. But it would buy far more than a pastry from a vendor. Of gold and good weight, it could keep a person very well for at least a month. How curious.

Enthusiasm lighting his face, Oliver stepped nearer. "Where'd it come from?"

Joslyn smiled. "If I did not know better, I would say it had fallen from the sky."

Oliver searched the ceiling overhead. "Did it not?"

"Methinks more likely it was caught in the folds of the gown."

"Oh." He was obviously disappointed.

Joslyn ruffled his hair. Then, thinking she would give the coin to Liam when next she saw him, she secreted it in the clothes chest and finished dressing.

"A'most forgot," Oliver said as they started down the corridor toward the stairs.

"Forgot what?" Joslyn asked.

"Papa's dead."

Her heart thudded. Halting, she stared after her son as he continued on ahead of her. "Oliver," she called to him, her voice hardly more than a breath.

He looked around. "Hmm?"

"Come, I need to speak to you."

"I'm hungry," he reminded her.

"I know, but 'twill take only a moment."

Obedient, though obviously unhappy about it, he trudged back to where she stood.

Lowering herself beside him, Joslyn brushed the hair out of his eyes and asked, "Who told you your father had died?"

"Unca Liam."

Her muscles clenched. The man had no right to speak to her son of the death of his father. It was her place to do that, not Liam Fawke's. She'd had every intention of telling Oliver just as soon as they were settled at Ashlingford. Joslyn drew a steadying breath. "And what did he tell you?"

Oliver scratched his head. "That Papa fell off his horse, an' that's how he died."

"Anything else?"

"Papa's in heaven." Oliver wagged a finger toward the ceiling. "A war'r for God."

Heaven. A warrior for God. Joslyn found it hard to believe those words had come from Liam. Though she trusted he would say naught hateful of his departed brother to Oliver, never would she have expected him to say kind words about him. "Your Uncle Liam said that?" she asked.

"Aye, but he won't be my papa."

Joslyn forced a smile to her lips. "You asked him to be your papa?"

"Uh-huh, but he jus' gonna be my friend."

Part of her was angry with Liam for his interference, but another part was touched by the kind light he had cast on Maynard.

"We eat now?" Oliver asked.

Joslyn nodded.

He turned and scurried toward the stairs.

"Go slowly," Joslyn said.

"I will."

Joslyn reflected on what her son had told her as she followed him down the stairs and into the hall. It was empty but for two servants, who were busy spreading fresh rushes, and Oliver, who stood in the middle of it looking lost. As at Rosemoor, the simple morning meal was served at the first breaking of day. For the luxury of sleeping in an extra hour or two, Joslyn and Oliver would have to seek their bread and cheese in the kitchens.

"This way," Joslyn called to Oliver.

He trailed her down a corridor that wafted sweetly of preparations already begun for the noon meal. "Ooh," he breathed as he stepped into the large room behind her.

Looking down, Joslyn saw wonder in his eyes as they went from servants to worktables to cavernous fireplaces, where great iron cauldrons hung by hook and chain.

How humble Rosemoor was compared to Ashlingford, Joslyn thought.

"Seems a sweet child," one of the kitchen maids said, unaware that Joslyn and Oliver had entered the kitchen.

"Aye, not like his father," another agreed.

The woman kneading dough a table away snorted loudly. "Too young to tell. Likely he'll prove himself more than worthy of his father's seed."

They spoke of Oliver, Joslyn realized with dismay. However, rather than retreat as she was inclined to do, she stepped forward, knowing there would be no better time to assert herself as mother of the heir of Ashlingford.

Several of the kitchen maids looked up, and those who did not were nudged into noticing who had come into their midst.

Oliver was the first to break the silence. "Whatcha makin'?" he asked, gripping the edge of the table and going up on tiptoe to peer at the woman who kneaded dough, the same who had made the derogatory comment about him.

The maid looked from Oliver to his mother, frowned over Joslyn's attire, then dropped her gaze back to the child. "Bread," she said.

"I taste?" Oliver asked.

The woman's lids fluttered with surprise. "I would let ye, child, but 'tis not yet baked."

"That's a'right. Like it that way."

A tight smile squeezed onto her lips. "Ye do?"

"Uh-huh."

She glanced at where Joslyn stood watching the exchange. "'Tis all right does he have a pinch, my lady?"

"Aye, but just that," Joslyn said, pleased that Oliver had managed to turn the woman's bitter mouth into one almost sweet.

"Ye wished something, milady?"

Joslyn looked to the kitchen maid who had come to stand beside her. "Aye, some bread and cheese for my son and me to break our fast," she said.

With a bob of her head, the woman turned away.

A short time later, Joslyn and Oliver set about satisfying their hunger beneath the watch of the servants, who tried to hide their curiosity behind their tasks. Hardly a word did any of them speak, and the few snippets exchanged were too hushed for Joslyn to hear what was being said. But she didn't really need to, for it was certainly about her and her son.

As Joslyn popped the last crust of bread into her mouth, she looked up to see Emma enter the kitchens.

Smiling at Oliver, the old woman walked to where he sat perched upon the stool beside his mother. "You are near ready?" she asked.

With a nod, Oliver swallowed the last of his mouthful, glanced at Joslyn, and said, "Full."

Wondering what he was ready for, Joslyn brushed the crumbs from his mouth and lifted him down to the floor. "You have planned something?" she asked Emma.

"Aye, the little lord and I are going to explore the castle this morn, aren't we, Oliver?"

An eager smile leapt onto his face. "Aye, explorin'!"

"You would join us, my lady?"

Joslyn would have, but in this she saw an opportunity to seek out Liam and confront him on his having told Oliver of his father's death. "Mayhap I will join you later," she said. "There are some things I need to do first."

Emma nodded and stepped back to consider Joslyn's attire. "Better too large than too small," she mused. "Thus I can alter it to fit."

Joslyn looked down her front. "It will suffice until my own garments are cleaned."

"Aye, but you did not bring much with you, lady," Emma reminded her. "You will need more than what you have brought to be the lady of Ashlingford."

"I am sure my father will send the rest of my garments soon," Joslyn said. "And Oliver's."

Emma looked skeptical, as if she doubted that Joslyn's manor attire would be appropriate for Ashlingford. And perhaps it wouldn't be, Joslyn thought. Though these things fit poorly, they were fashioned of the finest fabric and worked with such detail they had to have cost dearly. In fact, she did not think her entire wardrobe could have cost what this one outfit must have. "Whose garments are these?" she asked.

"They were the Lady Anya's."

Joslyn glimpsed on Emma's face a fleeting emotion she could not identify. Bitterness, perhaps? Dislike? Certainly not regret. Had her husband's mother been as disliked as he? Joslyn wondered. Had there never been peace at Ashlingford?

"You are being most patient, my boy," Emma said to Oliver. "Should we go?"

"Aye, now." He gave her skirts a tug.

Emma looked back at Joslyn. "Do join us when you are able to," she said. Then, taking Oliver's small hand in hers, she started for the door.

"I will see you later, Oliver," Joslyn called after him.

He looked over his shoulder, smiled and said, "Later, Mama."

And now for Liam, Joslyn thought, as she watched the door close behind Emma and Oliver.

Leaving the kitchens by way of the back door, she stepped out into sunshine tempered by a slight breeze. The herbal garden to her right, the flower garden to her left, she paused a moment to enjoy the sight and then continued out into the bustle of the inner bailey.

As much a curiosity here as she had been in the kitchens, Joslyn walked among people who spoke behind their hands and scrutinized her as if she meant trouble for them.

Time, she reminded herself. That was all it would take for her and Oliver to be accepted.

Crossing the drawbridge into the outer bailey and still finding no sight of Liam, she approached one of the men-at-arms. "Do you know where I might find Lord Fawke?" she asked.

"He is gone, my lady."

Gone. Surely he could not mean Liam had already left for Thornemede. He would not have without first . . . Nay, Liam Fawke owed her no parting words, she reminded herself. He would come and go as he pleased without warning or farewell.

"Gone where?" she asked.

"The fields, my lady. He ought to be back ere nightfall."

She could wait until he returned, Joslyn knew, but then she might not have the opportunity to speak with him in private. "I would like to go to him," she decided.

The man's eyes widened. "My lady?"

"Would you arrange it?"

"But—"

"You will accompany me, of course," she said, knowing that regardless of her station at Ashlingford, she would not be allowed to ride from the castle unescorted.

"I first must speak with the captain of the guard, my lady," the man said.

Joslyn nodded. "And then we shall be on our way."

14

As she rode through the countryside, Joslyn beheld much of the beauty fatigue had blinded her to yesterday. Pushing up through the earth was woodruff, fennel, daisies, and the flourishing plants of sown crops. Overhead, birds joyously soared the clear skies and called to one another with voices sweet and melodious. Along the roadside, hares and other small animals bounded through the grass. And in the fields, villagers coaxed life from the earth as their children made games of chasing off the birds who sought to steal their sown labor.

Everything felt new, Joslyn thought, just as heaven had meant it to be. Reining in her palfrey alongside her three escorts, she watched one of the workers of an immense fallow field tramp toward them.

"Has Lord Fawke been here?" one of the men-at-arms called to him when he was within hearing distance.

"Aye, and still is," he answered. Turning, he pointed to the farthest corner of the field, where a handful of workers were plowing up a strip of earth. "There."

Joslyn was relieved to have found him. At each of the three previous fields, she had been told he had already gone on to the next. "You may await me here," she instructed her escorts. "I shall not take long."

As she rode the perimeter of the field, Joslyn searched for the telltale red of Liam's hair. However, though a horse that must have been his stood nearby, there was no sign of him.

Frowning, she settled her gaze upon the workers. One man grasped the handles of the plow, his great body forcing it to follow alongside the strip of land previously turned. He was assisted in his labor by another ahead of him, who drove the team of oxen by whip and bellow, and four behind— two men and two women—who wielded clubs to break up the clods the plow cut from the hard earth.

It was strenuous work, Joslyn knew. Though she had never done any of it herself, as a child she had often watched the villagers toil in the fields of their lord—

She looked sharply at the plowman a second time. He wore a hood, its loose ties flapping against his chest as he thrust the plow ahead of him. His tunic, near all of it darkened by perspiration, clung to his broad shoulders, followed the contours of his muscled torso, tapered downward past his abdomen and hips, and molded to muscled thighs that strained with each step he took.

With each step Liam Fawke took, Joslyn acknowledged the man for who he was. As that unwelcome part of her stirred, she pondered why he did the work of the common man. After all, no lord was expected to actually work the land himself. . . .

Liam might never have looked up, so intent was he on the plow, if not for George. The man leading the oxen was first to catch sight of the figure riding toward them. Lowering his whip, he and the beasts ground to a halt. Almost immediately, the workers with their clubs also paused to take notice of the lady.

"God almighty," Liam muttered. He had left the castle early today for just this reason. Joslyn Fawke. After another restless night filled with visions of her surrender and vivid remembrances of the taste and feel of her, he had risen and gone straight to the fields. Now here she was destroying what little peace he had found. But he knew why she had come.

Liam released the plow handles, rubbed a forearm across his beaded brow, and propped his soiled hands on his hips to stare at her as she approached.

"I would speak with you, Lord Fawke," she said as she drew near.

He withheld his reply until she was close enough for him to see the clear amber of her eyes. Then he said, "I trust 'tis a matter most pressing that brings you into the fields, Lady Joslyn."

Looking far too lovely in gold-trimmed green, she drew to a halt a short distance away. "It is."

He looked over his shoulder. "Take the plow, Henry," he called to the one he had relieved of it earlier.

With a nod, the thickset man laid his clod-breaking club aside and started forward.

Knowing that with dirt and perspiration covering him he appeared as much the commoner as any of the others, Liam strode the unbroken ground to where Joslyn awaited him.

From her perch atop her palfrey, she looked down on him, but not with the distaste many a lady would have—and neither was her face drawn with anger as he would have expected. Instead, out of the depths of her eyes shone curiosity.

"What is it you want?" he demanded, sorely wishing she were the unbecoming waif she had been at Rosemoor, when she had been covered in near as much earth as he was now.

She glanced past him to the workers. "Can we not speak elsewhere?"

Though the plow was moving again, they were still an object of interest to the villagers. Still, Liam would not have cared had not the task required the closest attention if none were to fall peril to it. "The reins," he said, lifting a hand to accept them from Joslyn.

Wordlessly, she laid the leather strap across his palm.

Off the field and toward the wood Liam led her horse, his mind going ahead of him to the icy stream where he could refresh himself and wash off some of the dirt.

"This will do," Joslyn said as the trees of the wood rose up before them.

"A bit farther," Liam said over his shoulder.

"Lord Fawke, it would be unseemly for me to go into the wood with you without an escort."

He could not say she hadn't cause to be worried considering what had thus far passed between them—and most especially what had not—but if she was going to take him from the field, he would at least use the time well. "No more unseemly than your seeking me out among the fields rather than awaiting my return to the castle," he said.

She had no reply for that.

Sighting the stream, Liam dropped the reins and, without a backward glance, walked to where the water ran cold and shallow as the devil's heart. "Speak to me, Lady Joslyn," he invited as he lowered himself beside the stream.

After a moment, she said, "You had no right."

Nay, he hadn't, but that was before Ivo had jumped in to answer a question Liam had intended to evade. Tugging off the hood that plastered the hair to his head, he tossed it to the side and plunged his hands into the water. "To—?" he asked, purposely obtuse.

"To tell Oliver of his father's death, of course. It was my place to do so, not yours."

For the moment, Liam put aside the fact that it was Ivo who had done the telling. He splashed the water over his face and head, pausing to relish the shock of it against his heated skin. Nay, it was colder than the devil's heart, he decided, though not quite as cold as Ivo's.

"Lord Fawke, why did you tell my son of his father's death?"

He could just as easily accept the blame as given, Liam thought. After all, the responsibility was his for not having anticipated that, in showing Oliver his father's solar, the boy would ask uncomfortable questions. However, if Joslyn was seriously to consider his warnings about Ivo, she needed to know the truth.

"I explained it to him," he admitted, "but you are wrong in assuming it was I who told him."

"I do not understand."

"Aye, you do."

A moment later, she asked, "Father Ivo?"

As she had her answer, Liam returned to his bathing and, without regard for her presence, dragged the tunic over his head. Behind, he heard Joslyn draw a sharp breath—as if she had never before seen a man's naked flesh, he thought wryly. Bared to the waist, he began scooping water over his shoulders and chest.

"I will go now," Joslyn said.

The heat of his body greatly dissipated, much of the perspiration and dust rinsed away, Liam stood and turned to face her. "That is all you wished to speak to me about?" he asked.

A blush stole up her neck. Quickly, she turned her attention to the reins she held and pretended an interest in them. "I would thank you, Lord Fawke, for being gentle in telling Oliver of his father's death," she said, "though I must admit it surprised me to hear Maynard had gone to heaven. Imagine, a warrior for God."

Bunching his tunic, Liam used it to blot the moisture from his face. "To be honest would have been cruel," he said.

She allowed his remark to pass without comment.

Wiping the tunic down his chest and abdomen, Liam asked, "Why did you not tell him of Maynard's death?"

Joslyn looked sideways at him, then back down. "I thought it best that we first settle in at Ashlingford. It . . . it was not pressing."

Not pressing because Oliver had known so little of his father he could not possibly feel the loss of him, Liam wanted to say. "What did Ivo tell you about Maynard's death?" he asked.

She started to look toward him again but caught herself. "That he rode from the castle drunk," she said. "That a fall from his horse caused his death."

Knowing Ivo as he did, Liam was sure there was more to it. "What else did he tell you?"

"That . . . "

"That?" he prompted.

She shook her head. "It does not matter. Truly."

Irritation flaring, Liam strode the floor of the wood and caught hold of Joslyn's arm. "It *does* matter," he said. "What did he tell you?"

She glanced from his hand upon her to his eyes. "That though you did not kill Maynard, you are as responsible as if you had."

Liam released her. At least he could content himself with knowing the treacherous Ivo so well. "You ought to be on your way," he said, and turned and started back toward the stream.

"Is it true?" she asked, need in her voice to be told otherwise.

He halted, briefly considered her words, then continued on.

Why would he not defend himself? Joslyn wondered. Surely he knew his uncle had cast him in the worst light. She dismounted and followed him. "I wish to know the truth," she said, but it was as if she was not even there.

His back to her, Liam bent and snatched up the hood he had earlier tossed aside. "Return to the castle, Joslyn," he ordered.

Refusing him, she closed the distance between them and came to stand at his back. "I am done thinking the worst of you, Liam Fawke," she said. She laid a hand upon his shoulder, but in the next instant pulled it back with the realization of what she did. To touch him would only lead her in one of two directions—rejection, as he had shown her at the king's palace, or further humiliation in his arms.

She drew a deep breath. "Though for years I lived in fear of your one day coming to Rosemoor, I know now that my fears were unfounded—that what Maynard told me of you cannot be true. I beseech you, tell me of his death so I may put it to rest forevermore."

He turned around, but whether or not he intended to oblige her was not to be known, at least not immediately. With sudden recognition lighting his eyes, he reached forward and grasped between thumb and forefinger the sleeve of the gown she wore.

"Anya's!" he said.

The backs of his fingers brushing Joslyn's breast caused awakening to tremble through her. "Emma brought these things to me," she breathed. "My own garments are being laundered."

Liam captured her gaze. "I do not wish ever again to see you wearing them."

Baffled, Joslyn said, "'Tis true they do not fit well, but Emma says they can be altered—"

"If you need gowns, they will be made new," Liam said, his voice carefully controlled.

Joslyn shook her head. "I do not understand." Though she knew Maynard's mother had been instrumental in securing Ashlingford for her legitimate son, was Liam's anger so great toward the woman that he could not even bear to look upon garments she had worn?

Liam dropped his arm back to his side. "Suffice it to say that had Anya Fawke been born a man it would have been difficult to tell her apart from Ivo," he said.

That explained some of it, though what was unspoken must surely make more sense. "If it so pleases you," Joslyn said, "when my own gowns are returned I shall give these back to Emma."

"It pleases me."

She clasped her hands before her. "And now will you speak to me of Maynard's death?"

Liam considered her request a moment, then walked past her and lowered himself to sit before a great gnarled oak. It was some moments before he spoke. "Each time Maynard returned to Ashlingford," he began, "there were always arguments. It was the same that last night he rode out from the castle."

"About money," Joslyn supplied, remembering what Ivo had told her.

"Aye, he wanted more."

"For his gambling?"

"Of course. There was a game in London he wished to join."

Fleetingly, Joslyn wondered if it was the same game that had delayed her father's receipt of her message. Taking a step toward Liam, she asked, "And you refused him?"

Liam turned the hood in his hands, studied it a moment, and then tilted his head back against the oak. "Nay, I did not. Ashlingford was Maynard's, and as such he had a right to its profits."

This was certainly not the impression Ivo had left her with. "But?" Joslyn prompted.

"But not to the extent that his habit depleted the coffers. I would not—could not allow him to reduce Ashlingford to the same state it was in when I returned to manage it for him."

"What happened?"

Though Liam's gaze held hers, a distance came into his eyes. "Maynard was angry," he said. "At supper, he drank heavily and cursed me for treating him as if he were a child. In the end, though, he agreed to the sum I proposed—a rather large sum—though he said it would never be enough. I was filling his purse when he struck me."

"He struck you?" Joslyn gasped. Though Maynard had been a good-sized man, he had not been as large as Liam. She simply could not imagine him landing a blow on his brother.

"From behind," Liam explained, a wry smile lifting his mouth. "With a fire iron."

Joslyn could not help but be shamed by the dishonorable act of the man who had fathered Oliver. But then, he had not been an honorable man.

"When finally I roused," Liam continued, "it was to discover him gone from the castle."

"And all the barony's monies with him."

"All that was in the one chest. Had he known where I kept the other, I am sure he would have taken that as well."

"Did you give chase?"

He shook his head. "I should have, but I was weary of dealing with him. Too, though I knew funds would be scarce in the months ahead, there was still enough left to manage the barony until the next harvest. It seemed best to let him go and deal with him later."

Selfish Maynard, Joslyn thought. The same man who, when her father had been unable to pay his gambling debt to him, had demanded Humphrey Reynard's only daughter in marriage—half the debt settled upon consummation of their union, the other half upon the birth of a male child. How Joslyn had rejoiced when the midwife raised up the babe and showed her he was born a boy. Her duty done, her father's debt settled, she had welcomed Oliver into her arms and heart with the blessed knowledge that never again would she have to receive Maynard in her bed—a vow she had extracted from him the night he had come to her to settle the first half of the debt.

Realizing her thoughts had carried her away, Joslyn looked back at Liam and found his gaze intent on her. "How did he meet his death, Liam?" she asked.

His eyebrows drew together. "As Oliver told you, he took a fall from his horse."

She had done it again, Joslyn realized with a jolt of embarrassment. She had addressed him with the familiarity of a loved one. "That night?" she asked.

"Aye, he strayed from the road—assuredly the drink in him—and went down in a ravine."

Remembering Ivo's comment that Maynard had died in his arms, Joslyn asked, "Who was it that found him? Father Ivo?"

As she watched, Liam again slipped inside himself to that place of Maynard's death. "Nay, Maynard walked back to the castle himself," he said, a tightness entering his voice. "He was halfway to death when I carried him to his solar."

Joslyn felt a sadness she had not expected. "He died shortly thereafter?"

"Nay, he lingered until Ivo was summoned to his side, that he might bear witness for him to the existence and naming of his heir. Your son."

Oliver, who had taken everything from him just as Maynard had planned it. Drawn to Liam, Joslyn stepped nearer him. "I am sorry," she said.

He swept his gaze back to her, causing her footsteps to fall silent. "Why?" he asked. "Because your son is legitimate? Because he prevailed over a bastard?"

There was bitterness in his voice, though not as deep as it had been in the king's presence. "Though I can do naught about it," she said, "I know now that you were cheated. That Ashlingford should have been yours." His eyes upon her making her uncomfortable, she looked down at her hands. "And that you are not responsible for Maynard's death."

He laughed at that, surprising Joslyn into looking at him again. Then, his laughter subsiding, he said, "But I *am* responsible, at least in part."

Joslyn shook her head. "How can that be?"

The silence surrounding Liam grew so long Joslyn began to think he had no intention of explaining himself, but then he spoke.

"My father loved me as he never loved the son born to him in wedlock," he said. "He favored me, the child he had gotten on a common Irishwoman, a woman he had loved and would have given up the barony for in order to wed, had she not died a few hours after birthing me." He paused a moment before continuing. "Following my mother's death, my father wed Anya, the woman he had for years been betrothed to, but though she and others wished me to be sent to live among the villeins as so many bastards of nobles are, my father refused them and raised me up in the castle as if I were legitimate born. Never did he make any attempt to hide his feelings for me from his wife, nor his preference for his "little bastard" when Anya bore him Maynard. You see, it was something Maynard had to contend with all his life, something neither Anya nor Ivo would let him forget." Liam pushed a hand through his hair. "It turned him to drinking and gambling, which is why he is dead now, isn't it? Thus you see my part in it."

Glancing from the hard-set jaw and the eyes closed in pain to the fists clenched upon the hood, Joslyn felt the feelings he fought—feelings he did not wish to have for the brother who had so terribly wronged him. As Queen Philippa had said, Liam's had been a hard life. True, he'd had his father's love, but with it had come the burden of what he had taken from Maynard in having it and, too, the hate and resentment of others for being so loved.

Joslyn knew she must have walked to where Liam sat, but could not remember doing so. Sinking to her knees beside him, she reached out as she should not have and placed her hand upon his shoulder.

Immediately, his eyes sprang open, but before he could cut her with his angry words, she entreated,

"Do not say I cannot feel for you, for I do. I feel your pain as surely as if it were my own. I . . . I wish you freed of it."

Surprisingly, his eyes did not fill with offense. "And how do you propose to free me?" he asked, too softly.

Though Joslyn sensed danger in being so near him, especially in touching him, she ignored the warnings. "Though I know not all of what has gone before me," she said, "it cannot be your fault that Maynard drank and gambled to excess. The blame lies with him, with Anya and Ivo, and even your father, but not with you, Liam."

Doubt in his eyes, he leaned toward her, causing the muscles of his shoulder to flex beneath her palm. "Is it guilt that speaks from your mouth?" he asked, his breath warm upon her brow, his eyes probing hers to the depths of her soul.

Guilt? For having birthed Oliver to take Liam's place as baron of Ashlingford? Nay, if it was guilt, surely regret would follow, and never would she regret her son, who was all the good that had been of Maynard. "Not guilt," she said, wishing Liam would not come so close. It was far too disturbing.

He pressed nearer. "Then what is it you feel for me? What makes you care?"

Her heart was beating much too fast. Joslyn removed her hand from his shoulder and clasped it with the other in her lap. What *did* she feel for him? Compassion? Pity? Love? With that last shaking her as she had not been shaken in a long time, she dropped her gaze to her hands. Where had such a foolish thought come from? Of course she did not love Liam. How could she?

Gently, he lifted her chin. "What, Joslyn?" he asked again, his eyes searching.

Knowing that if she examined too deeply what she felt for him she might confess to something far more damaging, Joslyn swallowed and said, "Compassion. That is what I feel for you." Then she watched and waited for his anger to rise. But it did not.

As if outside himself—or perhaps it was inside he had gone—Liam lowered his eyes to her mouth and then to the rise and fall of her breasts. "I would rather you desire me," he said, his voice a caress that raised the fine hairs covering Joslyn's arms.

The breath trembled out of her. Lord, but she did desire him! Surely he knew. After all, when last they had been so near she had been ready to give herself to him, and most likely would have had he not—

Remembering the humiliation of how he had brought her to surrender only to cast her aside, Joslyn wrenched her chin free of his grasp. "Ah, nay," she exclaimed, falling back on her heels. "I will not allow you to do this to me again." Desperate to be away from him, and from all he was capable of making her feel, she pushed to her feet. However, she had taken only one step back when he caught her wrist. She gasped. "Let me go, Liam!"

He rose to his knees and pulled her toward him. "This time we will finish it, Joslyn," he said. "My vow to you."

Finish it? Then he would not leave her wanting as before? Barely had she thought the thought when the feel of him swept her toward a place void of reasoning. As he urged her down beside him, she felt first the muscles of his chest against her woman's place, then the hard flat of his abdomen, and last his arousal.

Joslyn fought to resist him, but it was too late. She burned, like never before. An exquisite ache engulfed her, her breasts strained to know his touch, and a need to be filled and filled again seized her.

"I want you, Joslyn." He spoke low, the green of his eyes eclipsed by the black. "Pray, do not deny me."

The feel of him against her—the strength and power in that part of him she longed to take inside her—made it difficult to breathe. She wanted him too, she admitted to herself. More than anything, she wished to know the answer to this incredible need he had awakened within her. But would the truth of it be as sweet as the longing?

As if her silence was consent, Liam lowered his head and grazed his lips across hers. "Kiss me, Joslyn," he murmured. "That's it. Open your mouth."

Though a small voice warned her otherwise, she barely heard it above the passion breaking over her. Trembling as Liam swept his tongue across hers, she closed her eyes, leaned into him, and curled her fingers into his flesh.

"Aye, Jos," he rasped, then deepened the kiss with a hunger that grew him harder against her.

She was melting, Joslyn realized, like honey set too long in the sun. Feeling Liam's hands move over her—the curve of her breast, her waist, her buttocks—she did what she would never have believed herself capable of. She began touching him as well.

Slowly, she drew a hand down his chest, over the swells of his abdomen, then lower. . . . Sliding it inward to where their bodies pressed his manhood between them, she lightly ran her fingers up the length of him held back only by the fabric of his braies.

A tortured sound escaped him. "God, Joslyn," he growled against her mouth.

Realizing through the desire enfolding her what she did—Joslyn Fawke touching a man as she had never touched one before, wanting him as she'd never wanted any other—she experienced a moment of consternation. But then her body guided her to thrill to the lips Liam trailed from her mouth down her neck.

She dropped her head back. "Liam," she said on a sigh.

He pushed her gown away, then put his lips against her bared shoulder.

Joslyn's breath was coming fast and shallow. She squeezed her closed eyes tighter. How long ere he laid her back? she wondered. How long before they joined as man and woman? Soon, she hoped. Soon.

Fitting his hand to her hip, Liam slowly glided it down her thigh to the ground and lifted her skirts. He touched the bare flesh of her inner thigh, lingered over it, and began stroking his fingers upward.

Joslyn knew what he sought and, knowing, pressed her hips nearer his as she held to that part of him which would soon make them one. However, though she thought herself ready for his touch, when he feathered over her woman's place she jerked against him.

And then his fingers found their goal.

Joslyn tried to hold back her cry of pleasure, but it parted her lips and sailed upon the air.

"Are you ready for me, Joslyn?" Liam asked, his voice grown as deep as that place inside her none but he had ever touched.

She opened her eyes and looked into a face become so familiar it was as if she had always known it, from the strong line of his mouth to the red hair falling over his brow. With no words to answer him, she nodded.

Still touching her with one hand, Liam lifted the other and pulled the string of his braies. They slid off one hip, then the other, and a moment later freed him.

Joslyn would not have thought herself so bold, but she lowered her eyes to gaze upon that part of a man she had never seen before. True, she was no maiden, but it had been dark. . . .

Liam's mouth claiming hers thrust the memories out of reach. It was no gentle kiss, though. Indeed, it was almost savage. However, rather than frighten Joslyn, it stole her breath.

Hungrily, he kissed her down to the ground, and when she lay in his shadow he pulled her skirts high.

Feeling no shame, wanting only to complete what had been begun between them days past in a London alleyway, Joslyn instinctively arched her lower body and brushed against him.

Liam groaned, then pressed himself to her entrance. "Once," he murmured thickly. "'Tis all it will take, Joslyn. I promise you."

That his words made it past the needs of her body was nothing short of a miracle, but somehow they filtered into Joslyn's mind. What did he mean?

she wondered. That after making love to her once, he would be sated and have no further need of her? That he could walk away from her forever? Aye, she concluded with a heart suddenly torn, there was no other meaning behind what he had said. He wanted her, and though he thought that lying with her once would be enough for him, she knew it would leave her with such a raw hurt she might never heal.

Liam was only a breath back from entering her when she twisted her body sideways. "Do not," she managed to say past the tearful lump in her throat.

Instantly, he stilled. "What is this?" he demanded.

Refusing to look at him, for she had no wish to suffer the anger that would come into his eyes if it was not already there, Joslyn said, "Release me. We . . . cannot do this."

"But we have done it, Joslyn," he rumbled.

Shaking her head, she began pushing her skirts back down. "No more," she said. "'Tis a mistake."

Though she resisted, Liam pulled her chin around. "What do you mean 'a mistake'?" His eyes raked hers. "We both want it. Where is the mistake in that?"

"I do not want it," she said.

His nostrils flared. "Little liar."

He was right—she was a liar, but only in part. Though she did yearn to know him intimately, she wanted more than that. More than what he wanted. "Let me up," she said again.

His jaw clenched, Liam stared down at her. "We are not finished," he said, and lowered his head to recapture her mouth.

Caught between the passion he caused to flicker back to life and the hurt of his words, Joslyn squeezed her eyes closed. She could not do this. She mustn't. But how to deny him—and herself?

The same as he had denied her the last time he had touched her like this. . . . Remembering what he had said that had wrenched her with such incredible pain, Joslyn grasped hold of it and shifted her mouth from beneath his. "You will hate yourself do you lie with me, Liam," she said, "for you forget that I was Maynard's first."

He covered her mouth again, but only for an instant before he pulled back. "God, but you are near as cruel as I, Joslyn Fawke," he swore beneath his breath.

Expecting his loathing to pour out upon her, Joslyn steeled herself for it. However, nowhere was that emotion evident on his face. In fact, the only expression he wore was one not unlike regret.

"What is it?" she asked.

He rolled off her. "You are right, I would hate myself." He tied up his braies. "Though not for the reason you believe."

Not for having been Maynard's first? Joslyn wondered. Was that what he meant? Or did she misunderstand?

Liam stood. "'Tis past time you were back to the castle," he said, and surprised her by offering her his hand.

Wishing he would explain himself, Joslyn stared at it a long moment—his large calloused palm, the long fingers tapering to blunt fingertips that only moments before had touched her private place.

"Come," Liam said.

Remembering herself, Joslyn placed her hand in his and, without effort, was drawn up beside him.

Immediately he released her, snatched his hood and tunic from the ground, pulled one on after the other, and started out of the wood. However, he had gone only a short distance when he broke his stride and looked back at where she had yet to move. "Make haste, Lady Joslyn," he said, once again formal. "No need to give the villagers anything more to make rumors of."

They had been in the wood a long time, she realized with dismay. But worse than the talk of villagers, would the men-at-arms ponder aloud on what she and Liam had been doing so long out of their sight? If so, surely word would reach Ivo, and she would be made to suffer his ridicule yet again.

Resenting the priest for knowing what was her desire, and wishing there was some way she might rid herself of him, Joslyn lifted her skirts and hurried to where her palfrey patiently awaited her.

Behind the plow once again, his loins still heavy with want, Liam watched Joslyn ride away. God, but he had been so near to having her—and would have, had he not voiced what he'd so wanted to believe: that in filling her once he would exorcise his desire for her forever. He had hurt her with that, though he had not realized it until, desperate to stay him from ravaging her, she had reminded him that she had been Maynard's. As if it would repulse him. And God, but it should have!

Seeking an outlet for the anger he turned on himself, Liam thrust his body forward with the plow. He had to get away from Ashlingford, and soon.

15

Liam was gone.

Joslyn had known it the moment she'd lifted her head from the pillow this morn. Though hardly a word had passed between them for over a week, his imminent departure had been in the air yesterday. During and following supper, through the tense silence prompted by Ivo's presence, Joslyn had watched Liam as he'd talked at length with the knights, the servants, and the steward. She'd been unable to interpret much of their conversation, but still she had known. And now he was gone with nary a word of parting. It shouldn't hurt, she told herself, but it did.

"Unca Liam'll come back, won' he, Father Ivo?" Oliver asked.

Remembering Emma's promise to bring Oliver to her following morning mass, Joslyn searched past those going out of the sanctuary before her and caught a glimpse of her son's upturned face below the figure of the priest.

Ivo had positioned himself outside the doors to acknowledge the dozen or more filing out of the chapel—from their demeanor, every one of them grateful that his monotonous delivery was finished. Now, as Joslyn watched, he bent down to the boy's level.

How would he answer Oliver's question? she wondered, with no small amount of misgiving. Would he speak ill of Liam? Would he tell Oliver his wish that Liam might never return?

"At least Father Warren believed his own sermons," one knight ahead of Joslyn grumbled to another.

The second knight nodded. "I am told Ivo gave him no warning—simply came to him before mass this morn and told him to leave."

Joslyn frowned. During the service she had fleetingly wondered at the absence of the other priest but, guessing the man was simply not feeling well, had thought no more on it. Now she knew how wrong she had been. Ivo had installed himself in Father Warren's place—as soon as Liam had departed. It could only mean he intended to continue on at Ashlingford. Inwardly, Joslyn groaned.

At her approach, Ivo straightened from Oliver. "Lady Joslyn," he said, inclining his head.

"Father Ivo."

He smiled, though the gesture was strained with what could only be displeasure. "Your son wishes to know when William will return," he said. "'Twould seem he has grown quite fond of him."

"Not Wil'm," Oliver protested. "Unca Liam."

Ivo's brow creased, but he said nothing.

Laying her hand atop Oliver's head, Joslyn

explained. "Father Ivo prefers to call Lord Fawke by his English name, William. 'Tis just another name for him."

Oliver looked up at her. "I like Liam better. You, Mama?"

"I do too," she answered.

"Wanna see what he left me?" he asked, excitement quivering on the edge of his voice.

Only then did Joslyn notice the arm he hid behind his back. She smiled. "Aye, show me."

With a flourish, Oliver swung his arm up and whipped the air with his newly fashioned scroug stick. "For my top," he said, with as much pride as she'd ever heard in his voice.

"Ah, 'tis handsome," Joslyn said, admiring the branch Liam had pared of its smaller limbs. "'Twas kind of Lord Fawke, wasn't it?"

Oliver's head bobbed up and down. "An' know where he left it?"

"With Emma?"

"Nay, un'er my pillow."

Under his pillow. Meaning . . . while she had slept, Liam had come into her chamber to place the stick beneath Oliver's pillow. Had he seen her in naught but her chemise, the covers kicked down around her feet as she'd awakened? She swallowed hard. "What a nice surprise, Oliver. You must remember to thank Lord Fawke when next he comes."

He nodded. "I will."

Attempting nonchalance, Joslyn looked back at Ivo. "And how did you answer my son when he asked if Lord Fawke would return?"

His eyes were like flint as he replied, "I told him that William would return. He always does."

Obviously much to his regret. Joslyn nodded and reached to take Oliver's hand.

"We need to speak, Lady Joslyn," Ivo said.

She wasn't surprised. But much as she would have liked to refuse him, she knew it would be better to have it over and done with. "Oliver," she said, "there is something Father Ivo and I must discuss. Why don't you practice with your top, and when I am finished we will explore the cellars."

He nodded and turned to where Emma stood outside the chapel. "Wanna see me spin my top?" he asked.

"Of course I do." Emma held out her hand to him.

Returning to the chapel, Joslyn crossed to the bench she had occupied during mass and lowered herself back to it.

Ivo closed the chapel doors and walked past her to the altar.

"Yes, Father?" Joslyn prompted, knowing it was Liam's visit to her chamber he wished to address.

After a long moment, he turned to face her. "You have not heeded my warning."

"Your warning?"

"Come, Lady Joslyn, surely 'tis not necessary for me to remind you of your talk in the wood with William a sennight past."

He knew more than she had expected. Although Joslyn had hoped that his silence these past days meant the contrary, it now appeared he had merely been waiting for the right opportunity to confront her.

"Or did you even talk?" Ivo asked knowingly.

"Of course we talked," Joslyn said, indignant.

Ivo seemed not at all put off. Stepping toward her, he said softly, "But then you sinned, didn't you, Joslyn Fawke?"

He was only guessing, she knew, but he had guessed right. She had known Liam's touch, though not as Ivo implied. Raising her chin, she said, "Believe what you wish, Father Ivo. Now good day." She rose from the bench and started toward the door.

"Understand this, Lady Joslyn," he called after her. "If your wanton behavior continues—and William's— you will leave me no choice but to appeal to the bishop for relief."

She turned back around. "What is it you are threatening?"

"I threaten naught." He clasped his hands together. "I am simply telling you what I intend to do if you do not cease with William."

"You will go to the bishop?"

"I will."

"And tell him what?"

As if the battle were his, Ivo smiled. "What has gone between you and William, of course."

"You do not know what has gone between us," she said, her dislike of this man growing stronger with each passing moment. "You only believe you do."

Ivo's nostrils flared. "I know that you have lain with your husband's brother," he said. "Your brother now, Lady Joslyn. A sin for which punishment is due."

What punishment would he call for? she wondered. A flogging? The humiliation of being pilloried for all to scorn? Worse, a far-reaching pilgrimage of penance that would see her torn from Oliver?

Refusing to give in to fear, Joslyn shook her head.

"Nay, Father Ivo, you are wrong. I have not lain with Liam Fawke, and if you speak such to the bishop"— There was only one thing she knew that might deter him—"I will myself seek an audience with him that he might be advised of how holy his holy man really is."

Ivo's eyes narrowed. "I do not know what you speak of, Lady Joslyn."

"Aye, you do. The raid, Father Ivo."

Something flashed in his gaze—alarm?—but he hid it behind scorn. "You refer to my use of the sword," he said, though there was question in his voice.

Joslyn refused him an answer. Let him ponder whether it was the letting of blood she referred to or his being the one responsible for the raid—or both— she thought.

"Sometimes circumstances dictate unusual measures," Ivo said, in an obvious attempt to prod a response from her.

"As they do now," Joslyn said. "And now that we understand each other, I bid you good day." Half expecting him to call her on her threat, she turned away. But he let her go.

Joslyn returned to her chamber, and only when the door was closed behind her did she release her breath. Though time would tell whether or not Ivo regarded her threat as real, one thing was certain— she had this day made herself an enemy.

Thornemede.

Liam stood on the threshold looking into a hall that might once have been preceded by the word "great" but was now so utterly decrepit it was little more than a hovel.

"And this I am lord of," he murmured.

"It does not get any better, does it?" Sir John asked, referring to all else they had seen of Thornemede this past hour.

All else but the fairly impressive number of sheep that had grazed the fields, Liam thought. Here was wool that could be exported, and the profits would begin to fill the barony's empty coffers—but only just. As for the rest of Thornemede, the two villages they had paused at on their way to the castle had been sparsely peopled, and those who had come out of their homes to receive them had seemed dismal and dejected. Most of the fields they passed had long been without the turning of a plow, the majority of the roads were in disrepair, and the rest of the castle was no better than this hall.

With its stinking moat, crumbling outer wall, inner buildings that looked near to collapsing, and the waste of humans and animals everywhere one stepped, Thornemede was worse than even he had imagined it could be. Too, though it was still occupied by the servants and retainers of the departed baron, it appeared that as many as half had left in search of another lord to pledge their services to.

Had they gone from the barony before Sir Robert had carried them the message of who their new lord was, Liam wondered, or afterward? In the next instant, he chastised himself for asking so foolish a question. As no attempt had been made to put order to Thornemede in anticipation of his arrival, it could not have been more clear that he was as unwelcome here as he had been at Ashlingford as a child. It didn't matter, though; he would bring every last one of Thornemede's people back. Still, anger coursed through his veins.

Damn King Edward to hell, he silently cursed, and damn himself for having allowed vengeance to sway him to the king's proposal. Then, suddenly, he laughed at the folly of it. As before, his destiny was another's, just as he had vowed it would never be again. Liam Fawke, bastard of Montgomery Fawke, was baron of Thornemede—lord of the thorn, lord of naught.

Slapping his palm to the outerwork of the donjon, Liam repressed his mock mirth and said, "Ah, but as King Edward attested, 'tis of stone and sturdy."

Sir John arched an eyebrow at him.

Looking behind to the dozen Ashlingford men he had chosen to accompany him to Thornemede, Liam saw concern in their eyes. Very likely they thought him building to the Irish in him, he mused, and were steeling themselves for the eruption of his anger. But he was in control—or nearly so.

As the men were his for only a short time ere he must return them to Ashlingford—and Sir John to Duns Castle—Liam decided it was time to put them to use. But first there was one thing he needed to tend to: the children. Lowering his gaze to where the three stood uncertain at the bottom of the steps, he forced a smile. Then he looked to the squire who stood nearby. "Take them into the garden," he said, and added, "providing there is one."

"And if there is not, my lord?"

"Occupy them. Just do not bring them into the hall until I am finished."

The squire nodded, and gestured for the children to follow him.

Had he made a mistake in bringing them? Liam wondered. Though they had only known village life, Thornemede was hardly any better than the wattle-and-daub house they had been fostered in these past years, and certainly less hospitable. Something, though—a need to be certain they were cared for as they deserved to be—had made him bring them with him to Thornemede.

Venting a harsh sigh, Liam stepped into the hall. "Let us be done with it," he said, and strode forward. Ignoring the curious servants who peered at him from the far end of the hall, Liam headed for the clutter of tables and benches that were strewn with knights and men-at-arms. A few had dragged themselves awake amid the commotion of bustling servants, but the others persisted in the bowels of drunken sleep.

Liam seized hold of one man's shoulder and rolled him off his bench. With a thud that shuddered the floorboards, the large man fell to the mildewed rushes. Whether he was a knight or a man-at-arms, was impossible to tell, for there was no longer any distinction between the two classes.

His groan far outweighing the complaining of his companions, who were similarly being awakened, the man forced his lids open. "Whaddya want?" he demanded, his words a drunken slur.

"On your feet!" Liam ordered. "Now!"

The man frowned. "And who might ye be?"

"I am Lord Liam Fawke," Liam said, the title feeling strange upon his tongue. "Baron of Thornemede."

The man's gaze turned insolent. "Ah, the bastard Irish," he said, too drunk to worry what his punishment might be for speaking aloud his loathing.

"On your feet!" Liam repeated.

After a long moment, the man heaved himself onto his side and stood to a height that bettered Liam by several inches.

"What is your name?" Liam asked.

As the great man folded his arms across his chest, the movement caused him to sway, first right, then left. "Gunter Welling," he said, and braced his legs farther apart in an attempt to steady himself. "I am captain of the guard of Thornemede."

"You will address me either as Lord Fawke or as 'my lord,'" Liam reminded him.

"Will I?"

"You will—or suffer the consequences."

Gunter arched a bushy eyebrow. "That so?"

He was drunk, Liam reminded himself. "Are you challenging me, Welling?" he asked.

The man smiled. "Ah, but I know my place, Fawke. What I'm wonderin' is: Do you know yours?"

A murmur went around the hall as Thornemede's retainers speculated on the price the soldier would pay for his belligerence.

Knowing that how he handled this man would set the pattern for his rule of the barony, Liam stepped nearer Gunter. "I am your lord, Welling," he said. "*That* is my place. However, if you wish to challenge me, I would be more than willing to teach you a lesson in humility." He rested his hand upon his sword hilt.

Gunter followed the movement, and though his jaw moved from side to side he said no more.

"I thought not," Liam said. "I will give you a quarter hour to gather your guard in the outer bailey, Welling, and for every one that is absent I will take it out of your pay. Am I understood?"

Gunter's eyebrows descended, but whatever his feelings, he did not speak them aloud. Instead, he stepped past Liam, called to the men-at-arms who had gathered across the hall, and walked outside.

It was a beginning, Liam thought. Though the captain of the guard did not like him, he would come to respect the new lord of Thornemede.

And now for the knights.

16

How much longer would Liam keep himself from Ashlingford? Joslyn wondered as she entered the hall with Oliver fast asleep in her arms. It was nearly two weeks since he had left, and though she had thought he would have returned by now, he continued to manage Ashlingford through a messenger sent daily between the two baronies. Although Joslyn would admit it to no one, his absence made her feel almost empty.

Suddenly, Emma appeared before her. "Come, let us sit and talk a moment," she suggested.

Joslyn allowed the woman to guide her across the hall to a padded bench before the hearth. Gratefully, she sank down upon it and settled Oliver against her shoulder. During the past three hours, they had explored every building, corner, and crack of the outer bailey, and now she was tired.

Emma smiled. "Wore you thin, did he?"

Joslyn returned the smile. "And himself. My father says he is much like I was at his age."

Emma raised an eyebrow. "I was thinking he reminded me of Liam, though the boy was a bit older than Oliver when I first came to Ashlingford."

Joslyn would not have expected such a comparison. "Oliver does not remind you of his father?" she asked.

"Aye, a bit, but as a child Maynard was more quiet than Oliver—more into himself, though not in a bad way, mind you. He just did not have the confidence of Liam."

Which Emma also saw in Oliver. "Why do you think that is so?" Joslyn asked, though she guessed it was as Liam had told her: their father had preferred the misbegotten over the legitimate son, which neither Anya nor Ivo had allowed Maynard to forget.

Emma sighed. "Ah, lady, there is much you will never know of Ashlingford—that you do not need to know."

Feeling the woman's withdrawal, Joslyn leaned toward her. "I have waited patiently these past weeks for you to tell me something of the Fawkes. I hardly knew the man I married, and now what I thought I knew of him has come to naught. All he told me were lies. I beseech you, help me, that I may come to understand who it was that fathered Oliver."

"Of course you need to know," Emma conceded, "but just as important as knowing who sired a child upon you, I will tell you so that when the castle folk begin wagging their tongues about Maynard you will understand what it was that made him so."

She paused a moment before beginning her tale.

"Maynard was a sweet child—in that, very like Oliver. Unfortunately, his father did all but ignore him from the day he was born. You see, it was Liam whom Montgomery Fawke loved, and it was as if in loving his misbegotten son he had no love left for any other. Not his wife, Anya, and not Maynard."

There was pain in what Emma said—a deep pain, Joslyn realized.

"Maynard sensed it," she continued, "even when he was too young to understand it. So, he turned to Liam for affection."

"Liam?" Joslyn repeated. It was hard to believe Maynard would ever have looked to his hated brother for emotional support.

"Aye, there was a time when the two brothers cared for each other—when the innocence of childhood was theirs to hide behind, but then they grew up."

Huddling closer to the fire, Emma turned her gaze to the flames. "From the day Maynard was born, Anya worked to keep him from Liam—to draw a distinction between the legitimate and the illegitimate so there would never be a question as to who was the rightful heir of Ashlingford. Then, when Maynard turned two and began attaching himself to Liam, she forbade him to go anywhere near his older brother. That did not stop him, though, nor did Anya's punishment when she caught them playing together. Maynard's need for love was that strong."

"But what of his mother's love?" Joslyn asked. "And Father Ivo? He seems to have cared greatly for Maynard."

Emma glanced at her, and looked back at the fire. "Anya did not love Maynard," she said, a bitter smile drawing her mouth tight. "To her, he was little more than a means of taking Ashlingford from Liam. As for Ivo"—she paused a long moment—"he treated

Maynard as if he were his own son, but Ivo did not know how to love him. And like Anya, he was always more concerned with Maynard as heir than as a child in need of love and affection."

Joslyn felt she had come to know Maynard better these past weeks than ever before—first through Liam's telling of his death, and now through Emma's telling of his early life. "It must have hurt him deeply."

Tears gathering in her eyes, Emma bent her head as if to hide them.

"You loved him, didn't you, Emma." It was more statement that question.

A tremble went through the older woman. "I did. At my own breast I nursed him to walking. My days were his days, my nights his. Hardly was he ever out of my sight, except when I allowed him to steal away with Liam. He was my boy, and I loved him as if he were mine to call 'son.'" A fat tear slid off her lashes and dropped to her lap. "I had thought my love would be great enough that he would not miss his mother's or his father's, but it wasn't—though methinks it might have been had Anya and Ivo only let him be."

Drawing a deep breath, Emma wiped her eyes.

"Worshiping Liam as he did," she continued, "'tis likely Maynard would have been content to walk in his brother's shadow evermore had he not heard every day what Liam had stolen from him and would steal when their father died. More and more time he began to spend with Ivo in study, and by the summer of his seventh year I had lost nearly all of him. A year later, I was to him no more than a woman who served him, and Liam an obstacle in his path to the barony."

Emma covered her face with her hands. "I tried," she mumbled, "but I could not bring him back."

Joslyn's heart went out to her. Sliding nearer, she put her free arm around the woman's quaking shoulders. "You cannot blame yourself," she said. "Some things only God can undo, and when He leaves them be, it is only that something better will come of the bad."

Emma looked up at her. "He was not evil, my lady. 'Tis true that many were the terrible things he did as he grew into a man, but he was not evil. I swear. Not my boy."

"I believe you," Joslyn said.

Emma eased against her.

Oblivious to Emma's revelations, Oliver continued to sleep against his mother as she sat silent beside the older woman.

"Is it true Maynard promised Ashlingford to Liam in exchange for his management of the estates?" Joslyn asked, though in her heart she already knew the answer.

Emma sighed. "Aye, he did, not only in my presence but before all his knights."

Relieved, yet not, Joslyn looked down into Oliver's face. He was so beautiful, she thought, his cherub cheeks rosy, his lashes long and sweeping— so utterly innocent of the treachery that had won him what should have been another's. What would he say to all this if he were old enough to understand? If he were old enough to have made the decision himself whether or not to take up the barony of Ashlingford?

Joslyn looked into Emma's eyes. "Then Ashlingford should be Liam's," she concluded, "not Oliver's."

"It should always have been Liam's. Never should King Edward have bestowed it upon Maynard."

"But he did."

Emma nodded. "He did, and it was a mistake. More mistake than you can ever know, Lady Joslyn."

But she did know, Joslyn thought. "I have been told that before Maynard called Liam back to Ashlingford, he had nearly laid the barony to ruin," she said.

"Aye, ruin. Were it not for the winnings Liam brought with him from the tournaments, 'tis uncertain what would have become of Ashlingford."

"He put his own money into the barony?" Joslyn asked with disbelief.

"And why would he not?" Emma said. "After all, he believed it would one day be his."

Then the money Maynard had time and again taken from Ashlingford had not been his to take, Joslyn realized. Liam could have refused him outright—and perhaps should have.

As if knowing what thoughts ran through Joslyn's head, Emma said, "I have not lied to you, lady. I spoke true when I told you that Liam and Maynard once held great affection for each other. True, it died in Maynard, but never did Liam stop caring for his brother."

It all made sense now, Joslyn realized. Though Liam had expressed little more than contempt for his brother, pain had shone from him when he had talked of Maynard's death. "He blames himself for who Maynard became," she said, "and for his death."

"Liam?"

Joslyn nodded.

A small smile drifted onto Emma's lips, replacing the sadness that had been there before it. "You two have been talking, eh?"

Joslyn's defenses went up, but then she reminded herself it was Emma she spoke to, not Ivo. "Some," she said.

Emma's smile grew larger. "That's good, though it surprises me he would say anything to you—that he would say anything to anyone. With the exception of that anger of his, Liam is not one to let his feelings be known."

Yet he had let them be known to her, Joslyn thought. What was she to make of that?

"He must like you," Emma said, "though he would not tell you that, of course."

A liking, aye, but of the flesh, not the heart, Joslyn thought. Still, it did not explain why Liam had exposed himself to her. . . .

"For certain, he has taken a liking to the little one here," Emma said, looking upon Oliver.

Joslyn nodded. "It sometimes makes me pause to remember my fear of Liam. I thought he intended to murder Oliver and myself to gain Ashlingford."

"'Tis what Maynard warned you of, is it not?" Emma asked.

"Aye," Joslyn said, then shook her head. "And I believed him."

It was Emma's turn to offer comfort. Squeezing a hand over Joslyn's, she said, "What is important is that you now know different. There is naught for you to fear at Ashlingford."

Joslyn started to agree, but then remembered the one person who had replaced Liam in her fears. "Naught but Father Ivo," she said.

Emma sat straighter. "Has he done something?"

"He has accused me of lying with Liam."

"And how did you reply?"

Joslyn was almost ashamed to admit it. "With a threat of my own, but I do not know if it will deter him, for I have no proof."

"As he has no proof of what he accuses you of, is that not right, Lady Joslyn?"

"You are asking if I have lain with Liam," Joslyn said. "I have not."

Emma stood. "I will speak with Father Ivo," she said. "Worry no more on it, lady."

Joslyn looked up at her. "But what can you do?"

Smoothing her skirts, Emma said, "I have known Ivo since he was a young man foundering with his faith. We understand each other very well."

Puzzled, but knowing it was all the explanation she would get, Joslyn did not press as she would have liked to. "Thank you, Emma," she said.

With a nod, the old woman slowly bent and pecked a kiss upon Oliver's brow. "This child will make everything right," she said as she drew back. "You will see."

Did she mean Oliver's little-boy charm would bring the castle folk around? Joslyn wondered as she watched Emma walk to the stairs. Or was it that he had touched some part of Liam thought to be untouchable?

She sighed. Whatever it was, she prayed Emma was right.

"I could kill you," Ivo said, as he mercilessly gripped her fleshy upper arm.

Emma did not even flinch. "You have tried before." Her voice was infuriatingly level. "But 'twas not me who died, was it?"

Wishing to be rid of her forever, Ivo squeezed her arm as if it were her neck beneath his fingers. "Bitch!"

Emma arched an eyebrow. "Hardly the priest today, are you, dear Ivo? What would the good bishop think if he came upon you now?"

Ivo thought of his dagger where it hung from the silken girdle of his vestments. Ere the old hag could let out a single sound of protest, it could be planted in her breast. And that would be the end of her. Of course, it would not be the end of the writings he had numerous times searched for and never found. Even worse, he might never see the money due him. Christ's blood! Would it never end? "Where is the coin?" he demanded.

She cocked her head innocently. "Ah, that."

"That!" Ivo shouted. "Where is it?"

Though he still held her, Emma took a step back from him and reached inside the full bodice of her gown. She pulled out a small pouch and tossed it to the floor.

"That is not all of it," he said.

She smiled. "Of course not. I may be lowborn, but I have learned the price of my own existence. You will have it all—bit by bit—but not before I have lived out the rest of my life."

With a curse that, had God been listening, would have brought the walls down around them, Ivo thrust her away from him. "You've served your usefulness, old woman," he said. "What more have you left to live for? Just die!"

"Die?" she scoffed. "When there's Oliver? Nay, Ivo, I will go when I am ready, and not a moment before."

His head reeling with every blasphemous word and curse he had ever had inside him, Ivo swung away. "Leave me," he said.

"You will leave Joslyn be," she reminded him, "and Liam?"

"What choice have I?"

"That is true," she said, "but still I would have your word."

His word. As if there were any truth behind it, Ivo thought. So easy to give and even easier to take back. He faced her again. "You have it," he said, then back-handed the air. "Now leave me, hag!"

Emma bowed her head. "As always, I am most grateful, Father," she said, her mockery nearly causing Ivo to lose the last thread of his control. She passed down the aisle between the two rows of benches and a moment later pulled the chapel door closed behind her.

How Ivo fought the urge! He even clasped his hands before his face as if in prayer. But when he knew Emma was gone far enough from the chapel not to hear it, he yielded. Tearing the cloth from the altar, he gloried in the crash of the chalice thrown against the far wall and the lesser clamor of the half-dozen relics that followed it. But that was not enough. Never was it enough. However, rather than destroy the chapel as was his greatest desire at the moment, he swung back to the bare altar, lifted his fists high, and prostrated himself upon the floor.

"Lord, Lord!" he cried. "Smite my enemies. Free me of every last one of them. Give me what is mine!"

His only answer was a surge of light in the chapel, as if a wind had blown through it and breathed on the candles.

Lifting his head, he glanced right and left, but did not see God as he was so sure he would one day see Him. "Patience," he muttered to himself. Soon enough the way would be pointed out to him, and then never again would he be forced to yield to Emma's demands—nor to the bastard and his whore.

Beginning to smile, Ivo rolled onto his back, extended his arms to either side of him as if he were laid upon the cross, and stared at the beams overhead. Really, Emma had gained little in threatening to expose him, he consoled himself. Since Joslyn's threat to carry her tale to the bishop was quite possibly real, he'd already decided against going to the holy man to seek her punishment and Liam's—at least until he had firm evidence. God, but it was maddening that Joslyn had enlisted the old woman's help. Absolutely maddening. Lord, to be rid of Emma!

Groping for the chain of his crucifix, Ivo closed his eyes on the knowledge that when the time was right—and it would come right eventually—he would have his justice. Then he slept.

The embers were hungry, shooting flames up from their dying depths to lap at the ivory parchment. Aroused, the fire crawled around the edges of the document, then jumped and flickered across the writing.

As Liam watched, he thought again of the contents of the missive. It had come this noon from Sir Hugh,

Ashlingford's steward, a trusted man who kept Liam informed of all the goings-on at the barony during his absence.

The news sent this day did not really surprise Liam, considering Ivo had weeks ago forced Father Warren out of his position as castle priest, but it angered him. The mere thought of Ivo taking the lord's solar for himself was near enough to send Liam calling for his destrier. But he would not, for did he leave Thornemede now, no worse mistake could he make. Aye, he would return to Ashlingford, but not before his position here was more secure.

The flame having expended itself on the document, it fell back to the embers, danced a moment on the surface, and withdrew beneath the red glow. Liam stared at the fragile, blackened sheet it left behind.

Gone was all evidence of his correspondence with the steward. Although they communicated regularly regarding the state of Ashlingford, it would not do for others to know that Ivo was more a matter of discussion than the state of the demesne. And not just that he had taken the lord's chamber.

As Maynard would have been certain to tell Ivo where he'd secreted the coins he stole the night he had ridden drunk into the ravine, Liam knew his uncle would eventually seek to retrieve them. Thus, per Liam's instructions, each time Ivo left the castle he was followed. Unfortunately, according to Sir Hugh's report, naught had come of those few times Ivo had ridden out. But he could not resist much longer, Liam knew—unless, of course, he had somehow managed to lay hands on the money without anyone's knowledge. For this reason, Liam had ordered a search of Ivo's belongings, which was the last item the steward addressed in his report. No coins had been found.

With a sigh, Liam turned from the hearth, walked back to the table, and lowered himself into the lord's high seat.

17

Sensing that she was no longer alone, Joslyn looked up from the dirt she spread with her bare hands to the man who stood in the doorway.

Liam stared back at her with a gaze so intense it momentarily stopped her breath. He was remembering, she knew, just as she did herself.

She sank back onto her heels. It was four weeks to the day since he had departed the barony, though it seemed far longer than that. Indeed, in thinking on his absence just this morn, she had wondered if he intended to manage Ashlingford from a distance indefinitely. But he had returned, and with him he'd brought the feelings that neither one of them dared fuel.

Lifting his gaze from Joslyn, Liam straightened, but rather than step into the garden as she expected him to, he turned and walked back into the donjon.

For a long moment, Joslyn stared at the space he had filled, now utterly empty. Why had he come to the garden if not to speak with her? she wondered. And why had he left without so much as a word? Confused, she rose from among the thorn of flowering rosebushes and made her way down the stone-laid path that bent its way through the garden.

So intent was Joslyn on Liam that she nearly collided with the cook, who had come out of the kitchens. "I am sorry," she said, stepping out of the man's way.

A fortnight past, this same man would simply have glowered at her and continued on, but things were beginning to change for the better. "And what is on yer mind this fine day, my lady?" he asked, a glimmer of a smile in his eyes.

Ever since Joslyn had begun overseeing meals as the lady of Ashlingford, that glimmer had grown brighter. Soon, it would reach the man's lips, she was certain, for it had no other place to go. "Lord Fawke has returned," she said. "As he is likely to have brought several men with him, you will need to add to the nooning meal. Mayhap some salted fish, onion tarts, and . . . spiced pears?"

"We haven't any pears till the morrow, my lady."

"Apples, then?"

"Aye, we've those."

"Good," Joslyn said. "'Tis in your hands."

The man inclined his head and continued on his way.

Joslyn found Liam in the great hall. With his back to her, he reached for the leather-bound ledger that sat open before the steward, pulled it across the table, and bent his head to the figures there.

"'Tis all there, my lord," the steward said. "As the

far column reflects, I have deducted from the total receipts the tenth that is to be paid to you per the king's decree—after his taxes have first been satisfied, of course."

"'Tis a goodly sum," Liam said.

Though Joslyn knew she ought to continue up the stairs and make herself more presentable, she ignored propriety. After all, it was not as if Liam had not already seen her in her gardening attire. "So, you are returned to us, Lord Fawke," she said, as she advanced on him.

He stilled, then looked over his shoulder at her. "You thought I would not?"

"I was beginning to wonder."

He regarded her a moment before returning his attention to the steward. "I would like to compare last year's receipts to this year's, Sir Hugh," he said, "and the year before."

"Now, my lord?"

"Now."

Frowning, the man nodded and stood. "I will collect the ledgers for you." Then he departed.

When the last of the steward's footfalls resounded around the hall, Liam turned to Joslyn and leaned back against the edge of the table. He crossed his arms over his chest and met her gaze.

Only then did she see the fatigue etched around his eyes. From a distance she had not noticed, but it was there—and in the grooves alongside his mouth. Was this a result of the weight of Thornemede upon him? she wondered.

"'Tis good to know my absence was noticed," Liam said.

Knowing he implied that she had missed him, she

clasped her hands at her waist and said, "Oliver speaks often of you. It seems he has taken quite a liking to his uncle."

The corners of his mouth turned up slightly. "And you have not?"

She groped for a reply. "You are always welcome at Ashlingford, Lord Fawke," she said, trying to maintain a composure that threatened to slip. "Surely you know that."

Whether or not he did, he did not say. Instead, he eyed her soiled garments. "We have been here before, have we not, Lady Joslyn?" he mused.

She had known he would not forget that first encounter in the gardens of Rosemoor.

"Yet this time you've no rake to fend me off." The light of humor entered Liam's eyes.

How strange and rare, that humor, Joslyn reflected, warming to it even though it was at her expense. "And why would I need to fend you off?" she asked.

He looked around the hall. "We are alone, are we not?"

A dangerous thing considering what had gone between them those other times they'd been alone. Though she knew her attempt to turn the conversation would be obvious, Joslyn said, "Your jaw has not mended well." The many scars crossing it were not as smooth as one would expect from the fine needle that had stitched the gashes closed.

Thoughtfully, Liam stroked his fingers across his jaw. "Nay, it has not," he said, and abruptly dropped his arm back to his side. Capturing Joslyn's gaze, he stared at her a long moment. "You torment me," he said finally. "But you know that, don't you, Joslyn?"

She blinked. "I do not understand."

"Aye, you do. 'Tis the same for you—even if you will not admit it."

She held his stare as long as she could and then looked away. "It is wrong," she said. "Wrong for us even to speak of it."

Stepping forward, Liam lifted her chin. "I thought in staying away it would end," he said, "but still I cannot lie down at night without want of you."

"And you think once with me will end it?" she asked, though it pained her to repeat what he had said to her in the wood.

He surprised her by shaking his head. "'Tis what I want, but I do not believe it."

Hope flickered through Joslyn. Mayhap Liam loved her as she—

It was the closest she had come to admitting it to herself, she realized. And a foolish thing it was to do. "Your uncle believes we have already lain together," she said. "He has threatened to go to the bishop and tell him of it, do we not cease. He will seek our punishment, Liam."

A different kind of light leapt into his eyes. "And what did you say to him?"

"I denied it, of course. Then I . . . it was not Christian of me, but I told him that if he went to the bishop, so would I. I said I would tell of the raid upon our party."

"That it was Ivo who was responsible."

Joslyn shook her head. "I did not say it, but methinks he understood my meaning."

Liam was silent a long moment. "That will only stop him for so long," he said. He dropped his hand from her and turned away. "The old devil. From the day of my birth he has stood between me and what is mine."

What was his? Joslyn could not believe she had heard right. Surely he did not include her in those things that belonged to him. Nay, certainly not.

The truth was, somewhere along the way Liam *had* come to think of her as his. Realizing it only after it was too late to catch back the damning words, he looked around at Joslyn and saw from her expression that what he said had not escaped her.

"I want you, Joslyn," he said. Aye, that was it, he assured himself. It was only desire for her that made him speak so foolishly. "But I will not risk the wrath of the church upon either of us to have you. All Ivo needs is proof. Then, regardless of your threat, he will go to the bishop. My uncle will rest only when he is dead—or when he has finally rid himself of me and, in doing so, gained control of Ashlingford. 'Tis only a matter of which will happen first."

As he watched, a questioning look grew on Joslyn's face. "Though I have learned much these past weeks," she said, "I do not understand why he hates you so. 'Tis not as if you took the barony from him."

"But I did."

"You did? But even had your father denied you, there would still have been Maynard to succeed him."

The memories of the past burdening him, Liam lowered himself to the bench. "It needs explaining," he said.

"It does," Joslyn agreed.

"Although my father loved my mother, he knew he could not wed her if he was to remain the heir of Ashlingford; grandfather would not have allowed it.

Thus, he determined to keep her as his leman after he had fulfilled his obligation of wedding Anya, to whom he was betrothed. However, my mother loved him too much to share him with another. She was entering her ninth month of pregnancy when she fled the barony. Though my father tried to deny his feelings for her, in the end he decided to relinquish his claim upon Ashlingford and go in search of her so they might wed."

"Which meant Ivo would become baron when their father died."

"Aye, and for a fortnight he put aside his priest's vestments to hold dearly to the only thing he had ever wanted in life."

Joslyn seated herself on the bench beside Liam. "Your father returned, though."

Her nearness tempting him to reach out to her, Liam curled his fingers into his palms. "He found my mother the day before she gave birth to me, but I came too soon for him to wed her that I might be born legitimate. She died hours later in his arms." Although Liam had not known his mother, he always felt a certain sadness when he thought of her death—most likely a result of his father's sorrow. "If not for me, my father would not have returned to Ashlingford, but in me he saw a chance to right the wrongs done my mother. Determined that I would one day succeed him, he brought me with him to the barony."

"His father took him back as heir?" Joslyn asked.

"Aye, knowing that Ivo was not fit to hold the title, he set aside the second son and welcomed back the first."

"But the old baron could not have been pleased to learn that your father intended for you to succeed him," she said. "If he would not allow him to wed a commoner and continue as heir, surely he would have refused you."

"A half-Irish bastard," Liam supplied. "Only after the old man died, a year later, and my father had wed Anya did he make it known that I would be baron after him. Thus, there was none to oppose him, excepting Ivo and Anya, of course, and he was certain that did they dispute my right when he died, the king would still accept me as baron."

Joslyn contemplated what he had told her. "Anya must have hated you."

Remembering her many cruelties—the vicious words, the pinches and slaps, the degradation, Liam said, "No more than Ivo, though I cannot say she did not have every right to despise me. After all, I was taking from her by taking from Maynard."

A movement in Joslyn's lap drew Liam's gaze to her hands, clenched in her skirts, as if it was the only way she could prevent herself from touching him. He had done that to her, he realized. He had rejected her goodness. But it was best this way. Wasn't it?

Following his gaze, Joslyn stilled her hands. "'Twas what your father wanted," she said. "It was not your decision to make. Just as it was not mine to make whether or not Oliver should be baron of Ashlingford."

In the next instant, Liam did something he would never have thought himself capable of. He reached out to her. Covering her hands with his, he said, "I know that now, Joslyn. Forgive me for having believed that in wedding Maynard you were the same as he. I was wrong."

The brilliant gaze she lifted to him was made even

brighter by the tears that sprang to her eyes. "Naught to forgive," she whispered, "only to be understood. And I do understand, Liam."

He resisted, but in the end he smoothed back the black hair falling over her brow and leaned forward. Though he expected her to turn from him, she didn't. Instead, she parted her lips.

Liam lowered his head. So sweet, he thought as he gently tasted her—like the first day of spring after the cruelest of winters.

He should have ended it there, should have drawn back ere she touched her tongue to his, but he did not. Roused and roused again, he circled his tongue around hers, then drew her into his mouth. The little breath Joslyn gasped excited him further. He wanted her—and no other. Inch by aching inch, he wished to slide her garments up her ankles, her calves, her trembling thighs, her woman's place . . . and when finally she stood naked before him, he would lay her down and slowly learn every sweet curve and hollow of her. She would be his.

"My lord?"

It was a voice Liam could not ignore, for it had no place where he and Joslyn were headed. Feeling her stiffen, he pulled back and stood.

There, lingering on the bottom step of the stairs, was Sir Hugh. Though he was not one to be easily addled, his discomfort at having come upon them in such a compromising position was obvious. Flushed from the top of his shaved pate to the collar of his tunic, the steward looked anywhere but at them.

Glancing back at Joslyn, Liam saw the fear on her face.

God's wounds! he cursed. It had been a fool thing

to do, especially in a place where the chance of being come upon was so great. It could even have been Ivo who had discovered them. "You need not worry," he said to her, and strode across the hall to the steward. "I trust you will be discreet about whatever you have seen this day," he said.

Sir Hugh raised an eyebrow. "But I have seen naught, my lord," he said with all earnestness. "I know not what you refer to."

In other words, what he had seen would never be told. "I am mistaken, then," Liam said. The matter laid to rest, he nodded to the ledgers the man held. "I wish totals month by month," he instructed, "and then a comparison across the last three years."

The steward descended the last step. "I will figure it right away, my lord."

Liam turned on his heel. "And now I've other matters to attend to," he said. As he strode from the hall, he saw that Joslyn had risen from the bench and now stood with her back to him, affecting an interest in the tapestry that hung behind the high table.

Liam was drawn to her, wanting badly to reassure her that what had passed between them would remain their secret. However, as they had already come too near to exposing themselves, he continued past her and outside. He would ride this want out of him, he told himself, and only when it was gone would he return.

Her emotions in upheaval, Joslyn avoided the steward's path and made her way to her chamber. There, Oliver napped, and in a chair beside the hearth Emma dozed, watching over him as if it filled a part of her that had long been empty. She truly loved Oliver. It was almost as if he were her own.

Warmed, though still filled with misgivings that vied with treacherous longings, Joslyn walked to the window and leaned into its shallow embrasure. It took her but a moment to pick out Liam as he crossed the inner bailey, for his red hair shone like a beacon until he disappeared from sight.

She was in love, she finally admitted it. It had to be that elusive thing she had only heard spoken of, for never before had she felt this way about another: a oneness, as if Liam would always be with her, even if he did not share her feelings.

"If. . . . " She chided herself. Never would he love her. Perhaps if Maynard did not stand between them, it would have been different, but he was there—evidenced in the beautiful child of their union. Aye, Liam wanted her, and must hate himself for it, but that was the extent of his feelings for her. And it was not enough.

18

He was drenched. Village to village, field to field, Liam had attempted to ride the need for Joslyn out of him, as he'd vowed to do ere returning to the castle. As the sky loosed sheets of chill rain upon him, his body eased, but that was not the only relief he sought. He wished Joslyn gone from his thoughts— just as he'd wished her gone from them this past month while at Thornemede—but as he had failed then, he failed now. She was in him and would not be driven out.

Tossing the reins to a waiting squire, Liam left his curses in the mud that sucked at his boots and took the steps to the donjon two at a time. Inside, a porter reached to a table set nearby. "A towel, my lord," he said, and draped one over Liam's shoulders.

Liam strode toward those seated around the great hearth, all of them having fallen silent with his arrival: Joslyn, Emma, Ivo, and a multitude of others, including knights, men-at-arms, and servants.

"Unca Liam!" an ardent childish voice exclaimed.

Oliver emerged from between his mother and Emma and ran toward him.

For the briefest of moments, Joslyn looked Liam in the eye; then she turned her face back to the fire. Still, it was enough for Liam to see her distress. Was it Ivo? Had the old devil learned what had happened between them this day and made more of his threats?

Looking to where his uncle sat, Liam saw what he had not noticed when he'd first come into the hall—Ivo's awkward attempt at filling the lord's high seat that had been brought down from the raised dais. God almighty! He had no right—

"You came back!" Oliver cried, nearly upon him.

Knowing this was neither the time nor place to speak against Ivo's brazen claim, Liam focused on the little boy. Some good came of everything, he thought, as he glimpsed shades of a young Maynard in Oliver. However, for only a moment did he allow himself to be pulled back in time. He had no use for such memories.

Hunkering down, he caught Oliver in his arms. "You've grown," he said.

"Uh-huh," Oliver replied. "Lots." Drawing back a space, he looked up. "How come you're all wet, Unca Liam?"

Grinning, Liam set the boy back from him. "I was out fighting that bear again, and it started raining in the middle of the battle."

Oliver breathed a sound of awe. "Really?"

"'Tis true," Liam said, and began toweling his hair.

"Wish I coulda seen it."

"You think so, hmm?"

The boy nodded vigorously.

With a chuckle, Liam ruffled his hair and then straightened.

"Oh," Oliver blurted. "Mama said to thank you for my stick."

"Did she?" Liam mused, remembering the night he had come into her chamber to leave it for Oliver.

"Uh-huh. Thank you, Unca Liam."

He smiled down at the boy. "I am glad it pleases you." He continued to the hearth, only to discover a certain grimness about those who sat before it. And at their center was seated a bedraggled Sir Gregory, also recently out of the rain.

Having received the knight's missive earlier in the week stating that he was healed of the wounds he had acquired during the raid, and announcing that during his protracted stay at Settling Castle he had won the hand of the lord's eldest daughter, Liam had not expected Sir Gregory to return to Ashlingford so soon, if at all. "So you are back from Settling," he said, savoring the warmth of the fire.

A shiver of cold shook Sir Gregory. "I arrived less than an hour ere you, Lord Fawke."

As at Thornemede, each time Liam heard his name linked with the title he had waited so long for, he felt an overwhelming urge to look behind him—as if he might discover his father there. As if Montgomery Fawke still lived. Lowering himself into the chair a servant brought for him, Liam said, "Unless you catch your death of cold, it looks as if you will live."

Those gathered around the fire exchanged knowing glances—except for Ivo, who sat silently fingering the chain of his crucifix. It was on Liam's tongue to demand an explanation for their peculiar behavior when Joslyn spoke up.

"Emma, would you take Oliver up to bed?" she asked.

"Of course."

Oliver groaned. "Wanna wait till dark."

"Nay, Oliver, 'tis time." Joslyn spoke firmly. "First a hug, and then off you go." She held out her arms to him.

Oliver glanced at Liam.

"Do as your mother says," Liam said, though as soon as the words were out he wondered how it had fallen to him to back Joslyn.

Heaving a hefty sigh, Oliver accepted her hug and looked again to Liam. "Tell me a story, Unca Liam?" he asked.

"Aye, but not tonight."

"When?"

"Tomorrow night, hmm?"

Oliver smiled. "A'right," he said, and followed Emma from the hall and up the stairs.

"Now I would know why you all sit here looking as if someone has died," Liam said. "Speak."

With naught to temper the serious set of his face, Sir Gregory leaned forward in his chair. "It has come, my lord," he said, his voice thick with foreboding. "The plague has arrived in England."

Liam's first thought was for Joslyn. Looking at where she sat across from him staring into the fire, he saw fear in her eyes. Doubtless, she was imagining losing everything dear to her: Oliver. Lord, were it not for their audience, he would take her in his arms, he thought. More than anything, he wanted to wipe away that fear.

"Did you not hear me, Lord Fawke?" Sir Gregory asked. "I said, the plague has come."

Liam shifted his gaze to the knight. He had known the disease would reach them eventually but had prayed for more time. "I heard you," Liam said. "What else do you know of it?"

Sinking back in his chair, the knight shrugged his weary shoulders. "There is not much to tell, really. Two days past, word reached Settling that it came in through Melcombe Regis at Dorset on a ship bearing a man stricken with it. Within days, a local died from it."

"Only one?"

"Nay. Several after him, and still others are dying now."

"Know you how many?"

Sir Gregory frowned. "Several, is all I was told."

As shown by the silence that followed, everyone in the hall was painfully aware of what this meant. Of those the plague struck, few survived. And those it overlooked were left with the painful loss of their loved ones. It was merciless, caring not whether one was noble or peasant, male or female, adult or child.

Liam thought ahead to the preparations that needed to be made. A physician must be found for Thornemede, more clerics to ease the dying, areas of quarantine designated, food supplies—

"'Tis God's wrath come upon us," Ivo said suddenly. "Divine retribution for our sins."

Instantly, a dozen pairs of fearful eyes looked to the priest, imploring guidance from a man incapable of guiding anyone. It nearly made Liam laugh. Strange, he thought, how fear had a way of leading astray those who were usually shrewd. They might as well look to the devil for salvation.

Basking in the attention that was so rarely given him, Ivo warmed to his role. "Sinners," he went on, his gaze touching first Liam and Joslyn before moving to the others. "They have brought this on themselves, angering God with their lies and deceptions, their greed and lust. Wicked, I say."

Though it was the same view the church embraced—that the plague was poured out by the hand of God—Liam knew Ivo was speaking more to him and Joslyn than to any of the others. In an effort to hold himself in his chair, that he would not leap out of it and do his uncle harm, he clenched his fists tighter.

"God will smite them all with the festering ill of the plague," Ivo continued. He looked heavenward. "Like leaves in autumn, the sinners will fall dead to the ground until His earth is cleansed of every last one of them—man, woman, *and child*."

The murmur of men went around the hearth, followed by the weeping of the women servants—most loudly those who were mothers.

Though Joslyn avoided his gaze, Liam saw the moisture gathering in her eyes. He looked across at Ivo. "Is it not your duty to counsel hope, priest?" he demanded.

Ivo draped his wrists over the chair arms and leaned back. "You would not have me lie, would you, William?" he asked. "'Tis true what I speak. You know it yourself. The dead will pile so deep there will not be enough ground in which to bury them."

Liam was not sure which angered him more, the

fear Ivo seemed determined to infect everyone with or his air of superiority as he reclined in the lord's high seat. Damnation, but the man was infuriating! However, before he could formulate a reply past the flurry of his emotions, Ivo had turned his attention elsewhere.

"Are you a sinner?" he demanded of the serving maid to his right.

The woman nodded.

"Have you children?"

A great glistening tear trickled down her face. "Two, Father."

Ivo slammed his palms on the arms of the chair. "Repent, I say—all of you—and mayhap God will spare your pitiful existence. *And* that of your children." As the serving maid fell to her knees beside him, mumbling incoherently, he swung his head around and looked from one person to the next until his gaze fell upon Joslyn. Long and thorough he considered her while she refused to look down, even though the weight of his gaze and the accusation in it must have made her wish to.

He wouldn't dare, Liam told himself. For all Ivo's animosity, he was too prudent to bring his accusations against Joslyn in the presence of the castle folk—most especially with Liam looking on.

"Are you a sinner, Joslyn Fawke?" Ivo finally asked.

The muscles in Liam's clenched fists strained. Ivo knew his bounds, and he had just come up against them. Certainly he would not cross them.

Though Joslyn's eyes widened, no words passed her lips.

"Aye, you are," Ivo said with certainty. "You lust

for the forbidden, your own husband's brother." He pointed to Liam. "Bastard though he is."

Ivo indeed dared, and in daring had gone too far.

Liam lunged out of his chair. This time he would do what should have been done years ago. He would wring the life out of the devil no matter the consequences. No matter the bloody church.

Seeing his nephew hurtling down upon him, Ivo screeched and fumbled backward in the chair, but there was nowhere for him to go.

With a snarl, Liam grasped his uncle by the neck of his robes, dragged him up out of the high seat, and flung him to the floor—ready to extract what was due him from this man who had made him suffer for so many years.

Ivo must have known his life was forfeit, for he played the priest no longer. Leaving his holy dignity among the rushes, he scrambled onto all fours, leapt to his feet, and from somewhere in his robes brought forth a wicked dagger. "Come on, bastard," he dared. "Come on!" With a maniacal laugh, he slashed the air before him.

Liam's own dagger pressed against his back where it was girded on his belt. He considered it but knew that only the feel of Ivo's neck beneath his hands would do. Stepping forward, he ducked the dagger thrust toward him and countered with a blow to his uncle's middle. Quick on his feet, Ivo sidestepped. Quicker, Liam swung his body right and landed an elbow to Ivo's gut.

Sucking in a breath, the priest stumbled back. "Send you to . . . hell for that," he gasped.

Liam moved in, his eagerness laying him open to the blade Ivo swept down upon him. Liam saw it coming but had only enough time to turn his shoulder to it and prevent it from entering his heart. Skittering down his arm, the blade opened his tunic and scored the flesh beneath.

The wound was minor, Liam told himself. He hardly felt it.

Triumphant, Ivo raised his dagger high as if to show everyone the blood that colored his blade.

Now Ivo had left himself open, and Liam took quick advantage of it. With one thrust of his body, he knocked the dagger from his uncle's hand, with another, he sent him down among the rushes again. Then he was upon him. His greater weight pinning Ivo, he reached for the priest's neck and closed his fingers around it.

Disbelief in his eyes, Ivo strained beneath Liam, and with his hands attempted to pry the vise from around his throat. But Liam was determined. Soon it would be over.

"Liam."

He did not hear Joslyn at first, with the blood pounding loudly through his ears.

Dropping to her knees, she gripped his arm. "Pray, Liam, do not," she beseeched him. "Do not do this."

He shifted his gaze from his uncle's hideously gaping mouth to Joslyn's, which trembled with fear.

She shook her head. "'Twill be the end of you," she whispered.

He didn't care. What had he to live for anyway? What better end to his life than to free himself—and Joslyn—of this devil?

"Please," she pleaded. The tears she had earlier denied began to fall. Suddenly, Liam realized that though he would regret allowing Ivo to live, his regret would be deeper yet did he kill his uncle with Joslyn looking on.

Turning from her, he stared hard at Ivo's bulging eyes, crimson face, and lolling tongue. Then he loosened his fingers and drew back.

Ivo's jaw worked uselessly until he finally managed to pull air into his lungs.

Liam was not finished. There was one thing he still had to do. He seized the chain with its gold jewel-encrusted crucifix from around his uncle's neck and wrenched it free. There was naught Ivo could do or say, only watch in horror as Liam flung his prized possession across the room and into the fire.

Then Liam stood and reached down to urge Joslyn to her feet. As she rose beside him, he saw gratitude and something else shining bright from her eyes, but there was no time to ponder it.

"You . . . " Ivo gasped. He managed to sit up.

"False priest," Liam said between gritted teeth. "You will leave Ashlingford this night. No more will I tolerate you." Gripping Joslyn's elbow, he turned her back toward the hearth.

"I will have you . . . have you excommunicated for this!" Ivo shouted. "You have laid hand to a holy man once too often, you spawn of the devil."

Liam turned to face him again. "And who will bear witness for you?" he asked.

Ivo indicated those who watched from the hearth. "Every one of them, you fool."

Liam looked back at the castle folk. Were they still loyal to him? he wondered. Or perhaps the question was whether or not they would risk the wrath of a God they believed already angry with them to stand

loyal to a man who was not—and would never be—
their lord.

They knew what he asked of them, and though
they were slow to respond, they turned away and
began dispersing. So they stood with him.

The steward had not moved from his place, however. He crossed his arms over his chest and stared at
Ivo a long moment before looking to Liam.

Having made it to his feet, Ivo started forward. "I
need only one witness," he said, as he pinned Sir
Hugh with his gaze. "Only one."

"What have you seen this eve, Sir Hugh?" Liam
asked.

"Only a man I thought to be a priest attack a baron
of King Edward and cut him," he replied. "Had I not
seen it with my own eyes, I would not have believed
it."

Liam felt the tension ease from Joslyn. The steward was simply enjoying himself, seeking retribution for these past weeks he had been forced
beneath Ivo's scrutiny. True, this would be the
extent of his indulgence, for Ivo's money had
earned him many friends in the church willing to
overlook his "little transgressions," but it made the
steward smile—and smile wider with Ivo's reaction
to it.

"To hell I damn you!" Ivo cursed. "Every last one
of you."

Liam pushed Joslyn toward the stairs. "Go to
Oliver," he said.

She complied without a word.

Liam looked back at his uncle.

In that moment, there was nothing about Ivo that
could be likened to God. Indeed, he looked all the

devil, with his hair strewn across his brow, his eyes like pits of burning tar, and his upper lip curled beneath his flared nostrils.

"I give you five minutes to take what is yours—and only yours," Liam said. "And if you are not gone by then, I will throw you out myself."

"Bastard," Ivo hissed. "I will see you dead for this."

"I am sure you will try," Liam said. He called for two knights to escort his uncle to retrieve his belongings.

Instantly, Ivo's demeanor changed. "'Tis raining!" he cried, stumbling back a step.

"Of course it is," Liam said. "We *are* in England."

"And 'tis night. You would not send a holy man—" As if remembering who it was he spoke to, Ivo amended his words. "You would not send a man out in such weather with darkness upon him?"

"I would," Liam said. "Do you wish to take your belongings with you or leave them behind?"

He had no choice, and he knew it. The ugliness rising on his face again, he stared a long moment at Liam. Then he located his dagger among the rushes, wiped its blade upon his robes, and fingered the mark left by his nephew's blood. "There will come another time," he warned, "and it will be the last."

Ignoring him, Liam addressed the two knights. "Do not turn your backs on him. I wish no more blood shed this eve."

With a nod, they motioned for Ivo to precede them up the stairs.

As the priest passed Liam, he veered toward the hearth.

Liam had known he would not leave without first attempting to reclaim his crucifix—or whatever was left of it. "Leave it!" he shouted.

"But 'tis my gold," Ivo said. "My jewels."

"No more. You now have four minutes left to you, *uncle*."

His color deepening, Ivo turned stiffly from the hearth and went up the stairs.

When he was gone from sight, Liam crossed to the serving maid who had fallen to her knees beside Ivo. He offered her a hand up, and timidly she accepted.

"Do not despair," he said.

Though fear still shone out of her eyes, she nodded.

Turning away, Liam called the steward to him. "Sir Hugh."

"My lord?" the man asked.

"What think you of a ride?"

Hugh arched a questioning eyebrow.

"If Ivo does not already have the coin, he will collect it ere he leaves," Liam explained.

The steward nodded. "I am not fond of the wet," he said, "but I do fancy a bit of fresh air."

Liam smiled. "Then follow him."

"And if he collects it, my lord?"

Despite the great amount involved, it was not worth a man's life, Liam thought, for in Ivo's state of mind he would not hesitate to murder. "If he collects it, follow him to his destination," he said, "and then return to Ashlingford. I will go for it myself."

Hugh inclined his head and left to do Liam's bidding.

*   *   *

Joslyn was kneeling beside Oliver's pallet, with Emma standing over her shoulder, when the door opened. She did not fear, though, for without turning she knew it was Liam come to her.

The old woman was the first to acknowledge him. "Ivo is gone?" she asked.

"Soon," Liam said.

"'Tis good," Emma murmured, "for now. But he will return."

Liam made no comment. "I would speak with Lady Joslyn alone," he said.

"You think it wise?" Emma asked.

Wise? Joslyn wondered. What worse could be said of her than what Ivo had accused her of in front of the castle folk? "Do not fret, Emma," she said. "It matters not what might be said of me."

With a sigh, the old woman tucked the blanket more securely around Oliver and pecked a kiss upon his smooth brow. Then she left them, closing the door behind her.

There was something so comforting in Liam's presence, Joslyn thought, as he drew closer. It nearly warmed the chill that news of the plague had caused to spread throughout her. Nearly, but not quite. Drawing a shaky breath, she said, "Will Oliver pay for my sins, Liam?"

His warm hand closed over her shoulder. "It is not by God's hand the plague has come, Joslyn," he said. "'Tis a sickness, that is all."

"Then even had I not sinned, my son might still be stricken?" She shook her head. "'Tis of no comfort, Liam. I might as well be the sinner I am."

Sliding his hand down her arm, he urged her to stand. "How have you sinned, Joslyn?" he asked. "You have not lain with me as Ivo believes."

Lord, how she wanted to turn into his arms and put her head on his shoulder, to accept the comfort he offered and for just a few moments forget what lay ahead.

"How, Joslyn?" Liam prodded.

Looking over her shoulder, she met his eyes. "By wanting you," she said with painful honesty. "And if that alone does not condemn me in the eyes of the church, then my allowing you to touch me—almost giving myself to you—does." She squeezed her eyes closed. "Through Maynard you are my brother, Liam."

Gently, he pulled her around to face him. "There is no blood between us," he pointed out. "Though you were wed to Maynard, with whom I shared a father, it does not make you of my flesh nor I of yours."

She looked into his eyes, which were lit by candlelight—green and deep as they searched her face. How she wanted to close the space between them and lean into his strength. To feel his arms come around her. To be loved. She shook her head. Had ever a greater fool of a woman been born? "But the laws of consanguinity say otherwise," she said. "We should not even be here in this chamber together."

Daring the laws of the church, Liam pulled her closer. "Such laws were originally intended for those of close blood ties," he said, "such as King Edward and his queen, who are cousins. The irony of it is that though they truly are related—and closely—still they were allowed to wed, and with the full blessing of the pope. All it took was enough gold to buy the law away. The laws are now only a means of lining the coffers of the church, especially with regards to those who are related only by marriage." He shook his head. "Nay, Joslyn, what we have done is not wrong."

Fleetingly, she wondered if it would be possible to buy dispensation that would free her to wed Liam as it had freed King Edward and Philippa. However, she quickly shoved the thought aside, for no good would come of such ponderings. "In my fear I am made foolish," she said, and looked back at Oliver. "I cannot lose him. He is all I have."

Liam pulled her chin back around. "He will be fine, Joslyn. I give you my word."

A sad smile tugged at her mouth. "How can you make such promises? No one knows whom the plague will choose to lay in the grave. It might even choose you, Liam . . . or me. It might take all of us."

With his thumb he traced the bow of her upper lip to the corner of her mouth. "I won't allow it to touch you, Joslyn," he said softly.

"But you do not know—"

Laying his fingers against her lips, he shook his head. "My word," he said.

And he always kept his word. . . .

Angling his head, Liam slid his fingers from her mouth to the undercurve of her jaw and kissed her fleetingly. "One day you will be mine, Joslyn," he murmured, then he drew back and turned to the door.

Joslyn ached to call him back to her—to bury

herself forever in his arms—but she had to let him go. When he was gone, she whispered into the terrible solitude of her chamber, "I love you, Liam Fawke."

19

"He knew I was following him, my lord," Hugh said. "He had to have known."

"He made no stops?"

"None. He rode directly to the abbey."

And he was probably this moment in audience with the abbot, Liam knew. What would be the result of that meeting? Would the abbot attempt to intervene on Ivo's behalf? "Return to the donjon and get some sleep, Hugh," he said. "'Twas a long night and day for you."

The man made no pretext of declining. Soaked through from the rain that still fell, dark shadows beneath his eyes from twenty or more hours of riding without stop, he nodded and tramped over the dank straw to go out through the stable doors. His departure blew in a gust of rain and fresh air that for a few moments masked the smell of horses before the door was pushed closed again.

For several minutes Liam stood silent with the

horses—his thoughts heavy upon Ivo—and then he pulled open the shuttered window and looked onto the bailey. It was empty of both beast and man, all having sought shelter on this second day of heavy rain.

As the news of the coming plague had spread rapidly among the castle folk and then to the outlying villages, Liam guessed that many men and women were spending their idle hours on their knees. If the plague swept over England as it had the Mediterranean lands, and most recently France, they had cause to pray: far more than the threat of a harvest spoiled by the rot of rain, the plague was to be taken seriously. However, as Liam knew from having followed its progress through the other countries it had ravaged, once the plague took hold on this island kingdom, prayers would soon turn to apathy. Some people would be so fatally resigned to death they would use what they believed to be their last living days to indulge in debauchery and excess; others would seek to escape by fleeing farther north. The result in both cases would be crops wasting in the fields and cattle left to wander untended over the countryside.

Liam could not allow that to happen, for in that direction lay ruin. The plague would pass, but not the devastation left in its wake if the villagers of Ashlingford stopped living in order to die. Whatever it took, he would keep them working so that when the worst was over they would have something left to them. It was important to establish areas of quarantine as early as possible. Though some scoffed at the idea, saying it was a useless measure—naught held back the dread disease—it was said by others that separating the sick from the well controlled its spread. But if quarantine did fail in preventing sickness, it had another use, Liam knew. Moving plague-stricken victims elsewhere helped to keep those who were well from brooding about those who were dying. This would help to suppress panic and hold people to the land longer than otherwise.

Aye, there was much work to be done at Ashlingford, Liam thought, and in the next instant was reminded that not only this barony needed to be secured but his own as well. Thornemede.

Wiping his hand across a face that had grown moist with the rain slanting through the window, Liam turned his thoughts to his own barony. Though he was confident he could lessen the impact of the plague on Ashlingford, what of Thornemede? In the past month of hard work he had made progress with the folk, especially those villagers he had worked side by side with in the fields, but still he was not accepted as their lord. If the plague struck before he gained their loyalty and trust, the cause of Thornemede would be lost— goaded further by his absences from the barony when he tended to his duties at Ashlingford. There could be no more fertile a ground for division and dissension.

Shoving a hand through his hair, Liam settled it at the back of his tense neck. Even now he ought to be riding to Thornemede, and would have done so had he not been waiting for Sir Hugh's return.

With a growl, he dropped his arm back to his side. If he had refused the king's offer of Thornemede and returned to the tournaments instead, none of this would have fallen to him. He would have started living his own life, setting a course for the years he had left to him.

Years without Joslyn. He let the thought slip in. Aye, had it gone different, he would not now know these feelings she roused in him: want, longing, a warmth he had never felt for any woman. It wasn't just desire, as he would like to believe. It went deeper than the animal in him. But how deep? His heart? Had Liam Fawke fallen in love with a woman forbidden him? As soon as the question came into his mind, he tossed it out. Impossible. It wasn't in him to love.

Thrusting the shutters closed, he strode from the stables and out into the rain. At the donjon, he was once again received with a towel. Leaving it draped over his shoulders, he crossed the hall.

"We leave on the half hour," he called to the Thornemede knights, who sat warming themselves with mulled wine and a roaring fire. Though he continued to the stairs without pause, he could hear the grumbling of the men who had accompanied him to Ashlingford. Doubtless, none of them saw a good reason for leaving on a rainy day that was already drawing to a close.

Liam ascended to his chamber, opened the door, and stepped inside.

It was a small room and not well lit, but it was the place where he had laid his head since childhood—and where he had kept the Ashlingford monies safe from Maynard when he had managed the barony for him.

After changing into dry garments, Liam pulled the bed away from the wall and lowered himself to his haunches. Loosening a nondescript block of stone from the others, he reached in the wall to drag out the coffer containing the bulk of what remained of Ashlingford's revenues. It was this Maynard had sought when he had followed Liam up to his chamber that fateful evening, but fortunately for Ashlingford, Liam had paid his brother out of coins he kept in the chest that held his clothes. Unfortunately, there had been too large a sum there, a sum that would shortly be in Ivo's hands if it was not there already.

He unlocked the coffer, counted out enough to pay the accounts of the barony for the next month, and placed the coins in a leather pouch. As he must leave this day, it would be Hugh's to dispense, but Liam knew he needn't worry over the steward's honesty. The monies would go where they were owed, allowing Liam to return to Thornemede to continue his work there.

Liam locked the chest and lifted it back into its vault.

"Unca Liam?" A small uncertain voice spoke from the doorway.

He had been careless, Liam thought, as he looked around. He could not remember having closed the door, let alone securing it. Maynard's death and Ivo's removal from Ashlingford yesterday had lulled him into a false sense of security. "What are you doing up here, Oliver?"

The little boy took a single step forward. "Lookin' for you," he said, and tipped his head to the side. "What's that?" He pointed to the hole in the wall that had yet to be filled.

What was he to tell him? Liam wondered: the

truth—that this was where all the wealth of Ashlingford was hidden—or a lie that would ease little of the boy's curiosity? He beckoned. "Come closer, Oliver."

The child hurried forward eagerly. "Can I see?" he asked, already bending down to peer into the hole.

"Of course."

"There's a box in there!"

"That's right, a secret box."

Bent over, his hands upon his knees, Oliver looked back at Liam. "A secret?" he whispered with anticipation.

Liam nodded. "Have you ever had a secret, Oliver?"

He thought a long moment and then beamed. "Uh-huh."

"What was it?"

Wrinkling his nose, Oliver shook his head. "Can't tell, 'cause it's a secret."

That was good, Liam thought, though was it good enough? After all, Oliver was just a child. He could reveal something as important as this without realizing it.

He could take the coffer with him to Thornemede, Liam supposed, but with the next thought he decided it wasn't necessary. Now that he no longer had either Maynard or Ivo to worry over, the measures he had previously taken were not so pressing. Still . . .

"I've a secret to share with you, Oliver," Liam said. "Can you keep it?"

"Uh-huh. Keep it good."

Liam smiled. "This is a special hiding place." He nodded to the hole. "Only I know of it—and now you. It's important that no one else learns of it. Do you understand?"

"Uh-huh. But why?"

"Because there are some who might wish to take from us what is hidden here. We don't want that, do we?"

Vigorously, Oliver shook his head. "Uh-uh," he said, then asked, "What's in the box, Unca Liam?"

"Coins, Oliver. Money that will one day be yours when you are a grown man."

Oliver's eyebrows shot up. "Lotsa money?"

"Aye."

After a thoughtful moment, Oliver said, "Emma's got money too. I seen it."

"I'm sure she does," Liam said. What little came the woman's way, she had always been careful to hold on to. "Now, have I your word that this secret shall remain between only us?"

"Uh-huh. Promise."

Liam ruffled Oliver's hair, then reached beside him and lifted the stone. Under Oliver's intense scrutiny, he fitted it into place.

"If anything should ever happen to me," Liam said as he stood, "you may tell your mother of our secret." It was actually good that Oliver had come upon him, he thought, for till now he had entrusted no one with the location of Ashlingford's wealth.

Oliver frowned. "What's gonna happen to you, Unca Liam?"

Straightening, Liam pushed the bed back into place. "Naught that I know of, but if your mother should need coin and I am not here to give it to her, I wish you to bring her to this chamber and show her the stone. Will you do that for me?"

Oliver nodded. "You not leavin' again, are you, Unca Liam?"

There was such concern in his eyes that Liam felt as if he were betraying the boy. Still, there was little he could do. He had to leave. Bending down, he said, "I'm afraid so. My own barony needs tending to."

Oliver looked down. "But you promised," he mumbled.

Liam cupped a hand over his shoulder. "Promised?"

Oliver's eyes were filled with tears when he looked up. "My story, Unca Liam . . .'member?"

He hadn't—and felt like an unfeeling fool. "Ah, about the bear."

Oliver nodded, hope replacing the tears in his eyes.

How he wanted to keep his word to him, Liam thought. But he couldn't. "I'm sorry, Oliver," he said. "If I could, I would stay and tell you the story, but I cannot. I must leave today."

"Don' want you to go," Oliver said. Lowering his head, he stared at his hands. "Want you to stay."

"I will be back, and when I return, I'll tell you the story, hmm?"

From beneath his sweeping lashes, Oliver regarded Liam a long moment. Then, unexpectedly, he stepped forward and put his little arms around him. "A'right, Unca Liam," he said, trying very hard to be brave.

Feeling nearly as awkward as that first time Oliver had inched his way onto his lap, Liam was slow to respond. But then he wrapped his arms around the little boy.

"Love you, Unca Liam." Oliver spoke into Liam's chest.

Liam felt his heart opening, after having been closed a very long time. "I love you too, Oliver," he said.

The little boy pulled back. "And my mama?" he asked, his eyes growing wide. "You love her too?"

Not sure whether or not it was true, but knowing the boy needed it affirmed, Liam nodded.

Oliver beamed.

Liam scooped him up and settled him in the bend of his arm. It was time to leave. "You will wave me away?" he asked as he crossed the chamber.

"Aye." Oliver draped an arm around his neck. "Till I can't see you no more."

Liam smiled. Out in the dim corridor, he pulled the door closed and went down two floors to the great hall where he found the Thornemede knights awaiting him.

"Where is your mother?" Liam asked.

"With Cook," Oliver said. "Why?"

"I should also bid her farewell, don't you think?"

Oliver nodded.

Halfway across the hall, Liam was stopped by the appearance of Emma.

"I was wondering where you'd gotten to, Oliver," she said, wagging a finger at him. "Found your Uncle Liam, did you?"

"Aye, an' he told me a secret."

Liam tensed.

"Ah," Emma replied. "Then you know you cannot tell it, don't you?"

"Can't tell." To demonstrate, Oliver pressed his lips tightly together.

Emma chuckled. "Come, my boy." She reached to take him from Liam. "No doubt your uncle has some tasks to tend to ere he rides for Thornemede."

The old woman was a godsend, Liam thought, as he handed Oliver into her arms, for now he could have a few minutes alone with Joslyn.

"Unca Liam wants me to wave him away," Oliver protested. "Don' you?" He looked back at Liam.

"When I am ready to leave," he said. "Soon."

Stepping past them, Liam walked from the hall into the kitchens. However, Joslyn was nowhere to be seen among the haze of heat hanging over the large room. "Where is the Lady Joslyn?" he asked.

"Gone below, my lord," a kitchen maid answered.

"Aye, and in quite a dither," Cook added.

Liam frowned. "Something is amiss?"

The cook scowled. "Only what she makes it to be. Imagine, gettin' upset over the leavin's of a rat." He nodded to a sack of flour poured out onto a nearby table. "You'd think she'd never seen 'em before."

It was commonplace for rodents and insects to find their way into the stores of the cellar, but Liam could understand Joslyn's concern. Though no one truly knew how the plague spread, one thing was certain: Where there was uncleanliness, and an abundance of rodents to feed on the filth, the plague took the most lives.

Turning away, Liam left the kitchens and descended the steps to the cellar. He heard Joslyn before he saw her, her breathing heavy as if she labored. Skirting barrels of untapped ale, he found her among the sacks of grain.

"Joslyn," he said as he advanced on her.

So intent was Joslyn on restacking the sacks away from the wall that she did not hear Liam or sense his nearness as she usually did these days. However, the next time he called to her she heard him. Flushed from exertion, she swung around. "I did not hear you come down," she said.

Liam lifted the sack she held from her and, in doing so, brushed his fingers across her forearms. "You ought not to be lifting these," he said, and laid the flour atop the new pile.

The brief contact caused Joslyn's pulse to accelerate. Trying to calm it, she busied her hands with the veil on her head, which had slipped sideways. "The rats are getting into the grain," she said.

"And you thought you would chase them out?"

Joslyn smoothed her hands down her skirts and looked up at Liam. "With the grain away from the wall, they have no place to hide. 'Tis how I kept them from the stores at Rosemoor—that and a dozen cats, of course."

Liam's eyes drifted to her mouth. "A good thought," he mused, "but you needn't do it yourself. I will send some men down to help you."

What did he intend? Joslyn wondered. To kiss her again? "We will also need more cats." She spoke far too quickly.

His gaze steady on her mouth, he nodded. "I'm sure they can be found." Then, to her surprise, he lifted a hand and brushed his thumb beneath her bottom lip. "You are working too hard, Joslyn," he said, showing her the dark smudge she had not known she wore on her face.

Having believed Liam's intentions quite different from what they had turned out to be, Joslyn nearly laughed at herself—and might have anyway, had she not been swept with sudden realization. "You are leaving," she said.

He lowered his arm back to his side. "I am."

"But you have been here hardly more than a day."

"Aye, but if word of the plague has not already reached Thornemede, it will soon. I am needed there."

What Joslyn wanted to say was that he was needed here too, but that would not do. Instead, she pretended a calm she did not feel. "Night is nearing. Can you not leave come morning?"

He shook his head. "I should have left hours ago."

Gone so soon. . . . But maybe it was better, Joslyn told herself, for otherwise her sin might be all the greater.

"I will return in a fortnight," Liam said. "Should you need to send me a message, you may do so through Sir Hugh's man."

"I will," Joslyn said, though she could not imagine what she might need to apprise him of.

Liam lifted a purse from his belt. "Sir Hugh sleeps now," he said. "When he awakens, I would have you give him this."

Joslyn accepted the purse from Liam.

"For the month's expenditures," Liam explained.

She looked down at the purse. From its weight, it held a good deal of money. "I will give it to him."

There followed a long silence, broken only when Liam finally spoke. "You are frightened."

Joslyn sighed. Never had she been much good at hiding her feelings. Tilting her head back, she met his gaze. "Do you realize we do not even have a priest to lay to rest those who will die?" she asked.

Liam nodded. "I have told Sir Hugh to send for Father Warren. Once he learns Ivo has gone from Ashlingford, I am certain he will return."

It was something, at least. Joslyn forced a smile. "I thank you."

Frowning, he searched her face long and hard, then reached forward and caught her hand in his. "Promise me something, Joslyn," he said.

Stirring softly—uncertainly—she looked into his eyes, to find a tenderness there she would not have thought possible had she not seen it for herself. What did it mean? "Aye?" she asked.

Liam bent his head near hers. "Promise me you will be strong," he said. "Do you allow the people of Ashlingford to know your fear, their own fear will be that much greater. You are their lady now, and in the months to come they will look to you whenever their faith wavers. You must be strong for them—and for Oliver. Can you do that for me?"

Realizing her love for him was far greater than her fear, Joslyn nodded. "For you, I will do it."

Emotions flickered in the depths of his eyes. "Do you love me, Joslyn?" he asked.

She knew she ought to be ashamed to have such a question put to her, but it seemed a natural thing for him to ask. She nodded.

Drawing a deep breath, Liam leaned forward and pressed his lips to her brow. "Do not forget your promise to me," he said, and turned away.

Liam looked back. It was something he'd never done when riding away from Ashlingford—no doubt a superstition of his Irish forebears that ran through his blood—but the urge was too strong to deny.

Did she watch him? he wondered as he picked out the donjon rising above the castle walls. From her chamber did she look out across the bailey to the land beyond where he and his men rode? Or was she still in the cellar crying the tears he had known she would cry?

Feeling an ache deep in his center, Liam turned his mount toward Thornemede.

20

The plague had entered England from the south, where most of the people who had left Thornemede had gone. Now they eagerly turned their feet north to Thornemede again, in hopes of escaping the dread sickness.

But they would not escape, Liam knew, for the plague was steadily working its way northward, and it was only a matter of time before it reached them. When it did, the difficulty would be in holding people to the land when they wanted to flee farther north.

In the meantime, Liam kept the villeins occupied in the fields. Because they had been neglected, there was a great deal of plowing to be done if the yield of the land was to increase. Then there were the villeins' own small plots and the communal village strips to be tended. The crops would be small, Liam knew, providing scarce sustenance throughout the winter to come. Still, the people would not starve, for Liam would provide for their needs. He had made them that promise and would keep it even if it meant spending every last coin he had left.

Liam laid aside his quill, and read through the missive he intended to send to Sir Hugh. The steward reported that all was progressing well at Ashlingford, so Liam had decided against returning when he had said. He would instead remain at Thornemede another week, to Lammas, the day that marked the beginning of harvest. This way he could assure himself that those who had recently returned to the barony were settled in and knew their places. Always, he felt it was better to assert his authority sooner than later.

Liam rolled the parchment, added some melted wax, and pressed it with his signet ring to seal the document closed. Then he called to Sir Hugh's messenger, who had sat patiently this past half hour awaiting his response.

The man hurried to Liam's side and left the hall moments later.

Liam stood and in that moment felt an ache in every limb. Though he had always prided himself on knowing the land as well as those who worked it for him, never had he toiled so hard in his life. With nearly every daylight hour spent in the fields, either supervising the work or doing it himself, there was hardly time to sleep. And he could not rest now.

He stepped out of the donjon and into the uncertain sunlight of a day that wished to rain but could not quite squeeze the moisture from its scattered clouds.

They had been fortunate these past weeks, Liam reflected. Whereas other parts of England continued to suffer unusually heavy rainfall, by the time the clouds converged upon this region, there was usually not much rain left in them. Had there been, the coming harvest would assuredly be one of rot. As Liam was depending on the grain he could purchase from Ashlingford to fill his stores for the coming winter, the weather was as much a concern for Thornemede as it was for the other barony.

With another six hours remaining of daylight, Liam struck out across the bailey.

"My lord." A woman acknowledged him as she approached.

It was Maeve, the woman he had selected to care for Maynard's children. Of a kind and generous nature, she had accepted them as if they were her own and they had taken equally to her—especially little Gertrude.

Liam inclined his head and crossed to the stables, where a squire held his mount in readiness for him. He swung himself into the saddle.

"You would like company, my lord?" the squire asked, indicating his own horse, tethered nearby.

"Nay, I will not be needing you," Liam said. "The remainder of the day is yours." Guiding his mount forward, he proceeded toward the open portcullis and, as he approached, caught the eye of Gunter, the captain of the guard, where he stood conversing with one of his men.

Liam stared at him, and after a moment's hesitation the man nodded his head in acknowledgment of the lord of Thornemede.

It was progress. Though Gunter continued to put up a stubborn fight to maintain his dislike for the Irish bastard now made his lord, every day saw him lose just a bit more ground.

Liam turned his thoughts back to the barony. More time, he told himself. That was all he needed. But would the plague deny him? Walking his horse over the drawbridge, he set off across Thornemede land. His land.

"I am sorry, my lady," Sir Hugh said, upon reading Liam's message that eve. "But 'tis only another sennight, after all."

Beside him, Father Warren offered her his sympathetic gaze.

The priest understood more than the steward what Liam's delay meant to her, Joslyn thought, for just a week past she had sought him out to confess her love for Liam. However, instead of thundering condemning words upon her head as Ivo would have done, he had listened and, when she was finished, assured her that all would come right in the end. What he had meant, Joslyn had not understood, but she had been too relieved by unburdening herself to ask for an explanation.

She sighed. Only this noon she had received a message that her brother, Richard, was returned to Rosemoor. At last, he and her father had set aside their differences that together they could deal with whatever effects the plague might have on the village and manor when it spread there. With this wonderful news in hand, Joslyn had spent the past hours feeling light as a puff of air, but what had lifted her even higher was her belief that Liam was returning to Ashlingford on the morrow. But no more.

Joslyn passed the parchment back to the steward

and turned away. What was she to tell Oliver? she wondered. All day long, up until this eve when she had put him down, he had spoken of naught else but the return of his Unca Liam and the bear tale he had waited a "hundred years" to hear. How was she to tell him he must now wait another fifty years—or, in her time, a sennight? Lord, she herself ached at the thought of waiting yet another week to see Liam again. Another week!

Her feet feeling as if shod in lead, Joslyn mounted the stairs. In the morn, she would break the news to Oliver.

"My lady!" Emma gasped, having appeared without warning upon the stairs above Joslyn.

She should have heard the woman coming, Joslyn knew, but her mind had been elsewhere. "Something is wrong?" she asked, noticing the high color on the old woman's cheekbones and her quickened breathing.

"Naught amiss, my lady," Emma said, looking down to watch her hands as she brushed imaginary lint from her skirts. "I just . . . just thought I would sneak myself something to eat ere bedding down."

How odd, Joslyn thought—not only the rush Emma was in but that she came down to nibble something before retiring for the night. It was not at all like her.

Curiosity and suspicion mingling, Joslyn said, "If you would like, I will join you."

"Of course I would like it," Emma said, "but I can see you are tired." She shook her head. "Nay, Lady Joslyn, you ought to be in bed, not gabbing with an old woman like me."

Joslyn nearly pressed it, but then decided it would

only turn Emma's suspicion back on her. "Aye, you are right," she said, continuing up the stairs. "I am quite spent. Good eve, then."

"Good eve," Emma echoed, and descended past Joslyn to the hall.

Once the woman was out of sight, Joslyn paused and turned around. There she waited a long moment—listening—and then started down again.

The kitchens were dark, as was the cellar, when Joslyn went to check the door that led down into it. Had the old woman gone to the garden then? she wondered. What would she be doing outside in the middle of night?

Joslyn's heart sped as she tiptoed farther down the corridor to the outside door, which she found was not seated in the jamb.

She released her held breath. Aye, Emma had left the donjon. But why? Leaning forward, Joslyn placed her ear to the crack of the door and listened. Suddenly, the sound of clinking coins reached her ears. She stilled.

"That is all?" a male voice hissed.

"For now." Emma's soft voice reached Joslyn's ears.

"You old bitch," the man said louder. "I ought to—"

"Aye, do it, Ivo. Do it and let me watch from heaven your descent into hell."

Fear shot up Joslyn's spine. Ivo had returned. Lord, how had he gained the castle walls without being seen? Had Emma let him in?

"Heaven?" Ivo scoffed. "You are no more destined there than the Irish bastard is."

"And you think you are? You delude yourself, dear

Ivo, for 'tis the devil who will take you, not the Lord. And I pray God it will be soon."

A slap upon flesh resounded through the garden. Though Emma made no sound, Joslyn knew Ivo had struck her. Anger firing her, she seized hold of the door handle.

"I am tired of your blackmail, you—" Ivo's voice broke off as the door creaked wide and slammed against the inner wall.

"Do you lay another hand to her, I will call the guard," Joslyn warned as she stepped out into the moonlight.

"Ah, Lady Joslyn," Ivo said, his shadow breaking from Emma's as he stepped forward. "I was thinking what a pity it would be if I did not see you ere I departed."

Joslyn hurried down the path toward him.

"Nay, Lady Joslyn," Emma called to her, "return to the donjon! Ivo is now leaving."

It was a warning Joslyn should have heeded, for a moment later Ivo lunged forward and caught her to him with a blade in hand. Pressing it to her throat, he put his mouth to her ear and said, "You have failed me, Lady Joslyn, but more, you have failed your son. Do you know the price of failure? God's price?"

Joslyn strained to free herself. "Let me go, false priest!" she demanded.

He tightened his arm around her. "You are spending far too much time with that bastard between your legs, my dear," he said. "Why, I could swear it was he who just spoke out of your mouth. False priest indeed."

"Release me!"

His lips touched her ear. "But I am not done with you," he said.

Repulsed, Joslyn raised her foot high. "Aye, you are," she said, and stamped down on his instep.

A gust of breath expelled from Ivo's mouth, followed by the curses of an ungodly man. Then the point of the blade pierced Joslyn's skin.

She cried out with the pain. Was it the great vein he had cut? she wondered frantically as she felt blood trickle down her skin. Would her life be severed from her as Ivo had severed it from the brigand Liam had attempted to coax the truth from all those weeks past?

"Release her, Ivo," Emma commanded, appearing beside them, "else I swear you will see no more of your precious coin."

"As meager as you dole it out, I cannot say that worries me, Emma."

"I will give it all to you," she said, turning desperate. "Release her and I will fetch it now. I swear."

He sighed. "How sweet your pleading to my ears, Emma. Do continue."

She gripped his arm that still held the blade against Joslyn's neck. "And the writings. I will give those to you as well."

"The writings?" he repeated. "But you told me they were elsewhere, Emma." He tut-tutted. "Now what am I to believe?"

A myriad of questions eclipsing her pain, Joslyn waded through the puzzle that was being spoken around her. The coin. Was it that which Maynard had stolen from Ashlingford? If so, how had it come into the old woman's hands? And what writings did she speak of? Joslyn had thought Emma did not know how to write.

"Fetch them," Ivo said. "The coin . . . *and* the writings."

"And you will release Lady Joslyn unharmed?"

"Always looking for assurances, aren't you, fool woman?"

Emma nodded. "Always."

He chuckled. "Aye, I give you my word."

Turning toward the donjon, Emma hurried down the path.

"Your word!" Joslyn scoffed. "You will slit both our throats once you have that which you seek."

"As I said, the old woman is a fool." He lifted his head and called across the garden. "Hurry, Emma. I grow impatient."

"Nay!" Joslyn cried out. "Do not, Emma. He will—" Unexpected light straining into the garden stole the rest of her words.

"What goes?" a gruff voice demanded from the doorway. Sir Hugh.

As Ivo wrenched Joslyn around to act as his shield, Emma let out a cry of dismay and stumbled to a halt before the steward and Father Warren, who stood behind him.

"Ivo!" Hugh said, recognizing him even in the shadows.

"The old hag has something to retrieve for me," Ivo said. "Let her past, and when she returns I will be on my way."

Sir Hugh's eyes narrowed.

"Pray, Sir Hugh," Emma pleaded. "He will kill Lady Joslyn, do you not allow me to bring him what he asks for."

Pushing past the steward, Father Warren stepped down into the garden. "How can you threaten death, garbed in the raiments of the holy church?" he demanded.

"Ah, so the little priest is returned to Ashlingford," Ivo said with a sneer.

Ignoring the taunt, Father Warren demanded, "Unhand Lady Joslyn."

"And if I do not?"

"'Tis the bishop you will answer to for your ungodly behavior."

Ivo chuckled derisively. "You think me a fool to believe you will not go to him anyway? Nay, Father Warren, I am not leaving without that which belongs to me. Fetch it, Emma."

A long silence followed, and then Sir Hugh finally said, "Bring him what he asks for."

His words caused Ivo to relax his hold on Joslyn a bit, but it was enough for her to take advantage of it. Spinning around, she brought her knee up into his groin.

Ivo's tormented cry split the air a moment before he lurched backward.

Released, Joslyn jumped back from him.

"Bitch!" Ivo groaned, his face contorted with pain.

"You are a disgrace, *Father* Ivo," Joslyn said, hating him more with every breath she took. "A pestilence upon the church. A degenerate. A—"

"Lady Joslyn," Hugh called to her, "stand back!"

Aye, it was foolish what she did, she realized. At any moment Ivo could recover sufficiently to attack her again. However, the warning came almost too late.

Having dragged himself upright, Ivo lifted his dagger and charged her.

But Sir Hugh reached Joslyn first. Thrusting her

aside, he swept his weapon in an arc before him. An instant later, he was rewarded by Ivo's yell of pain.

It all happened too suddenly for Joslyn to determine the extent of the priest's injury, but she glimpsed his stunned face a moment before he turned and ran.

Sir Hugh gave chase. He turned out of the garden, shouting to alert the guards of the intruder in their midst.

Joslyn would have followed if not for Emma and Father Warren's sudden appearance at her side.

"My lady, are you well?" the old woman asked.

Joslyn touched the wound at the side of her neck. "I am. Fortunately, 'twould seem Sir Hugh is as deft with a dagger as he is with those numbers of his."

Emma cupped a hand beneath Joslyn's elbow. "Come. I will tend to your cut," she said.

Joslyn shook her head. "I will await Sir Hugh's return."

As if the old woman knew it was an argument she could not win, she dropped her hand.

The steward reappeared shortly to an audience swelled by the ranks of household servants, who had come out of the donjon to discover the cause of the commotion.

"You have captured him?" Joslyn asked.

Sir Hugh looked regretful. "I am sorry, my lady. He has escaped."

"Escaped?"

"He scaled the wall ere I or the any of the men-at-arms could reach him."

"But he was wounded."

"Aye, I cut his arm, but not deeply."

Fearful, Joslyn said, "He will return."

"Not if he is found. I have sent a dozen men-at-arms after him."

Joslyn's relief was fleeting. They would not find him, she knew. With Liam, perhaps, but not without him.

"Let us go to the kitchens and I will tend your wound," Emma said again.

For the first time, Joslyn looked across at the servants, who made no attempt to hide their concern for her. They cared, she realized, joy momentarily supplanting pain and fear. Somewhere along the way they had come to accept her, which meant they would one day accept Oliver as their lord. "You may all return to your beds," she said.

As they drifted out of the garden, Joslyn returned her gaze to the old woman. "We should talk," she said.

Emma nodded. "We should."

"How is it you had the coin, Emma?" Joslyn asked.

"The coin?" Sir Hugh repeated.

As he was trusted by Liam, Joslyn had asked him—and Father Warren, as well—to remain while she and Emma spoke.

"The coin my husband stole from Ashlingford ere he died," Joslyn explained. It felt bitter on her tongue to call Maynard that.

"And 'tis you who had it, Emma?" Hugh asked, sudden interest in his voice.

The old woman put the lid on the salve she had applied to Joslyn's wound. "Still do," she replied. "Most of it. 'Tis what Ivo came for."

In the lighted kitchen room, Joslyn noticed for the

first time the flushed imprint of Ivo's hand across Emma's face. It was faded somewhat, but as it was still visible, she knew he must have struck her hard.

"How did you come by the coin?" Sir Hugh asked.

Emma sighed. "I've a terrible penchant for listening when I should not. When I knew Maynard had fallen from his horse and was dying"—she paused to swallow hard—"I went directly to him. As I approached his chamber, I heard him and Ivo talking about the coin. I stood without until Maynard told Ivo where he had hidden it."

"And where was that?" Sir Hugh asked.

"In the chapel of the old village."

Joslyn frowned. "The old village?"

It was Father Warren who answered her query. "Aye. A score of years past, a fire went through the village of Belle Glen and burnt all to the ground save the chapel. Even though it was fired as well, the walls remained standing."

"Where in the chapel, Emma?" Hugh pressed.

She looked past Joslyn to where he sat. "Under the floorboards beneath the altar."

"Of course," he murmured, then said, "The chapel is not far from the ravine Maynard fell into."

"And when Ivo rode immediately to Rosemoor with Liam, you went to the chapel and retrieved it yourself," Joslyn concluded.

"I did," Emma admitted, "and would eventually have returned it to Liam, had I not seen a better use for it."

"Protecting Liam and me," Joslyn said knowingly.

Emma closed her lids briefly over her weary eyes. "God will not reward me for it," she said, then looked back at Joslyn, "but that is what I did. I could not allow Ivo to carry tales to the bishop of sins you had not committed. He is an evil man, Lady Joslyn. Every day that passes he grows closer to the devil and farther from God."

"Where is the coin?" Sir Hugh asked.

"Sewn into the hems of Lady Anya's old gowns," Emma said. "That is where you will find it." She turned to bandaging Joslyn's throat.

Until now, Joslyn had completely forgotten the coin that had struck her brow the day she had donned one of Anya's gowns. Emma must have overlooked it when she had emptied the hem for Joslyn to use the garment.

"What of the writings, Emma?" Joslyn asked. "What were you referring to?"

Emma's laughter was dry. "That is an old piece of our past," she said. "Far too old to mention."

"But important enough that Ivo wanted it."

Emma shrugged. "Not only is Ivo ungodly, he is a superstitious old fool."

"Still, I would know," Joslyn pressed.

Standing back, Emma surveyed her work, then nodded. "That should do," she said.

"Emma." Joslyn tried again.

The old woman shook her head. "I am sorry, my lady. That remains between Ivo and me."

Joslyn knew she was meddling, but whatever the writings consisted of, they had seemed as important to Ivo as the money had been—perhaps more.

Sir Hugh scraped his stool back. "I must prepare a missive to send to Lord Fawke straightaway," he said.

"Whatever for?" Emma asked. "He is coming on the morrow."

Joslyn shook her head. "Nay, he is not. He sent

word that it will be yet another sennight ere he returns to Ashlingford." She looked around at the steward. "You needn't write, Sir Hugh. On the morrow I will myself take word to him of what has happened."

"You?" he asked.

"Aye, if he will not come to Ashlingford, I will go to Thornemede."

"Nay, lady, if Ivo is not found this eve, he may still be out there on the morrow."

"Then I will need a sizable escort, won't I? Would you arrange it for me?"

"The baron will not like this. I am certain he would prefer that you remain at Ashlingford."

"You are right," Joslyn agreed, "but still I am going."

Hugh sighed. "I will arrange an escort for you, lady," he said, and strode toward the door.

"And I must prepare a report for the bishop," Father Warren announced. "I am sure he will be most interested in knowing how Father Ivo represents the holy church." He stepped down from his stool and followed the steward.

Would it do any good? Joslyn wondered fleetingly. Then she remembered what she had yet to say to the steward. "Sir Hugh!" she called after him.

He paused with his hand on the door. "My lady?"

"I have not thanked you for saving my life. Know that I am indebted to you. If . . . if ever there is anything I can do to repay you, you will tell me, won't you?"

He was slow in answering, but when he did, there was emotion in his voice. "That I was given the opportunity to save your life is payment enough," he said. "'Tis not often a knight who has taken up books for his living is able to experience again that which made him first turn to the sword."

There was longing in the words he spoke, as if it was not his choice to post entries and work numbers the rest of his life. Did his true desire lie in the weapons of warfare and the thundering of a horse beneath him? "Still, I am indebted," Joslyn said.

He nodded, opened the door, and stepped out into the corridor, with Father Warren following close behind.

Joslyn looked back at Emma. "I also must thank you for protecting Liam and me."

A wistful expression on her face, Emma lifted a hand and brushed the hair back from Joslyn's brow. "I knew love once," she said, "or at least thought I did. I understand, Lady Joslyn." Then she turned, gathered the pot of salve and strips of linen from the table behind them, and left the room.

Thoughtful, Joslyn extinguished the torches and went up to her chamber. A short time later, she lowered her head to her pillow and lay on her side facing the wall, staring at the familiar shadows. Ere the first light tumbled through the window, she would be on her way to Thornemede to deliver Liam news of what had occurred here this night—but that was not all. She knew it was probably a mistake for her to go, but when her life had hung on the end of Ivo's blade she had known for certain how terrible it would be not ever to have known Liam as a woman. Though the laws of the church sought to keep them apart, just once she would surrender to him, that the rest of her life she would have the memory to pass the lonely years.

Dragging the covers up around her shoulders, Joslyn closed her eyes and for the first time in weeks dropped into sleep without the usual hours of tossing and twisting among the bedclothes.

21

Joslyn Fawke rode at the center of the men, her plaited hair having escaped the covering of her veil. Before her sat the small figure of Oliver.

Lord, what was she doing here? Liam wondered. What had made her leave the safety and comfort of Ashlingford to journey to backward little Thornemede? Surely she did not come only because he had sent word he would not be returning to Ashlingford for another sennight. Or did she? After all, she had admitted to loving him.

Liam slowed his horse as the riders neared.

"Lord Fawke," an Ashlingford knight called to him, "we bring the Lady Joslyn and her son to you."

Keeping his gaze from her even though he knew she sought his, Liam asked, "And who gave you such orders?"

"I did," Joslyn spoke up, guiding her palfrey forward.

She *was* lady of Ashlingford, Liam conceded, and

therefore no one could prevent her from making the ride. He looked across at her and only then noticed the bandage about her neck.

In spite of his concern, he felt her presence begin to move through him. Her brilliant amber eyes spoke to him of things they should not, and her softly parted lips invited him to taste them. She was more beautiful than the flower she smelled of. And he was the thorn to her rose . . .

God's wounds! Liam cursed himself. It mattered not how long he stayed away from her, still this hunger grew. Taking firm hold of his feelings, he asked, "For what reason have you come, Lady Joslyn?"

Oliver chose that moment to stir in his mother's arms. Lifting his head from her breast, he looked across at Liam, and a moment later reached out to him. "Unca Liam," he said, his small voice roughened by sleep. "I wanna ride with you."

Liam was struck with wonder. Never would he have believed there would come a time when Oliver would reach to him with those same wanting arms he reached out to his mother. Lord, never had he believed anyone would! He looked at Joslyn and, receiving her nod, guided his horse alongside them.

The mere brush of his leg against hers caused the fires to stir within him as Liam lifted Oliver from her. A moment later, small arms went around his neck.

"Missed you," Oliver said. "You miss me?"

Liam could not help but smile. "I did," he admitted.

Oliver drew back. A pleased expression on his face, he asked, "Gonna tell me my story now?"

"Here?" Liam asked. "Now?"

The little boy bobbed his head up and down.

What was happening to him? Liam wondered. He was actually entertaining the thought of relating his tale to a child in the presence of Ashlingford's fighting men. "Very well," he agreed, ignoring the questioning gazes that fell upon him. "I will tell you on the ride back to the castle."

Beaming, Oliver looked past him. "That your castle?" he asked.

"Aye, 'tis Thornemede."

Oliver considered it a bit longer, then crinkled his nose. "It's big, Unca Liam," he said, "but why it's not pretty like Ashaford?"

His leg still riding Joslyn's, Liam felt her stiffen. "'Tis older than Ashlingford by nearly a hundred years, and it has not been taken care of as it should have been."

"Like you took care of Ashaford?"

This time the knights and men-at-arms stirred nervously, and though they had good reason to believe the man who should have been their lord would react with anger, Liam felt only a dull ache. "Aye, like I took care of Ashlingford."

Turning in Liam's arms, Oliver slipped down in the saddle before him. "You gonna fix it, aren't you, Unca Liam?"

Liam put his arm around the boy. "I am," he said, and turned his gaze on the others. "There is drink to be had in my hall," he announced. "Lady Joslyn and I will follow."

For men who had ridden all morn—likely without pause—it was a welcome invitation. Eagerly, they directed their horses around Liam and Joslyn and spurred the animals away.

Taking his reins in hand, Liam looked back at Joslyn. Though her explanation for coming to Thornemede would have to wait until Oliver was otherwise occupied, he asked, "Is it Ivo?"

She nodded.

The muscles throughout his body tightening, Liam turned his horse back toward the castle and began weaving his story for an intent Oliver. Though there was still tale left to tell when he halted his horse before the donjon, Oliver did not complain when he was told that the remainder would have to wait until bedtime. Liam set the boy upon his feet, watched him scramble up the steps, and turned to Joslyn where she sat atop her palfrey.

He reached to lift her down, and she came easily into his arms—as if it was where she longed to be. Liam lowered her to the ground and held her a bit longer than necessary before taking her elbow and guiding her up the steps.

How would she react to Thornemede? he wondered. He had seen the appreciation in her eyes when she had stood in the hall of Ashlingford, but though these past weeks had seen many improvements made to Thornemede's hall, it still did not compare.

The first thing that struck Joslyn when she entered was not the shabbiness but the sweet laughter of children that somehow rose above the talk of men.

"Oliver has found some children to play with," she said, her eyes lighting on her son where he stood with three others. It pleased her. Unfortunately, at Ashlingford there was not much opportunity for him to be around other children, and as he had spent quite a bit of time with the village youngsters at Rosemoor, he had sorely missed them.

As they crossed the hall, Liam removed his hand from her. "The little girl is Gertrude," he said, a tightness in his voice that had not been there before. "The two boys are Michael and Emrys."

Frowning, Joslyn asked, "Servants' children?"

"Nay," Liam said, offering no explanation.

But explanation was not needed, as Joslyn saw a moment later. Up close, the children were as beautiful as Oliver, and their marked resemblance to him impossible to overlook—especially that golden hair. Even had Joslyn wished to ignore it, she could not. These were Maynard's offspring. They had to be.

She swallowed hard. It wasn't that she hadn't expected Maynard to have fathered illegitimate children, just that she had not been prepared for the encounter. Had she loved Maynard as she found herself loving Liam now, it would have hurt indescribably—especially as the little girl had obviously been born some months after Oliver. Instead, all she felt was sadness for these unacknowledged children.

Becoming aware of Liam watching her, she met his intense gaze. He was waiting for her reaction to the bastards of her deceased husband, she realized. Did he think she would respond to them as Anya had to him? Even if she felt hurt, never would she direct it toward these innocents. "You should have told me," she said.

He shifted his gaze back to the children. "There was not time."

"I know I gave you no warning that I was coming to Thornemede—I could not," Joslyn said. "But you could have told me when last you were at Ashlingford."

His eyes studying her, he said, "It seemed an unnecessary burden to put upon you. Most women do not wish to know their husbands as they truly are."

She almost laughed at that. "Do you think me blind, Liam? Ignorant? I knew Maynard was not faithful to me. Even at Rosemoor he found women who were more than willing. " She looked away.

Liam's hand settling on her shoulder was too much comfort. "I am sorry," he said.

Joslyn took a steadying breath. "The only pain is the humiliation. Truly." Then, eager to abandon the topic, she said, "These children." She nodded to where they stood with Oliver at the base of the stairs. "Surely Maynard did not come all the way to Thornemede."

"Nay, he did not. They were sown on Ashlingford women. I brought them with me when I came here."

But why? Joslyn wondered. She looked up at Liam. "And their mothers too?" she asked.

He shook his head. "They have no mothers. Gertrude was abandoned, and the boys' mothers are dead—one in birthing, the other by the plow."

"Why would you do it, Liam? They are not your responsibility."

"Are they not? I am their uncle, Joslyn, just as I am Oliver's."

Her heart swelled for this man. She had not chosen to love him, but she could not stop herself. "Do they know that?" she asked.

"I have told them, but I do not think they understand."

"What will you do with them?"

Liam's gaze grew distant. "When Thornemede is completely mine—its people and its land—I will place them with a family."

"Together?"

"I would not separate them."

Joslyn nodded. "Are there any others? Any more of Maynard's children?"

"Five that are known, but there are certain to be more."

"Where are they?" she asked.

"With their mothers still. But enough of this. Now I would know your reason for coming to Thornemede."

Catching movement out of the corner of her eye, Joslyn looked back toward the children and watched as Oliver took the little girl's hand in his. She smiled.

"Joslyn." Liam prompted her.

"If there is someone who can watch Oliver, it would be best if we spoke elsewhere," she said.

"Maeve will watch him," Liam said. He indicated a woman who stood to the side, her gaze intent on the children. "She cares for Gertrude and the boys."

"Very well," Joslyn said.

Liam motioned her toward the steps. "Come."

Upstairs, Joslyn stepped ahead of him into the chamber he took her to. It was the lord's solar—where Liam slept—she realized, as her gaze fell upon the screen behind which the great bed lay. Sensation rippled over her spine, followed by apprehension. She swallowed. Though last night she had dreamed of being here with Liam, uncertainty now crept in.

"Sit down." Liam indicated the chairs before the hearth.

Joslyn chose one with its back to the screened-off bed.

"Now tell me," he said as he lowered himself opposite.

"Ivo returned to Ashlingford," she began, and explained what had followed the priest's return.

"I will kill him," Liam said when she finished telling him of her encounter with his uncle. His eyes were cold with purpose. "The church be damned. I will put him in his grave myself."

Reaching to where he sat in the chair before her, Joslyn laid her hand upon his arm. "Do not speak so, Liam. I am well—truly—and Emma seems none the worse for her encounter with him."

He stared at her a moment before shifting his gaze to the bandage around her neck.

Joslyn could almost feel the calloused pads of his fingertips move over her skin, causing her to warm inside and out. If only he would touch her, make her feel a woman again!

With a growl, Liam shot upright. "God, Joslyn, why did you not go for help?" he demanded.

"I know I should have, but when I heard him strike Emma, I . . . " She shook her head. "I just did not think."

"Nay, you did not," he agreed. Turning away, he paced across the chamber and, upon reaching the door, paused there a moment before swinging around to face her again. "He could have killed you!"

Much as she would have liked to deny it, as she

had once denied Ivo was capable of setting the brigands upon them, Joslyn no longer could. "I know," she said.

Liam shoved a hand through his hair. "Tell me the rest of it," he commanded. "Did they find Ivo?"

"Nay, though they searched through the night."

Of course not. Liam nearly said it aloud. Ivo had been long gone ere the Ashlingford men had even put foot to stirrup. But he was still out there and would soon enough reappear. If only he could keep Joslyn and Oliver here with him! He entertained the idea momentarily before rejecting it. Nay, their places were at Ashlingford, not in the ruins of Thornemede.

Liam counted himself ten times a fool for not having questioned Oliver further when the little boy had mentioned he'd seen Emma's money. He had let an important fact slip by without a single moment's consideration. Was this what yearning did to a man? he wondered. Did it so dull his instincts and senses that he thought with the mind of a lovesick youth rather than that of a man who had been trained to watch his back? If so, he would soon be dead, for there seemed no end to his desire for Joslyn. "Where is the money now?" he asked.

Joslyn must have been deep in thought herself, for it took her a moment to respond. "Sir Hugh has retrieved it and locked it in his chest."

Liam nodded. "That is good."

Joslyn stood and stepped toward him. "Liam, what if Ivo comes again?"

He met her gaze. "I will not lie to you, Joslyn. He *will* come again, which is why you must take no more unnecessary chances with either yourself or Oliver."

"As I did in coming here."

He inclined his head. "Aye, though at least you were wise enough to gather a sizable escort."

She halted a short distance from him. "Sir Hugh is the one who insisted on so great a number," she said. "I did not believe half as many were needed."

Liam had walked away from her, so he would not have to smell the tempting sweetness of her skin. Now it wafted to his senses like the strongest wine. His gaze was drawn to the screen he'd erected around the bed. True, it effectively divided the chamber in two so that this half could be used for receiving visitors, but it was no place for him to be with Joslyn. What had he been thinking to bring her here? He ought to have taken her to the garden that was no longer a garden . . . the kitchens . . . the inner bailey—anywhere but here. He fought the longing to close the distance between them, but in the end his feet carried him forward.

Standing over Joslyn, he looked down into her upturned face. "I am sorry he hurt you," he said. Lightly, he touched the bandage at her neck. "If only I had been there to stop him."

She stared at him with those magnificent amber eyes.

It was too much. His loins rising with need, Liam cried, "Damn!"

Joslyn blinked with surprise. "What is it?" she asked.

Before the last of his defenses came crashing down, he pulled his hand back. "'Tis only you, Joslyn," he said. He swung around and walked away. "Now let us return to the hall."

There was silence until he was almost to the door. Then Joslyn broke it.

"Nay," she said softly, that one word stirring him as if it were her hands upon him.

Halting, Liam turned and saw that she stood exactly where he had left her. And in her eyes was the light of a woman who wanted more from him than the mere caress of fingers. Joslyn Fawke was ready to give herself.

Though Liam's body rose eagerly to wrest control from his mind, he forced himself to listen to reason. There were harvests to be brought in, the dread plague to be overcome, and Ivo, who still waited to bring the church down upon them. God, any excuse that he would not have to acknowledge what he felt for her, for once he lay with her he would have to admit it—even if only to himself.

"Dinner is shortly to be served," he said, and pivoted again. Walking away from her was one of the hardest things he had ever done, especially when her hurt reached out to him, but he could not allow himself to turn back to her.

It was hard and lumpy as only a well-worn, understuffed mattress could be, but Joslyn hardly felt the discomfort as she lay in the dark with naught but her aching thoughts for company.

She sighed, the small sound large in the quiet of the chamber she and Oliver had been given. If only she could stop thinking about Liam! If only she could push out the pain that filled her so completely.

Stifling the groan that rose to her lips, she turned from her back to her side, bunched the flat pillow beneath her head, and again tried to settle down to sleep. However, it refused her as surely as Liam had. He still wanted her—that had not changed, she knew—yet when she had finally gathered the courage to all but offer herself to him, he had shunned her. Why?

Joslyn huddled more deeply in the bedclothes. She ought to have returned to Ashlingford this afternoon following the meal, she told herself. Instead, she had endured the rest of a day turned miserable and stayed the night as originally planned. The only good to come of the journey to Thornemede was that Oliver was finally content. Having heard the rest of his story ere bedding down for the night, he had fallen asleep with a smile on his face.

If only Liam would be as willing to make her smile, too!

Standing on the roof of the gatehouse the next morning, Liam watched the Ashlingford party disappear from sight—Joslyn with them. Then he closed his eyes against the truth. But it was useless. Even though he had not lain with Joslyn, he could no longer deny his feelings for her.

There was only one thing to do. He returned to the hall and wrote a missive.

22

Blessedly, the harvest was in, and still the plague had yet to descend on Ashlingford. Blessedly. Though Joslyn suffered no illusions that it might pass them by unscathed, she was grateful it held back long enough to bring in the grain that would sustain them throughout the winter.

"God answers prayers," she murmured to herself. "Just not all of them."

Turning into the winds that blew down from the north, she made no attempt to catch back her hood when it was swept from her head, or to prevent the blustering air from rearranging her veil and hair. Instead, she stared across the landscape to the patterned fields. Sheep wandered over them, grazing on the stubble left by the cattle that had foraged there first. This was the last day for the animals to fatten themselves; on the morrow, the plow would once again be put to the earth so that winter cereal crops could be planted for the following year. This meant Liam would soon be returning—might even now be riding from Thornemede to oversee the first breaking of ground.

Beneath her mantle, Joslyn hugged her arms about her. She almost wished he wouldn't return. Though it was now more than two months since she had visited Thornemede, the pain of his rejection had not lessened. Rather, with each trip he had made to Ashlingford since, it had grown because of the distance he kept from her.

But it was better this way, Joslyn tried to convince herself. After all, she and Liam had no future beyond, perhaps, one night of passion. And even if it were to become more than that, Liam would eventually wed another to produce his own heirs, someone more suitable than the widow of the brother who had betrayed him.

Squaring her shoulders, Joslyn tugged the reins to bring her mount around. In the next instant, a feeling of being watched came over her—and not from behind where her four escorts waited.

Looking right, she swept her gaze up the knoll from which the deepening of autumn had cleared the green grasses. There, at the top, sat a lone rider, his robes flapping in the wind, his silvered dark hair blowing across his face, and the hilt of a sword jutting from the scabbard swung low on his hip. He stared at her.

Ivo had returned, just as Liam had said he would.

Fear closing around Joslyn's throat, she jerked her head around to search out her escorts. They were exactly where she had left them, huddled at the edge of the wood where the wind was not so harsh. Lord, she had not realized how far she'd ridden from them. And as none of them were looking her way, they had no idea of the danger she had put herself in by seeking these few minutes of solitude.

Looking back at Ivo, Joslyn saw he had not moved from his place. Nay, he was in no hurry, for even if she could convince her gentle palfrey to put everything it had into flight, Ivo's warhorse would reach her before any of the Ashlingford men.

There was her meat dagger suspended from her girdle, she reminded herself, but she knew Ivo would slit her throat before she could raise it from beneath her mantle. She might as well attempt the escape he expected.

Joslyn caught hold of that last thought and turned it over. Aye, it was exactly what he waited for—to chase her down in sport. Why not do the unexpected? Why not go to him willingly? What it would gain her, she wasn't sure, but it was certain to unsettle him enough that there might be opportunity in it.

Keeping her face impassive in spite of her heart's pounding, Joslyn urged her horse toward the knoll at a leisurely pace. Although tempted to look behind to see whether or not her escorts had yet noticed what transpired, she did not.

"Father Ivo!" she called out in greeting as she directed her palfrey up the incline toward him.

"Father?" he repeated, his eyes narrowing. "Why so formal, dear Joslyn? 'Tis no longer necessary. Surely you know that."

Naturally, it was she he blamed for his defrocking. "You still wear the robes of a holy man," she pointed out, "even though you are excommunicated."

His smile hideous, he stared at her with all the hate and venom of the devil himself. "Excommunicated," he repeated. "I prefer the word 'unchurched.' 'Tis not so . . . permanent."

As Joslyn drew near him, nausea churned her stomach. "But it *is* permanent," she said. "The church

will not allow you back after what you have done—
and all those things you did before."

"Ah, Joslyn, are you really so naive? All it takes is
money."

"Which you do not have," she countered, reining
in her mount before him.

He leaned forward in the saddle. "But I will have
it. 'Tis why I have watched you these past weeks. I
knew you would eventually leave yourself open. And
so you have."

He'd been watching her—had seen her make these
rides over the demesne lands day after day. The
knowledge chilled Joslyn. Beginning to panic, she
started to look around.

"Do not," Ivo snapped.

Swinging her gaze back to him, she found he had
turned his attention to the men beyond her.

"They are coming," he informed her.

As he seemed in no hurry, it must mean the
Ashlingford knights had just noticed them atop the
knoll, Joslyn thought. Ivo had time to do with her
what he wished.

"They cannot help you," he murmured. "You know
that though, don't you?"

But could she help herself? Joslyn wondered, still
finding naught in the situation that might save her. "It
would have been in vain to try to outrun you," she
said. "I knew you would kill me either way."

Ivo stared at her a long moment before beckoning
her closer.

Fighting down the urge to spur her mount past
him—a gesture even more useless now than when
there had been distance between them—Joslyn guided
her palfrey alongside his destrier.

Ivo bent near her, fanning her with breath made fetid by strong drink. "Even I know you do not give up so easily, Joslyn. Let me see what you've hidden beneath your mantle."

Wondering how long ago he'd partaken of the alcohol, what effects it yet had on him, and how she was going to use it to her advantage, Joslyn stalled for time. "Why do you not just kill me?" she asked.

Ivo unsheathed his dagger. "You will not die this day," he said. "As I told you, I must have the money that is due me, and I can hardly lay my hands on it with you dead—at least, it would be less convenient to do so."

Of course. "Then you will hold me for the money," Joslyn said.

He looked up from fingering the honed blade of his dagger. "The bastard comes on this day or the morrow, does he not?"

"You know he does."

Ivo chuckled. "That I do. It could not have worked out better, really, for otherwise there would be the delay of sending for him." Suddenly, he frowned. "He *will* give me the money, don't you think, Joslyn? What I mean to say is, does he like it well enough between your legs that he will pay to have you returned to his bed?"

Joslyn nearly denied that she and Liam had been together as Ivo believed but, knowing it would be futile, refused him an answer.

He sighed. "Aye, William will give me the money, and when I have it . . . " He left the rest unspoken.

He would kill her, Joslyn knew, just as he would have that night in the garden had he secured the gold and Emma's writings. She swallowed. The only comfort was that she had more time than she'd believed. But what to do with it?

"Come, come, do not be modest," Ivo said. "Open your mantle for me."

As Joslyn bent her head to part the woolen garment, she grazed her chin on the brooch that held it closed at the neck, its spiked pin pleated through the thick fabric. In the next instant, she knew what to do. True, the brooch was not much of a weapon, but it was certainly unexpected. Although she had intended simply to open the mantle for Ivo to inspect her person, she unhinged the brooch, pulled the pin free, and pushed the garment off her shoulders.

Whether or not Ivo thought it unusual that she revealed herself in such a manner was impossible to tell, but when next he spoke, it was as if he thought nothing of it. "How fares Oliver?" he asked, as he looked her over.

It was no idle conversation, Joslyn realized, the sarcasm having slipped from his voice. He truly was interested. "He is well," she said, catching the first sounds of the Ashlingford knights as they neared. "Just turned three." Lowering her hand to her side—out of Ivo's sight—she turned the pin of the brooch upright.

"A year nearer to becoming the baron of all this," Ivo murmured. "Is this what you were thinking to stick in my back?" He lifted her meat dagger from its sheath. "This dull thing?"

"If I could, I would use it to cut your heart out," Joslyn replied, revulsion weakening her composure.

However, as Ivo's attention was once again captured by the advancing riders, he hardly seemed to notice. "Ah, here they come now. A bit late, wouldn't you agree?"

From the sound of hooves, Joslyn gauged that the

Ashlingford knights were near enough to help her—
providing she could evade Ivo's dagger.

"Come onto my destrier," Ivo ordered, thrusting a
hand toward her. "Now."

Nay, she was not going with him—at least not
alive. Feigning compliance, she turned her body
toward him and lifted her arm as if she meant to take
his hand. However, before he could see what was in
her own hand, she reached over and planted the pin
in his destrier's backside.

As she had hoped, the animal's response was
immediate and violent, giving Joslyn barely enough
space to dig her heels into her palfrey's sides.
Fortunately, the little horse responded quickly and
carried her out of reach of the great angry beast and
Ivo's sweeping dagger.

Hearing a shout, Joslyn looked over her shoulder
and for a brief moment met Ivo's gaze, which was
filled with disbelief and rage: She had bettered him a
second time, something he found incomprehensible.
He clutched the destrier's neck as it surged sideways
in an attempt to escape the pain. However, finding no
relief, the horse lunged back onto its hind legs and
pummeled the air. It was Ivo's undoing. Though he
struggled to hold on, the destrier wanted to throw
him off, and a moment later succeeded in doing so.

Only when Ivo hit the earth did Joslyn halt her palfrey
and pull it around. From the distance she had gained,
she watched and waited for him to rise. But he did not—
even when the Ashlingford knights surrounded him.

Had the destrier thrown him far and hard enough
to break his body? Was he dead? Though Joslyn
would have preferred to go nowhere near him again,
she urged her mount forward.

"You are unharmed, my lady?" Sir Gregory inquired as she came alongside him.

She nodded and then looked upon the man who lay sprawled at a most peculiar angle on the ground.

Though Ivo was not dead, he gazed up at the world with dying eyes. Something vital had broken in his evil body. Pulling his gaze from the sky, he looked from one knight to the next until he came to Joslyn. Then he managed a twisted smile. "Now look what you have wrought," he said, his voice strained.

In that instant, Joslyn realized she had indeed killed him. Although she had only been defending her life, in her bid to escape she had laid the ground for all this. She felt sickened. Never would she have believed that she would be responsible for the death of another. "You gave me no choice," she finally replied.

"But death, Joslyn? Am I truly deserving of this?"

Drawing a long breath, she raised her chin. "At least you will not be able to hurt anyone ever again."

He closed his eyes—rested them—and then looked at her again. "Do one thing for me?" he whispered.

She said nothing, waiting to hear his request.

"When Oliver is old enough to understand, tell him I loved him. That it was for him I did what I did—to secure his future. Will you do that for me, Joslyn?"

Ivo loved Oliver? Joslyn was shocked at the thought that this man loved anyone other than himself. True, he had seemed to care somewhat for Oliver, but never would she have called it love. And how could she put the burden of those things Ivo had done on her son? She shook her head. "I am sorry, Ivo," she said, "but I will not do that for you."

His nostrils flared. "Whore," he cried in a hoarse voice. "It should be you here, not me."

And might have been. . . . Her stomach soured, her head beginning to spin as her entire body was overcome with weakness, Joslyn was grateful for the horse beneath her. Had she been standing, she was sure her knees would have given way.

In the silence that followed Ivo's taunt, one of the knights dismounted, drew his dagger, and stepped to where Ivo lay. For a long moment, he stared down at him, and then he said, "'Tis merciful to speedily deliver a dying man from his . . . " He paused to ponder the rest of it. "What was it you called it, Father Ivo?"

Knowing what was to be done, Joslyn pulled the reins left and urged her palfrey around. She had seen enough for one day.

"Tortured end?" She heard the knight continue his mockery. "That's it, isn't it, *Father*?"

The knight's words echoed through Ivo's flickering mind as he looked up at the man who stood ready to dispatch him to what he belatedly prayed would be heaven. Ah, yes, how could he have forgotten? This knight had been present not so long ago when Ivo had spoken those words himself—having severed the life of the brigand who intended to expose his scheme to William. Ironic, wasn't it?

However, it was naught compared to the irony of this fate he shared with Maynard, who had also met his end being thrown from a horse. It was as it should be, though, he conceded. Father and son.

He never felt the blade. One moment he was following its descent toward him, and the next he was dropping through an inky blackness that was one moment comfortingly warm and the next turned fiery.

*   *   *

"My lord, make haste!" a man-at-arms called to Liam.

Liam turned to face the anxious man who stood on the threshold of Ashlingford's hall. Then, without asking what it was he was being called to witness, he strode back the way he had come and stepped into a day he had just ridden out of.

Though the wind was cold with the threat of an early winter, Liam hardly had time to acknowledge it before his gaze was drawn to the portion of outer bailey that was visible through the open portal of the inner wall.

There rode five, among them Joslyn, with her head bent against the wind and her hand clasping the neck of her mantle closed. A moment later, Liam realized there were six, if one included the robed figure draped over the back of a destrier being led by a knight. Ivo's destrier.

Thinking he imagined it, or that perhaps he had not yet awakened from last eve's sleep and this was but a dream, Liam stood rooted to the landing outside the donjon. But it all was too clear to be conjured by his mind, the wind too piercing and the sounds of horses and men too sharp to be illusory. Ivo was returning to Ashlingford, and from the flaccid lie of his body he could not be anything other than dead.

Liam's thoughts leapt to Joslyn. What had she to do with this? he wondered, as he hurriedly descended the steps. Had Ivo set upon her, thus earning himself death at the hands of one of the knights? Had she been hurt?

As she entered the inner bailey, Joslyn eased Liam's worries by lifting her head and looking straight at him. However, though she did not appear to be injured, there was a distant look in her eyes.

"Lord Fawke," Sir Gregory called to him, drawing in his reins before the donjon.

Though Liam wanted only to go to Joslyn, the knight's voice reminded him that there was first something he needed to do: acknowledge the dead that was of his blood. He stepped past the knight toward the destrier that had been Ivo's both prized and abused possession.

Nervously, the great horse rolled its eyes at him, then sidestepped as if preparing itself for a more violent retreat.

"It's over, boy," Liam murmured. Over for both of them. Although after the years of persecution it seemed hardly possible, Ivo would plague neither of them again.

Liam looked past the horse's head to the body hung over the saddle. Blood matted the dark hair that fell forward to cover his uncle's face, but there was something more to his death than that, Liam instinctively knew. "Ivo," he whispered as he looked upon his uncle's stillness. No answer was forthcoming, nor was one expected.

Knowing the destrier awaited its unburdening, Liam began loosening the knots of the rope that held his uncle to the saddle. Then he lifted Ivo onto his shoulder. "Sir Gregory," he said as he carried his uncle past the knight. "See that the horse is penned and then return to the donjon straightaway."

"Aye, my lord."

"And the rest of you as well," Liam said to the other three.

There was a murmur of assent.

Liam lowered his uncle to the ground at the base of the donjon steps, then straightened to look down upon him. Ivo's face was gray, its color having flowed out through the slit in his neck to stain the front of his priestly robes dark red. The last of him had flowed out with it, Liam knew, but what circumstances had led to the unholy man's leaving himself vulnerable to another's blade?

Feeling watched on all sides, Liam looked up the steps and saw that Father Warren, Sir Hugh, and Emma had come out from the donjon to discover what had disturbed a day already vexed by too much wind.

"Father Warren," Liam called to the priest.

The man met his gaze, lifted his flapping robes, and hurriedly began his descent. One step up from Ivo, he paused to look more closely upon the dead man; then he turned to Liam. "I am sorry, my son."

If he were truly sorry, he would certainly be the only one, Liam thought. "I am not," he replied. "See that my uncle is given a proper burial."

"Where would you have me bury him, my lord?" Father Warren asked.

"He is still a Fawke," Liam said, "and should be buried as one. Lay him beside Maynard."

The priest leaned near him. "Maynard's mother is already on one side of him," he reminded Liam in a low voice. "What of . . ." His gaze, drifting to where Joslyn was mounted, spoke the rest for him.

Liam could not imagine Joslyn ever taking her place beside Maynard. She did not belong anywhere near him, and he would not allow it. "Lay Ivo alongside his nephew," he said again.

Father Warren inclined his head.

Swinging around, Liam strode toward Joslyn, who had just dismounted. Continuing to hold her mantle closed, she walked toward the donjon with eyes cast down.

Liam intercepted her as she put her foot to the first step. "What is it?" he asked, cupping a hand beneath her elbow.

"I killed him, Liam," she said.

He could have asked more than a dozen questions based on that one statement, but his first concern was for Joslyn, whose trembling he felt through her mantle. "Come," he said. "We will warm you before the fire."

She nodded.

By the time they reached the landing, Liam was supporting a good deal of Joslyn's weight, but she pulled away from him when he turned to lift her into his arms.

"I couldn't stand that," she said, and stepped past him into the hall.

Liam let her go. She was hurting, he knew—not only from whatever had transpired this day, but from what had not transpired between the two of them these past months. She still loved him.

"It ends," Emma said suddenly. "Justice is finally done."

And so it was, Liam silently agreed. Still, he could not help but wonder again on the secret the old woman had held so close all these years—what those writings of hers contained. It hardly mattered now, though, he reminded himself, for no more would Ivo have to answer to them. No more need he fear them. It truly was over.

With that last thought, Liam entered the hall and found Joslyn sitting in a chair beside the hearth. Before her was Oliver, hopping from one foot to the other.

"Aye, you may," he heard Joslyn say, "but only one. Do you understand?"

"Uh-huh," the little boy answered. "One tart." Then, intent on the treat that awaited him in the kitchens, he hurried from the hall without noticing Liam.

It was better that way, Liam conceded, for he wanted to talk with Joslyn ere the knights assembled in the hall. Coming to stand before her, he said, "Tell me, Joslyn."

She was a long moment looking at the flames, but when she shifted her gaze to him, he saw that some of the light had returned to her eyes. Oliver had done that. "Ivo caught me out in the open," she said. "As I knew I could not outrun him, I thought to surprise him by going to him willingly."

Liam frowned. "Where was your escort?"

"'Tis not their fault"— she was quick to defend them— "but mine. Wishing some time alone, I rode ahead of them."

"And they allowed it?" Liam exclaimed.

"There seemed no harm in it."

Had there been a table nearby to pound his fists on, Liam knew he would have, for the Irish rose strong in him. "But there *was* harm in it!" he barked. "God, Joslyn, Ivo could have killed you."

"But instead I killed him," she reminded him, then looked back at the fire.

The small voice calmed Liam. "How did it happen?" he asked.

"My brooch. He never expected it."

Though Liam had seen that she held her mantle closed, too much had occupied his thoughts for him to question the reason she did not use a brooch. "You turned it on Ivo?"

"Nay, on his destrier."

She did not need to say anymore, for Liam could well imagine the destrier's reaction. "The horse threw him." He spoke his thoughts aloud.

She nodded. "Ivo fell wrong."

Then he had died nearly the same as Maynard, Liam realized.

"I did not mean for it to happen," Joslyn continued. "I was only trying to escape."

Were they alone—and they no longer were, with the arrival of three of the four knights in the hall— Liam would have given in to the urge to gather her in his arms. Instead, he said, "You are not to blame, Joslyn. Ivo brought this on himself."

Her smile was grim. "I know that, but still . . ." She shook her head.

"Go abovestairs and rest," Liam said.

Standing, she turned toward the stairs. However, she had taken only a step away from him when she looked over her shoulder. "You are not staying long, are you?" she asked.

He wasn't. Couldn't. "I will be here when you awaken." He attempted to reassure her.

Without another word, Joslyn crossed to the stairs and, and as if she were more Emma's age than her own, slowly went up the steps.

When she was gone from sight, Liam turned to the knights, who awaited his pronouncement upon them. They were ready, he saw, each steeled for the anger that was more than due them. "Come forward," he ordered.

They exchanged glances and stepped toward him.

23

She was not alone. Joslyn knew it even before she opened her eyes. She also knew it was not Emma or Oliver in her chamber with her. It was Liam.

Lifting her lids, she peered into the dimly lit room and saw Liam where he sat in the chair beside her bed. Why? she wondered. It was as if he watched over her, and that hardly seemed likely—not after all these months when he had gone out of his way to avoid her.

"Joslyn," he said.

He must have seen she'd awakened. "What are you doing here?" she asked.

He was silent a long moment, and then he lifted himself out of the chair. "Emma was concerned that you not awaken alone," he said. The light creeping onto the planes of his face showed signs of fatigue that Joslyn had not earlier noticed.

"Where is she?" Joslyn asked, surprised that it was not the old woman who had stayed with her, and that Liam had thought it his responsibility to do so.

"She and Oliver are asleep in my chamber. She thought it best that your rest not be disturbed."

As Oliver would certainly have disturbed it. But how long had Liam sat in that chair? Joslyn wondered. Hours? Against her will, her heart stirred at the thought that, unbeknownst to her, he had watched her sleep. Had he felt anything as he sat there? Had he wanted to touch her as he'd once wanted to? As she still wanted to touch him?

"I will leave you now," he said, shattering her imaginings.

As he turned away, Joslyn searched frantically for something that might delay him, but in the end there was only the truth. "I do not wish you to go," she said, hating herself for it but wanting too badly for him to stay to spare her pride. Pushing back the covers, she lowered her feet to the floor.

Liam shook his head. "I cannot stay."

Was it Maynard who still stood between them? Joslyn wondered. She remembered again the words Liam had spoken to her at Settling Castle and how dirty he had made her feel for having lain with her husband. Still, when news of the plague had arrived at Ashlingford, he had come to her and told her that one day she would be his. Had she misunderstood? If not, was it simply that Liam had decided he did not want her after all? She had to know.

Swallowing, she asked, "Do you still want me, Liam?"

He did not answer her.

"I know I was your brother's first," she said, "but there is naught I can do—"

Something in Liam's eyes changed, causing Joslyn to fall back a step. Then, suddenly, he pulled her against him. "Never were you Maynard's," he growled, his breathing turned shallow. "Never." Then, as swiftly as his anger had risen, it dropped away. "God's rood, but I was cruel to say those things to you, Joslyn."

"Then why?" she breathed, aching at every place they touched. "Why do you keep yourself from me— especially now when Ivo can no longer do us harm?"

Shaking his head, Liam set her back from him. "Don't you understand? He is gone, but the plague is not. There is much to do and not enough time to do it."

"Then you do still want me?"

"I told you one day you would be mine," he reminded her. "Naught has changed. When this black cloud no more hangs over England—"

"We might both be dead," she interrupted.

He issued a harsh sigh. "The time is not right, Joslyn."

Knowing she risked much—that he might turn from her again—she stepped forward and slid her arms around his neck. "It *is* right," she whispered, then raised herself up on her toes and softly pressed her lips against his.

Liam held himself from her a moment longer. Then a tormented groan escaped him and he closed his arms around her. "You are mine, Joslyn." He spoke against her mouth. "Mine." Suddenly, there was no one to stop him—not Ivo, not the church, not even the plague. Hungrily, he deepened the kiss.

For fear she might otherwise awaken to find herself dreaming, Joslyn strained toward him.

Instantly, Liam's body burgeoned against hers, but he prolonged the kiss until she began running her hands over him.

Joslyn did not think about what she did but allowed her passions to guide her where they chose. However, when she slid a hand between them and brushed Liam's rigid manhood, he put a quick end to it.

Dragging his mouth off hers, he swung her up into his arms and carried her back to the bed. "You are sure, Joslyn?" he asked before laying her down.

"I want to know you, Liam."

He brushed his mouth once more across hers, lowered her to the bed, and began drawing her chemise up. His fingers grazed the hose-covered flesh of her ankle, her calf, and the inside of her knee, but the moment he touched her thigh he pulled back.

God, no, Joslyn silently pleaded, do not let him stop now. Looking up at his face, which the dying torchlight flickered over, she asked. "Something is wrong?"

Reassuringly, he caressed the side of her face. "If I touch you any more I might not make it out of my own clothes," he said. "I do not want to rush this, Joslyn. I have waited too long to behave as if I were a rutting youth."

Relieved that he was not rejecting her again, Joslyn relaxed into the mattress and watched as he dragged his tunic off. As she had first seen him by the stream, he was magnificent bared, the muscles of his torso, shoulders, and arms flexing as he tossed the tunic aside. This time, though, Joslyn did not turn away. Instead, she looked long and lingering at him as he bent to remove his boots.

Without pausing to free the ties of his hose from his braies, Liam pulled them off as one and left them at his feet.

He was erect, Joslyn saw, his man's body ready for her woman's depths. But first there was her chemise to be shed. Aching to hold him inside her, she reached down and gathered a handful of her skirts. However, Liam closed his hand over hers, preventing her from pulling them up.

"I will do it," he said. He loosened her fingers and laid her hand back to her side. Putting one knee to the mattress, he raised his other leg and straddled her calves.

Joslyn swept her gaze down his body and trembled with the knowledge that now they would finally come together. Tonight she would know what it was like to make love to the man who held her heart. It had to be different from simply making a baby, she knew, for the feelings Liam's touch aroused promised far more than the pain she had known on her wedding night.

Smoothing his hands up over her legs, Liam slid his fingers into the tops of her hose, rolling them down and off her feet. The next time he touched her, it was flesh to flesh, and a moment later he bent his head to put his mouth to those places his hands had gone before him.

Joslyn shuddered as his lips moved intimately upward. However, upon reaching her inner thigh, Liam lifted his head, looked across the chemise that was bunched up around her hips, and met her gaze.

"I want to see all of you," he said, and pushed the garment upward.

As much as she was able to, Joslyn assisted him, and a short time later she lay as naked as he, her hair unplaited and spread across the pillow.

"You are beautiful, Joslyn," he murmured, his gaze traveling over her like tongues of flame.

It seemed so right to be here with him like this. Aching with want, she beseeched him. "Love me, Liam."

"'Tis what I want to do more than anything," he murmured. Lowering himself between her legs so that his manhood was pressed against her opening, he bent and pulled a nipple into his mouth.

Joslyn burned to have him inside her, and with the promise of it so near, a needful sound rose in her throat. She fought to hold onto it, but when Liam released the rigid nipple and moved to her other breast, it burst from her. "Liam!" she cried. Arching nearer him, she reached up and pushed her hands through his hair to hold him to her.

However, rather than enter her, he lifted himself away. "Turn over, Joslyn," he said, his breathing labored.

It took her a moment to rise above the needs of her body to understand what he said, but when she did, she thought she could not have heard right. Confused, she shook her head.

Liam offered no explanation—simply reached beneath her and eased her onto her belly.

The next sensation Joslyn felt was his lips against the cleavage of her buttocks. She quivered. Lord, but she had not known it was so sensitive there. As with all else Liam touched, it seemed connected with the fires of her woman's place, his touch causing her insides to convulse. From there, he worked his way up her back, with his hands, lips, tongue, and teeth, finding every sweet spot Joslyn had not known existed. By the time he finally reached her neck, his body splayed over hers, she thought she might scream with want.

He breathed her in. "At Rosemoor, your bed smelled of roses," he murmured into her ear, "and of you, Joslyn. When I lie awake at night, it haunts me."

She shuddered. She had not known Liam had gone

to her chamber. The thought heightened her desire. "Liam," she gasped, "I think I am dying."

"In a moment," he said, his voice so strained she hardly recognized it. Then, rolling her onto her back again, he entered her.

The pain was only slight, and then it faded as pleasure swept over Joslyn with the turbulence of a winter ocean.

Slowly, Liam slid himself more deeply into her.

Though it did not seem possible to be any more pleasurable, his movement made Joslyn want to cry out.

Once fully inside her, rigid and fiery where he settled himself, Liam stilled. "What do you feel, Joslyn?" he asked.

She did not at first understand what he was asking, but then her body whispered it to her. "As if I stand on the edge of something," she said. "Something so incredible I can never hope to touch it."

Liam drew his hands down her sides and gripped her hips. "But you will," he said. "I promise you that." He pulled back, causing her insides to ripple with sensation, then he thrust forward and touched the deepest part of her. And again.

Small sounds escaping her, Joslyn remained unmoving, allowing Liam to do with her what he knew far better than she. However, as the feeling increased, her body began moving with his—tentatively, until she found his cadence. Then, matching him, she started climbing toward something that more and more stole her breath the nearer she got to it.

"Joslyn," Liam groaned, and a moment later began moving faster.

Lord, but she had not known she was capable of

such feeling, she marveled, her body speaking to Liam's as if it had always known his. As if—

Joslyn thrust aside her ponderings and allowed Liam to pull her toward the precipice. The sensations he awakened swelled and began spinning around her. Then, just when she thought she might collapse, the last of her breath was snatched from her and she plummeted over the edge.

Throwing her head back, Joslyn cried out as her entire body was shaken by jolts of ecstasy she had never before felt. In their midst, she heard Liam's shout and felt him thrust one last time before shuddering inside her. One after the other, the tremors rocked Joslyn, but whether or not they were of her body or Liam's she could not distinguish. They had become one, and only when the tremors eased her down from the heights of passion they had scaled did she flow back into herself.

For what might have been an hour, neither of them spoke, and then Liam lifted his head and kissed her brow.

"I have never felt anything like that," Joslyn said.

"I know," he murmured. "It has never been this way for me either." Rolling off her, he leveraged himself onto an elbow and looked down at her.

"Truly?" she asked.

He nodded and slid a hand up over her belly and curved it around her breast. "I have found fulfillment in many women's arms," he admitted, "but none such as this."

What did he mean? Joslyn wondered. That his heart had been in it the same as hers? That it truly was love between them, and not just the act of sex? She wanted badly to ask him, to know what he felt for her, but the persistent voice in her head whispered that she was a hundred times a fool.

"I must know about your marriage, Joslyn," he said. "About you and Maynard."

The mention of his brother cooled the warmth from Joslyn's flushed skin. Why did Liam have to speak of him? Maynard had naught to do with what had just happened between them. "I do not wish to talk about it," she said.

"Though I can understand your reasons for not wanting to, I need to know."

She stared up into a face that was still handsome in spite of the scarred jaw. Forever, he would bear the marks of that day when Ivo had sought his death. But what was unseen were the scars Maynard had inflicted upon him. Aye, he ought to know.

With a sigh, Joslyn said, "You were right in believing I was naught more to your brother than a vessel for the child who would take Ashlingford from you. I knew it ere we wed, so it did not hurt—at least not as it would have, had I loved him."

Lightly, Liam skimmed his fingers down her arm. "Why did your father agree to such a marriage? Surely he could have found you someone more fitting—someone who would have made a life with you."

"He had no choice. You see, my father is near as obsessed with his games of chance as Maynard was." She tried to suppress the shiver that rose through her, but it trembled onto her limbs.

Reaching behind him, Liam pulled the coverlet over them both. "What do you mean he had no choice?" he asked.

"He and Maynard met in London—gambling, of course. Shortly thereafter, Maynard first journeyed to

Rosemoor. Though he joined my father and several others in gambling the day and night away, it seemed I could go nowhere without his eyes following me; 'tis a wonder he kept enough of his mind on the game to win. The following day I learned from my father that Maynard had inquired into my betrothal and, upon learning I was without contract, had offered to wed me himself."

"And your father agreed?"

Joslyn hugged the coverlet tighter to her. "He would have liked to," she said, "but he had made my mother a promise ere she died that I would be allowed to marry for love as she had."

"Yet you did not refuse Maynard."

"But I did. I did not love him, Liam, nor did I believe I ever would. Though my father was disappointed, he honored his vow to my mother and told Maynard I had declined."

"Then how is it you changed your mind?"

"Each time Maynard returned to Rosemoor, my father lost more to him, until one day there was not enough coin to pay the enormous debt."

Liam was silent for a minute, and then he said, "I see."

"I had no choice," she said, praying he would understand. "My father would have been ruined had I not agreed to the marriage. In exchange Maynard agreed to absolve my father of the debt, half of it once we were wed, the other half when I . . . when I produced a male child."

Liam lifted a hand to knead his brow. "God," he muttered.

Tears sprang to Joslyn's eyes. "What else was I to do? I could not allow my father to face such ruin when it was in my power to help him."

"Nay, Joslyn," he said, his gaze tender, "it is not that. It is what Maynard did to you. That you had to endure his attentions."

Relief flooded through her. So Liam was not revolted by her having sold herself. Still, she needed to explain further. "I only lay with him the one time," she said.

He frowned. "What are you talking about?"

"When I agreed to wed him, it was with the provision that during my pregnancy I would not be made to suffer his attentions and that, once he had his son, he would come no more to my bed. It angered him, but he conceded."

"Then Oliver was conceived your first time together?"

"Aye. An old midwife helped me determine the day to wed that I would be most fertile, gave me herbs to increase my fertility, and spoke words over me that the babe would be born a boy."

"And Maynard kept his word?"

"The day after we were wed, he left Rosemoor and did not come again until I was near five months into my pregnancy," she said. "As I was only beginning to swell, he did not believe I was with child and sought to gain my bed again. To convince him, my father sent for the midwife, and though she confirmed it, Maynard still tried to break his word. My father held him to it."

Liam smoothed the hair back from her brow. "I am sorry, Joslyn," he murmured. "It should never have happened."

"I am not sorry," she said. "It gave me Oliver." *And you*, she added silently, even if it was only for this one night. But she would not think of that now. . . .

Liam bent his head and caressed her mouth with his.

It kindled Joslyn—made her want to join with him again. And they did join again, and several times more throughout the night, until the first light of dawn crept into the chamber. Then, finally, she slept.

Joslyn was not surprised to awaken alone in her bed. After all, the sun was approaching noon when she lifted her head from the pillow.

Sitting up, she gazed at the confusion of covers, some spread around her, some fallen from the mattress to dust the rushes. Portions of the sheet were wound tight with the blanket, the blanket with the coverlet, and the coverlet with the sheet—all three connected in one way or another as if they had made love as vigorously as she and Liam had.

In spite of the telling tenderness between her legs, Joslyn smiled. Last night had been like no other. Last night she had fallen completely and wonderfully in love. True, she had loved Liam before, but their joining had sealed it for her forever.

For a long moment, Joslyn basked in the glow of that love, feeling as if her world was finally made perfect. Then reality intruded and reminded her that last night might never happen again. Even if it did, there was no future in it. Not only was their relationship forbidden by the church, but it could not truly be called a relationship when one loved and the other only desired.

Still, whatever she had of Liam she would take gratefully, for it was far more than she would have had if he had turned from her last night.

Smiling again, Joslyn disentangled her legs from the covers and lowered her feet to the floor. Knowing that Liam would already have been in the fields for hours, she quickly rinsed herself with cold water from the basin, dressed, and plaited her hair. Then she made her way belowstairs.

The hall was empty—at least, at first glance it appeared so. As Joslyn crossed toward the kitchens where she hoped to find a crust of bread and a chunk of cheese to ease her hunger, the rustle of parchment drew her attention to the hearth.

It was Emma, standing with her back to Joslyn, head bent over the fire she fed.

Curious, Joslyn approached her and, as she neared, heard Emma humming a child's song that Joslyn recognized as one her own mother had sung to her—something about a child's toys lost, found, then lost again. "Emma?" she said.

The old woman jerked her head around. "My lady!" She flapped a hand to her heart. "I did not know you had awakened."

"Aye, not long ago," Joslyn said, then glanced from the blackened remains of parchment upon the fire to the single sheet Emma held down by her side. "What are you burning?" she asked.

The old woman shifted from foot to foot. "Are you not hungry, my lady? I am sure Cook can find you something to eat that will keep you till nooning."

Joslyn shook her head. "Are they your writings?" she asked. "Those Ivo wanted?"

Emma clenched in her hand the one she had yet to burn. "Do not concern yourself, my lady," she said, her voice harsh with strain.

Joslyn was not normally one to pry, but something

told her that whatever Emma had used to check Ivo's behavior was not inconsequential and involved more than the two people who had been privy to it. "Tell me, Emma," she implored. "Surely there is no harm now that Ivo is dead."

As if fearing Joslyn intended to snatch the parchment from her, Emma stepped back. "Nay, they are no longer of any use—to me or anyone else," she said, her breathing turned quick and shallow. "As Ivo wanted them so badly, I thought I would . . . I would send them to hell with him."

Clearly, the woman was overwrought. Realizing she was responsible for the state Emma was working herself into, Joslyn conceded. "Very well. 'Tis yours to do with as you think best. I will not try to stop you."

Emma searched her face a long moment, as if she thought Joslyn meant to trick her. Then, with a bit of color returned to her cheeks, she crumpled the parchment into a ball and threw it into the fire. Instantly, it caught, and as the yellow flames licked up around it, turning it black, it slowly opened itself like a flower in spring bloom.

"Your secret is safe," Joslyn said.

"Aye," the old woman whispered, her gaze unwavering upon the charred remains. "As it should be."

The silence that followed was heavy—as if of grief and mourning—but Joslyn knew Emma did not lament the loss of Ivo. Mayhap the loss of something else, but not the false priest.

"Where is Oliver?" Joslyn asked.

"With his uncle in the fields," she replied. "As he wanted so badly to go with him, and 'twas such a beautiful day, Liam said he could."

Though the fields were not a safe place for children—especially when the plows were upon them—Joslyn knew Liam would not allow any harm to befall Oliver. Assured, she turned toward the kitchens, but then looked back around. "Join me?" she asked.

"Nay, methinks I will go rest now," Emma said.

"Are you ill?" Joslyn asked.

The old woman shook her head. "Just weary."

It had been a long day without Liam, made even longer when the Ashlingford men finally returned from working the demesne lands to sit at table for the evening meal. In the clamor that followed, there had been no time for Joslyn to speak to Liam—hardly enough to catch his eye, but when finally he looked her way he had offered her a tired smile. It was something.

Throughout the tedious ritual of supper, Joslyn had done her best to listen to Oliver's jovial accounting of the oxen, which he claimed were ten times as big as his uncle's horse, and the plows that "chewed up the dirt." Though her love for her son had not diminished with the new love blossoming for Liam, Joslyn felt divided. Despite Oliver's sparkling eyes and small face aglow with excitement, she had sought out Liam where he'd sat half a dozen down from her.

Now, though, she finally had him to herself in her chamber. Lifting her head from his shoulder, Joslyn propped her elbow beneath her and leaned across his body. "Liam," she whispered, "are you awake?"

Her words were met by silence, but just as she started to lie back down, he spoke. "I am. Are you?"

She smiled. "Only if this is not a dream."

Reaching up, he brushed the backs of his fingers down the side of her face. "I wonder that myself," he said.

His admission surprised her. She turned her head and pressed her lips to his palm. "What do you feel for me, Liam?" she asked. There. She had risked the question.

It was not light enough for her to read his expression, but she felt him stiffen. "I care for you, Joslyn," he finally spoke.

He cared, but did he love? "Is that all?" she asked.

Again he was silent. Then, rolling onto his side, he pulled her beneath him. "Nay, it is not," he murmured before dropping his head and closing his mouth over hers.

He *did* love her! Joslyn rejoiced with her body as she returned kiss for kiss, caress for caress, and, shortly, the sweet thrusts that made her cry out. More intense than before, Liam made aching love to her until she had thrice scaled the heights he held himself back from, and only then did he allow himself release.

Afterward, with her backside fit to Liam's front where he curled himself around her, Joslyn hugged to her the knowledge that he loved her—his body having spoken it even if he could not.

"How long will you be gone?" she asked, knowing they had only these last hours before dawn ere he left again for Thornemede.

"Winter comes," he said. "With the harvest in and the cereal crops soon to be sown, there will be little occasion for me to journey to Ashlingford. 'Twill likely be spring ere I am needed here again."

Joslyn could not imagine the long, lonely winter

months that lay ahead. "But you will come, won't you?" she asked.

His silence said otherwise. "I can make no promises, Joslyn," he told her at last. "Much depends on when the plague works its way here."

"Will we be together again like this?" she asked, telling herself that even if it was the last time, she must be content that at least they'd had this much.

"We should not be together like this now," he reminded her.

Forbidden.

"I know."

Curving an arm more tightly around her waist, Liam murmured into her hair, "Sleep now." Then, her question left painfully unanswered, he settled back upon the pillow.

The still of night enveloped them once again, and Joslyn closed her eyes, but her thoughts were too restless to allow her to sleep. As she lay awake beside Liam, one after the other she relived the memories made since he had first ridden on Rosemoor Manor. In each she saw how she had drawn nearer and nearer him until her fear of him had turned to love—a love so deep it filled her completely. Yet it hurt. She fervently wished there was some way they might spend the rest of their lives together. But it would take a miracle, and, sadly, these days God seemed not in the mood to grant any.

She sighed and shifted to settle more deeply against Liam. "I do love you," she whispered. "I will always love you."

24

Princess Joan was dead.

As with most talk of the plague, her death was spoken of in hushed tones in those places that were not yet touched by the darkness. However, in Dorset where the dread sickness now raged, the passing of the daughter of King Edward and Queen Philippa was certain to be told by voices loud with hysteria. After all, if those so near God were not to be spared, what hope had the common man?

Arresting his stride in the middle of the outer bailey, Liam pushed a hand through his hair. Now he better understood the reason Queen Philippa had yet to answer his missive. No doubt it would be some time ere she rose from her mourning to do so.

Though he had been headed for Thornemede's smithy when he overheard news of the princess's death, Liam turned instead to the one who had spoken of it.

The merchant was standing on the opposite side of

the table his goods were laid out upon, the women servants his captive audience. "'Tis true." he said. "'Twas this past August while she was in France that the plague took her."

"In France?" Maeve breathed.

The man nodded. "Journeyin' to marry the son of the king of Castile, she was."

Liam counted: three months. Though news was wont to travel slowly throughout England, he was surprised it had taken so long for something of such import to reach Thornemede.

Noticing Liam where he stood back from the others, the merchant straightened. "Ah, Lord Fawke." He raised his voice in greeting. "There is something I can show you?"

Liam was about to decline when something among the pieces of worked metal caught his eye: a brooch. Stepping forward, he lifted it to catch the light. It was simple, made special only by delicate petals fashioned of silver that enfolded each of four rubies. Roses.

"'Tis lovely, isn't it?" the merchant said.

Liam turned it over, unhinged the pin, and closed it again.

He wondered if Joslyn had replaced the one she'd lost in her bid to escape Ivo during the six weeks since last he had been at Ashlingford. In the next instant he abandoned such ponderings. Until he had his answer from the queen, it would not do for him to be sending Joslyn gifts. "Aye, lovely," he agreed, setting it back down.

"I will make you a good price, my lord," the man said.

Liam shook his head and turned away from the table. However, the appearance of Gertrude in his path broke his stride. He should have known she would be nearby, for though Michael and Emrys had taken to adventuring, the little girl was never far from Maeve's skirts. She smiled at him—a dimpling smile she had perfected these past months. It was effective whenever she wished to sit on his lap before the fire, ride on his shoulders, or search in his trencher for a tasty morsel.

"You would like something?" Liam asked.

She chewed her bottom lip a moment, then stepped forward and slipped her hand into his. "Over here, Uncle Liam," she said, tugging him left to where another merchant displayed various leather goods. Peering up over the edge of the table, she quickly found what she was looking for and tapped a finger to the toe of one of a pair of small goatskin slippers that were dyed red.

"Do you think they will fit, Gertie?" Liam asked.

She looked down at her feet, shod in plain brown slippers, studied them a moment, and nodded.

Liam lifted the slippers from the table. "And if I buy these for you, what think you I should buy for Michael and Emrys?" he asked.

She knew without thinking on it even a moment. "Michael wants a dagger like yours, sire." Fleetingly, she touched Liam's scabbard. "And Emrys—he wants a belt."

"How do you know that?"

She shrugged. "Just do."

Looking around, Liam searched the bailey and soon located Michael, who stood before the merchant whose table was set with various weapons, and Emrys farther down, doing his best to make a man's belt fit his boy's waist. "I see," he said, then turned his gaze to the stout woman behind the table.

She offered him a gap-toothed smile. "Slippers for yer little girl, my lord?" she asked.

His little girl, Liam mused. "Aye," he said.

The woman named a price.

Liam countered with an offer of half what she asked—still more than their worth.

The woman tried again, but Liam held firm and soon was helping Gertrude in donning her new slippers. With the proud little girl skipping before him, Liam crossed to where Michael stood hopeful and purchased a blunt-edged dagger for him. Then he bought Emrys a belt that had to be looped twice around his waist in order to fit.

"When I'm all grown up, it'll still fit," Emrys said, having refused the merchant's offer to shorten it for him.

"Aye, that it will," Liam said.

Michael admired his brother's belt and ran his fingers over it, and they both trotted off.

"Can I have a ride, Uncle Liam?" Gertrude asked, reminding him that she had remained behind.

"Later, hmm?" he said. "I've work to do now."

She nodded, too content with her red slippers to beseech him to change his mind.

He led Gertrude back to where Maeve waited alongside the table of the first merchant

The woman took Gertrude's hand. "Come, little one," she said. "We've pastries aplenty to stick our fingers into."

"Oh, can I?" the little girl cried.

"Aye, but you mustn't tell your Uncle Liam I allowed it," Maeve said, grinning at him over her shoulder as she led Gertrude away.

Liam's attention was drawn again to the brooch.

"It is of good weight, my lord," the merchant said, "and the rubies are of the highest quality."

Picking it up again, Liam ran his thumb over each gem. "'Tis Ashlingford you go to next?" he asked.

"Aye, my lord. Ashlingford on the morrow."

With a nod, Liam handed the brooch to the man. "Deliver this to Lady Joslyn Fawke for me," he said.

The merchant beamed. "I can do that, my lord. Any word you would have me deliver with it?"

Liam did not think long on it. "Just tell her 'tis from the baron of Thornemede."

It was the first Joslyn had heard from Liam in all these weeks. Her heart beating with wonderful excitement, she hurried to the donjon and ascended to her chamber two steps at a time. After closing the door behind her, she paused to eye the pouch she clutched and guess a moment as to its contents, then she dropped into the nearest chair and laid back the folds of leather.

She gasped. Blinking up at her as if with awakening eyes was a silver brooch set with rubies—four of them—each made as a rose. Beginning to smile, Joslyn lifted the brooch into the dusky light of an overcast day.

From the baron of Thornemede, the merchant had told her. When she had gone down to the bailey to purchase spices, candles, and other household items, she had not gone anywhere near the man's table. Thus, he had sought her out to deliver Liam's gift to her. There had been no message to accompany it, but none was needed. Liam's thoughtfulness spoke clearly enough.

Joslyn held the brooch close to her heart for several minutes. Then, removing one Emma had given her, she pushed the pin through the folds of her mantle.

In the past few weeks, the loneliness caused by Liam's absence had more than once made her question what he felt. Now Joslyn had her answer as she stared down at the brooch. It was beautiful, she thought, but the love behind it was its true beauty. She sighed. Whether he admitted it or not, he did love her.

Her day made light even if the sun was still shut out by clouds, Joslyn returned to the bailey to complete her purchases.

25

It came like the dark of the dead of night, and by morning nearly a score of villagers stood outside the castle gates waiting to be admitted.

As the men and women were ushered into the hall, nearly every one of them looking fit to panic, Joslyn sent Oliver abovestairs with Emma. It was the day they had all been waiting for with dread, and now that it was upon them, Joslyn knew it was time to keep the promise Liam had extracted from her—to be strong for these people who would one day call Oliver their lord.

"'Tis come," one of the women blurted. "God's fist has descended."

Leaning forward, Sir Hugh said, "Describe it to me, woman. How do you know?"

She stepped forward. "This past eve the marks came upon my husband. First the swelling, and now his entire body is covered with sores. He's heated somethin' terrible."

"How many more?" Sir Hugh asked, looking to the others.

"My boy's stricken," a man old enough to be a grandfather said. Wringing his hood between his hands, he asked, "He ain't gonna die, is he? He's my only boy, ye know."

Even the old man knew the answer to that. Once touched by the disease, it seemed only a miracle could save the person afflicted by it.

"Your son must be removed from your home," Sir Hugh said, speaking no lie, but neither stating the obvious. "All who fall ill to the plague will be taken immediately to the old village of Belle Glen."

Joslyn frowned. The name seemed familiar.

The village woman who had spoken first exclaimed, "Belle Glen? But 'tis burnt out. There is naught there but ashes."

Now Joslyn knew where she'd heard it spoken of before. It was the village where Maynard had hidden the money.

"This past summer, Lord Fawke had built there several buildings to house the sick," Sir Hugh said.

"I will be there to minister to the people" —Father Warren spoke up—"as will the physician and the good friars." He nodded to three robed men who stood solemn across the hall. Liam had sent them to Ashlingford two months past.

"'Tis as Lord Fawke has spoken," Joslyn said, looking from one face to the next and then beyond to the silent servants. "If we are to survive this plague, we must continue as if it were not with us—removing our ill to the sick houses as soon as the first symptoms appear and then taking up our tasks again." It was asking much, she knew, for it was said to take two or three months, and sometimes longer, for the plague to run its course. A long time to live among death and pretend one was not touched by it.

"But how do we know that removing them will make any difference in whether or not the rest of us live?" asked the old man who was about to lose his only son.

"We do not." Sir Hugh returned to the conversation. "But one thing is certain: If we keep them among us, there will be other deaths. If they are taken to Belle Glen, we might save lives."

All told, five known cases of the plague had sprung up overnight. The villagers, as calm as could be expected, left the castle to return home and convey their sick to Belle Glen.

Standing in her chamber looking out the window, Joslyn followed Father Warren's progress across the inner bailey to the outer, where two horses were saddled and waiting. Behind the priest trudged the physician, a man who had stood silent throughout the meeting in the hall. Though Joslyn did not know him well, for she'd had no occasion to call for him, she sensed something was amiss. It had been more his place to calm the villagers than Sir Hugh or herself, and yet he had kept silent, as if he were not a part of it.

Would he abandon Ashlingford? Word was that many priests and physicians were fleeing their duties to the dying for fear of being taken with the sickness themselves—especially as they seemed to fall to the plague more easily than others. It was a curious thing if one looked beyond the horror of it.

"Pray, do not go," Joslyn whispered. Though more and more it was apparent that physicians were powerless in combating the plague, their presence was still needed to ease the sufferring.

"Mama, when will Unca Liam come again?" Oliver asked.

He was sitting on the edge of the bed, tossing his top from one hand to the other. He was growing, his baby's face now that of a small boy's, his arms and legs lengthening to the point that new clothes would soon need to be sewn for him. His mind was grasping at things that last year had been quite beyond him. God, she prayed, don't let the plague come upon my little boy!

"Mama?"

"I do not know when your Uncle Liam is going to come again," she said.

He sighed. "Been a long time."

Aye, since Liam had sent her the brooch, three months had dragged by. "Mayhap he will come soon," she offered, though she did not believe it. Now that Ashlingford was under siege of the plague, it would not be long ere Thornemede also bowed to it. Liam would be needed there.

"Mama?"

"Hmm?"

"Why don't Unca Liam marry you?"

Joslyn could not have been more unsettled by his question. She searched for an answer, but he was still too young to understand. Hoping to evade his question, she said, "You would like him for a father, wouldn't you?"

He set his top in his lap and met her gaze. "Aye, then we could live together and I could play with Michael and Emrys . . . and that girl too."

"Gertrude?"

"Uh-huh."

Joslyn smiled. "That would be nice, wouldn't it?"

He nodded. "So why don't he marry you?"

She had known he would not so easily allow her to sidestep his question. "It . . . just is not possible, Oliver."

"But why?"

Knowing there was no way to make him understand, Joslyn shrugged. "I do not understand it myself. 'Tis just the way it is."

He considered her a long moment, then asked, "You love Unca Liam?"

Though to deny it might have ended the uncomfortable discussion, Joslyn could not lie to him. She stepped to the bed and sat down beside him. "I do," she said.

Oliver grinned the grin of one about to tell something he knew to a person who did not. "He loves you too," he said. "Now you can get married."

Joslyn frowned. "How do you know he loves me?"

"I asked him."

"When?"

Thoughtful, Oliver rubbed his thumb back and forth across his top. "Long time ago."

"And you are certain he said he loved me?"

Pursing his lips, Oliver jutted his chin up and down. "Uh-huh. He said."

If only Liam had said it to her, it would have meant so much. Of course, it was not as if his profession of love had been voluntary, she reminded herself. How else was he to have answered Oliver's question?

"Now you can marry," Oliver concluded.

Joslyn shook her head. "I'm sorry, Oliver, but we cannot."

The disappointment that rose on his face tugged at her heart. "Am I ever gonna have a father?" he asked.

Joslyn wanted to cry for him. He did need a father, but she simply could not imagine wedding anyone other than Liam. Still, she could not tell him that. She swallowed the lump that had risen to her throat. "We shall see," she said, then stood. "Now we ought to wash up ere we go to meal."

His mouth turned down, Oliver lifted his top from his lap and slid down the side of the bed to the floor. Then he followed Joslyn to the basin and in silence washed and dried his hands.

Liam was mounted at the head of four of his men and ready to ride when the villager stumbled over the drawbridge into the bailey.

"'Tis the plague, my lord." The young man spilled his terrible news. "My father's laid down with it—got swellings in his groin and boils about his chest." He thrust his forearm across his sweat-beaded brow. "And methinks my sister is with it, too."

The knights began to murmur in fear among themselves.

Liam gripped the reins. Lord, he'd thought he had time ere the disease spread to Thornemede, at least a few days in which to ride to Ashlingford to assist Sir Hugh with the sick there. And to see Joslyn. However, he could not leave now that the plague had raised up Thornemede's first victims. He would be needed here, and as Sir Hugh's missive had assured him all was yet under control at Ashlingford, he could not leave. "Are there any others?" he asked.

"Don't know of any more in my village, my lord. What are we to do?"

There might be others in the villages beyond his. If there were, more people would soon come to the castle seeking reassurance. "Those stricken must be taken to the sick house without delay," Liam said. "By dusk, a priest and a physician will be there to care for them."

He dismounted and passed the reins to the squire who came forward. Then he addressed the knights. "Take this man up with you and return him to his village. I will expect all of you to assist in moving his family."

Every one of them looked uncertain, knowing that to come into contact with the plague made them more vulnerable than otherwise. Aye, Liam thought, soon he would know whether or not their loyalty to him had grown strong enough these past months for them to brave his orders.

"Aye, my lord," the first knight answered. "'Tis done."

The others nodded.

Liam searched their faces for the lie, but though they were all burdened with misgivings, he was fairly certain they would obey. Minutes later, they all rode from the castle.

Exchanging glances with the captain of the guard where he stood before the open portcullis, Liam read unease that few would have noticed in his hard features before he turned to enter the donjon.

Liam hurriedly ascended the stairs past three floors to the rooftop, where he found Ahmad kneeling on his prayer rug facing Mecca.

"*Allah Akbar,*" the man said.

God is great, Liam translated, having heard it often during the month Ahmad had been at Thornemede.

The Arab's recitation continued a bit longer. Then he lowered his head, spoke more prayer, and resumed his upright position. More words passed his lips, followed by the act of complete submission. Prostrating himself so that his forehead, hands, knees, and toes were all in contact with the ground, he thrice repeated a line of prayer before sitting up again.

Liam had paid enormously to bring Ahmad to Thornemede after his search for a competent English physician had proven unsuccessful. He only hoped the Arab was as capable as the reputation that preceded him.

Though Ahmad had thus far kept much to himself, he seemed to put great thought in the little he spoke, exuding the wisdom of an older man even though he could not be more than five-and-thirty. Most importantly, he had managed to survive the ravages of the plague after treating a multitude of its victims—many successfully, Liam was told.

"It has come," Ahmad said, the deep accent of his own language making the English he spoke sound almost lyrical.

"It has," Liam replied.

Ahmad rose, bent and rolled his prayer rug, and pushed his feet into the shoes he had removed prior to prayer. "Then it is time. How many?" he asked.

"Two."

"And the signs?"

"Swellings, and one has sores."

Ahmad nodded. "They have been taken to the sick house?"

"They are being taken there now."

"Then that is where I am needed." Lowering his gaze, Ahmad stepped past Liam and toward the stairs.

"The friars will accompany you," Liam reminded him, and added, "and our priest."

Ahmad looked around. "As you wish," he said, and began the descent.

Feeling tired and older than his years, Liam followed Ahmad and, in the dim of the stairwell, found his thoughts turning to Joslyn. He had wanted to go to her this day, having been so long without her he felt almost numb. Of course, it was easier that way, but when the message had arrived telling of the plague come upon Ashlingford, the feelings had surged through him stronger than ever. If only there were some way he could be with her. . . .

He shook his head. The time was past. Unless he was truly needed at Ashlingford, he could not risk Thornemede to journey there.

As if to attest to the importance of his remaining here, a clamor of villagers awaited him when he stepped into the hall. More were afflicted—and it would only get worse as the days and weeks passed. He started toward them but paused when Ahmad appeared and beckoned to him with those expressive eyes of his.

Striding to where the physician stood before the stairs leading down to the storeroom, he said, "Ahmad?"

"You remember the powders?" the man asked.

How could he forget? Though he had questioned Ahmad's wanting them—and in such great quantities—the man had said only that the various powders, among them sulfur and arsenic, would be needed. Liam had doubted him but purchased them anyway. "I remember," he replied.

Ahmad lifted the sackcloths he held in one hand for Liam to see. "I have gathered some to take with me," he said. "As for the rest . . . " He thrust a rolled parchment toward Liam. "I have written down how to mix them and in what quantities."

Liam took the document. "And what would you have me do?"

"Four times a day the mixture is to be thrown upon the fires in the hall and the kitchen. Also, it should be portioned out to the villagers for use upon their own fires."

Liam had heard of such concoctions being used to reduce the risk of infection, but had also heard they did little more than sweeten the air. Of course, regardless of what it was mixed with, sulfur was not likely to smell pleasant, he reminded himself.

Sensing his doubt, Ahmad clasped Liam's wrist with unusual urgency. "Trust me in this, my friend. Though I have been ridiculed for my use of it, it does work."

"You are telling me it will keep the plague from entering here?" Liam asked.

Sadly, Ahmad shook his head. "Nay, it will still come, but fewer will be taken with it. You will do this?"

As there seemed naught to lose, Liam nodded. "I will."

Ahmad stretched his mouth almost to a smile. "You will see," he said, and a moment later he was gone from the hall.

Watching his retreat, Liam thoughtfully slapped

the rolled parchment onto his open palm. Weeks ago, the villagers had been told that the Arab physician would be treating those who fell ill. Although few had spoken against Ahmad at the time, Liam sensed there was going to be trouble.

"I am sorry, Joslyn," he murmured. She would have to be strong without him. In the next instant, Liam almost laughed at that. Of all women he had ever known, none were as strong as Joslyn. She would be fine, and when the worst was over, he would be with her again—even if Queen Philippa never answered his missive. Still, he would send another one today.

26

It was a fortnight before Liam received an answer to the missive he had sent with the powders to Ashlingford.

Our physician has fled, Sir Hugh wrote, *but it is just as well, for there was naught he could do to stop the course of this terrible disease.*

It was different at Thornemede. Though Ahmad had initially faced much distrust and opposition, he was more and more looked upon as God's healer. True, the dead now counted eighteen, but of those stricken, seven had fully recovered beneath the Muslim's ministrations—an unheard of number. And in that was both the good and bad. Emrys had survived four days of boils and fever, but Michael now rested beneath the dirt Liam had himself shoveled upon him.

Liam squeezed his eyes closed, the memory of it gripping him with such pain he wanted to cry out again as he had when Ahmad laid the boy's spent body in his arms. No more, though. He shook his thoughts free of Michael. There were other things more pressing that required his attention—such as Ashlingford.

But what was he to do? Sir Hugh had written that the powder mixture was being used on the fires in the castle and villages, and though there were still deaths, they had slowed. He had also asked that more powder be sent, as Ashlingford's supply was nearly depleted.

He would send them on the morrow, Liam decided. There was more that could be done for Ashlingford, he knew. The difficulty was that, in doing it, Thornemede was likely to suffer. But a few days was all it would take, he convinced himself, and then Ahmad would be back at Thornemede.

Stepping inside her chamber, Joslyn paused at the sight that greeted her. Though Oliver lay on his belly upon her bed, talking for the birch-carved soldier in his deepest voice and making horse sounds for the wooden destrier, Emma looked to have fallen asleep in the chair beside the brazier.

Joslyn frowned. It was not at all like the old woman to leave Oliver unattended, even in the same room. "Emma," she said as she stepped forward.

Turning onto his side, Oliver laid his head on his outstretched arm and looked across at her. "She is not feeling well," he said.

Joslyn's breath came out in a rush. But nay, she told herself, it must be something Emma had eaten. It had to be. Still, she could take no chances. "Oliver, will you go down to the hall and ask one of the men to come up?" she asked.

"All right," he said, starting to rise.

"Then take yourself to the kitchens and tell Cook I said you could have a treat, hmm?"

"Uh-huh."

Looking back at Emma, Joslyn saw that the woman's color was high. Not the plague, she silently pleaded as she halted before her. "Emma?" she said. Receiving no response, she leaned forward and shook the woman's shoulder.

Emma opened her eyes. "I don't know what . . . " she began, then shook her head. "I feel so warm, my lady, and all of me aches as if I were beaten."

"Have you any . . . swellings?" Joslyn asked.

Emma lifted her head. "Nay, my lady, 'tis not the plague," she said with certainty. "Just a fever. I'm sure it will pass in a day or so."

Joslyn was not so certain. "I am going to feel beneath your arms," she said. "Will you let me do that?"

Emma frowned. "You do not believe me?"

"I am not saying you lie," Joslyn hurriedly assured her. "I know you would not do that. 'Tis just that we must be certain."

Emma nodded and lifted an arm for Joslyn to feel beneath it.

Naught. "And the other arm," she said.

Emma complied.

Joslyn's probing fingers found a small mass in Emma's armpit. She was ill with the plague.

"'Tis tender," Emma breathed, her drawn face begging to be given any other explanation.

Battling the tears that stung the backs of her eyes,

Joslyn laid a hand to the woman's shoulder. "We must get you to Belle Glen," she said.

Emma dropped her head against the back of the chair. "'Tis my due," she said. "For all the lies."

Joslyn was about to offer reassurance—useless as it was—when Oliver's thready voice spoke from across the chamber.

"Mama," he said, "is Emma gonna be all right?"

Thinking he had returned from the hall, Joslyn jerked her head around. But he lay on the bed as if he had not moved from it. "Oliver, I asked you to go belowstairs," she reminded him, fear making her voice sharper than she intended.

"But I don't feel good," he said. "I got a fever too."

His child's voice speaking the words over and over in her head—louder each time—Joslyn's heart came crashing down. Not her boy, she silently pleaded. Dear God, not her little one.

"A fever?" Emma said, the dread in her voice a shadow of that which gripped Joslyn. "Nay . . . cannot be."

Her knees beginning to buckle beneath her, Joslyn gripped the back of the old woman's chair.

"'Tis just all the sweets he ate at the nooning meal," Emma pleaded.

A sob Joslyn could do naught to hold back burst from her throat.

"Mama?" Oliver croaked.

Though she wanted to fling herself toward him, to grab him up in her arms and run as far from here as she could, she knew it would only terrify him—and it would all be in vain. Joslyn bowed her head and jerkily rocked herself forward and backward on her heels. She would not cry, she told herself.

"Thirsty," Oliver said.

Lifting her head, she forced a smile that felt so taut she thought it might snap, stepped to the bed, and lowered herself to the mattress edge. Reaching forward, she gently pushed a lock of golden hair off his brow and felt the heat of him. "What would you like to drink?" she asked.

Oliver clutched his wooden toys against his chest. "Honey milk," he whispered. "Real cold, Mama."

Joslyn pulled the smile tauter. "I will get it for you, but first let us move you onto a pillow, hmm?"

He nodded.

Sliding her hands beneath his arms, she pulled him up the bed and settled his head upon her pillow, but her seeking fingers found no masses. Much as Joslyn wished to revel in their absence, it was too costly a hope, one that would cause her one moment to soar and in the next might plummet her further into despair. She must check the groin. But not now.

Pressing her lips to his brow, which had grown even warmer, she said, "I will be back in a moment with your drink."

"Am I very sick, Mama?" he asked.

Her mouth was going to break with the false smile she continued to hold on to, Joslyn thought. "Just a little," she said, "but you are going to be fine. Now I will fetch you that honey milk." As she turned toward the door, she looked at Emma.

Though the old woman had turned her head to the side, the stream of tears wetting her face was visible as she silently cried out a grief that was more for Oliver than herself.

Joslyn made it through the corridor and halfway

down the stairs. Then, turning to the wall, she slid down to her knees. "Why?" she whispered. "Why?" Though the tears burned her eyes and strained her throat, she refused to give in to them. She could not, for then Oliver would see and know her fear. She must be strong.

She dropped her chin to her chest. What had she done to deserve this? she demanded of God where He sat unmoved in His heavens. What sin so great that Oliver must—

Liam. A taunting voice spoke above her pain.

Shaking her head, she begged, "Punish me, but not like this, Lord. My life, not Oliver's." But it was useless. All the pleading in the world would not stop the plague from burying Oliver, just as it had not stopped it for those who had already died. Slumping back onto her heels, Joslyn shuddered a long sigh.

"My lady." A soft, uncertain voice spoke from below. "Is it your son?"

Joslyn looked upon the woman servant where she hovered a dozen steps below. "Aye, and Emma."

"You would have me send for some men to bring them down?"

That they might be taken to Belle Glen, Joslyn knew. "First I need some honey milk," she said.

"Aye, my lady, I will get it for you myself."

"And something for Emma."

With a nod, the woman hurried down the stairs and out of sight.

"'Tis an ugly place to die," Emma murmured past cracked lips.

Joslyn looked across at her. "Are you thirsty?"

she asked. Though loath to leave the vigil she had kept at her son's side since coming here yesterday, she was the only one left to tend Emma and Oliver. Father Warren and the two friars who had outlived the third were ministering to those in the other houses.

"I *should* be thirsty, shouldn't I?" Emma said. "Aye, I suppose I am."

Joslyn nodded. "I will bring you drink." Leaning forward, she smoothed the wet cloth across Oliver's raging brow. Though he was in a fever, she was grateful he finally slept. All through the night and into the morning he had tossed and turned, then kicked and flailed as the plague boils began to appear all over his body. "I will be back in a moment," she whispered, though she did not think he heard her.

Joslyn walked to the table that stood between the two pallets and filled a cup for Emma. However, the old woman took no more than a sip of the liquid.

"You should drink more," Joslyn urged her.

"Plenty," Emma said, and turned her head away.

With a sigh, Joslyn turned back to the table and set the cup down, and as she did so, the small pouch containing the mix of powders caught her eye. Reminded that it was time to dust the fire with them again, she glanced at Oliver to assure herself he was sleeping well, picked up the pouch, and walked to the fire pit. She poured out just enough to fill her cupped palm and tossed the powders upon the fire. The flames leapt higher, fuming a caustic odor upon the air.

"Lord, no more heat," Emma groaned from her pallet. "'Tis torture."

Hurriedly, Joslyn stepped to the woven shutters

and pushed them open. The air that gusted in was hardly fresh with the stench of the surrounding sick houses upon it, but more so than the air within the wattle-and-daub house. Chilled by it, Joslyn pulled her mantle around her shoulders and started to push the pin of her brooch through the folds of material. However, in the next instant she pulled her hand back to gaze upon Liam's gift.

It was all she had of him. All she would ever have of him, she reminded herself. It would be unbearable to lose Oliver, but even worse not to have the comfort of Liam's arms to give her something to live for. Her life would stretch into unending emptiness. Of course, God might not make her to suffer too long for her sins. Mayhap a day from now . . . a sennight . . . a fortnight and she would lie victim to the same which now took Oliver from her.

Gripping the brooch so tightly it hurt her hand, she leaned back against the wall and tilted her face up. She was tired, not from the sleepless night spent mopping Oliver's brow and whispering soothing words to him but from the pent-up emotions she had yet to release. So tired. . . .

27

The stench assailed Liam ere he was even fully into the blackened remains of the village. It was worse than he had heretofore experienced. Of course, for Ahmad it was more than familiar.

"There is much death here," the Arab said as he drew his mount alongside Liam's.

His thoughts occupied with the news of Oliver's and Emma's affliction, which he had received upon arriving at Ashlingford, Liam struggled up from them and met the man's gaze. "'Tis the reason I brought you here," he replied between clenched teeth.

Ahmad inclined his head. "If your holy men are receptive, I will instruct them as you have asked," he said, reminding Liam that what he accomplished here would only be effective if Father Warren and the friars were willing to continue the therapy once he returned to Thornemede.

Liam was the first to dismount. As he dropped to

the ground, Father Warren, followed by one of the friars, came out from the nearest sick house.

"Lord Fawke!" the priest exclaimed. "What do you at Belle Glen? We were not told you were coming. You . . . you should not be here."

It was the very reason he had left his men at Ashlingford. "Where is Lady Joslyn?" he asked.

"In the far house with her son and Emma," the priest said, nodding over his shoulder.

Liam called to Ahmad and strode with him toward the house the priest had indicated. Upon entering, his gaze fell first to Emma, where she lay on the near pallet, her face turned to the wall as she slept. On the next pallet was Oliver, and beside him knelt Joslyn. Her mantle was draped askew upon her shoulders and her black hair hung tousled down her back as she leaned over her son and spoke softly to him.

Nearing, Liam heard her reassuring words. "Mama's here," she said, unaware they were no longer alone. "Hush, my darling."

The strain in her voice dragged at Liam's emotions. For certain, she believed she was going to lose her son—and she had good reason to believe it—but if anyone could raise the little boy back up it was Ahmad.

Behind him, Liam heard the soft fall of the physician's feet, which a moment later was drowned out by Oliver's pained whimper. Kicking his legs beneath the sheet drawn up over him, he moaned, "Hot . . . hot."

Joslyn dipped her cloth in the basin beside her. "Hush," she soothed as she patted cool moisture upon his face. "Hush."

His long-drawn groan ending on a sigh, Oliver quieted.

Even with Liam's shadow falling past Joslyn and growing larger on the wall opposite, she still did not look around. Either she believed it was one of the holy men come, he thought, or else she was oblivious to anything beyond Oliver. Most likely the latter.

Coming to stand over her, Liam laid a hand upon her shoulder. "Joslyn," he said. Immediately, she stiffened beneath his fingers and remained still a long moment before looking around.

She had not slept in some time, he saw. Her skin was so pale as to appear bloodless, and the circles beneath her eyes so dark as to resemble smeared ash. Most of all, her eyes were so sorrowful there was hardly any of the brilliant amber left in them. The mourning had already begun.

Though Liam wanted more than anything to drag her into his arms and hold her, something told him she would not welcome it. "I have brought someone to help Oliver," he said. "And the others."

Silent, she continued to stare at him, her expression empty but for grief.

Wondering if she was reachable in that place she had retreated to inside herself, Liam lowered himself to his haunches, then gently gripped her shoulders and turned her toward him. "Did you hear me, Joslyn?" he asked.

She seemed to stare right through him, but her gaze wavered. "What are you doing here?" she asked.

Liam nodded to where Ahmad stood waiting to be summoned. "I have brought someone to help Oliver," he said again.

She looked past him, but whatever she thought of the man in Arab dress did not show on her face. Sinking back onto her heels, she turned to Oliver again. "Just tell me he is not going to die," she whispered, though it could not be said there was any hope in her plea.

Liam had avoided looking upon Oliver, as the memory of Michael was still too fresh, but now he did. His heart—the one that a year ago he had not believed he had—swelled with emotion. Though Michael's boils had been worse, it was still a terrible thing to behold, especially on one so young.

"Can you tell me that?" Joslyn asked, looking back at him.

"I cannot," he replied. "All we can do is try." Unable to resist, he lifted a hand and cupped it around her jaw.

Joslyn wrenched free of his touch and shot upright. "What do you care?" she demanded, hysteria on the edge of her voice. "All you must now do is wait for Oliver to die, and then all this will be yours." She threw her arms wide. "All of it."

His anger rising with him, Liam slowly straightened. "You know that is not what I want," he said. He tried to control his dangerous emotions by attributing Joslyn's behavior to grief.

"Isn't it? 'Tis what you have always wanted, and now, finally, you shall have it."

Grief, Liam told himself over and over as he fought the temper in him that threatened to erupt.

Joslyn lowered her head into her hands. "You have won, Liam Fawke," she said. "Neither Maynard nor Ivo can thwart you. Ashlingford is yours."

The silence that followed was so thick it pounded in Liam's ears. "Do you really believe that?" he growled. "That I want Oliver to die that I might have Ashlingford for myself?"

Joslyn's throat burned with the sobs she fought back, and her eyes stung with tears she refused to shed. She tried not to fall apart. Later, in the great solitude that would be hers, there would be time aplenty for it. Just not now. But she *was* falling apart, she realized—cracking into little pieces that would make her useless in caring for Oliver.

Suddenly, Liam's fingers gripped her flesh with barely restrained anger. He dragged her from the house and, once outside, pulled her around to face him. "Tell me, Joslyn," he said between clenched teeth. "Is that what you truly believe of me?"

Though what she wanted most was to find some corner to curl into—to drag her knees up to her chest and bury her face against them that she might cry out all this pain—she forced her gaze to Liam's.

"Which is it?" he demanded, his face flushed and pupils so enlarged there was hardly any green left to them. "Am I beast or not?"

As she looked up at him, the love she had tried to suppress ever since Oliver had fallen sick crept back into her heart.

But there was her sin, she sharply reminded herself. However, what she had said of him was false, spoken out of grief, fear, and these past months of unanswered longing.

The first tear fell. "I am sorry, Liam," she said. "'Tis grief that speaks such words from my mouth. Only grief."

His hold on her eased, and a moment later Joslyn was in his arms.

Sagging against Liam, she began to shake, then harder as the sobs she had so long suppressed burst from her and the scalding tears rushed from her eyes.

She cried for Oliver. For all the years before him he would never see. For the laughter she would no longer hear. For the sweetness of his freshly bathed skin she would no longer smell. For the little hand in hers she would no longer feel. For the hundreds of questions he would no longer ask. For this one light in her life blown out so cruelly.

How long she clung to Liam she could not have guessed, but when finally she sobbed her last, she opened her swollen eyes to discover herself cradled in Liam's arms where he sat with his back against a tree. Though she had not known it, sometime during her outpouring of grief, he had carried her to this place removed from the sick houses. Away from the dying. Away from her son.

"Oliver!" she gasped, pushing away from Liam. "I must return to him."

He tightened his arms around her. "He is being cared for, Joslyn," he assured her. "The physician I brought knows the plague well. He will know what to do for Oliver."

"But I—"

"Ahmad cast the sickness from Emrys, as well as from several others. You must leave him to his work."

The Arab had saved Emrys? Hoped flickered in her. Was it possible he could help Oliver as well? She looked into Liam's eyes and, finding the reassurance she needed there, eased her weariness against him.

Liam stroked a lock of hair back from her face and brushed the moisture from beneath her eyes. "It was a long time coming, wasn't it?" he asked.

Her tears. Aye, if one could say that the eternity

since discovering first Emma, and then Oliver, ill in her chamber was a long time. She nodded.

Liam stared at her a moment. "I would have come sooner, but it just was not possible."

"I knew you could not."

He raised her clenched hand, and only then did Joslyn realize what she still held. Slowly, he unfolded her fingers from the brooch, then lifted it from her to reveal the four distinct impressions made in her palm. Roses.

Liam captured her gaze again and then brought her hand to his mouth and pressed his lips to it. "I love you, Joslyn Fawke," he said.

Thinking she could not possibly have heard right—or else this was just a dream conjured by her sleep-deprived mind, she stared at him.

A small smile pulled at the corners of his mouth. "'Tis what you have been waiting to hear, is it not?" he asked.

Though Joslyn had thought her eyes too dry to have any crying left in them, the tears surged forth from whatever well lay hidden within her. Liam Fawke had spoken his love to her. Never mind that the love could never be acknowledged. "I did not believe you would ever say it," she murmured.

He trailed his lips downward, and kissed the inside of her wrist. "A year ago, I would not have believed it myself," he said, "but for months now, 'tis what I have wanted to do."

"Then why did you not?"

Lowering her arm to her side, he leaned his head back against the tree and sighed. "I just could not—and still I should not have told you."

She pulled away, better to see him. "Why? You know I love you."

"Aye, and I also know there is no future for us," he said, exposing the harsh truth.

She needed no one to tell her that. Although she would always hold in her heart the words of love he had spoken to her this day, she would never know the fulfillment of awakening beside him each morning, of bearing him children, of laughter and tears and a strong hand to hold to when life turned cruel, of growing old with him as the world grew new. . . .

She must return to Oliver. Raising herself out of Liam's lap, she said, "I have been gone too long."

He also stood, but he caught her hand as she started to turn away. "I will stay as long as you need me," he said.

But not forever. "And Thornemede?"

Drawing her nearer, he brushed his lips across hers. "It can wait," he said. Stepping back, he pulled her mantle closed, deftly fastened the brooch at the neck, and then took her hand and led her back to Belle Glen.

As Joslyn entered the sick house, a horribly acrid smell struck her like a slap in the face. Realizing that it came from where Oliver lay, she jerked free of Liam and ran forward. "What think you are doing?" she cried to the Arab, who was bent over her son.

"Joslyn!" Liam called after her.

She heard him, but it did not matter. Nearly upon the man, she stumbled to a halt when he suddenly straightened and showed her the iron he held. It glowed red at the tip. "He does not feel it, my lady," he assured her. "I have given him something so he will sleep."

Liam's hands fell heavily upon Joslyn's shoulders, preventing her from lunging forward and shoving the

strangely garbed man aside. "'Tis this that saved
Emrys," he said, his fingers tightening upon her.
"Trust me, Joslyn. If there is to be any hope for
Oliver, you must not interfere with Ahmad's work."

Trying to hear Liam despite the fear shrouding her,
Joslyn shuddered. Was it truly possible that this man
from a far-flung country could do what had not yet
been done at Ashlingford? Could he save Oliver? If
there was even one chance in a million, she must take
it. She swallowed, then said, "I want to see my son."

Ahmad's eyes lifted from Joslyn to where Liam
stood behind her, questioning him.

The Arab stepped aside.

Oliver lay unclad on the pallet, but though the
boils upon him had all been laid open, and many of
them cauterized, he looked to be resting quietly. Still,
it was frightful. Her little boy—

"The boils must be discharged, my lady," Ahmad
explained. "The poison let out."

Turning, she pressed her forehead to Liam's shoulder and gripped his tunic with desperate hands. "Do
not let him die," she pleaded. "I could not stand it."

Liam held her close and stroked a hand up and
down her back. "Ahmad will do all he can," he said.
He guided her across the room to an empty pallet and
pulled her down beside him. "Sleep," he said. "When
Oliver awakens, he will need you rested."

"I . . . do not think I can," she murmured.

"You must."

Shortly, Joslyn found the sleep she had not
believed she would.

Liam stayed with her, loath to let go of her, but then
Emma's groan sounded around the room. Gently, he
laid Joslyn down and strode to the old woman's pallet.

"Oliver," she rasped. "My boy."

Liam lowered himself beside her. "He is being tended to, Emma," he reassured her.

Frowning, she opened her eyes, as best she could. "Is it really you, Liam?" she asked, her hand searching across the sheet spread over her.

Reaching forward, he covered her gnarled fingers with his. "It is," he said.

Her face relaxed. "I knew you would come. You love them too much to stay away."

Knowing she referred to Joslyn and Oliver, he said, "I do."

"Is Oliver . . . better?" she asked.

"He is," Liam said, not knowing whether or not he lied, though it was likely he did. But it was what Emma needed to hear, and he saw no reason to withhold it.

Breathing a long sigh, she closed her lids again. "He is such a good boy," she murmured, "just like my Maynard was."

Refusing to think on what Maynard had later become, Liam asked, "Is there something I can get you, Emma? Are you thirsty?"

"Always," she whispered. "And I do hurt so."

Releasing her hand, Liam stood to go to the table where pitchers of drink were set. However, Ahmad had already seen to it. Carrying a cup filled only half full, the Arab stepped past Liam and went down beside Emma.

It was probably best that the old woman was too weary to open her eyes, Liam thought, for otherwise she would surely have been distressed by the strange face before her.

Though she seemed content with only a sip of the

drink, Ahmad continued to press it upon her until the cup was drained. Then he lowered her head back to the pallet and straightened.

"How is she?" Liam asked.

Ahmad shook his head. "I gave her a draught to ease the pain," he said, "but I fear I cannot save her. She will die ere morning."

Liam was not surprised, but still there was a great ache in him for this woman he had always cared for. "And Oliver?" he asked, glancing to where the boy lay so small and still upon the pallet.

"The night will tell," Ahmad said.

28

The night was long and grew longer, as Oliver's tormented cries and violent thrashing tested Joslyn's sanity. Though Liam urged her to sleep during those times of respite when Oliver fell into a restless slumber of his own, she couldn't. It seemed that all the Arab had done was for naught. Believing Oliver was soon to die, she refused to leave his side. He needed her, and she needed these last hours with him—painful as they were.

Hardly aware of Liam even though he hovered near her and his hand was often upon her shoulder, she knelt beside Oliver's pallet and allowed her tears to fall unchecked. She spoke softly to him and wet his brow whenever he awakened in the course of a fit.

Tending to those in the other sick houses, Ahmad came and went, sometimes frowning, sometimes shaking his head, but more often without expression. He forced drink on an incoherent Oliver, laid his cheek to the little boy's to assess the strength of his fever, applied salve to the cauterized boils, and mumbled words of his own language over him which Joslyn came to recognize as prayers.

And then the fever broke.

Falling back on his heels, Ahmad lowered his head. "*Allah Akbar.*" He spoke the words with a voice louder and stronger than Joslyn had heard from him before. Then he lifted his face and fastened his penetrating gaze upon her. "God is great," he said. "Your son will live."

Disbelieving, Joslyn stared at him a long moment, and then she looked behind to where Liam stood over her shoulder.

A smile coming out upon his drawn face, he nodded.

"'Tis true?" she breathed. She reached with trembling fingers and laid them on Oliver's forehead. Not yet cool, but the fire that had raged through him had abated considerably. He would live. Words of thanks upon her lips for Ahmad, she shifted her teary gaze to where he knelt opposite her, but found that he had gone.

Emotion nearly bursting from her, Joslyn lowered her face into her hands and cried aloud the tears of joy that minutes earlier had been tears of sorrow. As they poured from her, she silently thanked God, Whom she had spent these past hours accusing of having deserted Oliver. Through this man whose God was different from hers—though perhaps not—He had spared her son.

Joslyn's praise was interrupted by Emma's voice.

"Nay," she wailed. "Not my boy."

Looking up, Joslyn saw the old woman lift a feeble arm and shake her fist at the heavens. "Curse you!" she cried.

Realizing that Emma must think she wept over the death of Oliver, and not the life, Joslyn rose to go tell her different. However, Liam pressed her back down.

"I will tell her," he said.

Joslyn grasped Oliver's hand and reveled in the life which flowed through him.

Liam bent down beside Emma's pallet. "Emma," he said, "Oliver is well."

She tossed her head side to side, mumbled something, and moaned. "Do not lie to me. He is dead. I know it. My boy is dead."

"Nay, he is not. The fever has broken, Emma. Oliver will live."

She whimpered. "You think to spare me, dear Liam? Nay, I know the truth. I know the truth."

Was she in a state of delirium? Joslyn wondered.

Liam took hold of her shoulders. "Emma, listen to me," he said.

"You should know the truth now," she continued. "There's no one to protect any longer. No one. Ah, my poor Oliver. Ashlingford is yours, Liam. It has always been yours."

Or should have been, Joslyn thought. However, Emma's next words went far deeper than whether it was Liam or Maynard who'd had more right to the barony.

"As Maynard was not the true heir of Ashlingford," she said, "neither is his son."

A long, tense silence followed, and then Liam drew back from her. "What are you talking about?" he asked.

"I am so sorry, Liam. I did not wish to be a part of it. Never did I want it."

"A part of what?"

"The deception. The lies. Ivo and Anya."

Joslyn saw Liam's hands knot at his sides. "Tell me," he demanded.

"Ah, Liam, do you not see?" Emma cried. "I did not love Maynard only for the years he spent at my breast. I loved him as if he were my own son because he *was* my son. Mine and Ivo's. Born without vows."

The old woman's confession shook Joslyn like a high wind through a tree. If it were true, Liam and Maynard had been . . . cousins? Aye, cousins, meaning Maynard never had a true claim on Ashlingford. Thus, Oliver had no claim either. Dear God, the irony of it!

"You make no sense, old woman," Liam said sharply.

"Nay, I suppose not," she replied, her voice growing stronger and clearer with each word she spoke, as if the unburdening of her soul strengthened her. "Just as it makes no sense that I could ever have loved Ivo enough to allow him to get a child on me. But I did. Wrongly."

"Tell me the rest. All of it."

Joslyn could only imagine what Liam must be feeling to learn after all these years that, legitimate or not, he was the only one to have a true claim on Ashlingford. It had all been a lie: the lives of Emma, Ivo, Anya, and Maynard, and now, too, Oliver.

"I thought Ivo loved me," Emma said, as if unaware of the emotions seething through Liam. "He told me he did, and then—" A spasm of coughing came upon her. When next she talked, her voice was a shadow, so soft Joslyn had to strain to hear her. "He got me with child," she whispered.

"That child was Maynard."

She nodded. "I was so fearful. So ashamed. But Ivo told me all would be provided for. He knew of a noblewoman unable to conceive on her own who would take my babe when it was born and raise it up as hers if it was born a boy."

"Anya," Liam supplied.

Clearing her throat, Emma spoke more loudly. "He said her husband was angered because she had not yet conceived by him and had threatened that if she did not soon, he would rid himself of her."

A lie, Liam knew. Never would Montgomery Fawke have threatened such. It would have suited him well had he known Anya was barren, for he already had his heir in Liam.

"So I would not know disgrace in my village, Ivo sent me to work in the manor house of one of his acquaintances," Emma said, her voice graveled by lack of moisture. "Though I do not know what excuse Anya gave your father for birthing their child elsewhere, I learned that she left Ashlingford and went into confinement sometime during my fifth month of pregnancy."

Liam ground his jaws together. Though neither did he know what excuse Anya had made to his father, he clearly remembered the woman's absence several months before Maynard's birth. During that blessed time he had not had her to torment and chastise him.

"Though I knew I should not, I came to love the babe growing inside me," Emma continued, "but still I knew it would be better for my child to grow up a noble rather than a bastard. Thus, I prayed it would be born a boy and not a girl."

A bastard. With each element of Emma's story unfolding, Liam was more and more torn with anger.

As if the effort of telling her tale was growing too much for her, Emma breathed a ragged sigh. "I am so dry," she said. "Wet my lips, won't you, Liam?"

Though Liam knew he was watched, when he rose from beside Emma he did not look at Joslyn lest she read in his eyes the emotions swelling through him. They would frighten her. Pouring some wine, he returned to the old woman and held the cup to her dry, cracked lips.

Soon she continued her tale. "And then my babe was born: a boy. Anya and Ivo were waiting, but though they tried to take him from me, I could not let him go once I had held him."

"So you came to Ashlingford as his wet nurse."

Emma inclined her head. "Aye, they did not want me to, but I gave them no choice. I said I would tell of their lie if they tried to separate me from my child. Thus they brought me with them, and once at Ashlingford I began to see the reason for Maynard's being. It was no accident that Ivo impregnated me, Liam. It was part of a plan he and Anya had devised."

Liam did not need to be told what that plan was.

Lifting her head from the pillow, Emma clutched a handful of his tunic. "All either of them ever wanted Maynard for was to take the barony from you. Ivo because he could not have it for himself and Anya because even if she could have borne your father a child he would still have loved you better." With a weary groan, she let go of him and dropped her head back to the pillow. "Let me . . . let me rest a moment," she whispered, and closed her eyes.

Liam could not imagine how he had been so blind. How had his father not seen it? Ivo had always been too interested in Maynard, and Anya hardly at all. And then there was Emma, who had loved him like the son he truly was.

"Liam," Joslyn said softly. Having come around

Oliver's pallet, she laid a hand to his shoulder and lowered herself to her knees beside him. "I am so sorry. If I had known—"

"What?" he asked, the word sharp to his own ears.

She drew a deep breath. "I would not have made a choice for Oliver that was neither his nor mine to make. I would not have gone with Ivo to London."

Though Liam wanted to lash out at someone or something, he fought the anger threatening to consume him and grasped at the love he felt for Joslyn. "I know," he said.

She searched his face a long moment, and then an uncertain smile came to her lips. "'Tis yours, Liam," she said. "I will go before the king myself and bear witness to what Emma has said. Surely he cannot deny you now."

Nay, Liam did not believe Edward would refuse him Ashlingford a third time if he was told the truth.

"I must tell you the rest of it," Emma muttered.

Looking back at her, Liam saw that her eyes remained closed. Obviously, it required too much effort to open them.

"You knew what Ivo and Anya intended," he said, "and yet you went along with it. Why?"

"I loved my son, Liam. I wanted him to live the life of a noble, not a bastard. 'Twas for him I did it." She drew a breath that wheezed noisily down her throat. "When I learned that your father had no intention of naming Maynard his heir, but rather you, my conscience was greatly eased. I thought my son could still have the good of life and yet . . . and yet you would not be cheated out of what was truly yours."

"But when my father died, Ivo and Anya petitioned

the king to name Maynard as heir," Liam said. "Still you said naught."

Emma's face momentarily contorted as if with pain, but then eased again. "Never did I believe the barony would be awarded to Maynard," she said. "'Twas clear that your father wanted it for you and thought you the better choice—and you were. You may not believe me, Liam, but when Anya and Ivo returned from London with the king's decree, I threatened that if they did not recant Maynard's claim upon the barony I would tell both you and Maynard the truth of his birth. That I would stand witness for you."

"Then Maynard did not know he had been born of you and Ivo," Liam said.

Emma shook her head. "There were times I wanted to tell him—when he began to turn from me to Ivo, and then to Anya—but I feared that to do so might be the ruin of him, especially once he had grown to hate you so. To learn he was no more legitimate than you?" She sighed. "I could not."

Would things have gone any differently had Maynard known? Liam wondered. Would he have stepped down from the title that had not belonged to him? "How did Ivo and Anya respond to your threat?" he asked.

"They tried to kill me."

Beside him, Liam felt Joslyn stiffen. "Kill you?" he asked.

"Aye, they . . . poisoned my drink. But they did not know I saw them do it."

Now Liam understood Anya's sudden death, which had so closely followed his father's. "You switched your drink with Anya's, didn't you?" he asked.

"God will judge me for it, but 'tis true. When she was not looking, I poured mine into hers."

"And Ivo knew."

"He guessed afterward."

"Why did you not come to me and tell me of the deception?" Liam asked.

"How could I? Ivo would have retaliated by telling what I had done in escaping the death he and Anya planned for me. My sentence would have been death. And Maynard . . . he mourned Anya so terribly I could not hurt him further."

"And when he died?"

"Then there was Oliver." Her voice caught with a sob. "I loved him ere I even laid eyes upon him."

Thus, by her silence, she had once again denied Liam the barony. "What of the writings?" he asked. "What had they to do with this?"

"The poisoning of my drink was not the first plan Anya and Ivo devised to rid themselves of me. Almost from the moment I arrived at Ashlingford there were . . . incidents . . . that might have been the death of me had I not put an end to them."

"With the writings."

"Aye, I had a friar write the truth down for me when he came through on his way to London. I told him it was a confession I intended to present to your father." She cleared her throat with a cough. "He believed he was doing good, never knowing I intended to use it against Ivo and Anya to preserve my life."

Liam nearly asked why, then, Anya and Ivo would attempt to poison her knowing that the truth might come out, but he answered it himself. They'd had naught to lose, really. At least with Emma dead, there had been a chance of holding on to Ashlingford through Maynard, for the writings might not have fallen where they would do harm. With her alive, their secret was certain to have been told.

"When the writings were finished, I showed a page to Ivo and told him that upon my death the person who held them had instructions to deliver them to you."

"But you had them all along."

"There was no one I could trust."

Knowing it was all told, that Emma might find peace in having unburdened herself, Liam said, "Sleep now."

She turned her head toward him, but still her lids were too heavy to lift. "You . . . you forgive me, Liam, don't you? Never did I wish for you to be hurt as you have been. I swear it."

The Liam of old would have been furious with her—so much that it was not likely he would have been able to lie in telling her she was forgiven. But Joslyn at his side had tamed him. He leaned forward and squeezed Emma's hand. "All is forgiven," he said truthfully. "Now rest."

Her lined face relaxed. "You were always my boy, too," she murmured, and let go of consciousness.

Liam remained unmoving for some minutes before turning to Joslyn.

"She is going to die, isn't she?" she asked.

He nodded. "Ahmad says by morning." Standing, he reached down and helped her to her feet. "I must leave you now," he said.

Immediately, she was distressed. "You are returning to Thornemede?"

"Nay, I just need to leave this place for a while." To think, to work over the unexpected revelations of this night, and to vent whatever was left of his anger. "I will return in a few hours."

Joslyn looked uncertain.

"My vow to you," he said, then strode from the house into a darkness that would be touched by light within the hour.

Though Ahmad left Ashlingford three days later, Liam remained a sennight before announcing that he must also return to Thornemede. As Oliver was recovered enough to be brought back to the castle, and showed signs that he would soon be running about the donjon again, it was time.

Still warmed by the love she and Liam had shared on the night past, Joslyn walked beside him to where his men had already mounted. "When will you go to court?" she asked.

His gaze unmoving on his men, he said, "Never again if I can avoid it."

"I do not understand. Surely the king will wish to meet with you to—"

Abruptly, Liam halted his stride. Then he pulled her in front of him and tilted her face up. "I have no business with Edward," he said.

"No business?" She was confused. "But what of Ashlingford?"

"Ashlingford is Oliver's."

"Of course it is not!" Joslyn exclaimed. "'Tis yours, Liam."

With his thumb he smoothed the curve of her jaw. "I have Thornemede," he said. "I do not also need Ashlingford."

He was giving up Ashlingford to hold only Thornemede? It made no sense—especially as Thornemede was only a shadow of this, his birthright, not to mention that Ashlingford would still require his direction. "But Thornemede is hardly—"

"It will be," he interrupted. "In time, it will rise alongside Ashlingford."

What he spoke was true, Joslyn knew, for Liam was determined to make it happen, but that he would give up what was his? "'Tis not right, Liam," she persisted. "Ashlingford belongs to you."

The shadows cleared from his face as the rising sun flushed the sky with its glow. And in his eyes Joslyn saw the love.

"I love you, Joslyn," he said, "and Oliver. The truth is best buried with Emma, and that is where it shall remain."

He was protecting them, she realized. His love was that great. "You cannot," she said, his image blurring as her eyes washed with tears.

Uncaring who might see what he did, Liam lowered his head and kissed her gently. "But I have." He spoke against her lips. "Oliver will be lord of Ashlingford."

Her throat was bottled so tight with emotion, Joslyn could only stare at him.

"I will be back, Joslyn," he said. "I swear it. And when I come, it will be for you and Oliver." Then, kissing her one last time, he stepped past her and strode to his destrier.

Joslyn stared after him. What he intended, she did not know, but he would do as he said. He would find some way for them to be together.

29

The days passed, and when finally the plague had taken its last victim and people began to rise from beneath the mantle of fear that had hovered over them for three months, summer was nearly arrived. Though it was estimated that Ashlingford had lost a quarter of its population, and Thornemede somewhat less, they had won. Unlike other places across England, life was quick to resume its wonderfully normal pace. The lands were producing, the cattle tended, and there was plenty of food to be had for all.

Liam had done what he had sought to do. He had saved both baronies from ruin.

Lifting her chin from her knees, Joslyn turned her head toward the excited voice that called to her. Oliver.

His legs pumped vigorously as he climbed the knoll she had sat upon this past hour, watching the workers in the fields.

When he neared, Joslyn looked over his flushed

face. It was scarred from the boils Ahmad had opened, but they had healed well, and with time they were likely to fade almost completely.

He halted before her and rested his hands on his knees. "Mama, Uncle Liam is here!"

Joslyn had only a moment to sigh over the loss of the sweet "Unca" he had outgrown before the rest of what he said struck her. Liam had returned!

Had he come for her and Oliver as he'd said he would? Was it possible?

"And A-papa too," Oliver added.

Joslyn blinked. Her father was here? Baffled, she stood. "Where are they?"

"There," Oliver said, squinting as he pointed into the sun.

Joslyn shaded her eyes and saw three horsemen riding toward them. Three? "Is your Uncle Richard also with them?" she asked.

"I think that's his name," Oliver said, never having met Joslyn's brother.

What did it mean? Liam . . . her father . . . and Richard? Her heart beating faster, she lifted her skirts. "Come, Oliver," she said, and ran down the knoll.

Liam was the first to reach her. Swinging down from the saddle, he took her into his arms and held her tight.

As it was the first they had seen of each other since Liam had left Ashlingford following Oliver's recovery, they clung together for as long as the others permitted. Which was not long enough.

"You gonna get married?" Oliver asked, looking up at them with wide, hopeful eyes.

His question jarred Joslyn, but Liam exhibited not the least bit of discomfort. Sliding his hand into

Joslyn's, he knelt before the little boy. "You would like that?" he asked.

"Oh, aye!" Oliver breathed.

"Then we will have to do something about it, won't we?" Liam said. He ruffled Oliver's hair, then straightened and met Joslyn's imploring gaze. "I have come for you, Joslyn," he said.

Though she heard her father and brother rein in behind her, she simply could not look away from Liam. "Truly?" she whispered.

Liam smiled. "We are going to be married."

She had known he would find a way—that was what had sustained her these many weeks—but hearing it spoken was like a dream. Beautiful but unbelievable. "How?" she asked.

He brushed his mouth across hers. "I will tell you later. Now you must greet your father and your brother."

Hours later, as they lay entwined in Liam's bed, Joslyn asked again.

"'Twas with Queen Philippa's help," Liam said.

Joslyn was surprised. "The queen?"

"Aye, months ere the plague struck, I sent a missive to her asking for assistance in obtaining a dispensation from the pope."

Joslyn had not realized his feelings for her went that far back. It thrilled and touched her. "You have loved me a long time, haven't you, Liam?"

He trailed a finger down her arm. "Not long enough," he said.

A shiver of excitement shot through her. "And the pope agreed?"

"Aye, he has issued us a special dispensation that we might wed."

"But how? Are we not still brother and sister in the

eyes of the church?" Though what Emma had revealed proved them to be further removed—cousins by marriage—Liam had insisted that the truth remain buried with the old woman.

Propping himself up on an elbow, Liam looked down at her. "Nay, the pope has decreed otherwise. For a price, of course."

Liam had paid for the privilege of marrying her, then. "Is it a high price?" Joslyn asked.

He smiled. "Not for what I shall have in return. But it shall take some time to pay it."

"How long?"

He thought on it a moment. "Most likely ten or more years."

"Ten years?" Joslyn exclaimed.

Liam nodded. "Aye, 'tis an abbey the pope wants and an abbey I shall build him—at Belle Glen."

Though Joslyn could not even begin to imagine how much it would cost to build such an edifice, for certain Liam had paid dearly to wed her. "When did you receive the dispensation?" she asked.

"A sennight past."

She would not have expected him to keep the plan secret for so long. "A sennight!" she cried. "And you did not come then?"

"I would have," he said, stroking her loose hair, "but I had first to bring your father here. I thought you would wish him present when we spoke our vows."

"I . . . I am pleased you did," she said.

Liam returned his gaze to hers. "Ours is going to be a real marriage, Joslyn. Forever."

Forever. "I love you, Liam," she said.

He lowered his head. "And I you, Joslyn. I will love you for always."

Escape to Romance
and
WIN A YEAR OF ROMANCE!

Ten lucky winners will receive a free year of romance—*more than 30 free books*. Every book HarperMonogram publishes in 1997 will be delivered directly to your doorstep if you are one of the ten winners drawn at random.

Harper Monogram

Let HarperMonogram
Sweep You Away